ONE WRONG
WORD

Also by the same author

THE LINCOLNSHIRE
MURDER MYSTERY SERIES

Dead Spit

Seaside Snatch

Once Bitten

Dead Jealous

Or Not To Be

Twelve Days

Sacrificial Lamb

In Plain Sight

Tissue of Lies

Final Whistle

Reasons Why Not

Best Served Cold

Body of Evidence

Bitter End

You can contact the author on Facebook

LINCOLNSHIRE
MURDER MYSTERIES

ONE WRONG WORD

Cary Smith

ONE WRONG WORD

Copyright © 2022 Cary Smith

ISBN: 9798358890008

PublishNation, London
www.publishnation.co.uk

1

Spring 2022

James Gosney, mumbled profanities to himself under his breath using the very same bad language he knew the powers that be would sack him on the spot for, were they to catch him swearing out loud.

More than likely it'd be some shit of a whistle blower betraying him.

Knew deep down it was never right in the workplace in this day and age, and with women about doubly so. Stupid snowflakes and the woke brigade were forever making life worse and worse. Up in arms if you said boo to a goose and some of the silly tosspots who countered against ages old language even claimed to be men.

He'd read more than once and had even considered publishing the fact, how it is usually the more intelligent and prestigious in society who use what some old biddies call bad language. Decided in the end that'd be sailing too close to the wind under the circumstances.

As editor of the *Lincoln Leader* he was one short that morning. About to go to press and not only did he have a blank page but the contributor wouldn't answer her damn phone.

In shirt and collar to signify his status, James just pushed the mouse aside, sat back in Rachel Barnard's grey chair and blew out a big breath of utter frustration. 'Bugger, bugger, bugger!' he said banging the desk with his fist. 'Who's f...lipping idea was all this crap, anyway?' he asked nobody in particular even though he knew the answer.

'All what?' came across the newsroom.

'Bloody working from home....nonsense,' he managed to remove a word at the last second.

'Your mate Boris.'

'I know that!' he almost shouted. 'What dickhead put it in his head? Not got the gumption to think for himself that's for sure. Be some overpaid civil servant.'

'Chances are it'd be that Barnard Castle Cummings,' Tony Parker offered.

'Be that Sage lot of experts.'

'All to do with the pandemic,' Kevin butted in with his contribution.

'How much longer we gonna blame everything on soddin' Covid?'

'She still not answering?' was shirt-sleeved bearded Petra Vargic, peering up from what he was involved in.

'Nothing. Phone goes to voice mail. Nothing on here,' he tapped the monitor with his knuckle.

'Working on some'at yesterday when she came in.'

'Well, it's not here now!' James gasped and blew out a big breath. 'Done it again, silly cow,' he said in annoyance. 'How many times've I told her to back everything up. Send it to that....Cloud. But please, please, please don't leave it open for every nig-nog to steal.'

'Careful boss,' was Steve from the Sports Desk over by the window.

'What?'

'Racist.'

'What is?' Gosney almost shouted back down the newsroom.

'What you just said.'

'Don't be an arse, Steve. Look nig-nog up on Google.' he suggested and was back to his phone for one more try.

'You sure?' Daisy dared.

'Course I'm sure,' he sighed and shook his head as he punched the numbers too hard. 'Why you all gotta query every word I say eh? Last week's here and all her history backed-up, but nothing since. Not even a spare in case.'

Now it was nig-nog these idiots were using to denigrate basic language. He found it increasingly difficult at times to remain calm, to keep his opinions to himself. Anyway what sort of word was it, this woke nonsense? According to the dictionary it was a verb not an adjective, the past of wake.

2

'Has to be there, saw her working on summat the other day.'

'Could be she's at home re-writing it now as we speak,' Kevin Elphick offered. 'Desperate with a re-write, getting it all down fast, not answering her phone. Be a ping soon enough and there it'll be boss.'

'That went to legal. Nothing back I've seen as yet.'

'That the Coronation Street woman piece?'

Kevin nodded. 'Having a go about her writing her biography full of all the usual tick box celebrity garbage. Read one you've read them all. Worse pregnancy in the world. Mental health issues naturally these days, domestic abuse and now...Menopause.'

'What's Rache having a go about?' Tony queried.

'Saying she expected all the dirt on her ex,' Petra offered. 'Goes on about the abuse in airy fairy terms without mentioning his name. Now a year or two later there's no sight of anger in the book. Nothing about the effect it had on the kids. Rachel rightly criticizes her for taking time though to mention more than once she's planning a novel. Domestic abuse comes in all forms as we know. From having a bit of a moan, the bawling and shouting to a good kicking. All the book promo went on about how badly she suffered and had trouble making it to the studio sometimes. Book is nothing more than her having a bitch and a moan about him, before scurrying back to the menopause.'

'So you all think I've got nothing better to do than sit here waiting for a ......ping eh? Tell you what, how about one of you comes up with something to get me outta the....clag eh, rather than sitting there picking your noses.'

'Want me to search for a left over we didn't use?' Steve queried. 'Still got that piece about tantric influencers.'

'Be serious! Thought we spiked that nonsense days ago.' Surely somebody coming up with a decent filler would be a piece of piss, he said to himself, though not out loud to be met with disapproval by one or two of the snowflakes.

James Glover dropped the phone when it went to voice mail once again. 'Need more than a damn filler. Anything we spiked last week? Do a re-write. Need something pretty decent before we put this all to bed.'

'I'll have a look, boss. How about extending the piece about public's reaction to Boris and that Rishi Sunak's Partygate fines?'

Glover sighed. 'We put it in only because we were ordered to. Just powers that be having another knock at the Tories. More, and we'll bore the pants off the readers.' He looked across the room. 'What about that eating in bed one they shunted up?' James aimed at Daisy Lytton.

'Still working on it boss. Thought that was next week.'

'Must have a lifestyle gig sitting here somewhere we can use. Nothing too political under the circumstances, had enough of their lifestyles to cobble dogs with.'

'Got that Mary Portas book thing we never used.'

'What a good idea Petar, seeing as we've already got that Masterchef bloke's.'

'What about the piece on culture bearers?'

'And how many peasants out there'll fathom what that's all about? Always told her, run with something, anything was….'

'Better than nothing.'

'Talking to myself til I'm blue in the face, reckon. Keep a spare. Lose one you lose the lot. How many times d'I say that? Phoned since first thing, emailed, sent bloody texts. Nothing. What we got for her page Thursday? Absolutely bugger all.' he looked across at Steve Ronane. 'Any chance you've got the Imps goalie and manager having an affair?'

'Sorry. Late in the season bit short on scandal, all a bit quiet,' he said head down onto the Urban Dictionary.

'This page'll be more than quiet unless we get hold of the daft bitch.' tall James was on his feet scanning the room for any notion of input from his team.

'Tell me about that eating in bed survey,' he said to Daisy as he approached her.

'Got the basics from what they sent. I'm now looking at advice for the best crockery. Checking out firm pillows so you can sit up straight.'

'What about the food?' he insisted. 'You'd not catch me eating even a bag of crisps in bed.'

'Found out some have condiments on their bedside table,' from Daisy made him cringe.

4

James just blew out a breath and shook his head.'Get on with it,' he said checking his watch. 'Got time, need a hand Kev's not got much on.'

'Cuppa in bed on Sunday morning's about all I manage,' he reacted. 'But Sunday roast or Chicken and chips is nonsense.'

'Started looking at bed tables,' said Daisy. 'Want me to carry on with the stuff you'd need?'

'Just fill the damn page.'

'How often d'you have to wash the sheets?' balding Steve asked across the room.

'Noodles with chopsticks'd be a good one to try.'

'What the betting Just Eat'll deliver right to your bedroom soon if this carries on?'

'One thing I've got already,' was Daisy. 'Watching Netflix in bed with a screen nailed to the wall's brought all this bed scoffing on.'

'To my mind this business takes you away from the experience of enjoying good food'

'Boss,' said Daisy to catch his attention. 'I was planning to interview folk in the street see what they think.'

'Make 'em up. Mention the Stonebow nobody'll know the difference. Enough now,' was a louder James. 'Somebody come up with a stand-by filler, Petra give Daisy a hand if you would,' he said as he moved away. 'Time for a chat with lover boy,' he said as he walked off pushed the door too hard and strode through.

His editorial team said nothing but just almost in unison sat shaking their heads at yet another of his outbursts. Rachel they all knew would come up with something, even if it was a rushed re-constructed piece she'd send from home.

Nowadays the world of media was ruthless and competitive and James was not at all sure the lot he'd been saddled with were up to it.

First to speak Daisy Lytton warned: 'If he gets down there and find Sean's on a day off, could be another storm brewing.'

'She not put in leave you think?'

'Not mentioned to me.'

'Easy could, and he's just not bothered to check.'

5

'Tin hats on team, heads down.'

'Well I'll be buggered,' Steve announced for all to hear. 'He's absolutely right. A nig-nog is a foolish person, a raw and unskilled recruit. Listen to this. The phrase has no racist connotations despite appearances. It is in fact a Yorkshire term referring to a silly person, it does not derive from the n word.'

'I'm gobsmacked me.'

'Apology coming up if I must.'

'Yeh right.'

James Gosney always wondered how others in a similar position got on with peculiar foreign owners, the ones controlling the purse strings. Big football teams surely had to have a similar scenario and frequently had him wondering how they operate.

The paper and indeed the whole publishing group was now owned lock stock and barrel by the brothers. Not foreigners as such but their grandparents had arrived from Uganda a lifetime ago with bugger all in their pockets or so people back then were led to believe. Then at a drop of a hat started up businesses from scratch from these empty pockets.

He had no foreign born owners to handle, but he always had this feeling it might be how it was with that guy who owned Man City. Yanks pulling the Man United strings or the Chinese Fosun group in control of Wolves who for no reason a year or two back, sacked one of their best ever and most successful managers.

His bosses the Katushabe brothers were all about strict morals, a strange code of stringent ethics they lived. died and controlled their business empire by.

Every time he thought about it, James was reminded of the first time he'd come a cropper with all this righteous politics they held in such high esteem. "Goddamit" was all he'd said out of frustration and human trait during a meeting with them. Afterwards he'd been called in, made to feel truly ashamed and told that one more such acerbic use of language and he'd more than likely be shown the door.

Took James three days to discover the whole shamozzle had ridiculously been all about the first three letters of the word. For ages after he'd needed to double checked his work for the use, such as godsend and godforsaken.

From that day to this with frustration heaped on exasperation he'd been on the lookout for a new job, maybe an editorship in times of falling sales was out of the question. Being offered the possibility of a marketing role had certainly peaked his interest. No foreign buggers involved, and knew for certain he'd not have to suffer the indignities of being treated like a child. Something along those lines would certainly suit.

'Rachel?' he said when he reached Sean Joseph's work station and stood arms folded peering down.

'And?'

'So. Where is she?'

'I'm not her keeper.'

'No?' James chided. 'What she say at breakfast then?' fair haired slim Sean looked at him, sighed and blew out a breath. 'What you talk about, apart from....shoes an' shopping, eh?'

Sean had tried hard to fathom what was wrong with Gosney's attitude all the time? Was it any wonder his Rachel got so pissed off with him frequently with his ingrained inclination? Be exactly why she'd stayed at home, but he dare not say.

'Rice Crispies do the talking. My porridge stays pretty quiet most days,' was the web designer's sarcasm.

'Very funny, I don't think. Where is she and what's she doing? You must have some idea? This is not a game of hide and seek matey. Gotta bleep paper to get out and I need her stab at something, anything.'

'No idea. Sorry. She's working hard on something that I do know and you're the editor. Think I'm right in saying the ball's in your court James.'

'What she tell you she was doing?'

'Last saw her Sunday evening for an hour or so. Now, d'you mind if I get on?' and Sean was back to his work on screen.

'Thought you and her…'

'Pardon?' and Sean turned his head and sat back looking up at Gosney the editor of the *Lincoln Leader* weekly newspaper, but not his direct line manager.

7

'You either are or you aren't. Now give. C'mon, not got time to waste here. This is Wednesday in case you've forgotten, got a damn paper to get out. Mukisa'll not be too happy reading a blank page with his cornflakes tomorrow morning. "Oh sorry your highness, should be Rachel's page, only she decided to take a….day off," he mimicked. 'Yeh right.'

'Rachel Barnard is your responsibility,' Sean insisted. 'Yes, we plan to marry next year, but I'm not her keeper. She doesn't need my permission to work or not work. You decide,' he said pointing up at Gosney. 'What she does and where she goes has to be down to you, not me. Works here, works from home or out and about you know full well. Remember she wrote that series about women being controlled a while back and got awards? D'you seriously think I'd be that daft bearing in mind her platform with that eh?'

'Somebody must know... something,' he came far too close to swearing.

Sean knew she could very well be up to something James Gosney would not be happy about at all. Knew he had a need to tread carefully with what he said.

'Oh bugger it,' said Gosney as he turned. 'Old filler here we come, be like the soddin' BBC here comes a repeat.' and then turned back to Sean now head down back working. 'You hear a word,' he pointed vigorously. 'She send you love and kisses you let me know pronto, d'you hear?' was not responded to.

The house uphill she'd set her heart on Sean guessed was behind what she was doing and probably where her mind and work were right there and then.

All he knew was Rachel'd somehow hit on something she reckoned would put her in with a good chance of taking on the Features Editor role in the Katushabe's glossy monthly *Lincoln Now!* the brothers were planning a Spring launch for. The house she'd fallen in love with they both knew, had to be slightly out of their league moneywise but to be fair she was doing her level best to close the gap.

Sean had tried hard to get her to slow down, stop her burning the candle from both ends with little success. There appeared to be no stopping her once she got the bit between her teeth on a major story. Rachel's contract was as a Columnist and Features Writer for the Katushabe brothers and it paid well. Her secret freelance work under false names was a bonus Mukisa and Kaikara knew nothing about.

Back up with his team of journos, James Gosney tried to call her again. Sent a text when it went to voice mail, even hurried an email.

Time to hunt down a Rachel Barnard standby. Fill her page with some freelancer's less than sparkling effort. Do that and he knew questions would be asked on Thursday afternoon. Mukisa with his customary post-production questions would demand answers, about what he was not happy with this week. Be a good chance the phone chat from his pie in the sky office in Birmingham would be short and sweet. No well done, no praise he had never been the recipient of. Just to his mind any excuse for negativity in abundance. Produce less than a perfect edition due to a real lack of decent local news was at times unavoidable. Even so, there'd be a monumental inquest almost as if it was written in stone and mandatory. The why's and wherefores. An intriguing and at times controversial Barnard feature would James knew produce a storm of appreciation aimed in her direction alone.

With everybody so accountable, in his world of work if matters weren't wholly above board these days James knew a wrong word here or there would produce unimaginable costly consequences he had a serious need to avoid.

Sean Joseph could only surmise about Rachel's absence. Money, they say is the root of all evil but to his betrothed it was the journey to her new home.

2

Detective Sergeant Jacques Goodwin listened to *Radio Lincolnshire* as he headed up the A15 towards Brigg in light rain initially, on the Wednesday morning. Roads had become busier as the weather slowly improved. Knew the route well enough and the familiar straight Roman-like road heading north.

One ear on the sound of the Four Seasons and the other listening out for updates from his major incident destination. The rain had stopped before he'd taken the turn off to Brigg when he'd got a sideways glance of a rainbow out to the west. How many Code Reds had that been recently he'd asked himself more than once lately.

Off the A15 and along to Redbourne in North Lincolnshire he'd passed through many a time with Sally heading for the big garden centre in Brigg. Quiet, neat and tidy Redbourne village past the pub on the left and he was then talked in by Sandy MacLachlan having followed instructions to turn off along little more than a dirt track having spotted the 'Higgins' sign.

Back at Lincoln Central he'd just started his morning coffee and was in the process of checking the overnights, before his DI was ready for her morning briefing. Then out of the blue Code Red. Body. Unexplained.

By the time he turned his Saab onto the track as instructed by his big Scotch colleague, the Four Seasons had been replaced by some hip hop name he'd never heard of and after eight bars decided the he or she he hadn't as yet fathomed, were not to be encouraged and he switched off.

Some things never change in the world of murder investigation. Different locations, varying local plods ability, incompatible scenarios, unalike times of day and he was thankful this was early to mid-morning after coffee, and in this case he'd thankfully been warned about, an unknown to him pathologist.

Jake was not at all sure what he preferred. Urban or rural locations, both were good and bad, had advantages and disadvantages.

Urban meant spending time in many grotty and often disgusting places, having to come into contact with the way some people live he always found most unpleasant and depressing.. Advantages were of course plenty with CCTV, plenty more nosey people to witnesses and folk with opinions. More sights and sounds generally and social media activity. Another downside was the selfie brigade and the trolls taking pictures of anything and everything that moved.

The rural crime scene was better in that respect, but the disadvantages were a lack of CCTV, of people in general and out of the way places he's had to trudge to and from in the past. Neighbourhood watch as such was no longer an organized cohort but replaced by a tribe of busybodies who infrequently were able to assist.

It had been well less than an hour's drive for the Detective Sergeant from his desk in Lincoln Central police station to the small village and this farm Sandy MacLachlan had guided him to by phone.

Road Crime Unit car pointed him in the direction of a dirt track alongside a big field he'd been talked towards. The black van from the mortuary was as yet not in sight. Too quiet in fact for those with experience like Jake. No need for blue lights flashing, no armed response cops come to that, which is too frequently the case these days.

Off the road leading to the farm vehicle access was very limited to say the least. Where he'd parked on a nettle strewn verge he'd passed a squad car, CSI's van already there along with Sandy's motor and one he didn't recognize. He nipped between bushes and trees to a fenced-in big field he'd walked along.

The morning under-powered sun had emerged and was warming the Lincolnshire countryside set out before him. His immediate view was of a long sweeping slightly uphill vista across the green field, to sheep outlined against the limp blue sky.

One thing always remained exactly the same, and Goodwin second on the scene from the Major Incident Team had always wondered how much of it was used in a year.

Blue and white tape. Strung frequently upside down across a road, between buildings, hung from tree to tree, tied to lampposts, hung off telegraph poles. Dribs and drabs of which would more than likely remain there for months after.

There just off the muddy track was one of a team of white suited individuals working in and around what looked for all the world to be a drinking trough. All rusty and manky, donkey's years old with weeds in abundance was the locus.

Jake could see even from a few feet away freshly decked out in his white coverall, a body in the dirty trough.

Jake had crafted an inner sanctum to protect his family from the depravity he witnessed almost on a daily basis. A safe world his family and friends had never been offered the password to. This was yet another in a long line. Something else he couldn't take home and chat about with Sally over a glass of red.

His mind immediately made him look across the grass covered pathway to a wire fence strung from wooden posts. Beyond that a huge field and in the distance a good hundred yards away a good fifty or more sheep grazing. The smell of the countryside redolent in the air, not the manky wiff he often faced back in unsightly grotty areas of the city.

'How d'you do? I'll be finished soon,' said the new to the area Home Office Pathologist who Goodwin had up to that point never met before. 'Think our friends,' he gestured with his blue nitrile gloved hand, 'Will take a tad longer by the look of it,' was aimed at Shona Tate's CSI team members all decked out in white some on their hands and knees. 'Doctor Meller,' he said up to Goodwin from behind his horn-rimmed glasses and the pathologist's blue eyes peering just above the mask were on his. 'Marcus,' he added. 'Why do I always get introduced to people like this?' on his knees he mused up to the Detective Sergeant. 'This your gig?' was unusual but boss Darke would always remind anybody how such words and phrases are not the sole right of the young.

'Looks like it,' Jake answered. What a curious word to use. One Jake knew had so many definitions. True most people use gig as a performance by a musician or group which he assumed was his connotation. What about the racing boats he and Sally had seen in Cornwall or a harpoon of sorts used in fishing? 'Detective Sergeant Jacques Goodwin,' he said formally. 'Pleased to meet you. I'm the SIO. Call me Jake.'

The big Scotsman Detective Constable Alexander 'Sandy' MacLachlan had been first there as per usual, and would from this point on liaise between the various cohorts investigating on site.

Sandy looked at DS Goodwin's face with concern written all over it.

'Problem?' the Scot asked.

'She's the one with the problem,' was curt. A puff of breath blown out, a grimace of sorts as Jake peered down pondering. 'Too many women and for why. Sex is a major motive, but...he dress her again you think. What's the chances?'

'Unless she said nae.'

Another suck of air for Jake. 'Say yes you get raped, say no you get this. Hardly a fair swap. Call the boss,' he said pulling out his phone. 'Time to make a start, need to get this sorted and hunt down another bad boy.' He blew out a sigh of frustration. 'How far have we got?' Jake dared ask somebody he'd never worked with before. 'Any chance of the basic gist?' He asked down to Meller.

'Easy,' said Meller still with his head down checking the cadaver. 'Prior to PM of course it looks like asphyxia. Smack on the head, then choked to death I presume in that order, and not a chicken bone she had for tea.'

'Male...assailant?'

'Probably as you say, by the bruising.' Goodwin watched as the white suited figure with hood down glanced up over his glasses with a grim expression. 'Yesterday, day before.'

'Thanks doc. At least that's a start.'

'Best I can do for now you understand,' said Meller slowly getting to his feet. 'Female I say obviously from the look of her, but the way things are these days even that can be wrong. Aged twenty to thirty five,' he read. 'Fully clothed as you can see and

13

there's been no disturbance. Redhead, green eyes, freckles, if that helps. No make-up. Head wound as I say and strangulation all pre-full diagnosis.'

Meller closed the black notebook he slipped into his inside pocket. He gestured to Goodwin as if to say that's your lot. 'Enough for now?'

'Thanks doc.' Goodwin responded. 'Gives us something to go on. See you before you go,' said Jake and was about to head off to find Sandy but he stopped and turned back. 'Quick question. Why would you have a sheep trough the other side of the fence from the sheep?'

'Yours to wonder why,' this Meller quipped. 'Not hold water now that's for sure.'

Jake was still pondering the puzzle as he walked over to Sandy MacLachlan. There had been an air of practised efficiency about the suited and hooded Meller to please him.

'One guess,' said the grinning big Scot stood away from a couple of middle aged women and their dog to make Goodwin visibly sag with the hint of their in joke. He led Goodwin over to the pair stood with their brown and white dog on a lead. 'Yvonne Salter and Susan Jones,' MacLachlan introduced and Goodwin still wearing nitrile gloves shook hands. 'Come along here frequently for a walk with Basil here apparently. Not been for two or three days.'

'Last time was when, roughly?' Goodwin asked the women. With support still to arrive Jake was in need of witness accounts. These two would do for now.

'Back at the weekend,' said this Jones woman.

'You found her back at the weekend?' Goodwin threw back.

'No,' Jones insisted making it into a long word. 'Last time we were here,' said the squat woman, all bottom half wearing pretend denim trousers, a waistcoat over a pink and blue flowered blouse. Hair hung loose to her thin shoulders. 'Be where your people are now,' she gestured back down towards the copse. 'Basil barked as he does which is all he can manage nowadays. Damaged a paw a while back that's stopped his scampering and jumping about. Got to say we were pretty taken aback to say the least,' she put a hand up. 'Him up on his hind legs. Didn't touch a thing. In fact we stood back, put Basil on

14

his lead, maybe should've checked for vitals and all that business but it were such a shock.'

'You've no idea,' said the other woman and pushed out a breath as if she'd just dashed fifty metres.

'You did well,' Goodwin advised. 'Understand you'd not have helped her if you had.' Jake Goodwin left it at that and looked both ways along the hardy trodden path alongside fencing leading to a huge meadow with the sheep still grazing some way off. 'Excuse me for asking, and there's no concern but why here? Why bring your dog alongside a field with all those sheep.'

'Alright with Hube.'

'Hube?' Goodwin repeated with more than a hint of grimace.

'Sorry Hubert, Hube we call him. Know him and his good wife a good while really. Hubert Cutforth and knows Basil's bit long in the tooth to go worrying sheep,' said this Susan Jones.

'And not fit enough nowadays.'

'I phoned,' Jones added pulling her mobile from her jacket pocket for some reason.

'Well trained been to classes and all that,' this Salter went on. 'Just sniffs about does his business and we get a good walk. From the village along to hereabouts and back. Not worry sheep, in fact not worry anything but good with what he did.'

'Certainly. Thank you.' Jake considered thanking the dog for a split second but decided against it.

'What time we talking?' Sandy MacLachlan asked for confirmation for the Detective Sergeant.

'Be just after nine?' said Salter turning to her friend who just nodded slightly. 'Left home good while before. Takes ten or fifteen minutes to let him off the lead.'

'Yes. Got to be nine, quarter past.' Susan Jones added to what her friend had already said.

'Not seen a soul, sorry, which I 'spect is your next question,' was Yvonne Salter jumping the gun. There was no point in telling her this was not a recent event to banter about the village, but her big walking boots were a bit out of place for a morning walk with an unfit dog..

'Got the ladies' details,' said MacLachlan.

15

'Thank you both,' said Goodwin. 'Shouldn't need to trouble you any more, but if need be we have your details.'

'Home anytime, both retired now,' the taller of the women slipped in before they both turned and walked off chattering.

Both Jake and Sandy stood watching them wander off back down the path. 'One day I swear to god I'll write these all down. Got to be a few pennies for knowing how many cadavers have ever been found by dogs. Bet I've known half a dozen at least.' Jake sighed. 'House to house started do we know?'

'Nae uniforms arrive the now.' Sandy shook his head. 'Need to get a move on, Sarge,' he suggested. 'Nae be long before those two wifeys, the internet and the local grapevine shout the morbid news the trolls'll pick up on.'

'Wonder if house-to-house is worth it? Got to be between Sunday and now and doc reckons could be a couple of days. Monday latest maybe.'

'Houses a good stretch away before the turn off, all set back a bit. Cannae see from here abouts,' Sandy pointed after that Mrs Jones in the distance at the end of the field disappearing through a gap in the trees. 'She was right. Good while away.'

'This Hubert Cutforth, must be the farmer. You seen him yet? produced a shake of the head. 'Gotta be worth a tap eh?' Sandy nodded and pouted as he thought. 'Anybody else since you arrived?' Jake asked and Sandy shook his head again. 'That must help.' He sighed and looked all about. 'Back in town it'll be CCTV and witnesses. What we got?' he asked with a wry smile. 'Two women and a damn dog. Brilliant!'

'If there was something going on along here say, gotta be easily be spotted,' the big DC said. 'Small village and what's the betting nosy, going on paranoid. Along with all the social media, anybody know a chimney sweep business.'

'My parents suffer the same thing. One of the downsides about small rural communities. Stuff and nonsense like *Suspicious activity aware! New white transit, sound of door closing. Why no cops when you need one*,' Jake and Sandy chuckled at his example. 'Not to mention the daily rant about dog mess. Think you're right though, they'd have said.'

16

'Need to dae something. Facebook and the rest of they gubbins for starters. See if somebody spotted something or assumed they did. I'll call the new girl.'

'Alisha,' Jake reminded. 'Alisha O'Neill.' Sandy pulled out his phone as Jake moved away. 'Back to it,' Jake sighed deeply. 'Time to see what else the doc's got before he heads off.'

'Morgue van's here,' he said pointing through the trees at the bottom of the field as he waited for a reply. 'Didna take long.'

'They'll need to carry the body bag all the way down here,' said Jake pointing down the field once Sandy was off his phone. He just stood looking.'

'Could be worse boss,' brought Jake back to the here and now. 'Could be Ukraine.'

'Yeh,' he half chuckled. 'With a gun over my shoulder,' and shook his head. 'Ah well, need to keep trolls well away. Last we thing we need is the cadaver and black bag all across Twitter.'

Be only a matter of time Jake Goodwin knew, before a reporter got a wiff of something going on he could use and satisfy a website or two. They'd got time. Nearest had to be Brigg, Scunthorpe or a tidy stretch up from Lincoln.

'See Jamie's here and Guy French,' big Sandy said when he spotted the kitted up Detective Constables emerge through the trees.'Get them to lend you a hand,' Jake suggested as Sandy ushered the DCs over. He then briefed both detectives and Sandy to some extent on the current scenario, adding what he'd been told so far by the pathologist.

'We'll start house to house, while we wait. Early bird and all that.' Jake suggested as he led the others off down the side of the field. 'Do properties closest to the road. Uniforms on their way?' he checked with Sandy who nodded. 'They can do the pub, shop whatever they've got and anymore close enough.'

'Only seen t'pub.'

'Let's get this started I can give you a hand. Another tranche of troops turn up we can spread further out. Maybe Hibaldstow if need be,'

'Boring job, right enough.'

'But essential.'

17

'Aye. Isnae much fun anytime.'

'Farmer?' Sandy reminded.

'He'll not be going anywhere, 'sept milking cows. See any more troops can we get started further afield?'

'Sure thing.'

'There's a pub,' said the Scot. 'Spotted as I came in.'

'Don't bother with the farm I'll deal with that when I have a word. C'mon, the DS ushered them away..'

Walking away from a crime scene was frequently a break worth taking and as an opportunity to toss the white suit aside and turn his pretty blue shoes back to black.

As he strode off to find the first property on his side of the road which was a fair hike, the shoestring thought came to mind when there was still no sign of nosey-parkers. Character in the series had been called Shoestring. That had been the name of a down-at-heel private detective on the telly. He'd seen repeats of a year or two back on some channel. Jake chuckled to himself as he linked the two together. Down-at-heel would have him working on a Shoestring. Jake had a picture in his mind as they all walked off. Bit like the news when they say something's all washed up and show you pictures of the sea for no good reason. Be all part of the same arty-farty idea. Couldn't for the life of him remember the actor's name he'd seen in loads since.

3

Goodwin, MacLachlan, Hedley and French were all fully aware of the house-to-house guideline parameters. Knowledge of the times during which the pathologist had suggested the deed was done as far as he could, at such an early stage.

Times people may have visited the scene was it seemed at that juncture as the trodden grass pathway went little further, simply down to the two women and Basil.

Sightings were what they were after, as a useful adjunct with times and any other witnesses reporting the same events or people.

They all knew this was never an easy job to undertake with such little knowledge of events but timings were the driver as always.

'You took your bloody time,' was aimed at DS Jake Goodwin stood on the concrete path to the first property he was tackling down towards the pub, after he'd knocked the white PVC front door, warrant card held up. Had to be the impending boredom of the tedious necessity getting to him.

'I beg your pardon,' he said. 'Detective Sergeant Jacques…'

'Yeh, yeh, so what yer doin' 'bout all this then matey?'

'All this what, sir?'

'Bloody kids on them scooter whatsits. Made a right mess o' me car,' Jake was struggling to come to terms with as the man in a grubby t-shirt and inevitable grey jogging bottoms pushed past him. 'Look mate,' he said when he reached a dark green old Mazda Demio sat outside the garage.

'I think sir, you're under a misapprehension.'

'Look at this. Little shits!'

'Excuse me, sir,' said Jake as he looked at the scratches the oaf was pointing to. 'I'm here on a completely different matter. Now…'

'Hang on a minute. Called you lot bloody Sunday mate, 'bout this. What yer gonna do 'bout it now you bothered to get off yer arse?'

'Sir. Stop it right now. This,' Goodwin said moving into his space as the scratches were pointed at. 'Is a uniform matter. You need to call Brigg police station and get them to give you an Incident Number. I'm sure they'll deal with it, sir. If nothing else you can claim off your insurance.'

'You what?' was gasped enough for spittle to emerge. 'That where it were, up Brigg. Reckoned they'd send one of you fellas down.'

'Right here and now we're dealing with a major incident and we're going door-to-door asking what people like you may have seen over the past few days.'

'Oh that's it then eh?' was sighed. 'Not good enough eh livin' round here like,' he said looking along the quiet road. 'Bugger me!'

'Please sir. You need to understand we're doing door-to-door asking if you or your neighbours saw anything untoward say on Monday or Tuesday evening and night.'

'How much d'yer wanna know?'

'As much as you can tell us. And you are, sir?'

'What?'

'Your name, sir?' Goodwin posed with notebook at the ready.

'Ullyatt. Why d'you wanna know that?'

'So if we have any follow ups we know who to contact, sir. First name?'

'Micky'll do,' he grimaced. 'Right then,' he said and sat back on the car bonnet and folded his chubby arms. 'Seen 'em bout all weekend wizzin' up and down like bloody maniacs...' Goodwin had his hand in front of the man's face.

'Not Brigg kids on scooters. Major incident, sir,' he said firmly. 'The body of a young woman's been discovered close to Higgins Farm.'

'Well, bugger me boots!' he uttered and shook his head. 'So we's at the back o'the queue are we? Bloody hell fire. Shoulda bloody known wi'you lot.'

'Sir, a young woman is dead.'

20

'Nowt to do wi' me fella. Seen nothing like that, what yer take me for?'

'So,' said Goodwin. 'You complain about all this stuff going on but suddenly on Monday and Tuesday you saw nothing, noticed nobody. No strangers or vehicles unusual to the village. That what you're saying?' he peered down at his notes. 'Mr Ullyatt,' was louder to convey a message he doubted the goon would pick up on.

'Nobbut all this,' he said shoved himself off the car and ran his fingers down the passenger door again.

'I'll have a word,' said Goodwin. 'Be plenty of uniforms about in a while, one of them could pop round for a chat. But you still reckon you've seen nothing but these kids. How old we talking, sir?'

'Youngsters?'

'Age?'

'Easy be twelve or fourteen reckon. Little bloody toerags'

'I'll get somebody to pop round. You be here all day?' Goodwin queried as he produced a card he handed over.

'Yeh.'

'Thank you, sir. Most helpful.'

'Anybody we know?'

'Shouldn't imagine so, sir. Thank you for your time.' *Waste of time* he muttered as he turned to start walking down the path.

'Try catching criminals for a change!' followed the DS away. Jake's blood boiling at the utter stupidity of the man made no comment or physical indication he'd even heard the dope.

Goodwin might well have social and interpersonal un-PC quirks and is determined not to become a tick box copper.

House-to-house never changes, but had to be done and to some extent Ullyatt was typical. This was the initial fast-track response phase in the manual. After that encounter hoping to learn of anything significant was a vain hope.

Hunting for mention of a stranger, something different just in case, but Jake knew statistics told him seven out of ten women knew the person who killed them.

'Well I never,' this woman gasped hand to her mouth as soon as Goodwin explained his reason for calling at the lovely property. 'She alright?'

'I'm afraid not, madam. No.'

'Goodness me,' and wiped away a pretend tear as some go in for. Flicked fingers in front of her face'd be about as much as he could stand with a major incident to deal with.

'Just calling to ask if you might have seen something or somebody, maybe just a strange car on Monday or Tuesday evening. Even back as far as Sunday might be a possibility.'

'Be Sunday we see more going on, what with folk visiting and that. Those delivery people about more and more o'course.' she stopped to think. 'My hubby might, knows more about cars than me,' she smiled at. 'Can I get him to give you a call?' Jake Goodwin handed over his card. 'Higgins Farm you say?'

'Yes. On the outskirts.'

'No reason,' she said shaking her head. 'For him to go up that way wouldn't have thought.'

'Anyway, thanks for your help and if you'd mention I called to your husband?'

'Yes,' she said and waved his card. 'He's at work. But I'll tell him tonight.'

Next house a good fifty metres along the road was a no show and he got a thumbs down from Sandy further along as the big man crossed the road towards him.

'Waste of time so far,' he admitted. 'But got a dozen uniforms just turned up. I'll head back get them knocking. Do the pub and the rest.'

Jake looked left and right along the road. 'Tell you what, if somebody was about they'd stand out like a sore thumb. One road in and out by the look of it.'

'Next to nothing so far, but,' Sandy pulled a face. 'Isnae hardly any houses close enough to the road either to spot somebody.'

'I'll do two or three more,' Jake pointed. 'Down to that white one where they peter out. Need to get off to see the farmer before he clears off to market or whatever they do.'

They'd all through previous experiences been ready for the ludicrous responses as Jake had suffered. Sandy had, back up in

Scotland as a PC once knocked on a door as part of a major inquiry to be told by a woman she'd just burnt a fruit cake for the third time that week. Could Sandy help?

Almost every copper has such sad and annoying tales to tell. "Kittie my cat's been missing for two days...What you lot doing about the dog poo in the street...You got a number for DVLA?" the list goes on.

Next up was another woman, much younger this time and by her outfit and the glow about her she'd been working out. Be following some exercise video or daytime telly.

'Sorry to trouble you,' he said holding out his card she took and read. ' We're investigating a suspicious death locally and we're asking people if they've by chance seen anything unusual over the past three or four days. Vehicles, people maybe away from the norm?' The response initially was a grimacing negative look. 'Looking around the Higgins Farm area in particular.'

'See cars and vans but just passing by,' she offered. 'Most heading off into Hibaldstow or back to A15. This something we should be worrying about? Thinking of the kids.'

'It's very early days and the woman involved was not from around here, Just think from what we've gathered so far, the quiet location is the reason.'

'Thank goodness.'

'If anything comes to mind, we'd appreciate if you would give us a call. We're based down in Lincoln but here's my number,' and he handed over another card.

'Just never imagine do you?' she wiped sweat from her brow with her tanned hand. 'In a nice place like this.'

'No madam.'

Truth was in line of duty he came across suspicious deaths far too often and in the strangest of places.

Next was another woman, this one in an apron who felt the need to tell Jake she was making a walnut and pecan cake. Claimed she'd seen nothing, been told nothing but just had to have a bit of a moan about litter, to completely the wrong person.

Last but not least another woman who had just pulled up in her car, having been into Tescos in Brigg for a food shop, but not really of a mind or in the mood to chat. Getting stuff into the freezer was her overriding priority.

On his way back Jake asked one of the uniforms passing, if he'd spend a minute or two talking to that Micky Ullyatt at a house he pointed out to the Constable.

4

By the time uniforms arrived on scene, Jake had already decided to end his involvement in what was turning into, as was often the case, a thankless task. Most people they spoke with claimed they'd not seen or heard anything at all, or wouldn't admit to it if they had. One reckoned there'd been a white van at the far end of the village with two 'scruffy looking herberts' the day before and one woman said she'd seen a dark car not normally in the village she reckoned had to be up to no good.

Was this one of the major differences between urban and rural incidents? A lack of people meant there were less to witness events, less to offer something to those knocking on doors.

The village was not alone he knew. Jake's parents lived in a small village and his old man was always going on about what people claim to see they stick on social media, particularly in regard to what they consider to be strange vehicles. Then message the detail two hours later by which time they've skedaddled.

His dad had told him about people messaging on social media about a lost snake somebody had come across. People asking if the car boot sale is still on, and with a garage in the village some dope asking where they can get their car serviced. He was convinced too many people are unable to function on their own now they have Google to rescue them.

'I'm off to have a word or two with this,' Jake checked his notebook. 'This farmer boy Cutforth. But need to have a last word with the doc first.'

By the time he was back to Meller the whole scene had been secured and step plates put down by CSI along with a grizzle faced uniform with a scene log in operation.

Connor Mitchell the crime scene photog was there, now videoing the whole scene.

'There you are,' said Meller when Jake now without his white attire walked up to him, but stood well back. The body had gone, Meller's job for now appeared done. 'You'll need this,' the pathologist said as he walked to Jake and handed over a business card. 'Your CSI leader has the wallet from her pocket, bit of change and a hankie. No bag at all, and more importantly to you is no phone. If this was one of those foreign noir dramas there'd be no phone, no wallet and more than likely no hands, if you could see anything at all in the dark. So you got off light,' he joked. 'But I got one of these from the wallet, so now we know.'

'Journalist,' said Jake as he read. 'Features *Lincoln Leader.*' He looked up at white wild haired Meller and pulled a face.

'Problem?'

'Just the name,' he gestured towards his Scots colleague. 'Confusion heading our way. Rachel's the name of Sandy's wife,' Jake chuckled. 'But having said that, it rings a bell. Why?' Jake asked himself as well as the pathologist.

'Local paper.'

'Wallet in her pocket tells us she had no bag you think?'

'Could well be right, bit of an old fashioned thing handbags according to my youngest daughter. Go with hats and gloves so she reckons.' Meller grinned.

'Anything else since I've been gone?'

'Blood lividity is an issue. As you know she was face down but a quick check tells me blood has settled on her back. Means she was on her back a good while and more than twelve hours ago as it's permanent.'

'Useful.'

'Time for a cuppa,' said the medical man. 'Don't touch that,' he said pointing to the old trough. 'The CSI woman's got her eyes on it.'

'See you again, no doubt. Thanks for your help.'

As Meller turned to walk off it came to mind. 'Thinking aboot it,' said Sandy scrutinizing the card. 'I'm sure she's the one who writes that good stuff in the *Leader*,' he said to stop the medical man. 'My Rachel reads her every week.' He shrugged, and handed it back to Jake. 'But to be honest, what else is there in a local rag like a parish magazine at best. She writes about topical and controversial stuff and often than not, exposes wrong doers.'

'Might be just the motive we're looking for.'

'Tends to have a different perspective on things,' Meller suggested. 'Often critical of women and unusually so. Sort of thing my Katie and her friends love. Can't think of an example off the top of my head, just pick up from what she says, but as an example when some of these women talk tripe about men supposedly leaving their clothes on the bedroom floor or leaving the toilet seat up, she blames it all on women.'

'Sorry?' was all a confused and grimacing detective could come up with.

'Says its all down to women. As their mothers they're the ones who from an early age taught them right from wrong and how to behave.'

'Interesting angle.'

'Yeh. Sure that's her.' Meller said as Jake was looking down at the business card again and knew he had need to check with his Sally when he got a free moment. 'Women then?' said a smiling Meller. 'Possibility of woman against woman is a good start. Don't quote me on this,' he said pointing at Goodwin. 'Don't wish to spoil the party, but PM will reveal all, but asphyxiation looks to be at the hands of a man. I'll leave it with you,' he said and walked off.

It was a good quarter mile away from the site of the discovery and Jake had not bothered to motor round. Taking Jamie Hedley with him, on such a nice day he enjoyed the trudge around the big meadow and made his way along the lane which then became a gravel single-lane road, full of potholes.

The fairly remote nature of the area meant police were few and far between and Jake knew anybody within touching distance would by now have been roped in to assist. Chances were idiot motorists on the A15 would get away with all sorts for an hour or two with traffic cops joining in house-to-house.

The farmhouse as traditional as could be, with three large barns and what Jake guessed was a milking parlour and then acres and acres of open farmland.

From his perspective it was the right decision to get a better outlook than just driving in and out. See the lie of the land and as expected the scruffiness that often seems at home on farms.

He was met before he reached the door by 'Oi you! Where you off to?' asked a scruffily dressed man with a ruddy complexion.

'Your front door,' said Goodwin with his warrant card hoisted high, and Jamie Hedley followed suit. 'And you are?'

'Cutforth,' he said as he tried to read. 'Oh, sorry. Can't be too careful with what's gone on.'

'What has gone on exactly?'

'Woman's body they reckon,' told Goodwin word had already started its journey around the community.

'Anybody you know?'

'Told not,' he answered shortly stood there hands on hips with weathered skin of someone happier outdoors than in.

'By who?'

'People we know.'

'And who might they be, just out of interest?'

'Had Vonne and Susan round earlier on.'

'And what did they say exactly?' Goodwin posed.

'Due in for a bevvy. Fancy one?' was not an answer to the question.

'What did they say?'

'Not one of ours.'

'Not one of your what?' he persisted.

'Locals.'

'You talking tea?' Jake Goodwin decided it would hopefully also provide a better environment than stood out there in the dirty yard.

'Come on,' and Jake Goodwin and DC Hedley followed the stout plaid shirted man around the side of the house and he pushed open what turned out to be the kitchen door. Almost before the door was opened the smell of recent cooking reached his senses. Could be they were planning on fresh bread and soup for lunch. Lucky devils Jake thought. His lunch if he got any, would be just about anything unhealthy at all.

With the Code Red as soon as he'd arrived in MIT and headed off he'd left his pack-up in his work station drawer,

Jake knew he'd better scoff it when he got back to stop Sally having a bit of a moan. Again.

Bread or cake his redolent senses had suggested, with two saucepans on the Aga.. 'Nancy. This is one o'them from the police like. Checking what's been cracking off.'

'Mrs Cutforth?' Goodwin enquired as he proffered his hand. She was a well-built blue eyed woman, salt and pepper hair growing whiter by the day.

'Nancy please.'

'Sit down son, sit yoursen down,' and Hubert Cutforth was first to take his place at the big old wooden table on the red flagstone floor. Everything clean, controlled and in its place told Goodwin somebody was a good cook.

There he was in a place just as one would imagine. Big fireplace filled with a pile of logs, but not lit. Be trees on their land they'd cut down, probably from the very woods he'd come from. Big Aga he'd spotted first up and a Butler sink he knew as, but his Sally called them a Belfast. One of the big things on his wife's wish list for the new kitchen they planned.

'What's this about then, lad?'

'A woman has been…'

'Yeh. Vonne was saying.' Why ask when you already know the answer was so infuriating.

'There's a suspicious death alongside that big field where you keep sheep.'

'Too far a drag away that lad. Not see owt from here.'

'Thinking maybe Monday,' he pulled a face. 'Tuesday?'

'Monday?' he gasped and scrunched up his face as if Goodwin had asked what happened on the last Thursday in November 1984. 'Last Monday? This week?'

'Monday just gone. Couple of days ago.'

'Why?'

'We understand,' said Goodwin carefully. 'That is when the incident may well have taken place. Not absolutely cut and dried, but that's what we have to work on at this present time.'

'Do you know who she is?' Nancy Cutforth waiting for the blue kettle to boil, queried.

'We don't talk names until the relatives have been advised by our Family Liaison team. That can sometimes take a few days if people are away or family circumstances dictate.'

Cutforth was shaking his head the whole time Goodwin was explaining. 'Spring lambs lad. Put out onto fresh grass, no need to get off down there and any feeding's done at top there,' he said pointing in the general direction of the window and then looked across at his wife, as if seeking confirmation. 'Not been down...along where they walked the dog you mean?'

'Yes.'

'Nah, not been down there in what...' he blew out a breath noisily. 'Good few days or more.' He then went on for some reason to give a brief resume of how at that time of year the sheep were tended to and fed.

Nancy Cutforth brewed the tea and Jake Goodwin was not at all pleased he was unable to add milk to taste for himself rather than have a load poured in to drown it.

'You do this all the time?' this Nancy asked as she sat down and scraped her wooden chair forward, noisily on the tiled floor. Not dismal in any respect but a homely inviting room you'd want to linger in, especially when the cooking was fresh out the oven.

'Pretty much. Major Incidents anyway take up the majority of my time. Lot of paperwork these days.' Goodwin admitted and took a good sip. 'Help out with other departments as and when of course.'

'Bet you see some sights eh?' she suggested next.

'Not too good at times,' Hedley responded. 'Hardly something you want to take home to the family.'

'How many?'

'Just one. Tyler,' Goodwin guessed she was talking children. 'My wife Sally's a nurse at the County in Lincoln.'

'Angels,' was all Hubert said before he took a drink.

Jake knew this would never in a million years be home to a wide-screen TV and home cinema system along with surround sound speakers. Even though he'd not ventured further than the kitchen he couldn't imagine a satellite box along with games gizmos littering their front room.

There was no way these two decent people would sit in silence each mesmerized by WhatsApp or Snapchat or whatever was on trend that week, scoffing their way through a Just Eat delivery.

'Monday and Tuesday,' Goodwin reminded him. 'Assume you worked all day with all you must have on, but what about the evenings?'

'Monday be doin' me books. Nothin' much going on, nowt good on telly till later, what I do most weeks. Sort of chore you gotta do, and Monday's best time.'

'And Tuesday?'

'We make us way t'pub in Stow. Wheatsheaf for a bit of chinwag with a few mates and that. Pool League night; dunna play no more but always good craic. Missus drives of course, don't you duck?' a remark to always amuse Jake, as if without it he might pull out a tube for him to blow into.

'Thanks for that,' Goodwin made a quick note for future reference. 'And you?' he asked Nancy.

'Same. Monday in, Tuesday's me natter night right enough.'

'What sort of time are we talking about?'

'Be abouts eight.'

'Thanks,' said Goodwin. He'd not made a note but Cutforth had hands like plates of meat with big fat fingers and thumbs. Useful tools around some lass's neck but not too good with a Pool cue. 'One question I've been struggling with. The victim has been found in what looks like an old sheep trough.'

'We know.'

'You know?'

'Susan said,' was pretty obvious when he thought about it.

'Could you explain why you have a sheep trough the other side of the fence from the sheep?'

'Not ourn.'

'How d'you mean?'

'We bin here,' he hesitated and looked at Nancy. 'What twenty six odd year now?' he asked her.

'Early March,' she responded.

'When we took over place from Higgins,' told Goodwin why it was so named. 'Old man Higgins were a cattle man and trough were for them. We went for sheep and they're more

31

inquisitive and smaller could easy get in among brambles, not good for their fleece and in the woods thereabouts, so we put a fence up.' He blew out a breath. 'Ten, twelve year ago?' he asked his wife who nodded.

'That's why its old and tatty because its not used.'

'Right enough.'

'Don't know for certain but it could be our forensic team will want to remove the trough. All to do with DNA and that business. No problem I assume?'

'Nah. Our land see includes the wood not that it's any use to us, so just leave it for the wildlife they go on about these days. Prob'ly get a decent rabbit if us were bothered.'

'Just have to hope it stays dry which will mean our forensic team'll get finished quicker.'

'East wind'll keep it a bit chilly.'

'Old trough's no good to us,' said Nancy having just finished her cuppa. 'When it were first put where it is, trees were not so big, but these days even if we didn't have sheep be no good. Trees overhang so much now, rain'll not fill it.'

'Not humpin' buckets of water o'er there.'

Once his strong tea had been drunk, Hubert Cutforth insisted he gave Jake Goodwin who was pleased to leave the weak milky tea almost untouched, and Jamie Hedley a brief tour of the farm and facilities and in particular illustrated how from where they were based they could only see the tops of the trees in the wood where the woman had been discovered.

'Hear its all over the internet,' Nancy Cutforth offered walking with them. 'Not good for us, having this place splattered all over with the disgusting things they have on there.'

'You've seen it?'

'Friend phoned, bit worried like, asked if we were alright, what was going on.'

'It'll be something else tomorrow,' Goodwin offered, without disappointing them by reminding how every time the case comes to court they'd likely as not get a big mention, if not TV crews after their pennyworth.

'Thanks for that,' Goodwin said and shook hands with the man. 'There'll likely be officers over there at least the rest of

32

the day, maybe a while longer. Please,' he said sternly. 'Don't go poking about or allow anybody else to. Body'll likely be gone by now,' he hoped would allay their curiosity. 'Hear anything, please let me know,' he added and handed over his card.

As the pair strolled back to the blue and white taped off crime scene Jake knew they'd had to deal with similar cases in the past and in truth it was how most murders were. Crime he knew would never be overt in somewhere like Redbourne.

The person they were after was just like him or the farmer he'd just spent time with. but maybe not quite so scruffy. Usually nothing special about them, would easily blend into an environment with no discernible features. The sort you pass in the street any day, like the guy who delivers your Amazon goods, a barista in Starbucks, a barman or the plumber you call out to sort a leaking tap.

Leaving Sandy along with Jamie to do the co-ordinating bit along with Shona Tate the Senior Forensic Scene Manager and her CSI team. Jake headed off back towards Lincoln but when spotting somewhere to take a break he'd been to before, decided it was time for a bite to eat.

Parked up, stepped from his Saab and his phone rang.

'Yes boss?'

'Think I need to view the site.'

'Not much to see. Connor's got pics and video.'

'Seen all that. Even so. Darke says with her being high profile I need to be more hands on just in case.'

'Just in case what?'

'The media take on their anti stance again. Meet you in this Redbourne place?'

'Better bet,' he suggested as his situation came to mind. 'Meet at Uncle Henry's'

'Good choice.'

'Farm Shop on the main A15 drag.'

'Know it.'

'Meet there and I'll give you a tour for what it's worth. It's well sign posted.'

'Look out for me.'

That he'd do, after he'd had a bite to eat and a coke. Might even persuade the boss to stay a while for a decent coffee.

Unlike many Sergeants Inga'd had to deal with over the years, Jake Goodwin was always prepared to see the good in people. Generally decent human beings until some dramatic event, childhood abuse, or as is often the case bad parenting had pushed them in totally the wrong direction in life.

Jake organized coffees when she arrived and almost immediately true to form the peace was broken when Inga's phone rang. She answered and then mouthed "Shona" to him so he knew.

Jake listened into one half of the conversation and got a general grasp of the subject they were discussing.

'Something else to upset your farmer,' she said as she plonked her phone down on the table, then annoyingly took a sip of her coffee. 'That was Shona. You probably know already but one of her team, Liam Routledge suffers badly from hay fever in certain circumstances. Turns out the farm's one of them. She was asking about that...Tessa Hewitt, the forensic archeological expert I told you about. The one I met at that conference in Coventry if you remember. Shona reckons for Liam to be suffering as badly as he is, there may be something unusual and wonders if with it being so bad maybe our target whoever he or she might be, got pollen on their clothing.'

'Read somewhere certain type of nettles can be bad and there were nettles around the sheep trough. Bet us trampling on them has started him off. She want your professor to take a look?'

'Said I'd give her a call. Probably too busy but you never know.' Inga sipped more coffee, then scouped up her phone.

'And she can check Rachel Barnard's clothing at the same time.'

'No time like the present. Give Nicky a call,' Inga said as she got to her feet. 'Get her to give me Tessa's number from her card I've got in my drawer.'

5

Whilst pragmatic, some would say boring Jake Goodwin back at Lincoln Central was trying hard to deal with what little if anything the village house-to-house had produced so far.

Millie Barnard clasped her husband's hand tightly. Too tightly as she sat listening intently to the latest relayed news of what had happened to her youngest daughter.

The two Family Liaison Officers had never met the couple before so their task was a degree easier.

Women chosen in the main for their in-bred ability to be understanding, sensitive and good at washing up. This pair knew to record everything. In a murder investigation if its not written down, it never happened. Their role is always two-fold. Firstly to provide dedicated officers of some experience to act as a link between the family and the investigation team. As part of that remit was the transference of information in both directions. Second was all about emotional support, along with undertaking everyday tasks including in some cases shopping and cooking.

Millie Barnard was in a serious state of shock still, but having husband Derek at hand along with her second daughter Kathryn and lanky son who appeared to do little else than sniff, had to be some comfort.

Nettleham a large village complete with village green and beck in West Lindsey district, had been the Barnard family home location for a good few years.

'Who would want to do such a thing?' Derek Barnard asked across the tidy lounge to PC Julia Dring, who was probably sat in the very chair Rachel Barnard had sat in a good many times.

Julie was a softly spoken sympathetic eyed mother with a soft smile, one could imagine as a matron in some posh school.

This as ever was such a waste of life for no reason anybody had been as yet able to imagine.

'We don't I'm afraid have any further details,' Deanne replied quickly. Julia nodded although in truth she was not sure about anything much at all. 'But we can assure you every effort is being made right now by our experienced officers to catch whoever did this terrible thing.'

With her first class communication skills having been quickly recognized, Deanna Stamp had chosen to become a Family Liaison Officer for Lincoln County Police, after her probation.

'Loads too many nasty shits being let out too early,' said Derek suddenly. 'Slap on the wrist nonsense all they'll do, bloody do-gooders got us into all this mess. Stabbing decent folk right left and centre, bloody good slap when kids'd stop all that.'

'Derek please,' Millie implored.

'Well it's right,' he insisted. 'What's the bettin' eh, it's one o'those illegal shits? What you get with bloody Tories and all their law and order garbage. Who was it cut thousands off police, tell me that? A bloody Tory woman living in some leafy urban suburb down south some place. Not seen a glue sniffer in her life, spice'd be some crap her cook uses. What's the betting there's no skunk buggers down her road eh? Don't need so many police, nothing ever goes on.'

'I can assure you Mr Barnard, we will keep you well informed,' Motherly Julia slipped in in an attempt to calm him. 'As the investigation progresses we will be advised and we will tell you.'

Discovered out in the countryside up near Hibaldstow by a dog was at that point pretty much all the family knew.

Derek Barnard had asked twice were they absolutely sure it was his daughter.

A brief description Deanne had obtained about the body's clothing she had passed on in an attempt to answer his query. They had to remain vigilant in what they said as layering worry or fear onto grief was never a good recipe.

36

Receiving knowledge of Barnard's wallet complete with cards having been located seemed to satisfy him for the time being, but upset Millie Barnard even more.

'I expect,' Deanne joined in. 'Our detectives will in time wish to speak to you about the people your Rachel mixed with, associated with through her work and in fact even those she worked with.'

'What you suggesting lass?' this Derek was back.

'Through her work as an investigative journalist she must have come into contact with one or two unscrupulous characters' was the least provocative way she could describe the drugged-up scrotes and arseholes they dealt with on a daily basis.

'Not be her friends' said Millie, head down looking at the carpet through her tear filled eyes.

'Didn't say it was,' said Julia. 'Just that they'll wish to talk to everybody, cover all bases. Often the most unlikely characters in cases such as this.'

'Cut out yer Yankee tosh!' the two FLO's knew the anger was part and parcel of the grieving process they had to deal with one way or another in all its forms.

'Derek,' Deanna tried to be less formal as Julia did her best in trying to fathom what his last remark had been about. 'We are sorry for your loss but I hope you will appreciate there will be things our team of investigators will need to know. We'll be here as long as you feel you need us,' was aimed at them all sat there, but for the angry bereaved father in particular.

Millie Barnard yanked free from her husband's grip and pushed herself to her feet. 'Can't just sit here. I'll make some tea.'

'We've just had one mum.' Was true but Millie had hardly touched her mug full.

'I'll make another. This is my house and don't you forget it.'

She gave a shuddering sigh as if a thought had ridden right through her and for a moment Millie held onto the back of the chair nearest to her.

'Need a hand mum?'

Deanna saw Millie blink once or twice to prevent more tears, she then swallowed obviously before nodding her miserable preference. A way both PCs knew she would look and feel for many a long tortuous day.

This Derek Barnard was nice enough but to Julia he was a bit rough around the edges. She got the impression he'd been fairly good looking back when he and Millicent initially connected.

When the pair of PCs had first arrived there had been two small kids with Kathryn the eldest daughter, just about school age who'd been unceremoniously bundled off with some stout woman living nearby.

Julia joined Millie Barnard in the kitchen. 'I understand how difficult this must be for you, but please remember we are on your side.,' Millie looked at her with a weak smile. 'I'll do the washing up and we'll get this made.'

Julie headed off to collect the mugs, some had hardly touched and others still half full. Back in the kitchen Julia was at the sink washing them up, when at that that point Derek waltzed in.

'Shouldn't you be out there,' he said pointing towards the garden. 'Doing something useful for once, not sitting round here drinking our bloody tea.'

'Derek!' was loud. 'Just shut up and sit down.'

Julia was pleased she had not had to be the first to tell somebody like this Millie that their loved one was dead. The Interceptors trained for such eventualities had been on call on this occasion, making that dreadful knock on the door.

'Tell you what,' said Millie as her husband skulked back out. 'Let's cheer ourselves up with decent coffees. You do his tea; Derek's old fashioned like that, calls it devil's water. Two tea bags two sugars and just mention the milk to the mug', she grinned with.

'Want me to do it?' Julia asked.

'I'm okay thanks, I...I just can't believe she's gone.'

Normally Inga Larsson's morning briefing with Detective Superintendent Craig Darke always tended to be one sided. Her relating to him the state of play with whatever cases were taking priority. He on the other hand would remind her of the force's relevant strategies and impending changes. That morning it had started quite differently.

'As you know, we and the media have a mutual interaction as the basis of our relationship. They need us to provide something more interesting and at times exciting than more roadworks and the Council closing toilets. As we both know, we need them more these days through the various channels. Media for us all is more than just the local newspaper. We need them to inform, advise and pass on vital information. Today social media monitoring is part of that process. In this case,' he said pointing his finger. 'We need to tread a great deal more carefully.'

'Because of Rachel Barnard?'

'Exactly. She is one of theirs. To my mind, and talking to other senior officers they tend to agree the *Leader* and the likes of Twitter are most likely with the help of joe public, wanting to gain an advantage over other outlets. Don't allow them to use us, to steal off the cuff quotes and delve into what our priorities are and be ahead of the storm.'

Speech over, Inga then went through all the relevant points as normal and she was able with his words originally from above ringing in her ears, able to walk back along the corridor to the Incident Room.

The buzz of chatter quietened almost in sync with her appearance at the daily designated time. Larsson as she often did just looked around the Incident Room, regarding each member of her Major Incident Team present as they quietly waited for her latest update.

With that the door opened and in walked Sandy MacLachlan.

'You born in Bardney?' Jake called out.

'Explain,' Inga queried as Sandy looked bemused.

'You left the door open,' Jake told the big DC. 'Were you born in a barn, or around here Bardney.'

After he'd closed the door and she'd sighed and shook her head Inga began. 'Here we are once again,' she started with. 'Back to square one as you say with Operation Greeba.' Knew she had to explain. 'Greeba is a river the computer's returned us to. As we all know we're talking about a 29 year old journalist we've all probably read at one time or another. Know I have. Columnist and staff reporter for the *Lincoln Leader* no less, based out at Witham St Hughs if she's not working from home. Before we get down to the whys and wherefores I've decided to play this one differently. I've already passed this by the boss and in line with the force's diversity policy,' she smiled with. 'All interviews will be carried out by us women of this parish, to coin a phrase.'

'But I've already started,' Jake offered. Inga Larsson was not amused. Not a word in retort but the look told a story.

Detective Superintendent Craig Darke at their morning briefing could see Larsson was caught in a rock and a hard place dilemma. Yearning to be freed from her obligations for a while, yet fully aware the case was already in very capable and experienced hands with Goodwin having been on scene from the outset.

'Chance for me to keep my eye in at the same time,' was her diplomatic response.

'No PM for me then,' said a happy Jake.

'Probably right, think you're on tea duties this week!, she joked as her rebuttal.

Detective Sergeant Jake Goodwin heaved a sigh of relief to himself to some extent. Life of late had rushed him from one dead or badly damaged body to another in quick succession.

Totally unconnected yet all linked, too far apart physically and personally to anything, but a joint experience, the moment of death.

He'd carried out his duties in the same manner as always, but a change would he knew be as good as a rest, in from the field literally at times away from the guts and gore and repetitive waste of life.

Office bound he knew would be less grim, until the next time. The next call.

As was normal at the start of any major crime, extras had been brought in to assist with the inevitable increased workload. Prominent amongst them this time was DC Guy French from PHU who had proved very useful in the past.

Guy had for a few months worked under cover as part of a nationwide drugs bust and was already aware how this would be a wholly different ball game.

'When the Code Red sounded none of us were to know who, what, why or where. Now we do,' said Larsson just before she took a sip of coffee from her red mug on the desk she had propped herself against. 'Let me explain ladies and gentlemen. Rachel Barnard is a feature writer for the *Leader* and frequently takes an unusual stance against women. Personally I see this as quality diversity. I'm a female in a role previously held by men. Barnard's role includes criticizing people. Women as well as men. To some extent controversially at times, although I'm not one of them who thinks that way. For a random example I think I'm right in saying when there was a big fuss a few years back about a woman in Runcorn or somewhere murdered walking home on her own in the dark. Rachel Barnard most certainly let rip. Why was she on her own? Would any sensible woman go out on her own in the dark without letting anybody know? Why not catch a taxi, or a bus or go with friends? Why overload with gin to make yourself incapable of anything except sex, wear ridiculous clothes and shoes nobody can possibly run in? Yes,' said Inga to catch her breath. 'We all know we should be able to walk the streets day or night without the possibility some clown will come out of the shadows and attack us. Difference is she lived in the real world.'

'Think she mentioned the key business,' Nicky Scoley reminded. 'Am I right or was that someone else?'

'Sure she did. Thank you. That's what she based her piece on I seem to remember. There was a fuss made by some feminists about the fact all women nowadays always have to carry their keys in their hand for protection.' She looked at Michelle's grimace. 'Know where you're coming from.'

'Nobody I know has ever done that,' said the DC sat at the back. 'Think there was a similar attack down in London when some brought that up, but still nobody I know does it or ever has.'

'Exactly,' said Inga. 'That's what she based her article on I seem to remember now. Rumours about women behaving in a way they never do, and urban myths like that do so much damage.' She sipped her luke warm coffee.

'My mum,' said Michelle. 'I remember was amused by one piece she wrote about the menopause. At the time she was suffering from all the hot flushes symptoms and some celebrity of sorts looking for her fifteen minutes of fame to give her flagging career a boost. Made a big thing about the shame she felt having to admit her state to friends.'

'With this Rachel it was like having somebody on your side, reading her work at times. I'll miss it that's for sure.'

'Pithy and thought provoking comments and astute observations on life, were Rachel's hallmark.'

'See them all the time,' said Nicky. 'Keys and phone plonked on a table in Starbucks and off they trot to stand legs crossed chatting to the barista. Then wonder why the phone and keys have gone along with the car. Madness.'

'Jake,' from Inga ended that thread.

'Post mortem.' he said to bring them all back to the here and now. 'Will give us the detail, but a bash on the head and then strangled are the basics from the scene. Can I just say the Pathologist is new to the area and was fine with me, so no worries there like we've had with some. No sexual assault of any kind not unless he dressed her again neatly, no handbag and no phone. Wallet in her jeans pocket with all the usual credit and debit cards plus a bit of money. Just over forty quid I think CSI said, and her business cards,' he held one up. 'Reckons lividity tells us she was on her back a good while but face down in the trough.'

'Thanks Jake. Michelle. Family if you will.'

'Parents both alive and Family Liaison are with them. The Barnards. Husband and wife and just a teenage son remain in a 3 bedroomed house up in Nettleham. Rachel Barnard our victim has a sister,' she checked her notes. 'Kathryn living with her partner out at Bracebridge Heath. Barnard herself lived on her own in a town house off Rookery Lane, she's buying.'

'On her own? Interesting.'

'Hang on a sec. Then we have the boyfriend's name given to us by the parents,' Michelle went on. 'Sean Joseph. I've checked him out on social media. On it certainly, but not one with hundreds of followers and nothing untoward I have spotted so far. But only done Facebook and Twitter as yet. He lives with his mother on the Ermine close to Sabraon Barracks, and works with Barnard for the Katushabe group at their area headquarters down at Witham St Hughs. They as we know publish the *Lincoln Leader*, loads of local newspapers and one or two magazines.'

'Two journalists?'

'He's a web designer.'

'Working on something?'

Inga thought for a moment. 'Job for you Nicky. Head off down there, check the lie of the land, see who it is they are all working for and with and more important discover what it was Barnard was working on which may have upset somebody.'

'I'm interviewing this Sean Joseph in a bit,' the DI advised. 'Where is her car?' she aimed at Jake and Sandy MacLachlan. 'Once we have that, then ANPR it for its movements. I'll get her car info from this Joseph in a while or failing that DVLA. He must at least have her number if not the actual phone. I'll ring you with the detail and you can get the geeks to start a search for where she's been or where it is now,' she said glancing at her watch. 'Sandy, you finished up in Redbourne?'

'Pretty much. All they're doing now is scouring the woods and that field for her phone and handbag if the sheep haven't eaten it and anything else they can.'

'Good. Desk job for you Sandy. Delve as much as you can into what this Barnard woman was writing about. Hopefully we'll know more when Nicky comes back, but I'm sure there has to be some back issues still on the *Leader* website and social media may well give you a clue. If going back any amount of time proves an issue, nip up and get the Tech Crime Team to give you heads up on how they'd find previous issues.'

Before she left the confines of the MIT Incident Room, DS Nicky Scoley did two vital actions. Got herself a coffee which she took time over drinking to have a read of the *Lincoln Leader* website, just to familiarize herself with the media's version of events.

A murder investigation has been launched after the death under suspicious circumstances of a vital member of the Leader's team.

The victim, Rachel Barnard, was a well respected and popular feature writer for this newspaper and for the Katushabe group overall, and she will be most sadly missed.

Police were called at around 09.30hrs this morning to a report of an attack on a young woman.

At the scene, the Leader understands a woman in her late twenties was found to have died in an incident near to Higgins Farm a mile or so south of Hibaldstow.

As part of their initial inquiries, Lincoln County Police are appealing to members of the public to get in touch if they have CCTV, dashcam footage or any information from close to the A1206 from the A17 to Brigg overnight.

Detective Inspector Inga Larsson, head of the Major Incident Team, said today: 'All our thoughts are with the woman and her family and as a force we are doing our utmost to support them at this very difficult time.

Lincoln County Police wish to assure the public that this is an isolated incident.

Any information can, in such cases as this, prove useful to their major investigation and if you have information please call and give Incident No J2948.

News of the day was the arrival of a new DC joining the team as a replacement for Ruth Buchan. Having resigned from the force almost on whim she was apparently now living somewhere in Scotland with an airman from RAF Waddington who'd been posted and she'd shacked up with. Typical of her to do something like that just off the cuff in a moment.

Ruth had been in MIT when Michelle first arrived. Then moved down physically and career wise to PHU.

Now mixed race Bangladeshi and Irish Alisha O'Neill had been selected to join them. Stolen almost by the boss from downstairs. Operating in effect one short since Ruth had been moved together with the loss of her social media expertise, a new one with the interest and knowledge had been chosen unofficially.

DC Alisha O'Neill, recommended for her social media expertise by DCI Luke Stevens they could make use of rather than disturb the computer geeks upstairs with every little tiresome query.

6

Thursday 14th April

'We appreciate you coming in Mr Joseph under these unfortunate circumstances,' said Detective Constable Michelle Cooper chosen specifically to assist DI Inga Larsson as a result of time she had spent with the Family Liaison team.

Despite the need to use it, and keep tabs on content. To Larsson social media fuels a view of the world which is frequently harmful at best, and can so easily become dangerous and violent.

With Joseph there would necessarily be strict rules of interview initially to adhere to, under such conditions. 'May we as a force offer our sincere condolences, and assure you we will do our very best to deal with this matter as carefully as we are able. It will be necessary Mr Joseph for us to record our conversations. Do you have any objections bearing in mind you have chosen not to be represented?'

'Carry on.'

DC Cooper switched on the tape only. Using video at this juncture had been deemed unnecessarily intrusive at this stage by Larsson.

'Thank you,' said Larsson sat directly opposite the man who had to be early thirties, sandy haired and decently dressed having come straight from work. He was wearing what she knew to be what they call a dip dye hoodie. Darker almost navy at the bottom fading upwards. With a string tie neck. Jeans were blue as well and his loafer shoes were tan. 'Realize this is an emotional time for you but would you be able in your own time, to tell us about Rachel Barnard and your relationship in order to set the scene, so to speak?'

'Met through work actually in a roundabout sort of way,' he opened with. 'Then when *The Leader* was taken over, moved out of that big place they once had in town where they'd printed it when it was a daily and out where we are now. New people put all the management and graphics for this area's journals all into the same building. We got to know each other better as a result.'

'Do you live together?'

'No.'

'Any reason?' blonde Larsson inquired casually.

'Money,' was all he said and the pair waited. 'Rachel's got her heart set on a house, not any one in particular but style and location if you like she has a preference for. This is important to her and its now a case of saving up.' He stopped to blow out a deep sighed breath. 'Or should I say, was.'

Larsson allowed Joseph to gather his thoughts. 'Would not living apart be more expensive than say being together?'

'Live with my mother.'

'And that's the reason why you and Rachel didn't live together?' It was a small thing but Larsson had to ask herself why? Knew she'd need to check, but this getting pernickety about location had to be a British throwback to how people thought last century.

'Finance as I said.' He sat forward and placed his hands and arms on the grey table. 'Need somewhere for me mum, and rather than buy just any place for the three of us, I stay with her and Rachel has...had her own place down Rookery Lane. We gain by her staying there. The value of houses is going up by a good percent a year, compared with the piddly amount you get putting money in the bank. So,' he said and sat back and folded his arms. 'Our way of saving money. When the time comes, sell her place, and move into the new property with my mum, she'll make more than she would have done with the cash sat in a bank.'

'Are we to take it your mother lives alone?' Michelle Cooper slipped in.

'Yeh.'

'Long?'

'Getting on for a couple of year now.' Cooper was not planning to ask any more but it arrived after. 'Me old man got done by Covid fairly early on.'

'I'm sorry to hear that,' The DC with a warm shade of chestnut hair, scrubbed clear face to a degree with toffee-brown eyes, responded. 'Not been a good time for you eh?'

'You could say that.'

'Can we get round to the…'

'Look just let me explain,' Joseph interrupted Cooper. 'Me old man was a bit old fashioned and didn't believe in all that business of selling off council houses, and grandad absolutely hated that Thatcher woman. Which is what she lives in on the Ermine. Got it right pretty much as it turned out, nowadays you'd have a job on to get a council house, or social housing is it? Waiting list as long as your arm, but we can still house the boat people. Really supportive eh?' he smiled for the first time. 'Paying rent these days even for a council place is a good wack and if they'd bought she'd be in clover.'

'Can we move on Mr Joseph to…'

'Sean,' he announced.

Cooper was still back thinking about the living arrangements. This Joseph's mother was paying rent unnecessarily as well as for all the utilities, when if the three moved in together she'd have no need to. Why would you waste money or was this another left wing gesture she'd been born into?

'Thank you Sean,' was Inga Larsson as she checked her notes. 'Can we now look back to what you were doing say Monday through to Wednesday of this week, if you wouldn't mind?'

He took a moment or two to consider. 'Daytime pretty much as normal, usual Monday. Evening…' he just stopped and the detectives waited. 'Can I be honest with you here? I know I've not got Rachel to think of now but I'm still really worried about losing my job you see. Mum's only got a part-time one at the local shop and me being out of work'd make things a bit tough and it's not her fault. And with dad gone and all that,' he grimaced. 'You know?' he shrugged both shoulders with.

'Is your job in jeopardy?' Larsson, arms on the table asked.
'And if so, why?'

'Not right now, no. But…' he sat forward again and looked
at the Swede across the table. 'Time's been hard for her as you
can imagine and I need to save her from any more worry.' All
the more reason to have moved in with Rachel somewhere was
Larsson's immediate thought. 'How confidential is all this?'

'Depends. Depends what you admit to.'

'Don't know if you know or not but the group is owned by
two brothers. Ugandan originally so we're told and the
worrying thing is they have some very strict principles they live
and work by. Bit…well how shall I put this? Like those Amish
is as close as some people have got.' He screwed his eyes shut.
'They're not like those ultra orthodox Jews you see on the news
in black suits and wide-brimmed hats though.'

'The Haredi,' said Larsson.

'That's them. Tell you what. Put the Katushabe's in charge
of Covid and we'd've been far better off.'

'They strive to limit their contact with the outside world,'
the DI advised not wishing to go down the pandemic road.
'Surely the people you're talking about can't be like that. A
form of cult.'

'No. I'm just using them as an example of people with these
specific odd ways, thoughts and traditions. Except the
Katushabe brothers are almost the complete opposite in some
respects. In praise of women to a great degree, and has to be the
reason why such things as bad language will not be tolerated
under any circumstances. Nothing like those who insist to retain
control their second class citizen women wear a scarf or one of
those hajib things. To some extent that is why Rachel had the
role she did, and the non-sexist freedom she enjoyed is down to
them.'

'Freedom in what respect?'

'She pretty much chose what she'd write about. From time
to time head office in Birmingham gave her the heads up on
something they've come across she could get her teeth into.
James Gosney the Editor and the group features chap in
Birmingham come up with stuff of course, but apart from that it
was down to her. Locally we only handle the local news, most

of each issue comes down from head office. Sort of bland stories purporting to be local but never truly are.'

'This freedom, came from...the brothers you say? She must have got on well with them.' Now Larsson knew why frequently the *Leader* tended to get their knickers in a twist with regard to locations and sometimes she'd even wondered if the reporters had even visited the city. Now she knew, they'd probably not and why the same four or five names claimed to have contributed to news stories one after another.

'Yes and no. As a journalist Rachel'd had in the back of her mind for ages, to expose them one day.' A hand went up. 'Not now, not while we depend on them for our living, but they have been known to sack people almost on a whim sometimes or so we understand just because of a remark they've made or something in their personal life they're not happy with.' They waited for him. 'One guy got dumped overnight because he got done for drink driving. Not a driving job you understand making absolutely no difference to their business or his work. Think it was the fact he'd broken a law they take so very seriously. Cannabis warning and you're out on your ear as one bloke in Worcester discovered.'

Michelle Cooper sat there nodding her head aware her dad felt exactly the same.

'And why would you talking to us get you sacked?' Inga Larsson checked.

'Ah well,' he sighed again. 'In for a penny eh? Rachel was very ambitious and wanted a particular type of house uphill and we're saving like mad eventually for a family and a good future. I do web work on the side, in my own time.' He stopped to grin. 'Brothers get wind of that, be out the door faster than you can blink. Demanding total loyalty is another trait.'

'And you think what you tell us will get back to the paper's owners.'

'The Katushabe brothers. They're billionaires and Ugandan by birth, sort of fundamentalists or whatever they are. Not exactly a sect, but some of the staff reckon pretty damn close. Think if they could get away with it, they'd have us all dressed alike.'

'Let me assure you,' said Cooper. 'Unless it is something materially affecting the case concerning what happened to Rachel, you have no fear of who might be told what you say.'

'Fair enough.'

'So, where were we? Ah yes. Monday, you're at work you say.'

'Yeh, Normal day, normal Monday. Spoke with Rachel at work couple of times I think, then we spoke on the phone later when I was doing work on a website for a local builder all evening. Don't know what Rachel was doing, but...doesn't matter now, they can't sack her, but you see,' was sceptical and pulled a face of hesitancy before he went on. 'Rachel worked freelance for other publications under false names.'

'She worked as a freelance journalist you say?'

'No. She's a staff features writer who did forbidden work on the side. Columnists such as Rachel have a degree of longevity the other reporters lack. Well past the stage of her writing up on the hapless in court for selling Spice. She does all the investigating the paper wants, dealing particularly with feminine aspects.' He stopped to catch his breath.'She was batting for women by telling what they were doing wrong. A few home truths men dare not mention. At the same time because of that freedom of creating her own stories she then sold to all sorts of people, newspapers, magazines websites, agencies. But nobody knows. Has a list of people men and women she masqueraded as.'

'They vehemently support equality, yet at the same time encourage her to criticize women?'

'Discipline is almost a motto. Lambasting women for some of their attitudes is their way of encouraging more women to take self-discipline on board.' He smirked. 'Said they were odd didn't I?'

'Because of these...brothers? This is extra money to add to the pot to buy the house?'

'Exactly right.' Sean pulled a face. 'Why I say they should have been in charge of Covid, they'd've made the country more disciplined and react in the correct manner. Take responsibility. Don't get drunk and walk the streets half naked on you own. Be in charge of your life, not following some code of bad behaviour.'

'What were these other features she wrote, anything in particular? Controversial maybe?'

'Literally all sorts. Good few recently about how people are being conned on social media and stuff like by those phone calls telling you your National Insurance Number has been cloned and you need to pay HMRC a statutory fee for a new one. Press number one to send your cash down the drain.'

'We've got fraud people working on the very same thing,' Cooper admitted.

'All unbenown to the paper's publishers?'

'Wrote one or two for *The Leader* but more harder hitting ones for others.' He stopped for a second to collect his thoughts. 'They plan a new glossy magazine they're calling *Lincoln Now!* I've been working on.'

'Used to have something similar free at the garden centre.'

'Died an obvious death by purporting the represent the lives of a small and dwindling part of society. Too upmarket. This one will be for the man in the street not for the fancy dans going to balls and driving BMWs from their million pound homes.'

'Those who know who they are?'

'Exactly right. And the plan was for Rachel to write a few good major expose's to give the launch issue a big boost. Like one she wrote a year or two back about that slave trade statue business people were pulling down if you remember. Using a male pen-name, along the lines of Austel Rose or something like that was her way of remaining anonymous and encouraging readers to think it was written by a young male. The whole world knows there was criminal damage, but finding protesters who caused that damage not guilty was an error. You can break the law provided you give some cause as your reason was to her a dangerous precedent. She also if I remember rightly, suggested you cannot change history no matter how hard you try and to back that Rachel explained how the truth is in some areas of the world, the slave traders being demonized were themselves black. '

If true that was something to provide a motive, Cooper had not previously been aware of. 'Was writing such controversial stuff not risking everything?'

'People make a fortune dealing in drugs how dangerous are a few words compared with that?'

'Have to ask this. What was she currently working on?' she asked.

'Wish I knew.' He shrugged.

'Something big for this new magazine by any chance?'

'Look, any chance of a glass of water?' did not answer the question.

'No,' said Larsson nudging her young colleague. 'We can do better than that. We'll take a break and we'll order. Tea or coffee?'

'Strong tea,' said Sean. 'Just a tiny touch of milk please. No sugar.'

Conversation while Michelle Cooper was away between Larsson and Sean Joseph was all about the Katushabe brothers and their disciplined moral codes which continued over a tea and two coffees. Fifteen minutes later they had returned to the job in hand.

'So, you're saying you don't know what she was working on?'

'You thinking it might somehow be connected to...you know? What happened to her? If it was for *The Leader* it's got to be on her PC at work, otherwise her laptop at home, which it very well might,' said Sean Joseph quietly shaking his head at the thought of it. 'Want me to have a look?'

'Would you mind if we got our team to go through it? We'll talk to *The Leader* and borrow theirs at the same time. Who's best to talk to?'

'James Gosney, the Editor,' was a name mentioned at morning briefing Nicola Scoley was heading to talk to.

'And you don't know what she was working on?' He shook his head. 'Why?' Cooper asked. Here was a guy who claimed he had no idea what stories his girlfriend was working on and still lived at home with his mother when Barnard had a home of her own. Do couples really not talk? Was that in itself the basis of a good Barnard style feature?

'Way she worked.' His tendency to grimace and pull a face was a habit he used again. Larsson knew her team were aware of her theory about the guilty pulling faces to create time to think. 'If she had a fault,' said Sean head down. 'Rachel insisted everything we did was done her way. Just the way she was. Took a bit of getting used to. Got it from her old man, he's a bit like that.'

'Interesting.'

'Her work was very intense at times and she had to go where the story took her. Permanently had a bag packed in case she had to shoot off and I'd get a text saying off for a day or two. After all she was not just another journo like that Elphick and Daisy Lytton, who in effect do little more than localize others handiwork.'

'And you were happy with that?'

'Her work would have suffered had I kept her on a short rein.'

'Just out of interest, how well do you know the road to Brigg up through Redbourne and Hibaldstow?'

Sean Joseph chuckled. 'Quite good,' he said and continued to be amused. 'Only been through them of course, but if we're heading for the bridge we'd normally stick to the A15 or going further up cut across to the A1.' He leaned forward as if he had the need to insist on something. 'Think Rebourne's got a pub laid back a bit and Hibaldstow's quite a bit bigger with shops and a pub. Never stopped there, ever,' he said and tapped the table firmly with his index finger.

'So, when she wasn't at home you thought nothing of it?' was the change of subject to confuse.

'Just a quick text that's all. Remember she'd moved quickly from snippets of local crime into her investigative world and her popular column.' Joseph breathed out, bit his lip and Cooper guessed there was more.

'Take your time,' she encouraged.

'D'you know this might well be a very odd thing to say,' he went on. 'But Rachel'd absolutely loved to be investigating her own murder. Bigger bacon than all the scams Mrs Public loves.'

'Would you say she was controlling?' Larsson queried wondering of this was why he lived with his mummy?

Joseph laughed at the suggestion. 'Don't be silly. Nothing like that. Just a case of habits really, not much more than that. Could be to do with living on her own. Virtually everything she did, and her work was just one element. Know this might sound daft, but you peel potatoes Rachel's way, you make the bed her way and so on. Same thing applies to her work. When we first got together I could understand her not wanting to share her work with me. But now? Just the way she was. Sometimes got the feeling she was trying to protect me. In the end, always got to read her finished work first of course, before she'd punt it off.'

'Protect you from what?'

'Whatever she was exposing,' Sean Joseph said as if it was obvious.

'And we can find her features on *The Leader* website?'

'She's got them all on a few USB Memory Sticks. Want me to lend them to you?'

'Tell you what. We have a CSI team heading for her place as we speak. These Flash Drives easy to find?'

'You'll need a key.'

'Got one from her mother.' or at least Family Liaison had. 'Sorry.'

'She's got a different colour one for each publication she works for. Quite a few, must be at least eight or nine of them. Plus a couple of Minion figures too she uses.'

'You saying she wrote for eight or nine different publications?'

'Not all the time,' he smiled rather than laugh at the detective. 'She was able sometimes to re-write some stuff so it pertained to a particular niche subject. If one of the people being conned shall we say, fished for a hobby she's make a great deal more of that aspect even include fishing in the headline and sell it to a fishing magazine. For a normal run of the mill mag she'd tone down any reference to fishing. When I say fishing I'm talking about sitting on a river bank not fisching on the internet,' the detectives grinned at. 'Some mags she'd only written for a couple of times. Not constantly writing for eight. She'd be worn to a frazzle coping with that.'

'Our techy guys can join CSI there,' Larsson said and picked up her phone from the table. 'Excuse me,' she said to Joseph. 'Adrian, can you send somebody to pick up a load of USB sticks from an address in town. Shona's CSI lads should be there already.' She listened. 'Operation Greeba. Rachel Barnard.' Larsson stopped talking. 'Any problems give me a call,' she added and gave the address off Rookery Lane. 'Cheers. Talk to you later, I'll explain what they contain.'

'Her parents,' said Michelle Cooper the moment Inga Larsson put her phone down. 'Can we talk about them?'

'Clash of generations, but oddly so. He's only in his early fifties but he's more out of touch than my grandad was. Rachel and her dad are constantly at each other simply because of what she does, or rather how she does what she does. Her old man doesn't have a mobile,' Sean said and stopped. 'More than one row about *"Hi this is Rachel, can't take your call, right now"* gets him in a real tantrum for some reason. Almost as if he thinks it's aimed at him personally.' He grimaced again. 'More than once I've thought about getting one of those old phones with a dial but works the same as modern landlines, but guess that'd be taken the wrong way. Too much of a piss take.'

'But he's happy with the old engaged tone I take it?'

'Exactly.' There was a short pause before Joseph continued. 'Books to him are made of paper and real news is in a newspaper or on BBC. Tablet's something you get on prescription. Still insists he collects his paper prescription from the doctor and takes it to the chemist, all that sort of thing.'

'The clash to do with her work was?' Larsson as yet had not figured.

'Her working on a laptop all day, peering into a screen, constantly on her phone, interviewing people on Zoom, recording interviews on her phone rather than using a shorthand notebook, typewriter and all the rest of it.'

'But generally they're fine.'

'Yes. Just everyday basic good people to be honest. Ridiculous really, Millie's mother's got a mobile. Bit basic she uses to text, at least its a start.'

56

'Think that's us about done,' said a happy Larsson pleased to be back in the swing of things. 'Unless there's anything else?'

'No. But I'm sure something will come to mind when I get a chance to clear this,' he said and tapped his head.

'Our Tech Crime Team will pick up her laptop and those USB sticks. Imagine we'll be finished there by the end of the day, but I'll bell you with the all clear.'

'Happy with that?' Cooper checked.

'Fine,' said Sean Joseph almost reluctant to get to his feet.'Tell you what might help. One of those Minion sticks has got like a directory on it. About all she uses that one for. That'll tell you what's on each stick save you trudging through every one. Purple for stuff for the *Leader*, Blue for the *Peterborough Sentinel* and so on.'

When Jake Goodwin was told what had been said he wanted to add his two pennuth. 'Think I'm right in thinking those Ugandans came over here donkey's years ago and this lot could be part of that. Read somewhere they were housed in, think it was near here.'

'Hemswell,' said Nicky. 'Where the Sunday Market is. According to my dad.'

'Housed in RAF married quarters I seem to remember, ones the servicemen had just moved out of. Think they'd be grateful wouldn't you? No chance, complained about sub-standard accommodation.'

'Had the same year or two back with the illegal refugee boat people turning up in Kent in their dinghies. Then complained the military barracks were not fit for human occupation.'

'Allegedly.'

'See this morning there's talk of shipping asylum seekers to Rwanda. Some processing scheme.'

'At least we know what we're dealing with,' Jake sighed. 'But could be better. What I want to know is, how come ID cards never came in? More good deeds by the damn snowflakes, helping a constant rabble off those dinghies they turn up in then let them just disappear into the black economy. ID cards stop that happening right across Europe. And don't get me started on Brexit. Still don't understand why we ignored the obvious warnings.'

Some of the trolls nonsense on social media Alisha came across on a regular basis such as 'boks' and the awful 'Ma bit' while beavering away was always worth a shout. That morning she'd told the team about some woman asking if anybody knew of a plumber. To which one card had replied "Yes thanks." From that she'd come across the dope asking "Need a new tyre for my Peugeot. Any ideas?"

All of which Jake Goodwin could readily appreciate from the kind of dross his own father regularly told him about. "Has the chip van been yet?" was just the sort of drivel he could not abide.

Due to her dual ethnicity Alisha had always been used to different words and phrases being used at home. Her interest in urban speak the internet was full of, had first come to the fore from her phone.

She'd started when she got her first decent phone with help from friends by understanding the basic textese with the silliness of 'deckies' at Christmas and friends described for some reason as 'besties.' From there she'd gone on to understand 'fresh' as talk of an admired one, and to 'ma bit' or 'crib' for my home. Then onto BF, FYI, JK the no probs NP and B4e1, before everyone..

All triggered to some extent initially by her naively assuming lol meant lots of love only to discover how in that particular context it meant little old lady.

She'd almost had to teach herself to be a linguist when she realized it could well help with career advancement. Street talk, slang and she was constantly updating herself in the world of urban English. Now when required she had become an urban street translator for emails and on social media. One reason why she'd been snapped up for MIT.

Generally people suggest street talk is associated with people from the poorer end of the spectrum. Alisha knew different. Apart from being a way of taking less time and space when texting it was being used more and more by the criminal fraternity to hide their plans.

7

Dr Marcus Meller the newish on-call Home Office Pathologist who DS Jake Goodwin had met on site, was also new to DI Inga Larsson. If it were not for the scrubs and a scarlet bandana he added just before he commenced his work, Larsson could have quite easily have mistaken him for the cleaner. Mass of white uncombed hair all over his head and at least two days growth of beard was not how she normally spied such eloquent and professional people.

Cadaver on the block, blue sheet removed carefully from the body to allow Meller to commence his procedure. Blonde, attractive DI Inga Larsson in attendance and all dressed up in green too was pleased she'd remembered her Bergamot oil to rub under her nose. Even so, the disinfectant smells were always a stern reminder of where she was.

Stood there she recalled how Rachel Barnard had torn a strip off the anti vaxxers for being selfish along with Piers Corbyn. Who during one non-sensical protest had a friend suggest mask wearing gives you Alzheimer's. Extinction Rebellion were not forgotten who she had suggested should head off to China to assist with their climate change issues. Inga recalled the columnist also supported JK Rowling's stance on transgender issues. Including support for a woman losing and then winning on appeal her industrial tribunal case after she'd commented on transgender people.

Stood there waiting, she remembered there had been a time when her boss Detective Superintendent Craig Darke had taken on this onerous job. She had seen it back then as his way of keeping his hand in with case investigations. No mention today and she was on her own.

All the staff were in regulation scrubs, caps, gloves and masks. She was decked out the same and this Meller with his goggles sat on the top of his white haired head had his mortuary technician fussing around him with implements, bowls and a variety of specimen pouches, Inga was not looking forward to watching being used.

'Allow me to start with basics we do know. 29 year old Rachel June Barnard with identification provided by her father.' He peered at Inga over the top of his glasses and she nodded. 'Journalist with a firm of local, in fact national newspaper and magazine publishers. Discovered just off a pathway alongside a fence with a huge grass meadow beyond containing a flock of sheep.' He stopped for a moment. As if trying to remember. 'Lincoln Longwool if I'm not mistaken. Out on Higgins Farm,' he continued. 'A bit south of Hibaldstow and Brigg. Not far in fact as the crow flies from the A15. Somewhere according to her parents she has no known association with.' He looked at Larsson.

'We know nothing different, so far,' she came back with. 'But, having said that she was as you quite rightly say a journalist of some repute and we unfortunately have no idea so far what it was she was working on at the time.'

'What about her...editor...or?' Meller said as if he didn't fully understand.

'Personal Computer,' Larsson felt was best to use. 'Lacked very recent activity. With no evidence of a new article which he claims he doesn't understand. In fact he was expecting her distinctive column, a full page article for publication that very day.'

'First thing,' Meller went on with. 'I have to state is based upon my findings on site. She was laid face down in an old rusty animal feeding trough, between bushes with damage to the back of her head we will come to later. The trough has since been removed by the Crime Scene Investigators. Having said that. Initial examination back here has revealed brick dust in her hair we have sent for analysis. There is,' he said looking all around, to see if his team were paying attention. 'No sign of the brick itself with that providing us with possibility of the convenience of DNA. This may well be an old adage but it pertains in this instance. Absence of evidence is not evidence of absence. Somebody hit her that is for sure, she didn't smack her own head with a brick. Unless you know differently?' he asked Larsson.

'No. Some members of the CSI team have been there ever since and my last message just before I walked in here, stated that nothing like a brick has been discovered in the woods or the field so far. We have made arrangements for an expert on pollen to visit the site in a day or two as it is very prevalent in that area.'

'Thank you Detective Inspector. Yes, all the clothing has gone for analysis. Because of that and if such knowledge remains so, I will suggest the woman before us was killed elsewhere and quickly dumped where she was discovered, allegedly by a dog. Correct?' was also aimed at the DI.

'Indeed,' she responded. 'Two women from the nearby village out walking.'

'Redbourne?'

'Yes.'

'What else do we know?' Meller asked the gathered four and the DI. 'We know that is the most likely scenario simply because very little of the grass and shrubbery around the body and the trough had been disturbed. Yes, one or two people had walked close by of course such as the women and their dog and the first Police officers on site. No indication of an attack having taken place there, certainly no evidence of a struggle which the state of her clothing also is indicative of. I also understand the CSI photographer has clear defined photographs of the area, which is a useful tool to have.'

'Any reason for that?' the woman in Inga needed to know.

'As to why? Your guess is as good as mine. Likely framework is the locality of death is not anywhere she could be dumped without connection to the perpetrator or perpetrators. The attack zone was a better location I should imagine, on home territory is always a possibility people often use due to familiarity with their surroundings. Like football teams are generally better playing at home.'

'We're working on her phone for location.'

'Slim build,' he said for the microphone above his head as he went through a visual examination of the whole body laid out in front of him. 'Makes a nice change,' he said as with a wave of his hand his assistant rolled the cadaver over. 'Back scar, could be anything from a Nevis to something more serious. Check medical records,' was a message for his assistant.

'How long?' Inga needed to know as Barnard was laid back, face up.

'All indications suggest Monday, but Tuesday more likely. Not absolutely accurate until all the tox results come back, but I'd be concerned if it were any longer. If it was it could mean storage somewhere and frozen if any longer but that's not possible due to her known presence before then.' Was Larsson decided this a case of him hedging his bets by putting that fact on record.. 'Severe head injury, likely skull fracture we'll come to no doubt. Concussion of course always provides the perpetrator with the ideal opportunity for strangulation. Has a look of the heavy hand of a male,' Meller said as he moved the head to check both sides. 'Both with the head trauma and neck bruise markings.'

'This possible manslaughter?' she had to ask.

'No matter what this was all about. A lovers tiff, sex games outcome with no penetration, jealousy, even something gone wrong. The intention still was to kill. You do not do that much damage to a woman's throat unless you really mean it. Signs of pure hate.'

When this Marcus Meller got down to delving into Barnard's torso, Inga Larsson made her excuses and left. She had no reason to know what might have been going on inside her. They knew what killed her, they'd always known the basics back even when Sandy and Jake had seen her laid in that trough. Knowledge of what she had for tea was of little interest and would be in the report in any case.

She wished them all a happy Easter removed her scrubs and headed back.

If she'd stayed on there was very little she'd learn by watching him saw the poor woman open, weigh her heart and liver like the butcher does. As ever in the end it'd all be down to the toxicology and forensics. People handy with a microscope rather than a sharp saw.

Inga Larsson was always pleased to be able to just walk away from a post-mortem when it suited her. Back in the morgue they'd be invading the young woman and when they'd finished weighing her body parts and sown her back up, the poor lass would be wheeled off back to the refrigeration complex until such time as she could be moved by funeral directors. Or, an over keen defence lawyers for some evil bastard demanding a second opinion and out she'd be dragged for the sharps to cut her open once more.

Back at Lincoln Central Inga Larsson had an audience when she walked out from her small office in the corner, mug in hand and rested her backside against a table.

She took a drink. 'Must be the smell. Always gives me a thirst,' she said and placed the mug beside her. 'What the basic post mortem now tells us is a very likely rear fractured skull, on top of what we knew, probably done from behind she was unaware off or as she walked away, hit by a brick is a clue.' She put a hand up to stop Jake. 'CSI are still brick hunting and tox may well tell us if we're really lucky what type of brick and the manufacture info, but we'll have a wait for all that. Detritus dust from the brick embedded in her skull is what they're working on. This likely skull fracture, if that didn't kill her and tox will have the final say, takes us fairly and squarely to strangulation. As with all of this we'll know more of course when we get the pathologists full report now he's slicing her open. In addition an expert in pollen examination I met at a conference has agreed to check the site. But the fracture or dislocation of the upper cervical vertebrae could very well be the cause death rather than the strangulation. Lack of air.'

'Means,' said Jake as Inga went for another drink of her coffee. 'What the doc was saying on site could be right. She'd at the very least have lost her balance with that bash on her head and fell forward unconscious with no sign of putting her hands out to save herself. Knee on her chest and big hands did the rest.'

Sipping DI Inga Larsson put down her red mug once more.. 'No sexual goings on whatsoever thank the Lord. Not even the suggestion her clothes were disturbed.' She sighed.

'Means motive will be a struggle without a sex element,' butterscotch blonde DS Nicky Scoley suggested.

'I believe the clue has to be found in her written word if its not family, close friends or even Sean Joseph I'm tending to discount for a variety of reasons.'

'Not good on that front,' DS Nicky Scoley suggested. 'I'm heading upstairs after this guv, but word has it there's nothing much on the flash drives that Joseph told us about. ASBO got young Hari Mistry the hacker to have a look. Says they're just the features she'd written for various publications.'

'Nothing untoward from their perspective but what about content. Who or what has she written about, why has she named and shamed, who has now got his or her own back?' Inga sighed. 'I read two or three and so far just one name the Tech Crime Team are trying to hunt down if that was his real name. A Joshua Kemp running a scam who claimed he lived in Mauritius.'

'Good luck with that!' Nicky knew statistically some good many people would get scammed on line, when almost three million are taken down each year.

'Think somebody like Adrian'd get bored easily with gossipy magazine and paper stuff, but I'll get the USB sticks back or at least those they've finished with and I'll look at who else she slagged off.'

'Did she?' Jake asked quickly.

'Chances are. Anyway there's only one way to find out,' Nicky told him.

As with all cases of this severity and nature, press conferences were an inevitable evil to some extent, yet also a means to an end.

With the Katushabe Group's newspapers distributed all over the UK this was far more than a simple yellowbelly yokel murder for the greater world to generally ignore.

Inga Larsson dressed for the day in her best deep blue suit sat that afternoon alongside DS Craig Darke and Jo Neilson from the PR team, knew this was not just another major incident.

64

Each and every death is tragic in its own way and that morning as the requirements of the event were building in her mind her thoughts were elsewhere.

With Rachel Barnard's family and friends and in particular Sean Joseph who she had met and so far she regarded as a good man. Living at home at his age and in a relationship in this day and age was her one major concern.

Craig Darke rattled through the introductions and opening pleasantries.

'You all know why you are here this morning,' Darke continued with. 'For a good few of you this is yet another poignant moment in the methodology we employ in such situations. The whole purpose of this today is to bring you all up to date with the processes so far.' He then gestured to his Detective Inspector sat on his right. 'Inga Larsson the Senior Investigating Officer some of you will know, leading Operation Greeba.'

'With Rachel being a well known and respected member of this community,' Larsson opened with to appease the locals. 'You don't need me to tell you there are likely to be those in the wider community who would not be pleased with every word she wrote with such vigour. Acerbic wit and humour.' She put a hand up to stop any interruptions. 'I am willing to admit I read her column in the *Lincoln Leader* avidly each week.'

'Our understanding,' said Darke. 'At this juncture, as a result of the post mortem analysis so far is, that Rachel was somehow knocked unconscious, but we believe not where her body was discovered. She was then strangled.' Just as the Katushabe's *Lincoln Leader* reporter was about to interject, Darke beat him to it 'We know what was used to both make her unconscious and the system used in the asphyxiation process.'

The initial murmurs and whispers had not died down since the start, and Larsson wondered as she watched them, if they were in fact taking it all in. Some were, but not personally. Relying for the most part on the work being done by the whole paraphernalia of sound equipment, cameras and a proliferation of phones of all sizes and colours.

The Swedish born Detective Inspector began to scan the larger than normal throng. Had to be the same as when an

65

officer goes down. Here were journos of all shapes and sizes seizing on a piece of the action desperate for news of one of their own. But, Larsson surmised looking at them, how many of the locals would have been jealous of Barnard's high profile and they were quite possibly looking for a snippet they could use to bring her down in the public eye?

'We have a team of very...'

'Are you saying,' one young man interrupted as he sprung to his feet. 'You already know what weapon was used, yet you are keeping it to yourselves.?'

'You are, sir?' from Darke visibly annoyed the questioner.

'Tony Parker from the *Leader,*' he said as if it was obvious.

'*Lincoln Leader* I take it?' was a well used tactic a form of which Larsson had seen her boss use before at such times.

'What else?'

'*Lewes Leader, Linlithgow Leader?*' showed Darke had done his homework knowing there'd be a few from the local rag desperate to make their mark. For themselves and for their paper. 'In answer to your question, yes we do,' he went on. 'And we will know even more once that instrument in question has been thoroughly examined and investigated, along with the forensic analysis and toxicology reports when they come to hand.'

In this case Darke's experience told him he'd not get on the wrong side of the media. Alienating them, normally meant a distinct lack of coverage. This, one of their own was wholly different. Being belligerent and sarcastic would create no imbalance.

As if they knew he could be difficult to deal with, the hubbub levels dropped. If meeting the press did nothing else this bunch of amateur sleuths would remind all and sundry about the increasing crime rate, with them all permanently in need of something a bit more wholesome than mere gossip.

'It would seem from our inquiries that Rachel was targeted,' Larsson went on to say.

'What she working on d'you know?'

'You should know if anybody does, as some of you,' she pointed at the lone *Leader* reporter sat there, when she'd expected two or three of them. 'Worked with her. Rachel had as

66

we have all done at times, worked hard to investigate wrongdoings only for that work not to come to fruition and gets spiked. Something I've done many a time in this job. She tended, as a result of previous disappointments, we are reliably informed, to keep her next project very close to her chest.' Larsson hesitated, drew a breath and continued. 'We are currently reviewing her previous projects and work, and information has already come to hand which may or may not lead us to what was at the time of her death, the next expose.'

'You saying it's somebody from her past?' a woman in a vivid green jumper asked.

'Could well be, and that is the mainstay of our reasoning for inviting you here today. Ask if your readers and viewers will come forward if they are aware of any interviews she carried out recently no matter how minor or trivial they may appear, which as yet have not gone into print. Questions she asked, the people she asked, sought out, spoke to or mentioned.'

Larsson was decidedly more aware through previous experience than the public, that none of the hordes of social media sites, newspapers, websites or radio stations were renowned for telling the whole truth.

Why were they all there when she knew many of them would just make up what they didn't know as they went along? Using as graphic insinuations as was possible, aimed at their particular audience.

'Thank you,' said Darke. 'Please,' he made a long word. 'If you become party to such information, ensure we are made aware of at the earliest opportunity.' Jo had reminded them both the force are always in need of any leverage the media can provide.

'You all have my Incident Team's numbers,' said Larsson. 'Now, if there are any questions,' she asked but so wanted to add the word 'ridiculous. 'I'll wish you all a Happy Easter'.

'This another one to add to your growing list of unsolved?' some berk asked almost inevitably. 'How many's that now?'

'In case it has escaped your notice young man,' Darke retorted and pointed at the badly dressed goon. 'All these incidents are surprisingly not self-inflicted. Strange as it may seem, we don't go around killing innocent people at random

67

just to give us something to while away the time between our tea break and lunch.' The youth went to utter. 'Thank you all. Thank you for attending.'

Detective Superintendent Craig Darke walked steadily almost marched out of the room without a glance in any direction. Larsson was caught slightly by surprise just as reporters started to shout demanding answers and the sound of cameras hid the sound of his footsteps.

Larsson sat there, pleased with the sudden end to hack off this shower of shit, all desperate for a great deal more.

Back in the Incident Room with coffee she'd collected on the way up, after they'd spent fifteen minutes answering mainly nonsense, Inga briefed her team. 'Why would you call a dog Basil?' she asked and they all looked at her. 'At the end there, some Scunthorpe reporter asked the name of the dog who discovered Barnard's body,' she explained calmly. 'Then some wally wanted to know why they called the damn dog Basil!'

Sat up among the Digital Forensic guys who Nicky knew well, she always felt as though she had stepped from an inter-galactic space craft straight into another world. Downstairs there'd be coffee for most, tea for some now and again, an occasional soft drink and mandatory bottles of water. Up with the Tech Crime Team (TCT) it was always a strange concoction starting with head geek Adrian Simon Bruce Orford known as ASBO for obvious reasons, who only drank hot water, and in the main chewed liquorice. There were the hydration drinks, the usual energy assortment such as Carabao and one can of Hibiscus and Rose Seltzer she spotted. Sort of thing she's like to have a quick taste of one day, just out of curiosity.

That day sat alongside young Hari Mistry tasked with scouring the memory sticks from Rachel Barnard's home, he had a can of Pepsi Max which appeared quite sane considering.

Downstairs that morning chat among the team had been all about atrocities in Ukraine once more. Talk of Liverpool and Man City winning in the Champions League. Yet up with the Tech Crime Team no mention was ever made of local or international news. Sat there with Hari she wondered if he even

68

knew it was Maundy Thursday, and would he be tucking into a big chocolate egg.

'This woman of yours writes about anything and everything,' he told her. 'Nothing I've come across so far I'd bother myself with but guess you'd latch onto things like she writes for a women's magazine about sexism in the workplace and maternity issues.' He picked up the Orange Memory Stick. 'This is all the stuff for Womens' magazines,' next was the white one. 'This is where it gets a bit tasty as its her blog she fires to all and sundry, but to be honest stuff about pretending to be a first time gardener or suggesting a women only jogging club is never going to lead us where you want to be.'

'You've read them all?'

'Not every one,' he admitted. 'But you easy pick up the trend and anyway the front piece tells you where they're aimed, name of the publication and has an index listing each feature. Some only have one or two.' Hari stopped to take a swig of his drink. 'This is your best bet,' he said lifting a Minion Memory Stick in his fingers. 'This one here is an index of all of them, and I've got to say for efficiency give her top marks. After every feature at the end she details the publication and the date. Date she wrote it, and usefully all her contacts including phone numbers and even addresses appertaining to that particular article. Done one series on people who have been scammed on the internet, usually women, who all think they've fallen in love with some nasty shite from Outer Mongolia with a sick kid.'

'And need money.'

'Got it in one,' he shook his head. 'Some silly buggers lost a fortune.'

'Which one is that?' Nicky asked.

'Take him,' he said handing her the Minion stick. 'That's the overall index. No writing content, only info on the other sticks. Lists whats on each stick, except…' he stopped to drink. 'One missing, Lists nine on there, but the red one's missing.'

'Missing?'

'Well, we've not been given it shall we say. Davey went down there and brought everything back. No red stick when I went through this,' he handed 'Clive' the Minion to Nicky.

'How d'you know red is missing?'

'She tells you on Clive what's on each colour,' was obvious.
'How many are there?'

Hari named them as he counted them out. 'White, Orange, Pink, Black, Purple, Green, Yellow, Blue and the missing Red.'

'The one with the women being scammed is where?'

'Think that's Pink,' he grinned. 'For women more than likely despite what the PC brigade go on about.'

'Yeh,' Nicky sighed with frustration. 'True to form, and to be honest just as Rachel herself would go on about. Probably produced by a woman or designed by one, and dozy females buy them by the barrowload because they're a ghastly pink then march up and down with placards about sexism. A disease they pretty much create.' Nicky stopped. 'Sorry,' she offered and chuckled.

'Was that her problem?' he asked. 'Do we know what sex attacked her?'

'Not yet I don't think. Why?'

'Is that what this is all about? Women against a woman. There's loads go on and on about men with a succession of scurrilous untrue stories. Littering the internet. Then up pops this better educated Rachel and rather than defend their frequently hypocritical stance, she has a good go at them. Sort of as wake up call some have got upset about.'

'All the women I know absolutely love her. Says it as it is.'

'Just a thought,' he said as she motioned to move.

'Let me have the rest when you're done, and thanks Hari.' The sort of misspelled name she hated. That had been the first time he'd given his personal opinion about anything. At least she knew he had read what had been put in front of him.

8

Blonde attractive navy blue suited Detective Sergeant Nicola Scoley once refreshed was up to date with the media reaction, after scouring the *Leader*'s view in the latest edition.

Accompanied by DC Alisha O'Neill, she pulled up into one of the designated spaces in the small car park, reserved for 'Visitors.'

At the Katushabe Publishing Reception down in Witham St Hughs in a newish building on St Modwen Park industrial estate probably roughly where RAF Swinderby was once based, they parked up.

Being out that way was a reminder for Nicky, as she and Connor had visited the Aubourn Weir Loop from Witham on their bikes. Not done the whole circuit but this was a gentle reminder.

In the front door of the two storey uninspiring offices but functional build and design for whoever, rather than specifically for a newspaper. The pair were asked to wait by a sullen female whose body language radiated boredom as she lightly tapped her keyboard. Too heavily made up but with no piercings in places they could see..

Eventually a young woman in a far too short deep blue and cream check skirt appeared, claiming to be the Editor's secretary. She didn't bother to introduce herself, but Nicky read her badge as a matter of course. *Caz Nichols* it said which could be anything from Carole and Caroline to Casi, Camilla, Carrie or a Callie she'd once sadly come across.

Upstairs it was nothing like either of them imagined. Not packed with a noisy flurry of people typing or on phones, in fact at first guess there were less than a dozen people at the very most and any work commotion was off the moment the pair entered as if a switch had been flicked.

The female with bright red long nails ushered them into an office with big windows out to the main room and as they walked in a dark haired tall man just looked at them.

'Detective Sergeant Nicola Scoley and Detective Constable Alisha O'Neill,' the woman read from the cards they'd handed over downstairs, she then placed carefully onto the desk and departed in a flurry.

'James Gosney,' this thickset man said still seated and offered his hand across the desk, neither responded to as a matter of course. 'Good morning ladies. How may I help you as if I don't know.' His suit jacket was hung over the back of a spare chair in the corner and his pale green shirt had the sleeves rolled half way up his forearms.

'Sorry to meet you under such circumstances Mr Gosney,' said Scoley as she sat down on one of the two chairs already in place facing his desk littered with papers, as O'Neill did the same.

'Can we get you any refreshments, tea, coffee, orange?'

'No we're fine thank you,' Scoley responded as she looked across at him seated, a gold band on his wedding finger ticked a box. 'Would you be kind enough initially to give us a brief indication of Rachel Barnard's work, anything you know about her personal life. And in order to assist with our investigations, information on any particular matters she was working on at the time? We can of course redeem everything about her, but this way I'm sure you will agree is less invasive and less time consuming.'

'I can take all this business,' he said pointing at Scoley. 'But just go easy on her parents. Understand what I'm saying?' hinted at a form of threat.

'Family liaison are with them thank you.'

James Gosney sat back in his seat and proceeded to relate what little he knew or was willing to admit to about Rachel Barnard, her home life, and her family. He then added almost as an afterthought a slight reference to their Web Designer Sean Joseph. The way he quickly moved on told Scoley he was deliberately skirting around the matter.

Scoley found it interesting that no reference was made at that point to the fact this Sean Joseph had been due at Lincoln

Central earlier to be interviewed by the boss. Perhaps the web designer didn't come under his jurisdiction she decided, but simply wrote *'Joseph?'* in her notebook as a reminder..

'And what exactly was she working on at the time?'

'Allow me to explain her role,' he said and did so to a greater extent than was really necessary. She had her own caustic column in their weekly newspaper, created and wrote features for other newspapers in the group, plus magazines occasionally under the same ownership.

He then slipped in what appeared to be a deliberate downer that she was expected to take on basic mundane editing of news stories when she was there.

Hair smothered in gel Nicky could smell a mile off, which her mother would suggest was hiding something.

'How many people would work with or alongside Rachel Barnard?' Alisha O'Neill asked.

His reaction was disturbing to even Scoley let alone Alisha. 'Look for yourself,' he gestured out into the room. 'Got a newspaper to run, so if that's all,' he said directly to Scoley blanking O'Neill. 'In case you hadn't noticed,' he continued and got to his feet without having the decency to answer the question. He spoke looking down at Alisha. 'You sure you're up to all this?' he smirked.

'Think you need to slow down Mr Gosney, we're the ones with a great deal to get through,' said Scoley as she tried not to appear ruffled though inwardly she was seething at his attitude. The timbre in his voice said there was an issue with Alisha. No guesses for what that amounted to. *Arrogant and racist,* she left the words unspoken. With luck Alisha sat beside her was with her experience of being slighted, would be coping better.

'You'd better get on with it then, if you must.'

'We obviously need a list of the staff who had regular working and personal contact with Miss Barnard.' DS Scoley had sat across from a good few nasty scrotes who'd not caused her as much consternation as this man had done in one slight. An attitude his type groomed themselves into. This was not office banter the world accepts in the workplace, this was deliberate. 'A list if you will,' she added when there was no return. A demand rather than a request.

73

'Get them sent across,' he offered. 'Next week do? One good thing about having foreign owners, they don't get all tangled up in some of our stuff.'

'Excuse me!' from an angry Scoley was louder as she angled her head to one side. 'Need that list and their personal files, please Mr Gosney.' He'd deliberately snubbed Alisha and now this nasty was making excuses.

'I'll arrange that,' he said, sniffed and with his head gestured for the pair to leave.

'Today,' she said across to him as he rose in somewhat of a hurry. 'In fact now! If you'd be so kind.'

'I'm sorry,' he smirked as he opened the door and both detectives were on their feet. 'I've got thirty six pages to fill and it doesn't happen by magic. When I have the time, understand miss?'

'We're not going anywhere until you hand them over.'

'Who on earth do you think you're talking to?'

'You Mr Gosney,' was an erect Scoley standing firm unwilling to admit his supercilious tone had grated on her. 'This in case you hadn't noticed is a murder investigation and our requirements come before your local rag. It takes precedence over everything else including whatever you think just might be important. So yes, Mr Gosney it is you I'm talking to. Files now if you please,' she told him and stuck out her hand..

'Look ladies...'

'No Mr Gosney, you look,' feisty Scoley gritting her teeth pointed at him. 'We can do this one of two ways. You provide me with the files, not the complete files with all your annual reviews. Just their basic details, names, addresses, position held, basic employment history and the like, right here, right now or a team will be in here causing absolute mayhem.'

'Take time,' he sighed and shrugged with one hand still holding the door open. Something inside must have told him this was the wrong journey. Nicky spotted his shoulders slump inside his shirt to a degree as he expelled a breath quietly.'Go on then,' he then sighed more obviously. 'Anything else?' he asked and just stood there unmoved.

'Get along then,' and Scoley ironically gestured for him to leave. 'The data we require here and now has to include all the

74

staff who have any link whatsoever to Rachel Barnard and any other information we feel we need or I gain a warrant and a team of a dozen will be walking all over this place and next week's issue could well not reach the streets at all.'

'You wouldn't dare!'

'Try me.' Scoley saw him look to the side, noticing the rise and fall of his chest as he sighed in the knowledge she was suddenly in charge. In his own office. 'Not look good all over Twitter, but can you take that risk?' she stared at him until he reacted.

'If you insist,' he said releasing a breath.

'I do,' she shot back. 'Don't forget your own.'

'But...'

'But nothing. And while you're at it, we need space to work. Thank you.' Scoley smiled at him.

'You're not...?'

'Yes we are. Hurry along now if you will. We're not leaving until it's done.'

Scoley knew this was a critical moment. Despite her being aware Gosney was wearing a smile behind his mask of a face, he was within his rights to ask the pair of them to leave and entitled to call her boss or even the DI's boss for an explanation of her attitude. On the other hand he had a paper to edit and as a given he'd be a nosey parker. Scoley's next card was being aware he like so many in his trade would cheat and lie to gain an advantage.

She wondered if he was the one responsible for the shouty headlines the paper now carried as as matter of course to make themselves look cheap.

Ten minutes later this secretary Caz had found a desk in the far corner of the office they were led to and she then provided the pair with what appeared to be screen shots of pages from files. Gosney had not been seen since he'd trudged off and when she next spotted him he looked less of the creature they had first encountered. His cocky demeanour had shifted.

Nicky Scoley was used to seeing the change coming over someone when he or she are visited by the police. Some she knew being on home soil so to speak saw that, as in this case, as an advantage. The ship in full sail they had met was now drifting along nervously with a lack of wind.

She'd wondered about his hair from the outset and now had concluded it had been carefully dyed, to provide a self-serving look.

'Elphick,' said O'Neill and slid the sheet she was reading across to her left. 'What's he all about?'

Nicky Scoley did a quick scan of the basics. 'Do a check.'

Two minutes later and Alisha had the semblance of an answer. 'According to PNC,' she handed her phone to her DS. 'Done for possession three times and had a spell begging on the streets, all in Sutton Coldfield. Dropped out of university too.'

'Now doing what?' Scoley gulped and quickly looked around the big room in a vain attempt to spot the naughty boy they were reading about.

'Sub editor.'

'You're joking!' she responded in a whisper and immediately flicked her eyes left and right for tell-tale signs of people being nosy. 'Just shows you eh? Sounds more important than it probably is.'

There was nothing further of particular interest in the files but they took longer than was really necessary to annoy that Gosney chump. Even so there had been no further offer of refreshments.

Back with Gosney, back in his office and it was time for more questions.

'Could you explain the set-up here,' she gestured out to where they'd just been.

Sighing came first. 'Downstairs is all the admin, advertising and circulation people. Up here the editorial staff you've met and through the other end there,' he gestured.' We have web designers and our graphics people.'

'Thank you. Monday and Tuesday of this week,' she said.

'No,' Scoley hesitated. 'Tell you what Mr Gosney, how about you tell us what you did at the weekend and then on Monday and Tuesday.'

'You being serious? Me?'

Was that another smirk? Scoley felt a prickle of annoyance as if this male was trying his best to needle a mere woman.

'Of course.'

'What's my private life go to do with anything?'

'Everything.'

Attractive blonde Detective Sergeant Nicola Scoley was well aware especially in this particular case, the public egged on by the likes of Gosney and his team, will expect some sort of escalation in the investigation. As yet they had hardly broken the surface, but she knew those out in the office behind her would be planning all sorts to go to print with. A result they could one day fly from the chimney pots if they had any.

'Lucky for us an old friend had a cancellation for one of his Safari Tent units he owns out at Burgh le Marsh so with the kids off school we took up the option to spend a weekend glamping. Not sure the kids enjoyed the beds and no wi-fi as much as we did, but it made a nice change anyway.'

'This your family?'

'Who else?' he batted back.

'You didn't actually say. Monday and Tuesday next, apart from working here I assume?'

Gosney's brow had cleared as the conversation turned away to what he and his family had been doing, but Scoley surmised he was still not entirely happy with his situation.

'Let me explain. As you probably know we have local elections coming up early next month. This includes for the first time as part of the government's move to disestablish some areas away from government's Londoncentric confines in Whitehall, to more of their dissolved areas. Under that premise is the new election for an East Midlands Mayor. Can't imagine it will work in the same manner say as Mayor of London or Manchester which are more compact, but we will see.'

'You're not in favour?'

'Not a case of not being in favour, but I don't see it working across such a wide area from Lincoln here down to the other side of Leicester and over to the west but not including Nottingham. Be good if it does.'

'Carry on. You were saying about this election.'

'That's it,' he blew out the breath. 'Just ignore us eh? Give it a week or two and your lot'll be on bended knee desperate for our help when you've got nowhere yet again. Always to suit you lot. What about us getting a paper out eh? We can't just work when it suits your lot.'

'You know as well as I do,' said Scoley. 'We have to have a post mortem with any suspicious death. In addition there's all the forensics to be analyzed and toxicology can take days. When we know I'm sure our people will tell you. Now, this election, you were saying.'

Scoley knew they'd probably intruded upon the Barnard family's grief already, parked outside the house, borrowed a photo of her as a kid and hassled as many of her close friends and school chums as they could dig up.

'Just trying to explain about the procedure,' was his lack of patience showing once more. 'In accordance with what used to be called Purdah, the period immediately before an election has specific restrictions on communication activity imposed. That of course includes us. We're just a few weeks away from the election and if you like the door will be been shut in our face,' he smiled at his own phrase.

'You can't report.'

'Any actual news we can, but we are not permitted to offer candidates proactive publicity running up to the election.'

'And how does this involve Monday or Tuesday?'

'The powers that be…'

'This the Katushabe Brothers we're talking about, are we?'

'Of course,' was sharp from the annoyed. 'They have decided that any of their weeklies with a Thursday publishing day in the East Midlands, and there are eleven all told, will postpone publication until the Friday. That way we can print information on the election immediately after.'

'But not the result surely, that'll take a day or two.'

'With such a wide areas of course, but things like an exit poll'll all be on the web,' he admitted. 'But,' he hesitated. 'It means in our case we can on that Friday publish the reaction, thoughts and promises of the two main candidates. Even an exit poll if we've a mind to.'

'Only two?' Scoley knew there were five.

'Two who will more than likely win. Tory and Labour's choices. Rest'll lose their deposits I have no doubt. All a bit of a bunch of Raving Loonies to be fair.'

'We talking about election result without knowing a winner?' Scoley's dad Tom was not at all sure it was that cut and dried.

'Certainly. That's what I was doing. Getting the inside story, not the bland press releases everybody's been handed. What will you do first, what's the plan for your first hundred days? How do you plan to bring such a diverse large community together? All the ethnics down in Leicester and the white yellerbellies'll take some joining together. On the Friday you'll be able to see for yourself.'

Why did these people all have to follow the same pattern? What will they do first, apart from have a decent coffee and relax? Why 100 days? Like forever asking Olympic winners to bite the medal. And why play the race card? Again.

'Why Monday and Tuesday?'

'Busy day Wednesday putting the paper to bed. Interviewing both of them as near as dammit to the election as was possible, with their latest views landing on people's breakfast tables the next day, Friday morning. Bearing in mind the candidates busy schedules particularly with Easter coming in between.'

'Which was which?'

He peered at Scoley and although she was taking the lead would this man ever as much as look at Alisha? 'See what you mean. Of course. Monday was Raymond Earle down at his place in Melton Mowbray.' He stopped to look out into the main room. 'Sorry,' he said. 'Strange world we live in. There's Raymond Earle very left wing, Labourite through and through living in a magnificent converted barn down there, got to be worth twice what David Petrie probably paid, as nice as his place is of course.'

'Not always what it seems,' said Alisha.

'So, Monday down in Melton Mowbray and Tuesday back up here to talk to Petrie, both now in the can, just waiting.'

'Thank you,' said Scoley. She checked her notes. 'Can we talk about Kevin Elphick?' Gosney closed his eyes and sucked in a breath noisily through his teeth.

'Thought that might come up.'

'What does a sub-editor do exactly?' produced a reaction, when Gosney actually turned to look at Alisha. Scoley guessed

79

to do anything else could have been perceived as both downright rude and racist.

'Subby,' he said back to her which was unnecessary. 'They write of course but also check the written texts, are responsible for the correct grammar others use,' he wiggled his head about. 'Done electronically these days of course along with spelling. All part of the job. Plus, house style and general tone of the paper they're working on.'

'Kevin Elphick,' Scoley said. 'Tell me about him.'

'Goodness they say is next to godliness and allow me to tell you a story to illustrate that.' He sat back in his chair, elbows on the arms and finger tips touching. 'Precious the wife of one of our bosses Kaikara Katushabe was just out shopping in Sutton Coldfield near where they live and this,' he stopped to shake his head. 'Hoodlum, is a decent word to use,' he smiled. 'Sliced through the strap of her handbag she had over her shoulder, and ran off with it. Within seconds what Precious initially assumed at the time was an accomplice went haring off in the same direction. Turned out to be a young man squatting on the pavement begging, had seen what happened and gave chase. Caught him and literally frogmarched this….back to where by then a throng of people had gathered round.'

'Good Samaritan.'

'Indeed. We're all, so they say one pay day away from being where he was. Good example of the Katushabe way of doing things and the brothers took him under their wing. Turned out he'd been at university by chance studying for a journalism degree, got in with the wrong group, took drugs initially at a party to be in with the crowd to save being picked on and bullied. Our directors including their mother helped him turn his life around. Been with us about a year, moving over here from the West Midlands where he had encountered some bad vibes from people he'd once known.'

'Lucky for him he was studying something useful to the brothers.'

'Sorry. Many fingers in a good many pies. Whatever he was studying or was good at, they'd have found a place for him.'

'One last thing. We'd like to have a quick word with your staff out there individually,' Scoley gestured towards the window. 'Just in case they heard anything, knew something or somebody. We can talk to them out there, let you get on.' She stood up and without offering a hand over the desk and waited as Gosney scrambled to his feet.

'Wasn't so bad after all,' Alisha remarked sarcastically which Nicky Scoley loved.

They chatted with the whole team one by one, including Steven Ronane the sports reporter and Daisy Lytton the only female apart from Gosney's secretary and the girl on Reception they'd seen.

Having chatted to all the reporters it was what Nicky had surmised during the course of the interviews.. Not one of them was from Lincoln or anywhere near. All brought in like cheap foreign footballers. Told her a great deal about the rag. Why events are frequently misreported to have taken place somewhere completely wrong. Traffic reports detailing a road and a town where the two are never connected by any stretch of the imagination. Once reading about the cathedral suddenly being moved to the 'city centre' had amused and annoyed.

As she and Alisha left the building Scoley had expected a load more barbed comments and as they walked to the car, she felt to some extent a twinge of disappointment they'd not materialized. Aware all the time they were there he was wearing the air of someone answering questions under sufferance.

From there it was coffee time, almost across the road into the village and Latte and Americano for the pair sat out at The Market Lounge. A place to ponder recent events. Was he a typical narcissist, bigger on ego than brains? Somewhere really good Nicky and Connor had stopped off at once on a bike ride when they'd enjoyed lunch and another when looking for somewhere different just for coffees and snacks as now.

Enjoyable break over too quickly and it was time to head back up to Lincoln Central to report to the boss.

A clap of hands and 'This is how it is,' said James Gosney stepping from his inner sanctum. 'No more. Understand?' he told his team 'Done our duty talking to those two...' he stood there shaking his head with the inability to finish. 'How soddin' unimportant do they think we are eh? Just two bits of girls tells me one thing for absolute certain...'

'Bit o'goods though guv,' Ronane popped up with.

'Yeh,' he sighed at the interruption. 'Give you that,' he admitted. He was never about to admit they'd both been very easy on the eye. 'Anyway, where was I? Ah yes, by sending that dozy pair even though one was pretty tasty, they've decided we're not a critical part of their inquiry. One of them was even different gravy. Where were the real coppers eh? Important? Where was that Swedish tart they go on about?' was louder. 'This is *our* colleague and that makes it *our* story. So from now on we don't talk to the coppers any more, d'you hear? Have a word with legal see if we can organize an injunction to stop those busy bodies poking their noses into our business, our bread and butter. Anything we tell a couple like them two it'll more than like finish up all over the net, and we lose our advantage. This is not a twitter feed. This is the *Leader* first and foremost. This is *our* story, remember.'

'Press conferences? Petar Vargic asked. 'They mention anything?'

'Be silly,' Gosney scoffed. 'My guess is those two normally make the tea,' he thought was amusing. 'Tell you what Petar, you go,' Gosney told him. 'We'll not go mob handed and show how keen we are,' he pushed out a breath. 'This is our story and don't you forget it. We'll not get another like this in a long time. I want World Scoop in big letters as fast as you can.'

9

Having been with Jake when he'd interviewed Cutforth and his wife, Jamie was chosen to go up to Hibaldstow on a scouting mission and to check on the farmer's alibi.

He checked CCTV at a pub in Redbourne as he was passing but it was obviously too angled towards their car park.

Constantly on the lookout for others, he passed the site for skydiving, and eventually reached Hibaldstow further on with their Co-op and then his main target the Wheatsheaf Hotel.

Jamie parked up in their car park and entered by the rear door. Had a soft drink and sat in the bar just getting a feeling for the place. The range of food looked good and be somewhere decent to visit for a change. A Sunday Carvery looked to him to be particularly inviting. He found it interesting to discover the pub was closed on a Monday, linked nicely with the day the Cutforth couple claimed to have stayed at home doing admin.

Drink finished, it was time to talk to Dave the landlord who obviously knew the Cutforth and in addition confirmed it was indeed Pool League Night. He added that they were indeed regular Tuesday customers and he was willing to show to Hedley them sat in the bar that Tuesday on CCTV.

From there Jamie went for a drive and wander in the sunshine around the pleasant village he'd driven through a good few times. Starting at the rear of the pub he eventually turned round and reached Church Street which unsurprisingly had a church and the village hall. To counter the questions the boss might ask he mentally noted down the Fish Bar and Medical Centre and sight of an old windmill.

A fine assortment of houses and bungalows left and right got him thinking. Was this where Barnard's killer lived and why he knew about the sheep trough, and likely escape routes. Road heading to Sturton or Brigg he'd seen was a distinct possibility. Eventually coming close to the M180 and away.

On the way back to base he stopped at the Co-op for a sandwich and can he consumed in their car park.

Back at base DS Scoley was reporting back to the boss about the *Lincoln Leader* encounter.

Jamie sat down with DS Goodwin to go through all he'd discovered in and around Hibaldslow.

Jake Goodwin was impressed with Jamie having borrowed the CCTV disk from the Wheatsheaf pub and even got the geeks upstairs to take screen shots of the best images of the Cutforths sat at a table with two men and a woman and made a copy. They meant nothing.

'At the pub Dave Gibson said he knew the Cutforths, confirmed they're there most Tuesdays their Pool League Night but old Hubert's not played for a good few years.'

Jake admitted to Inga he had spotted as Jamie had, one or two cameras on private homes but as far as could be seen they were aimed down onto the front gardens or the drive in an attempt to catch intruders, rather than out onto the road to record passing traffic.

'Was telling me he went for a bit of a drive around after he left the pub instead of just heading back after. Proved he could make his way back here if he set his mind to it, by using back roads all the way. Means no cameras of course. Jamie reckons he went back to close to their farm and then drove all the way to Hackthorne before he jacked it in. Nipped across to Lincoln City's training place and RAF Scampton and just linked up with the A15. No cameras, apart no doubt on people's homes. Certainly no ANPR to give us reg numbers, owners and occupiers.' Jake went to get to his feet. 'One thought Jamie's had. What if she wrote something nasty about the village? Tells us why Hibaldstow was chosen to dump her body, be somewhere familiar.'

More trundling up the A15 for DC Jamie Hedley that evening, to take the disk back and just see if staff there recognized anybody unusual and get names.

'As the saying goes, more questions than answers down there,' Nicky Scoley reported to the DI. 'That Gosney, the Editor was certainly anti when we first arrived. Had this sort of how dare you attitude. As if he thought we were poking our noses into something not of our concern.'

'But you got there in the end?'

'As best we could. Gave us screen shots of their personal files. Just all the basics we were after. Given them to Jake to hand out for checking against PNC and the rest. As for Gosney himself, turns out he was interviewing the East Midlands Mayoral candidates. One Monday, one Tuesday.'

'Bit late,' Inga responded. 'Whole lot about them in the paper last week, week before. Got to be ten or a dozen standing.'

'This was just the Tory and Labour ones he reckons are the only viable candidates. He was telling me the *Leader* coming out on a Thursday will be delayed until the Friday after the election. Not so they can publish the result that could take all weekend, although all the other council results'll probably be in.' Scoley could see the inquisitive look on the boss's face. 'This is all, so he can publish a bang up to the minute news piece about the pair of them, probably an exit poll they're cobbling together. Says,' she pulled a face, 'otherwise everybody else will beat them to it.'

'Why go this week?' Inga asked. 'I sort of read bits last week, week before.'

'Rules are rules. Two week period of grace when they're not allowed to publish anything. So, he did them just before the deadline to get as close to polling day as he could. Everybody else'd get them after.'

'How few will bother to vote?'

'Still,' said Nicky with a cheeky smile. Knew her parents would and her two brothers. As a family they always voted. 'Got his mobile number just in case,' made Inga lean forward.

'I won't ask.' The cynical look Nicky'd seen many times before.

'Nipped off to get one of his minions to copy the files for us, phone just sat on his desk. So took the number. You never know.' She sat back and released a breath. 'That business with Alisha I was telling you about really got to me. Think I did it out of spite more than anything, a sort of I'll show you Mr Editor.'

'Covering all bases,' said a smiling Inga. 'At the same time.'

'As it says in the manual,' the butterscotch blonde quipped. 'Car was easy sat outside when we left, in the space marked Editor. We can if deemed necessary carry out ANPR checks with my friends down in Hendon, see if what he says is legit.'

'Not too bad a visit after all.''

'Except,' was a tad more solemn. 'As I was saying on the way in, he was not good at all with Alisha. Almost totally ignored her, but relented near the end, thinking maybe his conscience got the better of him.' She pulled a face. 'Played the I'm the king of the castle thing for all he was worth.'

'Tells us what we're dealing with. Guess being king bee's difficult to change.'

'Druggie worries me,' made Inga take notice. She related what she had been told about this Kevin Elphick going to the Katushabe's wife's defence. 'All sounds really good and feasible with what people say about the brothers' moralistic views, but Elphick's pupils were dilated when we interviewed him, and his eyes were slightly bloodshot.'

'Cocaine?'

'But still working there. In his defence maybe he's not out of the woods as yet, but Gosney did say he'd been there a year.'

'Why up here? Where's he from?'

'Sutton Coldfield area, where the Katushabes all live apparently.'

'Interesting.' Inga wondered if this Kevin Elphick fully understood the act of kindness shown on that one day. Any other street, any other time and chances are he'd still be begging, or dead.

'What d'you want done about this? One to keep up our sleeve maybe, quick sift through and his alibis seemed fairly normal. If he comes back on our radar could easy be drugs.'

'If he's still using, that'll put him back where he was, and if that happens wonder about these...Katushabe brothers. How will they react I wonder?'

'Not best pleased I imagine with their holier than thou business.'

'Back burner for now, but still get Jake to check him out.'

DC MacLachlan had sidled up to the boss's door listening to the women chatting.

'Jake and Michelle doing them one by one and Alisha's lending a hand as well as catching up on all of them on social media.'

'She alright you think?' a concerned Inga queried.

'Shrugged it off,' said Nicky. 'Guess she's used to it. I'm planning to take a closer look at the features Barnard's written. Got to be a clue there somewhere surely. Why else would anybody kill her? This could easily be some skurk getting their own back for something she wrote.' She pulled a face. 'Could be very caustic at times.'

'And not Sean Joseph you think?'

'No, he's good,' Inga said firmly. 'Indeed it was him gave us the link to her USB sticks, which is another way for us to be able to investigate first hand what she was working on. If he was making any attempt at hiding what she was up to, he'd never have done that.'

'Double bluff?'

'Really?' was grimaced. 'He's a graphic designer not an OCG criminal master mind.'

'This not some sort of dig at maybe some extreme political group?' was one idea from Sandy at the door suddenly. 'People like Gay Pride activists killing a woman doesna seem feasible but I think she had a lot to say about these transexuals at one time, my Rachel was saying. Then there's always political extremists she could have had a go at. National Action and that alias the Home Office banned a time back. Black Lives Matter for one, with their right wing stance along with all the environment factions. Nazis under one flag or other we still have here and back in the fatherland.'

'What about Taliban,' said a grinning Larsson. 'If we're not too careful we could go on.'

'Och aye. Be here all day with a motley crew like Al-Shabaab, Boko Haram and all the rest.'

'Can't imagine any of this is that political,' Nicky offered. 'Think with Rachel it was women who needed to watch their step, to up their game rather than Boris Johnson and his crew.'

'Not at all what she was into,' said Inga Larsson shaking her blonde head. 'Not that I've ever read anyway. Feminine angle is worth a check, sided with females but was also ultra critical of them at the same time when they say and do soppy things. Couldn't be doing with all the stupidity that goes on with some, day in day out.'

'I'll have a good read. Be something different from watching crap on the telly this evening.'

Inga Larsson sat back with a look on her face Scoley recognized from knowing the woman so well.

'Come on,' she encouraged. 'Out with it.'

'You know I had Sean Joseph here?' was a Larsson admittance rather than a question. 'Gave us a lot of useful info all about her USB Sticks, the ones Adrian's collected a bit earlier. Then just as he was leaving he just casually turned back and said. "Would her phone be any use to you?" I'm gobsmacked me!'

'Where'd that come from?' Nicky gasped with hand to mouth.

'Reckons it was on her kitchen table.'

'Anything on it?' Sandy probed.

'Adrian's got Dexter Hopwood delving into it, checking her contacts if nothing else. Need the provider to come up with the calls data as soon as.'

'She just forgot it you think?'

'Looks like it. Possibly got called out urgent. Always possible the killer called round, maybe...' Inga grimaced with her eyes shut trying to imagine somebody with a brick. 'According to Sean he'd not tried to open it, said he didn't know the password and anyway said he'd not be able to stand the sound of her voice. Which you can understand.' Inga sat forward. 'Do us a favour,' she said to Nicky. 'Take a copy of the list of the *Leader* phone numbers, take it up to Dexter. Got to be some from work; but whatever he'll give it all a good try.'

'Why didn't CSI discover the phone and where'd these flash drives appear from?'

'Sean told me Gosney sent him round to her place to check, when she didn't turn up for work.'

'This doon Rookery Lane?' was a Sandy query.

'Yes, having got no reply from her phone. Wondered if she was sick maybe. Bet Sharon Tate's blushing a bit. Barnard kept them in the freezer,' as Nicky went to respond, a chuckling Inga went on. 'Checked it myself. Flash drives are fine in a freezer providing you keep them dry, sterile and free from any contamination like your chicken legs,' she joked. 'Put them an a freezer bag they're okay.'

'Well, blow me down,' Nicky gasped her surprise. 'Why?' she asked abruptly.

'Security.'

'You learn something every day. My word,' she sat there shaking her blonde head.

'You've read her stuff,' Sandy slipped in to the boss. 'It's not all like that. One of the things my Rache reads in the *Leader* as well as matches and dispatches, but she just enjoys them. Never mentioned any of it might be a state secret.'

'You're forgetting something,' was Inga. 'Perhaps you don't know but she wrote for other magazines on the quiet under false names, to make extra money to buy her dream house.'

'So that's why the articles she wrote are a priority,' Sandy had deduced. 'If she felt the need to hide the drives like that.'

'Could be a major development. And now you have her sticks,' she said to Nicky, 'You can read them to your heart's content.'

'Always possible we may have to hand them out when Adrian and his team have had a quick scan to check for bugs. Getting on for a dozen I think Sean said, and there's a lot more than one article to each drive. Take a bit of going through. Have to assume it's something recent but you never know. If Barnard exposed somebody about some fraud or whatever. Slagged off a few bitter toerags, always possible he or she's been inside and just got out on licence maybe. Tracking her down through the paper would be fairly easy.'

'Revenge? Easy be.'

'Getting their own back.'

'Gotta be something pretty serious to go to those lengths though. Think we know what you'll be doing for a few evenings.'

'Glass of red, leave Connor to watch sport to his hearts content. Be good.'

'Could be what we're looking for.'

It was Good Friday but she wasn't missing anything important. Nicky'd delivered Easter Eggs to her brothers' kids earlier in the week so that was all done. She and Connor had bought a Dark Chocolate Egg for Sunday.

'If nothing else, means we can cross Sean Joseph off the small list.' Inga clapped her hands. 'Back to it folks, I'm off to see the boss and listen to him moaning about having to give another talk to another bunch of ladies who lunch.'

Larsson sat facing her monitor for a few moments, peering and asking questions of herself at the same time.

According to CSI Leicester's clever dick boffins, Rachel Barnard had been walloped over the back of her head with a 'Shire Blend Clamp Handmade Brick' and had to enhance their research ability included a PDF of a dozen or more of the bricks as an example.

She beckoned her deputy into her office, to read the email. Larsson heard a sigh escaping from Jake Goodwin stood beside her, she took to be a comment without any need for words.

She rubbed her forehead. To some extent this whole case had escalated into something more than a plain and simple murder for some ridiculous reason at a point in time as they often are. Had to be a whole lot more than just a simple falling out and anger getting the better of somebody.

'What about?' Larsson surmised. 'This is all connected somehow to the Leader and Barnard was an easy target? Just a thought.'

'Not something she wrote for the *Commercial Grower* about strawberries and greenhouses that's for sure.'

'Wouldn't bet on it! Some gardeners have funny ideas.'

'If it is something from the *Leader* and they get an inkling they're keeping themselves to themselves they'll all be looking over their shoulders for who's next.'

'Been thinking,' said Goodwin as he moved away to sit opposite. 'How about a former offender given a hard time by the paper, not necessarily by Barnard in particular. Our killer has no idea how to make contact with say a columnist for the Daily Mail or one of the big boys who also did a piece, but Barnard has a high profile locally and in magazines and has her pen picture against her weekly column.'

'Interesting thought.'

'Wouldn't they tell us?' Jake queried across the desk.

'And miss out on a scoop?'

'D'they still have such a thing these days with social media snapping everything up?'

'Worth a thought though.'

'From what Nicky was saying he was un-cooperative to say the least. Keeping things close to his chest.'

'Pity we have to wait for Thursday to come round.'

10

'You haven't run round have you?' as the back door was opened to James Gosney.

'Nice evening for a jog.'

'Everything alright Jimmy? Well, under the circumstances should I say,' James Gosney was asked by his long time friend as he was ushered in by the back door, slightly out of breath.

'Not that you'd notice,' he grinned with.

'In what way?' he asked as Gosney leant back against the pale grey shiny work surface.

'Crawling with bastard coppers, of course,' was far from the truth.

'Asking what, as if I don't know?' he surmised as the back door was closed.

'All the usual. Stuff they get off the telly. Where were you, what were you doing morning noon and bloody night. What was she working on? Writing for this bloody paper what d'you think?' he blew out a breath as he brushed a hand through his flattened dark brown hair. 'Had to poke their noses in all the staff's personal files for God's sake. What's her discipline record like? What time she go to the toilet? When she didn't show for work what did you do? Jesus Christ!' He blew out another breath. 'Had a fuckin' paper to get out missus that's what. What d'they expect me to do? I'm not her bloody nursemaid!.'

'You didn't? No Jimmy, please.''

'No, course not Charlie. God knows what tomorrow'll be like though.'

'They back tomorrow?' a slightly sweaty James was asked as he was ushered into the large lounge.

92

'God knows. Rachel's bedmate Sean's been down the cop shop apparently, back this afternoon. He's keeping his mouth shut, which doesn't help when we're desperate for an angle.'

'What's he got to say?'

'Not seen him. Pete Leyton told him to take time off, but think he's better with his head down than moping around at home.'

'They interviewing you all?' he was asked as they strolled away from the kitchen.

'Pretty much. Talked to my lot, took all their details away.'

'Be checking you all out, be that PNC business they do.'

'Good luck with that,' James scoffed. 'Don't know the Katushabe's like we do that's for sure. As if we'd dare employ any scallywag who'd only nicked a sweetie from the shop.'

'What they hope to gain? After all she didn't die at work. Not as if there's a health and safety element.'

'All about her work and her friends. What else can any of them say? I mean what could any of us say about some bod we work with? Be one of the others I'd not have a bloody clue. Not that I know much anyway.'

'But apart from all that?'

'Apart from all that and trying to get the damn paper out all at the same time. Course true to form her page as usual was bloody blank. Why's she always late?' He grimaced with. 'Had to get a couple of lads to cobble something together, went with that eating in bed fad in the end.'

'How d'you mean?' Charlie asked.

'Been all the rage for a while. Katushabe's sent a survey up and we turned it round to fill the hole.'

'You talking about having a cup of tea in bed?' he chuckled as if anything more was a ridiculous notion.

'No. Full works. Some goons even have salt and pepper on the bedside table. Sunday roast, pie and mash you name it.'

'Sorry mate. Find that concept too ghastly to comprehend. You do that?' he grimaced.

'No. What d'you take me for?'

'Think when I was sick as a kid, I had a boiled egg.' He just stood shaking hid head.

'Damn sure that nasty bitch having a go at me today with snide remarks, thinks we spend all week with our bloody feet up and come Wednesday morning throw the paper together.' He sighed and his head dropped. 'Good bollocking heading my way in the morning no doubt.'

'Why?'

'Do the brothers Grimm ever need an excuse? Hand-me-down stuff forced in the bloody paper every week I want nothing to do with. Something reminded me today about that mental health garbage, remember? When we had Covid still, hanging about and then Ukraine got lobbed in. Had to get one of the lads to do a piece on how these world events effect five year old's mental health.'

'Why on earth do people think anyone's interested in such piffle?' Charlie commented.

'Katushabes that's who,' said James as he dropped down heavily onto the big sofa. Coal fire embers unnecessarily still smoking in the grate for the time of year. 'What sort of shit's that eh? Asking me to tell adults to protect their kids from Putin,' he sighed with frustration.

'Snifter?' Charlie asked rather than comment further, as James' attitude appeared to have disappeared with a noisy sigh.

'Why not? Jogged over so the cops'll not pull me. Be good that, after the day I've had. Sorry sir, you're under arrest for driving a motor vehicle over the prescribed limit for alcohol...you're bloody fault officer, sending that blonde bitch round to hassle me all day,' even James himself had to snigger slightly.

'Good thinking. That'd get the Katushabes on their high horse.' James ran his index finger across his neck in a slashing action.

'As if they ever need an excuse. Dead staff's not quite what I need with them, what d'you reckon?'

'Weren't you planning to check the Katushabes out at one time? See what this over-egged moralistic quirk is all about?'

'Never got round to it to be honest. Told once if you remember, it's got something to do with some Eastern Orthodox Church offshoot from the 4th century think it was,

94

upon which they base these ridiculous moralistic values.' He pulled a face. 'Not absolutely sure though.'

'At least you know its not for much longer.'

'D'yer know every week when I do that final edit it always reminds me of the nonsense they spew out on the telly. All that stuff about scenes some people may find distressing, which never is of course as we all know its just fiction. Notice they hardly ever say that before the news which is often full of absolute mayhem.'

'Nanny state looking after snowflakes.'

'Makes you wonder how they've become so successful, with the types you have to deal with in business.'

'Never get in the Masons, that's for sure.'

'They still going?' James shrugged at.

'No idea,' he scoffed. 'All about care, respect and integrity somebody reckoned at one time. Eric Webb said he was planning to have a good look at the whys and wherefores after he got fired, but not heard from him since.'

'Remind me. What did he actually do?'

'Gave a photographer a hug and a peck on the cheek.'

'Male?'

'Yep,' James responded.

'Daft when every programme on the telly's got one.' Breath sucked in noisily. 'After the no hugging pandemic?'

'Like walking on thin ice with that lot at times. Leave everyday normal living at the door. All ye who enter here.'

'Including swearing.'

'For most it's nothing worse than everyday something and nothing, but. There was Danny Wilkins up in Bolton got done for speeding on the M6 and got fired by the brothers.'

'Driving job I assume?'

'No. Not at all. Perjury.'

'Explain.'

'Stopped by the cops doing over a ton. When it came to court he'd got a clever barrister to plead hardship. Pleaded how his elderly mother had no other relatives to care for her and claimed he got called out regularly in the middle of the night. Got points rather than a ban.'

'The perjury?'

'His mother and father are fit and well, and the Katushabe's knew it was just a bag of lies even if the magistrate believed his sob story. ' James grinned. 'Bragging how he got away with it didn't do his case much good. They just kicked him out when they heard.'

'Got to say James, I agree absolutely with that. Too many idiots driving round with dozens of points and pulling strokes like that. Be a man, hold your hands up. For goodness sake.'

'Bit like having Kaikara Katushabe as a back seat driver all the time though.' Gosney sniggered as his friend poured them each a gin and tonic.

'Plenty of tonic please Charlie,' produced a look in response.

'You're not in the pub now.'

'I know, but I've always gone down the lager route, don't need any more hassle at home thank you. Not as if I've not got enough at work.'

'This scoffing in bed. You being serious?'

'Had to rush it, but easy be something we can come back to. Sorry, but its too ridiculous for words.'

'Know who I met this week? Remember Ryan Tindall?'

'How could I forget.'

'Still doing the gumshoe routine.'

'Getting a bit old for all that surely. Why's he suddenly appeared?'

'Offered me scandalous and probably libelous info on somebody who shall remain nameless,' he winked.

'Be careful'

'All over the internet soon enough.'

'Bane of my life,' Gosney admitted. 'Have that kids mental health utter twaddle, and what does all that produce? Half-baked kids, no good to man or beast with a phone they won't let go of and bolted bedroom door.'

'Too busy watching porn.'

'Was it you who told me about the teacher saying he'd discovered kids in class with one eye on their phones watching porn?'

'Head teacher it was. And the Katushabes if you remember wouldn't publish. All arse about face to me.'

'And the other bane of your life, still nagging is she?'

'And the rest,' James admitted.

'You taking time off this weekend?'

'Monday to be with the kids. But the powers that be still expect us to be heads down.'

'Somebody was telling me this zealous religious fervour of theirs has pretty much been eroded by the young in Uganda these days.'

'Somebody told me they're mainly Catholics or Muslims.'

'Could be where the no alcohol comes from.'

'And no chocolate eggs.'

'This is a centuries old Christian offshoot we're talking about though.'

'Muslims are a bit anti women, more than a bit with the Taliban back. Never see any of them at a funeral. But you don't seem to have any of those sort of issues.'

'Ever respectful of women, bit over the top sometimes in fact. What's the guessing they'll want Daisy to cover her face next to protect her from something.'

'Is all this business a constant issue for you?' made Gosney shake his head, as his gin and tonic was handed down to him. 'I've always wondered why you don't get the staff together and decide how you wish to work,' his host suggested as he sat down. 'Set your own parameters, modern levels of behaviour, even language of you like. Bit of office banter never hurt anybody despite what snowflakes go on about. Then when the Katushabe's turn up you all go into your fundamental mode.'

'But for one thing,' James said before he took his first sip. 'Daisy Lytton.'

'Why? She gay or...?'

'Suspected.'

'And her problem is?'

'Religion,' James responded with.

'Not the...'

James' head shake stopped the remark and they both drank. 'This fruity?'

'Cotswold Wildflower. Bought a few when I was down the other week.'

'Good,' James said and pulled a face as he nodded.

'Religion?' was a reminder.

'Oh yeh. One of these born again Christian types. Be in church today of course and Sunday. Not stupid enough to add her to the rota. Bit worried the Katushabe's have planted her as a spy to be honest. One major clue is she's only average at best with her work and they always tend to go for top notch to be fair to them.'

'You think they'd stoop so low to infiltrate your daily workings?'

'No doubting that, as you'd know if you worked with them. No,' James stopped himself and looked down at his glass. 'Not work with them, work *for* them. There's a big difference.'

'Working towards the next billion no doubt.'

'Lost count at eight.'

'How would Daisy's religion be connected to some of their prudish off-the-wall Ugandan centuries old thinking?'

'Got notes at home I still have when I was checking her out. Load of gubbins about talking to Jesus.'

'As if he was sat on my sofa with a gin in his hand.'

'Exactly.'

'Like you a lot James, but Jesus you are not!'

'All about,' said a smiling Editor. 'Having a conversation with God.'

'Have to try that sometime when I'm on my own, see how I get on.'

'All happy clappy, singing along with a tambourine and a guitar probably.' James sipped, then when on hastily as if he'd just remembered something. 'Worry about Barnard too to some extent.'

'Why? Was she a strict Muslim or something?' was sneered.

'No. She and that Sean have been an item for at least a year, yet he still lives at home with his mummy.'

'Sounds like he's the one with a problem!'

'Wonder if she's the plant.'

'Now you're getting paranoid,' Charlie suggested and sipped. 'All very hocus-pocus to hide something?'

'Why not live together eh?' was shrugged by James sat forward arms on his thighs glass held in both hands. 'What stops people, other than having some religious belief? Maybe not them specifically but often parents constraints controlling them.'

'Maybe he beds down there regularly, you don't know about.'

'Nobody's heard mention of even a weekend away someplace.' James looked down at his hands around the crystal glass. 'Got to say in his defence he's good at his job. Brilliant idea to go with like a tabloid looking front like the *Sun* or *Metro* for *Lincoln Now!* Only trouble now is the hard hitting stories we planned to use have just gone up the spout. Thought she'd saved the ones she'd done but I can't find them.'

'You'll find another.'

'Not too sure about that.'

'One door closes remember and anyway its not for much longer.'

'You hope.'

'Hope doesn't come into it.'

'Just have to hope Mukisa has got someone somewhere he can pull out the bag, but I doubt it.' Gosney just shook his head. 'Or what's the betting they come up with another fucking toerag druggie one of them dragged off the streets or the bloody gutter somewhere?'

'You think they would?'

'Good chance. Remember Charlie, they're happy enough with Kevin Elphick,' made his friend sigh. 'Easy repeat the process to get more Brownie points from the damn do-gooders.'

'So, you're coming down on the side of the big Katushabe morality business? What does everybody else think?'

'All they come up with are nasty cracks about him, but apparently he was living with someone for a while before her.'

'Who?'

'Sean.'

'Phew!' He gasped. 'Thought you were on about Katushabes.'

'No chance,' James smiled with

'With her out the way now, keep your eye open for her replacement turning up in a burka or praying to the coffee machine!'

'Very good. I already do that when it dishes out the wrong thing! Funny you should mention that. Rudolf Toussaint the features guy from head office told me they're considering sending one of their top investigators up here, see if he or she can solve the crime before the cops.'

'All they can see are the tills ringing seems to me.' Charlie was back to his gin. 'You say you're still having trouble at home. Isn't it time you jacked in the five-a-side and found another interest.'

'Easier said than done. Not a good idea to choose something new such as playing Badminton and have Emily suggest she joins in, or join a crafting workshop.' He shrugged. 'What else is there? Know about football, can easy talk bollocks about what went on like the rest of them..'

'See what you mean.'

'Emily hates football, and anyway there's no connection. Stopped actually playing good year or two before we met, so she doesn't know any of my old team mates I meet up with.'

'And you still do all this secret drinking dens idea?'

'Don't want her knowing I go to one particular pub, then she gets talking to her mates who mention they go there. And never seen me or worse suggests she joins them. Be a right mess.'

'So, you set off like tonight and tell Emily you'll get a text on your way into town telling you where they're meeting tonight.'

'Pretty much'

'Seems a bit convoluted to me.'

'You don't have a wife to worry about.'

'Did away with all that nonsense a good while ago, thank you.'

'Have to change tack at some point. When Rowan reaches pub age you can bet your life I'll be encouraged to take him with me to meet my old mates,' he had to smile at the idea of.

'Time for another weekend away, what think you?' James was asked. 'I'm sure the Katushabe's can come up with a weekend course they insist all editors have to attend. What about advocating morals in your editorial?' amused himself. 'Thinking Lake District, what you reckon?' James was asked and his friend was back to the last of his gin and tonic.

'Guess what?' he came back with. 'Emily's got some off the wall ideas about holiday destinations,' he sucked in his breath. 'With a difference.'

'Go on.'

'Saw places on some programme she watched. Seemed keen at first on the suggestion she could stay in Whitby lighthouse, Two things though. Headline suggests that, but the truth is you stay in a lighthouse keepers cottage next door not in the lighthouse itself. Even so, sounds like a good place for my two,' he chuckled. 'On the edge of a cliff.'

'Hardly the sort of place you'd want to spend a fortnight.'

'They're all staycations seems to me.'

'Why d'you media people always latch onto such nonsense, like staycation?'

'Well...'

'Too busy trying to be on trend all the while seems to me. It's a holiday. It's nothing more than a simple few days away. A break, a weekend. Why make up a daft word?' He sipped gin. 'That's an ideas for the Katushabe's for a conference. How to eliminate looking daft with on trend garbage, like woak and doxing'

'That's the sort of nonsense they're into,' he reacted and ploughed on. 'There's a double decker bus in the Lake District if you're looking for somewhere up that way. One place in Cornwall I seem to remember sits on stilts. Sounded okay until Emily mentioned yoga and foraging.'

'Anywhere sensible?'

'Place that looks like an airship has landed and one campsite includes a helicopter..'

'Sounds more like it.'

'Another one has all sorts, like campavans in a field.'

'For a family of four?'

'Exactly.

'Something different to keep up our sleeve. Fancy that helicopter though. I'm free of family ties but even I need a change which as they say is as good as a rest, and my God you certainly will with what's going on. You sure you should be here, with what happened to Rachel and if there's trouble at home?'

'Need to get away from both. Breath of fresh air, clear my head and find my own space.'

'You'll get that alright out biking at your age.' Last dregs of gin and tonic sipped. 'You certainly need a break away not only from nosy parker coppers but from all your work hassle and to be honest I don't know how you stand it. Just get way away from a nagging wife and two teenage kids. On holiday what do you do?' James was asked firmly. 'You do what Emily wants, am I right? Because you're a soft bugger, go where she and the kids want and what do you do? You agree, like a bloody puppy dog. Right again?' James nodded slightly at the truth hurting. 'We need to be two grown men spending time doing what we want for once what pleases us, not doing what others think we need do, or in your case I should imagine, must do.'

'You thinking country cottage somewhere?'

'Out the way. Thinking maybe Windermere - seen a good one on line, or for a change what about a Pine Log Cabin near Keswick?'

'Using your alter ego again?'

'Arthur Ranking comes riding into town folks!' A glass was raised in James' direction. 'Another?'

'Not on a bike,' he chuntered. 'Lager if you've got one, then I'll smell like the pub she thinks I've been to.' James was left alone to ponder life and times and the likely onslaught he faced next morning.

Were he at home, apart from being alone in the spare room working, he'd be downstairs being offered another cup of tea or bored to tears thinking about work pretending to watch the most ridiculous of television channel hopping choices, one after another.

As if he was reading his mind the next question aimed at him was one answer to many issues in his life but included monumental issues to be faced.

James Gosney was looking for a life away from all this, but was this the answer to his dreams?

''How are we with the change of direction?' he was asked as half a pint of lager was handed down to him. Was it the gin effect or just that fire failing to go out which had made him warm?

'Still the same issues.'

'What happened to your power of persuasion then?'

'Not as easy as that.'

'Yes relocation could well be an issue I'll give you that. But....' another gin was started. 'How much easier will life be for us both? You, both professionally and personally. You'll not have to spend your life kowtowing to all this centuries old moralistic nonsense these people claim they live by, if in fact they do.'

'I'll give you the job of persuading Emily. You convince her disrupting the kids schooling will be better in the long term. Tell them they need to go to some strange place, more immigrants, more issues and all the hassle about making new friends. Anyway, how would Rowan contend with Leicester City compared with his beloved Imps?'

'Isn't that the point. Others always coming first no matter what.'

'They're my family.'

'Of course they are.' Fresh neat gin sipped. 'On the other hand you'd not have restless nights like you face right now,' was suggested as James got stuck into his pint.

'What utter garbage will that Mukisa Katushabe be spouting come tomorrow? When in this day and age he should know better. Pray to a fig tree if you wish, collect old lawnmowers or paper serviettes, but don't expect me to.'

'By the way. You expecting the law to return?'

'No bloody idea. Only worry is next time it could well be proper coppers not two fancy pieces like today.'

'Did they not say?'

'Just took the staff info with them, for what good that'll do them. Real stuff is down in Birmingham for madam Katushabe to scurry through, looking for one of us being late for school or dropping a lolly stick in the park,' made them both smile.

'Your alibi for Monday in case they ask?'

'You seeing them, then?'

'Not that I know of, but best be prepared.'

'Went to Melton Mowbray interviewing our friend Ray Earle.'

'Of course you did,' he said nodding. 'Worth going?'

'Not really. All the usual bluster but he lives well.'

'What a council house upbringing does for you. Government gives you everything from the day you're born. Maternity Leave, free school meals. Universal Credit…'

'Enough.'

'But you know what I mean. Anyway what's it like? Seen it from the outside of course.'

'Victorian looked to me, but what would I know. Over three floors but not sure what there is right at the top, apart from an attic maybe. Big lounge with bay window was all I got to see. Parking for half a dozen cars on the drive that's for sure. Extensive garden out the back I could see while he was spouting on.'

'Anything new?'

'No. Just the usual socialist propaganda and more tosh about welcoming immigrants into the fold. Boris wants to ship 'em off to Rwanda and silly buggers like Earl want as many as you like ramming the streets of Dover.'

'Him on the dockside saying, welcome. We've not had a terrorist attack this month.'

Charlie frequently wondered if his welcomed visitor was simply a very useful but social menace with his life of peeping and snooping. In exchange for what? An average salary and then now and again a good headline to be easily forgotten next day when another story winged its way in his direction. At least these days his hard work never finished up as nothing more than chip paper thanks to the torment of PC nimbys.

'Time to go,' James sighed and downed the last of his drink. 'Deadlines wait for no man. What I need is that tattooing where I can see it in the mirror every morning.'

11

Detective Sergeant Nicola Scoley looked at Mundin, a slip of a young woman and wondered exactly what she truly knew of the depths of despair and loneliness many have to live their lives surrounded by.

Chatting to the woman in the newsagents, or the chubby butcher was probably pretty much what she would do with her day. Never as far as Scoley could understand, was she having to deal with any of the atrocities goings on in the world out there.

Scoley guessed Lorna Mundin's average days would take their time depending on the weather. Bad weather would most probably stop Mundin from venturing forth to break the monotony of a long drag, or just to be able to partake of what was more than likely a form of routine. Monday to Friday would be nice.

Sort of day Nicky felt she could sometimes do with just for a break from the pressure and stress of work. Early morning, grabbed lunch if any at all and late nights for them both frequently. At least she had Easter Sunday with Connor to look forward to.

All that had to be the reason why. The reason behind her just giving away a huge chunk of money to a scoundrel, being a nice way to put it.

Sat there still waiting Nicky Scoley wondered what Rachel Barnard had really thought about this Mundin woman, other than what had been in her article.

'Sorry,' this Lorna said before she was seen. 'Billy needed feeding,' Nicky had no idea who or what Billy was. Bad news was the tea already had milk in it. Too much milk to Nicky's taste, who normally only give any hot drink the smallest of dribbles into a mug. That was another thing, the mug was missing and instead the high days and holidays dainty teacups maiden aunts go for were there on the coffee table, which was a pleasing sight. Poor drink but there being far less of it, would suffice.

'The article Rachel Barnard wrote about you, said right at the beginning you were in receipt of a fake phone call.'

'How was I to know that?' she came back with. Hair washed but looked dank and unkempt. 'Think that's something Rachel missed.'

'Fair enough. You received a call. Can you remember what was said?'

'A man.' Nicky waited. She knew that from the article the woman must surely still have a copy of. 'Well male voice, but these days you can never be sure.'

Was it not surprising this Lorna Mundin's story had been linked to another woman who had been tricked by the same fraudsters, if this was how little she had offered.

'And?'

'Told me my National Insurance Number's been compromised.'

'Before we move on to what happened next, can you tell me why you reacted as you did?'

'I was worried. Said I'd need to get a new number.'

'But,' Scoley sighed to herself. 'What did you need a new number for?' Her advantage was she's read Barnard's account and therefore knew the ins and outs.

'Everybody's got one. Because they said I'd be in trouble without one?'

'But, I think you're missing my point.' Arms resting on her knees she looked at Mundin. 'What did you need a National Insurance Number for?' and this thin woman looked at her as if she had two heads. 'As far as we can make out, you never used the one you had. In fact according to Rachel's article, you'd never used it because you'd never had a job and still haven't.. You were in the very fortunate position of not needing one, apart that is from helping your disabled mother. National Insurance numbers are all to do with employment. Why would you need another number you were never going to have any use for?'

'Because everybody has one.'

'Can we move on?' Scoley asked but it was never a question she wanted answering. 'Having lost money by pressing the key and becoming embroiled in what must have amounted to untold pressure to give up your bank details, did you later that year fall for a similar scam, this time connected to the Love Bug website?'

'How did you know about that?'

'Because if nothing else Rachel Barnard was very efficient in the way she constructed her newspaper articles. Not only did she at the end as a form of index list all contacts, phone numbers and where necessary email addresses and websites, she also as in your case we guess later, she added an addendum to your article stating how you had also appeared on a website as the victim in a similar scam very soon after.'

'Not the same.'

'I know they were not the same,' said Scoley, and in need of a drink no matter how milky the tea looked and likely tasted, she took a mouthfull. With cup back on the saucer she decided unless she wanted this all to drag on all afternoon it was time to tighten the screw. 'How much did you lose in both cases together?'

'Seventeen thousand pounds,' she just offered without a pause to consider. 'Well a bit over, actually.'

'And this was made up how?'

'Twelve hundred for the new National Insurance Number and…'

'You never got.'

'And,' Lorna went on. 'The rest I stupidly sent to Mauritius.'

'Mauritius?'

'Yes,' was almost whispered and for he first time Scoley saw emotion in her face.

'Tell me. What did you do about it all?'

'What could I do?'

'How about friends?'

'And admit it all? Would you admit to somebody you'd been that stupid?'

'You stayed silent to save face?' was answered with the slightest of nods. 'Did you contact Rachel Barnard at the *Lincoln Leader*?'

'No,' she shrugged with. 'Why would I?'

'Just wondered if by any chance you attached any blame to her for the second and worse scam.'

'How?'

'This Joshua Kemp I would suggest read what happened to you and saw you as a likely candidate for his Love Bug scam? Probably Googled National Insurance scams and your name popped up.'

'How would he?' she chuckled as if it was impossible. 'He lives in Mauritius and it was in that Lincoln paper.'

'You think.'

'What?' was all breath.

'Website you can easy pick up on anywhere, even Mauritius. Like everybody these days, the *Leader* has a website.'

'It was Port Louis'

If you say so. The look told Scoley this was one naive woman. alone in the world with no pals to call on or meet up with, and simply relied on the television, phone and the internet as her comfort blankets.

It would have been easy to offer her once more the advice Rachel had probably given her back then.

'Are you still on Facebook?

'Yes,' was timid and then Lorna set about her cup of weak but not very willing tea.

'Might I suggest, if you get any more messages or phone calls from people who appear to be even slightly dubious about, you do nothing. Message your friends on Facebook, tell them what happened, ask their opinion. How many Friends do you have on there?'

'Fourteen I think but only a few I know to speak to.'

'Get more Friends. The butcher, the baker and whoever you see on a regular basis, ask them, look them up and request. Have people you actually know. That way if you get more problems, you could for example message the local greengrocer and ask his opinion.'

Driving away back to Lincoln Central from Wragby, Nicky could see how easy it would have been for Rachel Barnard to become a sort of social worker.

Some scams she had exposed were cleverly organized. One was for somebody who had received a reply to an email they had innocently sent to a friend. The email address was correct and knowledge of the friend was there. Asking for a Google Play Gift Card to be sent to a friend for her birthday, because being away from home travelling the scammer pretending to be her friend, claimed he could not source one himself. The email address of course had been hacked. Barnard had discovered this was a regular scam as such Gift Cards can be easily converted to cash.

Had Rachel Barnard somehow, somewhere down the line become too involved, too entangled in somebody else's problems and in the background a scammer objected to her poking her nose in?

At home in her four-bedroom house she shared with Adam and daughter young Terése Danielle in Fiskerton on the outskirts of Lincoln, Inga Larsson had homework to do of sorts. Putting herself down to work on Easter Sunday would free others up to spend time with their families. With her physiotherapist husband in charge of all things domestic including lunch out for the three of them, she was sat at the dining room table with laptop and a glass of the remnants of a new red wine.

Time to delve into what Rachel Barnard had written which may well have got her into serious trouble.

Inga sat back and began to read.

As it turned out this column was all about her annoyance at the absurdity of these Gen X, Y and Z cohorts. In the same vein she exposed the absurdity of people suggesting Gen X eat less chips than previous generations. Who is it then who pack the queues at McDonalds? She'd then let rip at the Baby Boomers which as she carefully explained was completely out of date. The big baby boom had in fact been in the 1920s not after World War 2 and not as some claim 1960s.

Her asides at the end always made Inga chuckle. This time it was the Chinese and dozy women who came under attack.

TO THE OTHER SIDE. Did you know the Chinese government at one time banned appearances on television of celebrities they considered to be too effeminate?

They used the term "niang po" which is "girly girls" and tech companies apparently have fallen in line. Not at all sure it still operates, but try that here and some programmes would be badly hit. Beware the yellow peril chaps.

BAD NEWS WEEK. Did I read that right? Some dozy females are spending a month's salary on a love-coach course. This flim-flam industry they claim is booming.

I've heard enough awful stories about predators on dating sites, but this love-coach nonsense has to be manna from heaven for the nasty manipulative vultures we all hear about.

Need a love-tip ladies? Spend your money on shoes, handbags and gin, and as for love? B&Q it...do it yourself! As they say - its better to be safe than sorry.

Saturday evening at the end of a lovely family day, Inga was back to reading Barnard's work.

In one of the columns earlier in the year she'd read Barnard scoff at the idea of a period tracking app to enable women to plan their lives in line with their cycle.

Inga had to laugh at the idea of crooks deciding whether or not to batter an old lady and steal her pension having hacked into Inga's tracking app to check her status.

Time for a break and a sip or two more of her Australian Shiraz and Inga was no further forward. With no names mentioned in that article who was there who might hate her enough as a result of her taking the mickey, she sat there pondering? Good to read, interesting as always and very typical Barnard style along with a lovely sense of humour. Unlikely however to upset somebody enough to want her dead. Not even some doped-up GenZ chav who Rachel claimed some zombie had named Zoomers.

Only this Joshua Kemp had been mentioned and she knew from the info Rachel added to her work, she'd had him checked out. Action Fraud had been her first stop, she'd even gone through a reverse image search to discover the same photograph of this smiling goon appeared all over the internet in a variety of poses.

To her mind there surely was not just one person coming up with the cohorts Barnard pokes fun at, somebody who just might lose their cool. Indeed sat there out of interest she just checked out 'hullaballoo' and then generation cohorts. Rachel was right, they were a complete mess.

When she got into it being down to two Americans, she knew this surely was never the reason for Rachel being strangled. A stance she had surmised right from the outset. Discovery of' a 'Silent Generation,' based idiotically on the premise that one generation were seen and not heard, brought that episode of research to a conclusion.

Time to return to the sofa and patient Adam.

Around the same time, with Connor watching the FA Cup Semi-final Nicky Scoley too had decided to read some of Rachel Barnard's work just in case.

She'd checked the television schedules and all that did was remind her as she scanned, how this Barnard female apparently had once talked about the tokenistic casting of black people in programmes for which they were totally ill-suited. As a result according to her, that simply added to the division rather than the other way round.

Time for another of Barnard's columns. She started by arguing that critics who suggest she only deals with women being conned were far from the mark.

> MALE OF THE SPECIES is another subject some talk about on social media whenever my name is mentioned. Why is it always women being hoodwinked in my column they ask?

> Critics suggest how as a woman I should see the
> world from a different perspective. Suggesting my
> mention at one time of spiking drinks was aimed as a
> criticism of women although it was nothing of the sort.

From there Barnard had gone on about the young desperate for everything now and their constant Wows and Likes. How their life is put in the hands of influencers and she had even given an example of their nonsense.

> INTERNET NATIVE CONSUMERS. A generation
> who matured exploring their unique style of platforms.
> We young whet our appetite in order to create our on-
> line habit. Everything on this site is optimised with big
> data and contains great convos.

Time for Nicky to push her tablet to one side and think about what she had just read.

Nicky knew the boss was an avid reader of the Rachel Barnard's work and frequently, but not always, supported issues raised. This was particularly relevant with her Sexual Offence Officer's cap on. Sat there glass in hand pondering not the actual content, but how her frequent stance might well be received in some quarters.

There were a hundred and one campaigns and petitions being launched all the time for a whole variety of good reasons alongside total nonsense. Many of which in this day and age were organized by women, for women, often with their overworked hard done by attitude.

There were many causes both Nicky and Inga supported personally without going on a march or some sort of protest gathering.

Campaigns in support of a crack down on domestic abuse and the weak punishments handed down. An end to discrimination by gender they both supported naturally as they were both doing jobs held previously by men.. The campaign to make taking pictures of women breastfeeding illegal, misogyny in Parliament and more, were all on their list.

Was this, Nicky pondered, all about the criticism of women by Barnard, and one angry loose cannon was behind her murder. Were there those out there campaigning for complete bilge who had got so upset by Barnard taking the diversity route of criticizing both man and women their problem?

Sitting supping, her mother came to mind. Nicky wondered what Paula could so easily add to the list of excuses Barnard had come up with young people use to buying a house. Not from her mother, but the constant increase in drug driving brought that subject to mind, which she knew Paula would immediately link to Glastonbury. She smiled at thoughts of her then more than likely linking that to talk about the ghastly tattoos she thinks women pay an arm and a leg for to simply demean themselves.

Time to see if there was anything on the telly when money wasters such as expensive trainers, a watch to tell the time in Mombasa and designer jeans also came to mind. Last but not least the total waste of buying takeaways Paula as far as she knew had never ordered.

12

Thin evidence files for the case were so far leading them nowhere. At this rate Larsson knew she'd not even get to the stage where the CPS could pour cold water on her major pointers with their negative means to an end. Not enough substantiation to press charges, not that they had anybody in their sights to press charges against.

'Fed up, is one nice way of putting how you appear to be,' a listless Inga Larsson said to Nicky Scoley back down in the Incident Room on Monday morning half an hour after her trip up to see Hari Mistry.

'Not the only one,' Jake offered.

'I get so exasperated with people like this,' she sighed out a breath.

'Explain,' said her boss.

'Women falling for all this bollocks some shit from never never land comes out with.'

'These the scammed?'

'And now destitute. Beggars belief some of what I've read. Gave a few names to Dexter while I was upstairs see if he can throw any light on them. Trouble is if what they say is to be believed, none of them as far as I can make out are based here.'

'How bad have they been?' Inga asked casually. She as yet had not been able to uncover anything even slightly untoward and had decided it might be time to switch to another stick for her homework.

'Hundred grand one woman.'

'Really?' the DI drew in her breath as she shook her head. 'And Barnard exposed her?' was not really a question.

'Not exposed her as such. She'd obviously heard about a few cases on the grubby grapevine we call social media and these are it would appear, women in the main contacting her.'

'To confess?'

'If you like.'

'Did she pay them?' Inga checked.

'No idea, but if she did, that might be one angle as some of them are virtually penniless. Desperate for every last penny they can lay their hands on.'

'Was she aware and is this the very sort of motive we're looking for, do we think?'

'Woman A gets scammed, Barnard writes about her and the woman's secret is out. All her friends know it'd turn your life inside out. Divorce maybe and goodness knows.'

She looked at her DS. 'Motive for family and friends?'

'With that last one, she interviewed her right enough.' Nicky looked up at Inga. 'The Somalian or Indonesian she's exposed with her articles. They'd not be jumping with joy. What's the betting they've got plenty of contacts over here'

'Would it really bother somebody like that, living and operating from some crummy internet cafe, far far away? Anyhow surely he can just change names and get on with grabbing what he can out of the next frustrated old woman he comes across.'

'Or man.'

'How old is the next one?'

'Forty seven when the piece was written last year. Not that old. Can understand old lonely women being conned, all this technology takes some getting used to at my age, let alone compared to what they are used to.'

'Makes her a Generation X,' she chuckled with.

'Meant to tell you,' Scoley returned with quickly. 'After what you were saying I looked it all up. Somebody called,' she checked her notes in hand. 'McCrindle says the next lot will be Generation Beta and then it will be Gamma and Delta.'

'Why in that order?' Inga gasped. 'Why does nothing make sense when by rights it should be Charlie?'

'Because as you quite rightly say, it's complete tosh. Just a rag bag for some elements of the media to live by. Did the same with the names of viruses and got themselves in a real pickle at one point.'

Inga guessed there was more. 'Go on.'

'Took a break and went onto another stick which is one where she writes generally for magazines. Thrown up more possibilities. In one she was writing about somebody somewhere suggesting Ernest Hemingway had a form of transgender. As you can imagine that set her off. Basis of her attack were people who suggest such things to give their own lifestyle credibility for some peculiar reason. Barnard suggested it was,' she looked at a piece of paper in her hand. 'Utterly ludicrous nonsense.' Nicky looked up smiling 'Then asked who is next? Were Nelson and Marilyn Monroe gay and when is somebody about to reveal Tarzan was a paedophile,' she sniggered at as she shook her head. 'Finding these romance scammers who might have done her harm is one thing, but an article like that could stir up all sorts.'

'Some people have an obsession about old writers like Shakespeare, Chaucer and the like. Many more to go through?'

'One a week for two years on the *Leader* USB alone.' Inga turned to her other Detective Sergeant. 'And your boredom comes from…?'

'Wheatsheaf pub CCTV. Nice place according to Jamie and a menu I might have a look at. Nothing on PNC about any of the three who meet there regular as clockwork on Tuesdays. Cutforths. Richie Grummitt and his wife Doreen. Pig farmers from nearby, and a Joe Pickwell who the publican thinks works in IT in some way but said don't take that as gospel. None on PNC.'

'One door closes…'

'But somebody had to know Cutforth'd not be at home, just thought they might have some connection.'

'You know what they do on Tuesdays. Who else have they told over the months, maybe years?'

Jake Goodwin sighed.

Nicky Scoley saw the rounded shoulders heave up and sink down again, sat in the kitchen of this woman's Holbeach home. On Tuesday morning.

'Called him all the names under the sun,' she began. 'As you can imagine but…' she tailed off as if she had no wish to go over it one more time, then shrugged her shoulders lightly. 'Been a silly bugger eh?' and there was a meeting of eyes.

Dark haired Angela Kellihar according to Barnard's long article had received a text out of the blue in November 2021 suggesting she had missed a delivery by Royal Mail. 'Didn't think,' she'd told Rachel. 'Stuff I order on line comes from Amazon most of the time. Know who you're dealing with. Gets delivered by a nice man who always wears a black vest.'

Was to Nicky a very odd remark. Then according to Kellihar it was suggested to her she had to fork out a small fee to pay for the parcel to be delivered for a second time. Innocently she then followed the instructions on the text and in the end made payment.

Next thing was her bank calling to say there had been strange activity on her account and as a result it had been compromised. Whoever she spoke to persuaded Kellihar to ensure her money was safe, to clear her compromised account save for just £50, and transfer it all to a special account he gave her which the bank used on such occasions, to ensure people's savings were safe.

'Silly Bugger,' she'd called herself more than once when talking to Rachel and did so again to Scoley. Angela Kellihar had all her money in one account. Over £8,000 in all.

'Were you happy with what Rachel Barnard wrote?'

'It was alright.' lacked any enthusiasm.

'Only alright?'

'Well, me son says I should've kept quiet, says it'd make me a target for other people like that Jeremy from the Royal Mail or wherever he was.'

'He was not happy then?' Scoley probed gently and carefully.

'Got a bit of a thing about people like her, bloggers and writers who make money out of people's misfortune. Tells me its worse on the internet, not that I go looking for trouble on there. Eddie tells me to keep away from some of them sites.'

'Just out I of interest to clear up one or two points. Could you let me have your son's details?'

'Why?'

117

'Need it for my report,' Scoley answered calmly. 'I'm not allowed just to say your son wasn't too happy. Need a name. All about box ticking these days I'm afraid,' she fibbed. 'Go back with just this and I'll only have to give you a call anyway.'

The woman pulled a cotton handkerchief from the sleeve of her grey jumper and wiped her nose fleetingly, then kept it clamped in her fist for the next time.

According to the information detailed at the end of the article on the USB stick as she did as part of her process, Rachel explained how she had afterwards done her own investigation. She had concluded it was set up by a rogue employee at her bank who had set the whole thing up with fake texts purporting to be from Royal Mail to see who would bite. Set up a spurious account in each victim's name he controlled no doubt. Rachel concluded by suggesting poor Angela had not been the first and would not be the last.

13

Back at home base with just one or two names from Angela Kellihar she was able to pop upstairs for them to work on tracking down IP networks for the people involved. Checking them on the dark web and going through all their wondrous processes.

There for the first time she was introduced to Abby Warriner. Nicky didn't begin to understand half of what Abby Warriner the Telecoms Intel Researcher was telling her about her role. As the only female working among the seriously odd balls in the Tech Crime Team set-up, it was not a situation Nicky felt she would enjoy permanently.

Part of the East Midlands Phone Intelligence Team, she was tall and lean with fairly short neat carefully styled hair. A first class operator according to ASBO, had moved from Derby when the new post appeared at Lincoln Central. A move to suit Abby less than 20 miles from her girlfriend in Newark.

Nicky Scoley back down in the Incident Room was more interested in reading what Jake, Michelle and Alisha had discovered about the *Lincoln Leader* reporters.

Jake Goodwin had plumped for the Editor James Gosney for starters but all he discovered from the scant information provided was he had been born and bred near Norwich, gained an Honours Degree in Journalism, although where from was not specified. He had worked for the Katushabe Group in a number of positions for five years until he was chosen to take on the Editor role at the *Leader*. He was married without any mention of family, and on checking Jake became aware families were not included in anybody's data. He did however have one bad mark to his name. Speeding in 2014.

New to working with the MIT team on such an important case DC Alisha O'Neill having experienced James Gosney's racist attitude towards somebody of mixed race first hand, chose Daisy Lytton from the sheets Gosney had handed over.

Her reasoning was two-fold. Number one she was the only female apart from secretarial and admin staff such as those in advertising. circulation and subscriptions who were unlikely to have any close working relationship with Rachel Barnard. Secondly she was coloured.

She'd spoken to this Daisy when she was with Nicky Scoley at their offices, but they'd not pressurized the young woman about the colour issue or queried whether she had Ugandan origins or family connections of some form linked to the owners.

Reading the sheet photocopied for them provided little else. According to the one piece of paper she was originally from Newcastle-Under-Lyme, had excellent GCSE results and then A levels in Business Studies, Psychology and more importantly for publishers, English Language. She had not attended university and her employment record started and ended with the Katushabe Brothers. First in Stoke not that far from where she'd been brought up, then onto Wolverhampton and finally to the *Lincoln Leader*.

Alisha's gentle smile had faded as the initial introductions were replaced by questions and answers. How did this woman Alisha wondered to herself, get on with a possible racist or at least somebody with a tendency to racist bias on a daily basis? Or she pondered, and not for the first time, had she been mistaken. Was that just his way? Did she just happen to be the colour she was and he was more misogynistic by nature. Had his phrasing been all masculine by nature. If so, Nicky's not mentioned it or had not noticed. Was it simply a case of him being top dog, and having to be questioned by two female police officers simple went against the grain?

Alisha O'Neill was truly proud of her achievements within the force. Good to be one of those chosen specifically to be part of the team working round the clock to sort through what few clues had emerged so far.

She also knew how proud her mother would be when she heard.

It had been interesting to read about this motley crew at the paper, each one quite different in appearance and attitude. Tall and thin, plump and round, foreign and coloured. These were the very people doing their utmost to keep the Barnard case as high profile as they could. Extra sales meant extra income and provide a bounce in advertising revenue she guessed.

There was nothing on PNC and her social media site was quite sparce when Alisha checked out this Daisy Lytton. It was as if she had not bothered to make new 'friends' locally.

Best Alisha had discovered was this Daisy asking if anyone could repair a bike. A 'friend' had recently posted a photo of two young children sat up in bed watching television as if that was an everyday event. Why would you post such a thing was a question with her role she asked herself a dozen times a day. Don't put your daughter on the stage Mrs Worthington or even worse photos on the internet for paedos.

Then there was somebody asking her if they could take a mobility scooter on a bus. Just the sort of drivel Alisha was always amazed to read.

Whenever Alisha thought about this Daisy and those they were checking, a number of things came to mind. She double-checked with Nicky Scoley that she was not wrong in imagining none of the six they had spoken with had a visible tattoo. Although one had a beard, none of the men had anything like a bun or pony tail and this Daisy had been at the *Leader* for more than three years. Would she have stayed if there was a racist backdrop to working for Gosney?

Was all this part and parcel of the Katushabe doctrine? Beard for religious reasons maybe, no tattoos, no plucked eyebrows some guys even go for, no expensive daft hairstyles. Just the one female with overlong inhibiting painted nails.

Michelle for her part had looked at the Sports columnist Stephen Ronane and his writing she knew from her dad was almost entirely one club football orientated.

Even in the close season the lead story was something completely inconsequential about Lincoln City. Other football clubs in the county were given short shrift and she could remember when at one time her dad and a few of his friends had complained to the paper long before the Katushabes' took control about other sports never got a look in. Despite illustrating how some county sportsmen and women were often competing at a world level compared with Lincoln City in non-league backwater then, Ronane's predecessor simply would not admit to his lack of sports knowledge.

He was short and bald according to Alisha, and Michelle Cooper had found nothing untoward about him anywhere.

Tony Parker the Assistant Editor had been the only one to attend the press conference. A decision both DCS Craig Darke, DI Inga Scoley and their PR guru Jo Marcone had found intriguing and a mighty strange decision, they had to assume on the part of the Katushabes.

No mention of a wife or partner, but then the data in the other cases had only said specifically 'Married' when that was the case. Almost as if a partner was unacceptable or maybe the others really were just married or single living alone. Another one with nothing to report on or double check.

Petar Vargic was last but by no means least. Compared with the others on the block he was a new boy, in that he'd only joined the paper the previous April.

In his initial answers to almost every question about his alibis this one gave a lazy shrug and when not doing that at one point he scratched his nose as if time wasting.

Right at the finish he closed his eyes and breathed in deeply. As if to say "thank God for that!" he daren't utter out loud.

They'd all three spent valuable time trawling through the *Leader* editorial staff members' less than comprehensive employment records. Then cross referencing them through PNC and all the limitless stream of data available, before Alisha checked each of them out individually on social media.

'Floors all yours,' said Inga Larsson at afternoon briefing and took a pew as if she was one of the team.

'So far,' said Jake Goodwin, stood out front. 'For the most part it's been data gathering. Or as far as the journos at the *Leader* are concerned, a lack of.'

'Sorry to interrupt,' said an interrupting Larsson. 'Is that the Katushabe Brothers in action do we think? If you've been a naughty boy, if you've done something not within their strict boundaries then you're no longer working there.'

'Just one speeding has to be a bit more than somewhat unusual,' Jake responded. 'But to be honest we've not found anything untoward to set the alarm bells ringing. None of them out on licence, nobody wanted, none skipping bail and not one of them trying to hide the fact they're dealing or head of a drug cartel,' he offered amusingly for him.

'We just have the attitude of Gosney to concern us,' Nicky Scoley offered. 'You do have to wonder how that Daisy Lytton copes day to day if what Alisha and I experienced was his normal behaviour.'

'Unless that's just his way,' Alisha offered then grimaced.

'Part of the issue,' said Sandy MacLachlan. 'What's just office banter and what's a more serious issue? If I complained every time anybody took the piss for being a Scot, I'd be knocking on your door daily,' he aimed at the DI. 'Jokes about being sent back over the wall and too many Jocks down here isna funny the hundredth time. Jokes about what I wear under my kilt and crap about Scotland football is never ending and...'

'Thanks Sandy, now....'

'Sorry Sarge,' stopped Jake. 'Just haud your horses aye. Could easy take offence and suggest there's racist intent although to be fair some non-English shall we say, are more sensitive. Nae danger me having a moan but when we win Curling at the Olympics you all want to be a Jock.'

Jake hesitated to make sure Sandy had had his pennyworth. When he was younger having a French name had kids he was at school with endlessly calling him a frog, among other much nastier quips.

'Now it's time to dig a bit deeper into some of these people,' was Jake Goodwin bringing the chatter back to the plan for the next day. 'No suggestion there's anybody suddenly appearing over the horizon, so we'll stay close to home. Next up we'll start with the family,' he looked down at his notes. 'Millicent and Derek Barnard, married eldest daughter with two youngsters, and a son still living at home.' He looked at Michelle and Alisha, then checked visually with the Detective Inspector.

'Interesting? Rachel lived alone and her boyfriend is still with Mummy and her brother's the same.'

'Only fourteen.'

'Okay, sorry. How about we take the inner circle,' Inga reacted. 'And you and the lads deal with the outer fringes for starters?'

'Good thinking,' he said but was what he already planned for. 'You and Michelle ma'am, off then to Nettleham to speak with the parents. According to Family Liaison she's very nice but he can be a bit belligerent at times. Nicky, you take Alisha and talk to the sister, see what she knows.' He looked down at Sandy MacLachlan. 'From what we've been able to gather we have one bad apple in the *Leader* bunch.' Jake pulled a face. 'Don't tell the boss, but here's an idea,' he smiled at the big Scot.

'Go on,' Inga sighed sat there arms folded.

'This Kevin Elphick. One fly in their ointment, one with the murky past, been wondering about bringing a bit of pressure to bear. If the truth is they were all just fine with Rachel they'll not risk talking out of place and maybe upsetting these strange brothers. This Elphick could easy be the weak link. Stop him arriving at work. Give him illegal drug test.'

'There's mair to ploughing than whistling,' from Sandy few understood.

'With a bit of luck,' Jake went on. 'We can use a negative result if luck's on our side for once, force him to confess on what's been going on or we'll snitch on him with the Katushabe brothers. Don't see any other way of breaking down any wall of silence they've erected together, to protect themselves and retain their publishing advantage'.

'That breaks every rule in the book,' said Inga. 'Checking drug driving is an Interceptors matter Jake and as you know with due reason. You'll need more than good reason to get that past the Darke boss.'

'Always possible,' was Sandy. 'These deil's bairns have told them all to…'

'Hang on there. What's all this deil's bairns,' Jake struggled with.

'Devil's bairns, devil's children,' said Sandy as if it was obvious. 'Theys keeping it shut in order to retain the advantage. What they know they're keeping close to their chest, is a real possibility.'

'I'll do it,' said Jake looking down at Inga. 'Give me a bit of fresh air, and as I've been stuck back here they'll not know me. Never met any of them. Get one of the Interceptors to tag along and actually do the swab for me.'

'If you need to be incognito you could always hand him one of my cards.' said Jamie Hedley.

'Good thinking,' Jake responded with Inga Larsson shaking her head and listening to all this going back and forth. 'Then if he complains I can always say I was elsewhere and he's just making it up.'

'Thank you very much,' said Inga sarcastically. 'This'll go down really well along the corridor. I don't think.'

'Only kidding, but, ' Jake admitted and took a breath of hope. 'But to be honest we could easy do that, we have a reasonable excuse, but maybe not play the false card ploy.'

'I'll have a word, if you're serious.'

'I'm up for it. Got to take the gloss off the *Leader* somehow. Gotta be they know more than they're letting on aboot.'

'Remember,' said Nicky Scoley. 'To put it mildly. That interview with Gosney was far from easy.'

'Talking of Gosney,' said Jake back at his notes. 'Like the rest of that motley crew, looking for proof he did what he said he did. Did he go down to Melton Mowbray? Did he interview that...Petrie chap and that's just for starters.'

'Showed us on his PC what he'd written and saved ready for after the elections.'

'Fair enough,' said Jake. 'But it doesn't prove he interviewed them then. Bit like me saying I went to the pub.' He looked across at her. 'Nicky can you give Jamie the ANPR contact you have if you wouldn't mind, and that's one for you,' he told the Gainsborough man.

'Sure and remember after the interview I was so annoyed by his attitude I made a quick note of his car details,' she told Jamie.

'Useful.'

She gave the demure look Nicky knew she could use to good effect. 'Also got his phone number.'

'Know you're out and about with all this, but any chance?' Jake asked. 'If you could make a note of all the *Leader* numbers we need to look at for locations on that Monday and Tuesday, even the Sunday if we get shady alibis. See what your Tech Crime Team friends can get from the phone providers?'

'New Telecoms researcher woman upstairs,' Nicky reminded.

'Of course.'

'Might not get permission I know,' Inga offered. 'But if you plan to stop this Elphick, be a chance to get your hands on his phone. Make life easier upstairs if that Abby Warriner's got the real thing rather than just the number.' She scanned the room. 'Let's do it! Come on, get on with it.'

14

Inga Larsson and DC Michelle Cooper drove around the housing estate next morning and eventually discovered the correct address, pulled up outside the Barnard family home. Not a new-build but be what some call mid-century.

Facing the Barnards, Inga Larsson shivered as she recalled matters from other major incidents. Cases she'd been involved in. Not all involving death but all too often young women.

Millicent Barnard's voice was gentle, with a lilt of a west country accent Inga spied from her time at Bristol University. Her heart as ever went out to the woman with distress etched on her face.

The Detective Inspector asked after them both and their daughter Kathryn sat on the sofa with her mother who offered to make tea and disappeared.

She had been briefed by the Family Liaison pair including the pointless spelling of the daughter's name. Something Inga knew would annoyingly live with the one remaining daughter for a life time. At least she'd not suffer from wrong pronunciations as some suffer from endlessly

'I'm okay,' was all fair haired, head down, hands clasped together managed. 'Still not sleeping too well, suffering from shock the GP woman reckons,' Inga sensed there was more. 'She wasn't a bad person, you know. Our Rachel.'

'Nobody believes she was,' Larsson returned with quickly. 'Just that some of the people she more than likely had to deal with obviously were not.'

'Neighbours'll be asking more than likely. Nosy damn parkers,' this Derek Barnard offered. Larsson had no idea how they would know who they were, or even be interested.

It was never going to be easy talking to a recently bereaved woman about a successful daughter she doted on. What did this

Kathryn think of her sister forever in the limelight to a certain degree, was one matter to consider.

This bit of the job was something Larsson had always shied away from whenever possible, but having volunteered to be out leading her pack with this one, duty called. Her dipping out of bits she didn't fancy would not go down well with keen as mustard, play a straight bat Jake.

She'd spent too much time watching what effect bad things have on people's lives and those sat before her would be another example to add to the sad list.

According to Millie and her daughter there'd been nothing out of the ordinary over recent times. Nothing they could see Rachel had been that worried about. Neither were aware of any particular strangers she'd mentioned and no unscrupulous men she'd had to interview.

So far, Millie Barnard had answered all their questions honestly and carefully as far as the detectives were concerned or aware.

Talk of this Derek Barnard forever stroking his beard, being truculent had so far not borne fruit. He had remained silent for the majority of the time they were there. Chances are his thoughts Inga Larsson decided, would still be on those who carried out the horrendous attack on his daughter. A thought likely to remain with him for a good time yet.

There were of course parents who go through this whole process and eventually see somebody convicted of the murder and get slung in jail for a hefty term. Then fifteen, twenty years later when some Parole Board deem the culprit ready and fit to return to mainstream society with loads of restrictions and a tag most probably, the family are still there berating all and sundry. A reminder of just how long such events can linger and fester in people's minds.

Larsson sat there wondering what would be going through a father's mind at a time such as that. Thoughts of revenge most likely. What he imagined he would do to the perpetrator were he to get his hands on him, was not worth thinking about. To somebody like Derek Barnard the chances were he'd not have even considered the possibility it very well might be a woman.

The backdoor opened and suddenly stood in the doorway was a stout woman wearing a totally inappropriate white strappy top. Showing every lump, bump and unseemly bulge imaginable.

'Only just heard Mill. Sorry for yer loss,' this woman said as if she was the only person there. 'Horrible this, just terrible Mill. Anyway, hows you doing duck?' was thoughtless. Almost as if she'd just nipped round to ask her to go for a coffee.

'Excuse me Lynne,' said Derek. 'We're busy if you don't mind.'

'Alright, alright,' she sighed back. 'Just payin' me respects, see if there's owt I can do.'

'You can leave same way you came in,' he told her.

'Derek!' Millie snapped..

'Well it's right.'

Larsson watched this intruder with enough mascara to block out the light as her plucked eyebrows lifted slightly, to signify disapproval.

'You'll ne'er change him. What me ma always said. Bad uns always bad uns.'

'Lynne,' said Millie as Derek got to his feet. 'See you tomorrow eh? Be a pet.'

'Just checking there's nowt you need. Gotta say, you do look a bit peaky.'

'Excuse me,' was Larsson on her feet. 'Please do as you're asked and kindly leave,' was a demand without the need to raise her voice. Tone was sufficient.

'And you are?' this woman scoffed.

'Detective Inspector Inga Larsson,' she responded with warrant card pushed in front of the woman's face.

'What sorta names that eh?' she sniggered. 'Time you sorted all this out.'

'Thank you,' Larsson gestured towards the door as hapless Derek sank back into his chair.

'Need somethin', anythin' you call right?' The woman told Millie. 'Huh,' she murmured. 'Seeing as I'm not wanted.'

As Larsson regained her composure and her seat Kathryn was following this Lynne out. Inga had kept reminding herself to keep her tone light and understanding, and she hoped her intervention was seen the way it was intended.

'Talk to me about Sean,' Larsson suggested to get back to her questioning, with Kathryn she could hear out of the room boiling the kettle for the inevitable teas. 'He still lived at home we understand,' indeed from the horses mouth.

'Stupid woman that Glenda. Plays the Adam Faith card too often for my liking. People are sick up to here with it,' she said and gestured with a hand to her forehead just rustling her limp hair.

'Adam Faith?' Larsson shot back.

'Poor me,' Michelle aware she had to answer her query for the boss, with Millie looking across at Larsson. Her expression grim, probably due to the intrusion. The DI was none the wiser with the reply.

'Every time you bump into that Glenda, all you ever get is her tiresome medical history, every bump and bruise. What the doctor said, what's new pills she's on, how this aches and that hurts morning noon and night.'

'She did lose her husband,' Larsson recalled Sean saying.

'That's as maybe,' Barnard continued. 'If his old man were still alive, poor Sean'd still be tied to her apron strings. Always at her beck and call. Nivver let go that one.'

'Checked that one out first thing,' said Derek suddenly from his high back chair by the door. 'Can't be too careful lass.'

'How do you mean you checked him out?' The old adage spun to mind. Assume nothing, believe nothing and challenge everything she was doing right there and then.

'What they say innit? Keep your friends close but your enemies closer. They reckon more killings o'this sort get done by family than owt else,' he pushed out a scoffing breath. 'He'd not be family if his mother's got owt to do wi'it, but he's near enough to check out.'

'Derek, please understand. In cases such as this, frequently it is somebody known to the family,' she chose deliberately rather than use his daughter's name. 'If you've noticed something different or seen people acting out of character, you need to tell us.' He pulled a pouting face as his response. 'Who else,' Larsson asked of him. 'Have you been checking up on?'

'Bits an' pieces that's all.'

Larsson had already noted the hollows beneath this Derek's deep brown eyes below bushy unkempt eyebrows. If he was hiding something it meant their case journey would be turned on its head. This man sat there could be a real problem needing to be resolved and quickly.

'Asked about that ex o'hers, that whatshisname,' he said to his wife. 'Turned out he's on holiday some place,' he said as Kathryn appeared with two mugs of tea.

'I could have told you that!' was Millie. 'Bumped into his mum in town.'

'Turkey according to his mum', said their tea lady and was gone again to return with two more. Nothing was handed to her dad.

'Anybody else?' Larsson checked.

'Anyway,' said Millie as Kathryn joined her. 'Time you were going to work,' and Derek Barnard gave her a strange look Larsson considered for a moment.

'Anybody else, Derek?' Larsson persisted. 'You've been checking up on?'

'Nah. Who else is there, like? Be the lot she works with s'pose. All those media types. Bosses seem a mighty strange bunch that's for sure. Blinkin' heck, do they?'

Larsson already knew about the Katushabe effect and a good deal about Millicent Barnard from her Family Liaison girls. She worked full-time as an industrial cleaner. Heading up a small team, dealing with the aftermath of office and store closures. Then later getting then back spick and span for new incomers. The van she drives was sat out on the drive in front of an old, well used Allegro.

'Tell you this,' said Millie when Derek hadn't moved a muscle. 'Sean was her best friend. Yeh, fit and healthy and all those thingies going round inside gets some into trouble, but at the end of t'day that's why relationships last. Being best mates. Like me and old rat bag over there,' she gestured towards Derek. 'We're best pals eh?' she asked. 'And don't you dare say otherwise,' was good relationship banter. Larsson spotted a glimpse of a wistful expression in his eyes then he just pulled a face to say he'd not disagree.

131

'What is it you do exactly?' Cooper asked him. She'd also been briefed by the Family Liaison team report saying he worked for Curry's at their distribution centre in Newark.

'Work for Carphone Warehouse as a First Line Manager.'

'What does that entail?' was just plain curiosity.

'Supervise the running of my department.'

'And you work afternoons?' Larsson asked.

'Not normally,' he admitted. 'Senior me, usually days but wi'all this going on been put on afters. Two to nine-thirty for a week, depending what happens, like.'

She's never have guessed he was a techy. There was that faraway look again in Barnard's dark eyes. Something going on in his mind could only be bad news.

Bad could easily be because he was unwilling to share something critical, something he was planning given half a chance.

Rachel Barnard's death was no different from so many Michelle Cooper had dealt with in one form or another. Except this was not and never had been linked to any form of domestic abuse. Unless, it was Sean Joseph hiding bruises from the world.

The dead woman was at that age when such abuse these days seemed to Cooper to be part and parcel of relationships. Almost the accepted norm in some areas of society.

'Kathryn,' said Larsson as Derek Barnard scrambled to his feet and trudged out in his slippers. 'Tell me about your partner and what you both did this last Monday and Tuesday.'

Brown hair tied in a single plait she had hanging over her left shoulder and down in front. Long sleeved t-shirt, pale green around the shoulders, then dark green close to black, and blue jeans she's squeezed herself into.

'Nathan. Does double glazing for a place in Sleaford,' she offered freely. 'I do a few hours four days a week while kids are at school, helping out a friend who's got a small cafe. About it really. With two young kids, nights out are a bit few and far between; mostly weekends if we can get a babysitter,' she said and glanced at her mother who was not looking. 'Nathan'd be home sometime after six. Be getting the kids to bed and be at least nineish before we got to sit down to watch a bit of telly.

Nathan watches the news and what's in the papers usually and I do his pack-up,' she shrugged. 'Go to bed.' She grinned. 'Exciting life eh?'

'Quite normal, seems to me,' Larsson assured her. The DI turned back to Millie sat there mug in hands she'd not seen her drink from as yet. 'Has there ever been anything happen because of what Rachel wrote. Some of these con men she has exposed perhaps?'

Grimace, then 'Not that I knows of.'

'Any issues at work, not necessarily about who she wrote about?'

'Bit odd,' and at long last Millie Barnard sipped her tea which by that time was no more than cool. 'Bosses she works for.'

'In what way?' Larsson knew bits and bobs about.

'Very religious with lots of rules and regulations about what you can and connot say an' do. Derek says its all this politically correct nonsense, but he uses a stronger word than that,' she smiled slightly with.

'Mum,' said Kathryn beside her having only drunk half of her tea. 'According to Rachel they believe in some sort of moralistic ideal,' she told Larsson and Cooper. 'They believe God wants everybody to be good, be kind and fair to each other and one way they can do that is get rid of some of the nastiness. Things such as swearing in the workplace, won't allow any racism, probably because they're from...Uganda,' she got to after a moment. 'And sexism they're dead set against too. Think our Rachel was a good example of that, giving her the freedom with her own column which is often feminine flavoured rather than hoisting the job onto some bloke just because he's male. Some places I've worked could have done with a dose o'that.'

'You sort of in charge?' Millie asked.

'I'm the Senior Investigation Officer,' Larsson admitted. 'The Major Incident Team, is my responsibility. Think like so many other services and businesses we suffer from some odd ideas coming out from universities these days. As if tutors have been given free range' Smiling with this Kathryn, she suggested: 'Our fear is we'll have people like those intimacy co-ordinators telling us how to solve crimes.'

'And easy finish up with rapists and killers on every street corner.'

Legal issues were nothing knew to the DI. A nasty piece of work in a domestic dispute in Lincoln High Street a few months back had been charged but not prosecuted by the CPS, despite kicking his partner in the head.

Inga Larsson wondered sometimes if at times she cared too much for the innocents involved in such an investigation. One day a happy family she presumed this one was and now all this.

She'd spend days and weeks in some cases searching for just one person. Although a lone subject had been the target in all that time, and part of countless conversations and theories. Inga knew from experience she inevitably would in the end spend far less time with the guilty than she would as in this case, with the innocent tragic Barnards.

15

In the world of Inga Larsson and Craig Darke to a certain extent, very little was ever achieved by sheer chance, but every now and again there was a moment of inspiration out of the blue to prove useful.

Alexander 'Sandy' MacLachlan out and about doing jobs for Jake Goodwin decided to take that opportunity to drop off a bottle of Scotch his dad had given him. As big and burly a Scot as Sandy was, he'd never had a real appetite for his national drink, he'd promised it to a friend. To him Irn-Bru had always been a more acceptable north of the border product since he was young, selling more up there than Coca-Cola.. Wine and red in particular was his tipple of choice nowadays.

This was all a form of subterfuge. He'd done his level best over the years never to give his dad the impression he loved a wee dram. It was just assumed. Whenever he went home to Scotland or his parents ventured south it was always a decent Scotch as a gift from father to son. He'd never had the heart to explain how a bottle would last him a lifetime.

Mate Paul Scott was his usual recipient of the golden nectar and more of a connoisseur than Sandy would ever be.

In had been in his boot all week and then as he drove along Riseholme Road he realized he was in the vicinity not only of his pal Paul, but also the home of this Mayoral candidate mentioned back at Central.

Jake he knew was trying to organize a meet with this David Petrie, but so far he had proved elusive. Pressure of the upcoming election was the excuse and it may have to wait a week or two until he was installed or not as the new East Midlands Mayor.

A quick check back to the Incident Room and he headed for the address just to satisfy his own curiosity. He parked up in the

Pay and Display car park in Westgate and went for a casual stroll.

Lack of decent driveway or a pleasant garden of flowers and being terraced did not deter from the value of the place. In Bailgate it was just the sort of property estate agents would describe as a desired address.

Big three storey place right enough as he'd been told, and just one empty parking space outside.

Sandy walked on to Newport Arch a Roman gateway to give the impression of being a tourist without shorts, flip-flops, camera or daft hat. This was where the tourists flock to. Some even managing to climb Steep Hill, once dubbed Britain's Best Place.

Walking back from his saunter to nowhere his copper's nose spied CCTV cameras on one property close to this Petrie's place and another just a tad down the road towards the Castle, for his memory bank.

Be the sort of place where people think they've got stuff worth nicking or put up fake cameras to give the impression they have, which at times can be very annoying.

Back at base Sandy was able to report what he had discovered about Petrie and then sat delving into Zoopla and the Land Registry they had access to.

3-bedroomed terraced house over three floors as he'd seen. It at least had a back garden and the value in 2018 when Petrie bought it was just a tad over half a million. Principal en-suite bedroom on the second floor did not distract Sandy from the distinct lack of frontage.

Jake Goodwin in charge back at Central was still waiting for data back from ANPR down in Hendon on Gosney's car movements but he did have the initial Tech Crime Team's Track and Locate analysis of the Editor's phone whereabouts, at what they still considered to be the time of Rachel Barnard's demise.

Not having the actual phone, ASBO and his team of geeks including the new woman were unable to do any more than obtain a list of outgoing and incoming calls.

Jake knew from experience never to rub anybody off the Murder Board until there was absolute 100% proof of their inability to be the perpetrator by location or circumstance, witnesses, finger prints or DNA.

He'd done that with one case when he'd first been moved to MIT in Craig Darke's early days in charge and could still hear the bollocking he'd got to this day.

He now knew Gosney's phone had been down to Melton Mowbray, but there had been no calls. Hardly a surprise as he was driving and then would have been interviewing the Labour Mayorial candidate Raymond Earle. All he needed now was his car having pinged an ANPR on route and that was one he could push to one side.

Just a pity Sandy had not spotted Petrie's car parked at his home, he could have checked in readiness for placing him on the back burner too.

He altogether was going to be a more difficult prospect, apart from the fact he had remained elusive so far, not having his mobile number let alone the phone itself was a hindrance Jake could do without.

16

'What we up to today?' DI Inga Larsson asked Jake Goodwin the following morning early. Never imagined how Barnard would upset a farmer, but there you go. Box ticked for that pair.

'Unless he's the local romance scammer,' from Nicky made Larsson smile. 'Or been scammed.'

'We getting anywhere with her back story?'

'What else we got?' Nicky asked. 'Being upset by what she writes about people could so easily make somebody more than just a bit cross. If you're some bad boy deciding this is easy money and then you're plastered all over the local paper, that's gotta make somebody more than a bit upset. Particularly when their wife or partner finds out or gets the mickey taken out by her pals on social media. Seems to me we've not come across anybody else who could have reason to be that angry.'

'Seen this boss,?' Jake asked as he slipped his tablet in front of her.

NO GOOD NEWS
with *Rachel Barnard*

Despite extra resources and manpower having been made available to her, the *Leader* understands the Swedish Detective Inspector said to be in charge of the case appears to be no further forward in her homicide investigation for the killer of our sadly missed colleague and dear friend Rachel Barnard.

This, YOUR local paper, will not rest until the perpetrator is brought to justice and we can only hope this will be swift, as Rachel has now been dead for some time.

Jake knew this initial surge of interest from the media and the *Leader* in particular was to be expected with one of their own once more pictured with the short sharp news item on their website.

Shock and horror initially as with any attack was to be expected, but now that rag in particular had turned their attention to the understaffed and underfunded Lincoln County Police.

'Didn't expect anything else did we?' Larsson retorted having scanned it quickly and the DI was back to business. 'First thing to pass on is the toxicology report from the post mortem. Nothing untoward except for one bit of bad and one bit of good news. Cannabis in her blood and those clever sods have discovered what brick it was killed Rachel, but we're still waiting on tests on other artefacts from the scene..'

'A brick's a brick,' Jake gasped. 'The things people do for a living.'

'What about Sandy?' she said to Jake looking out into the Incident Room at nobody sat behind his monitor. 'Has he managed to fix it yet? Seeing that Petrie.'

'Still being awkward apparently offering what he described as a "minute or two of window in my important schedule." For now I'm putting it down to his work commitments and the election of course, but we'll see when Sandy's spoken with him'

'What about Jamie?'

'He's still working on ANPR data for Monday and Tuesday but they're very busy. Might just add this Petrie's motor to his workload if he seems a bit …'

'Why would he?'

'Why would he what?'

'Kill Barnard.'

'It's Gosney I'm checking up on. He gave interviewing this Petrie and the chap down in Melton Mowbray as his alibis remember.'

'But how did you jump to him giving a very plausible alibi to the alibi becoming a suspect.'

'Just need to assimilate what Sandy comes back with. Being a Mayor designate or whatever he is, doesn't make you innocent.'

'Nicky going through more of her writing?'

'Think she's getting sick of it. You can sometimes get too much of a good thing.' said Jake as he turned away. 'I'll be off.'

Big DC Alexander 'Sandy' MacLachlan knocked firmly on the door in Bailgate with having parked up in Westgate once again.

'Detective Constable?' he was asked as the black wooden door opened.

'Alexander MacLachlan,' said the DC as he stepped into the large uncluttered hall offering his warrant card as proof the man didn't even glance at.

'You're a long way from home son,' said this tall grey-haired distinguished Petrie, who MacLachlan followed into what looked like his election office, but by the furniture it had to be the dining room.'

'Fair bit.'

'What brings you down here?'

'Canny career move in a roundabout sort of way.'

'What can I do for you,' he said and glanced at a big watch on his wrist. 'Busy times eh?'

'Certainly. In such an inquiry as this, in this day and age we need to go through our procedures in a box ticking manner. People provide alibis, we need to check them.'

'Of course. How may I help or more to the point how on earth am I involved?' Petrie sucked in noisily. 'Nasty business, too bad, too bad indeed.'

'We have been given your name by James Gosney, Editor of the *Lincoln Leader* and...'

'Know James well of course. In my line of business guess that's a given.'

'He has offered you as his alibi for...'

'Alibi? James Gosney? What on earth has he go to do with all this nasty business?'

'The victim Rachel Barnard worked for the paper as you probably know.'

'Good column, or should I say interesting column. Always makes you think.'

'As I was saying,' MacLachlan went on. 'Because of where she worked, with our processes we've asked all the immediate staff to provide alibis for this past Monday and Tuesday. For an inquiry such as this, eliminating people is the best way of toning down volume of numbers to a more manageable size. Select the chaff from the wheat is how somebody once described it. Leaving us to arrest the wheat.'

'Shouldn't somebody who'd stoop this low be the chaff rather than the good wheat?' he thought was amusing.

'Probably. But remember we're after the prize candidate. But anyway, as I was saying Monday and Tuesday.'

'Be honest right now I'm seeing people all day every day. I know James as I say, and yes he's been here, interviewed me for their special day after edition but whether or not that was Monday or Tuesday I really couldn't say. Had meetings here most of the day Monday and on Tuesday there was quite a gathering in the evening.' He pulled a face. 'Could easily have been here, what with the cut off point for reporting now having passed. Yes he's probably right.'

'Another box ticked, thank you, sir.'

'Just take this morning, I had a breakfast planning meeting with two of my strategy colleagues before eight.' He smiled. 'Nothing pretentious you understand. Usually I rustle up toast and coffee but with the busy day ahead with food unlikely to be a priority I did make scrambled eggs.'

'Busy day then, sir?' said MacLachlan as he moved back towards the hall.

'You could say that. Look officer. We were eating and I had my speech on the table by me and somehow I dropped egg on it. Had to print off another copy. A matter most of us would consider innocuous, but the media seem to get some sort of thrill over such matters. Spot I'd spilt something on it they'd turn into their main focus rather than the content.

'The *Leader* you're talking about?'

'No. Not particularly. Just the media in general. Acting as if they would never allow such a thing to happen.'

'Busy day ahead then.'

'Off out now across to Mansfield for the afternoon and then Derby this evening. Briefing, public meeting and long drive back. Not to mention fax, phone and emails to deal with.'

'Not as easy as being Mayor of London I guess where nobody's much more than a Tube ride away.'

'You can say that again,' said David Petrie as he leant forward to pull open his front door. 'Case of getting used to it if I'm elected.'

'Thank you, sir.'

'Thank you, and good luck with your inquiries.'

Sandy strolled along back into Westgate close to where he had parked his car. Far enough away behind bushes with a busy car park at his rear not to be noticed, and if what he'd said was true he'd have time to nip for a coffee before part two.

Seventeen minutes he waited before Petrie's Mercedes-Benz GLA almost caught him out, turning right opposite the Prince of Wales Inn and heading close by, down Westgate to Burton Road and away.

Time for a coffee. He wandered still in sauntering tourist mode in the direction of the medieval Cathedral and Norman Castle housing a copy of the Magna Carta, before then turning right into Gordon Road and Bailgate Deli.

Sat outside he was able to people watch with an Americano in readiness for his next venture.

Break over, Sandy MacLachlan walked back to his previous location where he'd visited David Petrie, hoping he'd not suddenly re-appear, and the house almost opposite with the camera facing the road and part of the houses opposite with any luck.

'Yes?' was asked before the front door was fully open.

'Detective Constable Alexander MacLachlan,' he introduced with the warrant again.

'And?'

'Looking for a bit of assistance, sir if you would? Few nights ago there was a Millenium burglary doon the road,' he fibbed as he pointed back roughly in the direction of the Cathedral and Castle Square. 'Looking for any CCTV in the area.'

'No idea what you're on about. Say it again,' was pouted with the head shaking. 'In English.'

'Millenium burglary, sir,' Alexander lied without reacting to the sarcasm. 'It's where criminals break into a house sometimes stealing goods such a TVs but their main target is car keys to steal the car, which is what happened in this case.'

'You're a bloody long way from home. Claim you as foreign now do we?' The frequency of unnecessary attitude was generally on the increase and was best ignored.

'Yes and no sir. I live in Lincoln.'

'What, with that accent eh?'

'Galashiels actually, sir.'

'Galla what?'

'Galashiels. In the borders, south of Edinburgh.' He was sorely tempted to ask if he knew where the capital was.

'All sound the bloody same to me. Bet you're all for this independence racket eh?'

'I don't get involved in politics I'm afraid, sir.'

'Which way d'you vote?' seemed a ridiculous follow up question. 'For that Sturgeon tottie I bet, eh?' and winked.

'I didn't get a vote last time and in any future independence referendum, I can't imagine I'll get to vote.'

'Why not,' was sniggered.

'Voting is for people who live in Scotland if that's what you mean. I live in Lincoln.'

'Don't talk daft. You Scottish or not?'

'Yes I am sir, born and bred.'

'So you must get a bloody vote. Got pals in Spain get to vote over here.'

'Sorry no.'

'Why not?'

'Rules.'

'Eh?'

'If I lived in Scotland I'd get a vote. I've got a friend who was born and brought up in Liverpool but she married a Scot and has lived there for years. She gets a vote.'

'But not you?'

'That's right, sir.' MacLachlan hesitated to get his composure back. 'CCTV, sir,' he returned to. 'Wonder if we could borrow your disk or the one that was in use at the start of the week.'

'You sure that all went on?'

'Yes sir.'

'What d'you think you'll see?'

'With any luck, the car the burglars must have turned up in.'

'But you know what car's been stolen.'

'Yes, sir. But which way did they go, what sort of car do we look for having triggered ANPR? Did they switch plates, did it go east of west? Can we see anybody? Save us a good amount of man hours if we can get heads up, and we might get lucky with a shot of the driver.'

'Yeh, why not,' he sighed and ushered MacLachlan through to wait in the hall. On the return of this strange character in rolled up brown shirt sleeves and grubby jeans, handed over the disk, MacLachlan handed over a receipt and promised it would be copied and returned to him the next day.

As a precaution MacLachlan took a note of the name which he offered without any form of sarcasm to add to the address he already knew.

17

Sandy MacLachlan was straight up to the audio visual section of the Tech Crime Team's armoury. An array of dedicated equipment and associated computers he knew could easily handle the multivarious tapes, disks and USB stick from all types of businesses, people's homes along with retail shops and premises..

The big Scot was faced with all the sort of gadgetry Nicky Scoley was used to handling, and he was more than pleased to accept instruction before he settled down to view.

David Petrie's white Mercedes was parked just as it had been when he'd visited and stayed put throughout the sequence.

First up at around 18.45 was a woman in high heels appearing from the Newport Arch direction, carrying a folder under her arm who knocked on his door. Petrie opened it and let her in after they'd gone through the pretend kissy-kissy business. The freeze-frame technique explained to him by young Dexter Hopwood the Digital Forensic Analyst when he asked, was a godsend.

It was getting on for twenty minutes according to the disk before a car pulled up and two men got out. One in a suit, the other in jacket and trousers, no ties but they each had a briefcase. The car immediately moved off south.

At 19.23 an odd character compared to the previous three sauntered from the right. Dressed in a long sleeves t-shirt, unkempt jeans, white trainers with a lump of dark hair all over his head and down to his shoulders, this younger man was invited in.

He was there no more than a quarter of an hour and went away back to the right as he looked. Where had he come from, maybe he was young enough and fit enough to have walked up Steep Hill or along Eastgate. With a package under his arm it was as if he only called to pick something up. Next to leave was the woman a bit after ten and it was nearly 23.30 according to the disk before the two men headed off on foot quite possibly heading down into town.

Within fifteen minutes the lights had gone out and Sandy was ready for a break. In all cases he'd not seen where they all went apart from the woman heading for Newport, they'd all walked off in the same direction.

Next day saw Sandy MacLachlan scanning the CCTV disk the Tech Crime Team had copied from the one that Robert 'Bobby' Heard had lent him. When he dropped it off first thing in the morning the front door was opened by a wife far more attractive then he'd given Heard credit for.

Jamie Hedley was still working on ANPR data organized for him through Hendon contacts Nicky Scoley had been using for a good few years. They already had Sean Joseph's reg number and those working for the *Leader* which DC Guy French had obtained simply by parking up near to the newspaper at Witham St Hughs with mobile in hand in order to snap each person driving away in what particular car. Not as easy as it promised to be when Steve Ronane and Tony Parker left together in the same car. The former driving was a clue to ownership.

The stuff they'd received on car movements over the two days in question was a bit of a boring trawl though for Guy, especially when they all did exactly as they had said they did.

Entering Inga Larsson's office, Guy reacted to her hand gesture and took a seat to calmly wait for her phone conversation to finish.

'Yes, Guy, '

'Thanks ma'am,' he reacted when her call was over. There was a short pause before he continued. 'As you know I've matched them all to their cars. Even that Tony Parker who I missed first time round. Waited outside his home in Hykeham early and he's got a Renault to add to the list. I've started at the top with that James Gosney the Editor chappie. There's nothing like a Volvo.'

'How d'you mean. No Volvo?'

'ANPR have his number to check like all these others. Nothing. No alerts to say he's passed the cameras closest to the village or on the A1, so he's off the list.'

Inga lowered her head slightly and sat with her finger tips splayed across her forehead.

'Jake reckons you could, with a bit of planning, drive all the way from that...Higgins Farm place, all the way to probably somewhere like South Hykeham without triggering cameras. Not ours anyway.' She sighed, sat up straight and folded her arms.'Carry on,' lacked enthusiasm.

'I also ran a check on the cameras closest to where he lives and on Monday evening his Volvo passes the one on the by-pass going down to the Carholme roundabout a bit before one o'clock lunchtime. ANPR have got the car tracked all the way, and passes go again on his way back late that same night.'

'From Melton Mowbray was it?' she queried.

'Yes ma'am.'

'Any good news?' Guy answered with a sharp noisy intake of breath. 'Carry on then,' she reacted.

'On the Tuesday he gets home just after 18.30 and then it alerts one camera at 19.28 and but then does so again presumably on the way back from wherever he'd been at 19.53.'

DI Inga Larsson sighed her mood.

The boss had said how good Rachel Barnard's features in the *Lincoln Leader* and magazines were, long before her body had been discovered by Basil the dog.

This was especially true from a woman's perspective. Nicky having read a good few already now realized what she'd been missing. None of the tawdry misalignment of relationships so many women bleat on about. No scurrilous nonsense about odd-ball feminine rights and values except one feature she'd read by way of a change from the romance scammers, the boss knew about.

The content was she had quickly discovered so good, she could almost have written them herself. Were she that proficient.

Highlighted to Inga by a friend upon hearing the news it was Rachel writing a very poignant piece about the parental pressure to have children usually among immigrants, but now having increasingly transcended the cultural divides and classes. This all aggravated by a falling birth rate generally.

At the same time Rachel had investigated how young women want more from their men than just being a provider and protector. Something according to Rachel some men refuse to accede to.

This next one she was about to read in the vain hope somewhere she'd come across Rachel seriously upsetting somebody enough to want her killed. Up to that point she had concentrated on women being scammed on the internet, but now from something Connor had said it was time for a change.

Caffeine at hand, Snicker ready and she was settled in amongst the hubbub of case work going on all around her.

The latest column she's picked at random was all about dating scams. Involving women and men living in the county, but Barnard had changed all the names to protect them. Small amounts had been lost but there were people sadly losing tens of thousands to scammers. In some cases their life savings.

Sat there taking a break Nicky Scoley had to ask herself if any of what she'd read was true? Did these scammers just invent a new name for every conquest and choose a different part of the country from a map, therefore deliberately making it harder for people to get close.

There had been just a couple of these romance scams Rachel had written for the *Leader*. One living in Wittering just south of Stamford and another at Ingoldmells not that far from Skegness. Basically this was because they were the ones featuring Lincolnshire residents and where possible born and bred yellowbellies. Others of the same ilk were researched and devised by her for a romance magazine published by the Katushabe group.

In every case Nicky Scoley had come across so far, it had been a matter of changing the names to protect the innocent and she had to assume that was not only done to protect the people who had been scammed but also the conmen and women as their names were unlikely to be for real.

Not a lot of use if you are looking for a reason to kill somebody. One article she'd skipped through was Rachel talking about people making life changing decisions some for the better some for the worse. To gain the public's interest she'd included well known faces. Jerome Flynn was one example. A well know popular actor and singer who for ten years dropped out of the limelight. Then returned and had fortunately for him subsequently he'd been in the likes of Game Of Thrones. In an industry famous for there being no way back he'd proved it was possible.

Others she mentioned on the flip side of the coin included people who had quit successful bands to go solo and went from one miss to another, having made a decision they must regret. One away from showbiz was a bespoke baker who had been a chef and then using traditional time honoured methods created a thriving business making bespoke loaves of bread.

Suddenly as she reported he'd just upped and left. Very strangely he'd gone into what Rachel declared was the dubious and sceptical world of personal development. He'd claimed he'd been driven to do something right for him and said at the time he was as passionate about his new life as creating special loaves. Went on and on about finding himself. Something Nicky had never understood.

Rachel claimed she'd done as much research as she could, but he, his wife and young daughter had just disappeared. Somewhere living a life of utter regret.

By naming him had she aroused anger in a despondent possibly penniless man with a family to provide for, to do something he'd never consider as a great baker?

Nicky decided it was high time to change to another USB stick rather than continue down the same theme, and quite possibly a road to nowhere.

The green USB had just one major feature included and what caught her eye was the subject matter. Rachel had written in length about a subject Nicky had some interest in.

She'd never been on a dating website in her life, being very happy with partner Connor, but she had years back started to build her family tree. Nowadays it was something she went back to from time to time and did her best to add more relations to the various branches.

Being alone is the perfect pitch for a scammer and Nicky had already read other features on the same subject saying how if a scammer is told the subject has a close family and have been talking to them about the new man in their life, frequently they are gone in a flash.

This one was completely different and the woman who admitted to being scammed was not lonely; she was happily married with a family. Added to which this was not someone in search of romance. Simply wishing to develop her family tree which pricked Nicky interest.

Worst cases as Nicky had discovered are often women who hear of, or know somebody close who has genuinely found new love, new partner even husband on a dating site.

This was also not the case Nicky discovered with a Madeline Buchanan from near Rugby. Sat at home alone that evening with Connor out to meet his Camera Club mates.

18

Having worked on her own family tree in the past Nicky Scoley could see how doing so for future generations would be almost impossible to decipher when out of nowhere up pops a Bucking name. When double-barrelled became fashionable for some, she could recall from her past silliness such as Waddingham-Cottingham, but nowadays Nicky guessed. that would become Waddingcotting. Triple headers just don't bear thinking about.

Sat there with another glass of red waiting for Connor to arrive home, colleagues names came to mind. The boss and her husband would become Larking, Jake and Sally would do well with Goodway and she and Connor would be heading for Scomit, Scolmitch or Mitchsco. Maybe after all, Scoley-Mitchell might in her case prove preferable.

'Got somebody,' Nicky Scoley said at the door to Inga Larsson's small office on Friday morning before the DI had hardly taken her jacket off. 'Chances are it's not pucker, but wondered if it's worth the Tech Crime Team lads giving it a whirl? Got to be somebody like this,' she looked at her notes. 'What about this Ronan Colbert I was telling you about in that family tree business, as we don't appear to have anybody else in the frame. If nothing else, whoever it is will find it more than difficult doing it to some other poor soul, now its been in the magazine most of them subscribe to.'

'Worth a try,' said Inga. 'Because as you say, what else is there?'

'According to her notes Rachel passed her story and Madeline Buchanan's details to Action Fraud. According to subsequent notes, because I've got the feeling she was planning a follow up. Other people had queried his email address and then the Garda discovered he was using a number of aliases, and under his real name had been jailed for fraud some time ago'

'You got all this from the USB stick?'

'At the end of each article, think I told you before. She lists details of all her contacts, those she's spoken to, interviewed including phone numbers, email addresses the works, and adds cryptic comments at the end.'

'Bit like her articles. Sarcastic. Cynical very often but often really amusing. Carry on.'

'According to Rachel she thinks he probably regards this scamming as his job. What he does for a living. In this case there was none of the nonsense I've come across before from romance scammers, telling lonely women about having to work abroad. Getting his bank account frozen due to some customs violation somewhere or suddenly being in need of a load of cash for equipment he'd had stolen to finish his contract. Family needing urgent medical care is another he didn't use as an excuse but did say he was off sick.'

'What are Garda doing about him?'

'This scam is fairly new to them and I've yet to check, but even if they do arrest him it's only a scam. What'll that be, a fine over there? Even if they plan to take it further, chances are he's out on unconditional bail and...'

'Yeh, yeh...I'm ahead of you,' Inga grinned and shook her head. 'Jumped on a boat after he read the magazine. Drove over here and dealt with Rachel. Certainly has to be a serious possibility.'

'As you say we've got nobody else, and she's cut off his income supply.'

'Rachel wrote that piece towards the end of last year according to the index she adds to. In the end it was published in quite a few magazines earlier this year. But,' Nicky hesitated. 'Not all published in Ireland but surely he has to have a subscription.'

'You could check,' Nicky made a mental note of.

'Except under what name and if we go down the Border Force route, who was it booked on the ferry?'

'By now this Ronan Colbert or whoever he is, could well have been booted out of all the family history societies which will blow a big hole in his ambitions.'

'And his bank balance.'

'Nearly four grand's not as much as some I've come across, but if he was running ten at a time or more that adds up to a tidy sum. Good holiday money if he's not actually sick at all and got a proper job.'

'Evenings and weekends,' Inga nodded solemnly. 'Built himself up into some sort of go to clever dick with family history.'

'And these forlorn women do that, go to him and get stitched up.' Crossed legged Nicky blew out a breath and frowned. 'Got to admit I went back into all my own family history stuff last night after I read all this by Rachel. Had to pay a few bob to get back into the system in case I wanted to download, but anyway. When I was doing it seriously a year or two back there were forums I went on a few times, where people were asking all sorts.'

'Such as?'

'People on there with all the answers tend to specialize. Some morbid one's of course who have photos of gravestones, but then there are others who concentrate on military bits and pieces like cap badges they can recognize at a hundred paces, medals and the like. Who served with who and when.'

'Doing this as you say, this Ronan could be working loads all at the same time, surely. Even if he only picks up a few grand from each its a good way of getting on the housing ladder.'

'Bet that Madeline in effect paid for him to have weekends away, hotel, petrol, meals.'

'And probably took his wife and kids along.' Inga smiled and creases emerged around her mouth.

'Here's a question. Why would an Irishman dump her somewhere like Redbourne? How would he know about it?'

'Maybe just visiting, got relatives.'

'But what if he's not Irish at all? Ronan hints at Irish, where he says he is in Ireland. Could be out of Scunthorpe. Knows Redbourne and Hibaldstow like the back of his hand, maybe once worked for one of the farms, picking cauliflowers or whatever.'

'She never spoke to him, so if he's got a Lithuanian accent she's not to know.'

19

'Wait a moment,' said Inga Larsson to stop Michelle as she was about to walk into her office. Frustratingly the DI then set about logging in, checking her emails and stood there Michelle assumed even entered the password protected evidence file for the operation, while they waited for the drinks Alisha had been asked to get.

'You're right. It's on here about that...' she just shook her head. 'Oh dear. What a waste. Right. You were saying.' Michelle Cooper smiling held up her left hand and splayed her fingers. 'Oh my word,' Larsson gasped and was out of her chair to hold Michelle's fingers and inspect the diamond ring. 'How did this happen?'

'You say that as if I'm a scrote spinning you a yarn.'

'Sorry,' she said as she sat back down. 'Congratulations, well done. That's really good news. Didn't even know you were seeing anyone.'

'Kept it quiet,' Michelle admitted. 'Wasn't sure, all seemed too good to be true.'

'How d'you mean?' Inga asked and then took her first sip of coffee.

'Remember back during the Wickham case I had to interview those former students. Decided for some reason not to have a coffee with them. Decided to concentrate on what they were saying and I was free to make quick notes on my tablet. After I'd left them to chat, went for a walk and decided to nip into Costa in the High Street for a break. Place was packed, only two empty seats and this guy walks in and asks if the seat opposite me is free. The rest as they say in history.'

'You'll be looking for somewhere to live then.' Michelle shook her head. 'How d'you mean, no?'

'Not exactly. Matthew's an architect plus he and his retired dad renovate old houses. Week last Sunday he took me to see a house he'd rented out for a few years they've been doing up after the long term occupants moved away. Completely empty and I've got the job of furnishing it. We're moving in when I've got it sorted.'

'How d'you mean you weren't sure? I'd have bitten his hand off!' she chuckled.

'Why me?' Michelle needed a drink. 'Why is this really nice guy but a total stranger who's not on social media, making a hit on me?'

'And the policewoman inside told you beware.'

'Exactly. When you've worked in this sort of job you tend to be more than a little cautious.'

'But now you're fine.'

'Wondered why he was single,' she shrugged. 'Two reasons, he's been too busy working. Couple of days after we met he had to go to Holland for a week, plus he's renovating these old houses with his dad.'

'Still no reason not to have somebody in tow, you think?'

'That's what the negative me thought. Still in the back of my mind until his mother told me on the quiet how he'd been seeing this female for three or four months and she expected them to move in together when suddenly it all fell apart. Turns out he couldn't understand her mood swings and in the end she admitted she was taking drugs because it's what everybody does.'

'Cannabis, cocktails and hot tub lifestyle.'

'Cannabis before he met her and then all sorts. Gave her the heave ho sharpish, and concentrated on work and building his business empire as a way of getting over her. Stopped renting except for two because of all the hassle with tenants and now buys and sells.'

'Great. Really pleased for you. Wedding date?'

'Later in the year, but nothing stupid. None of that twenty grand nonsense.'

'Time to tell the team,' was Inga on her feet and heading to the Incident Room. As Michelle got to her feet her boss grabbed her and pulled her in for a hug.

Once the room had settled after the announcement, the ring had been inspected and congratulations had spread it was time for morning briefing. Inga's smile they knew was ominous when she treated them all to one of her pauses. 'Time for something completely different. Time for a long shot,' she saw the expected look on Jake Goodwin's face. Good copper, excellent detective, a decent man she'd trust with her life. Unfortunately at that moment she knew he was all for doing things by the book. Although every now and again he'd surprise her, but she guessed this was going to be a step too far. 'Nicky if you will,' she said and the blonde Detective Sergeant started to hand out sheets of paper to them all one by one as Inga perched herself on the edge of a work station.

'Time to have a read, and please read carefully, don't skip as I need you to take it all in. This is an original from one of Rachel Barnard's USB sticks. All to do with people being scammed out of a small fortune.'

She waited and so did Larsson until they were certain they understood.

'This was published in a family history magazine called *At A Distance* and in a number of other general publications owned by or linked to the Katushebe group.'

'All done?' Inga checked.

'Ronan Colbert,' said Nicky. 'But we have no idea if that is his real name. If that is where he comes from even in fact we know next to nothing, which unfortunately is often the case with these scammers.'

'Can I just say,' Larsson said. 'Most of the cases such as this one are to do with lonely women being scammed when they join on-line dating apps. This is different, this is to do with family history as you know. The woman who was scammed admitted she did gain from the information he provided, so one has to assume he has at least some knowledge of the subject.'

'There are perfectly legitimate forums linked to such research where people can go on, as I have done myself,' said Nicky Scoley. 'To get answers to difficult questions from the dark and distant past, before the internet and Google and before Encyclopedia Britannica. In many cases before people could read and write. People have been there before, done all the hard work other members can then benefit from.'

'Why are we doing this?' was Inga back asking her team. 'First answer is a question. What else do we have? Any likely candidates have alibis we've checked and in some cases double-checked. No previous histories of violence or threats anywhere any of us have come across. We have no new sources coming up with ideas apart that is, the usual crowd of dregs who always want to get involved in every homicide. How would an Irishman know about that old trough on the edge of that field near a small place like Hibaldstow? Not exactly on the tourist trail. Not on the Spires and Steeples, next door to the Cathedral or top of the Wolds.

'Lived there at one time maybe,' Nicky came back with before any of the team could guess. 'Grew up there, went to school up that way. If not that, perhaps he holidayed there, has family close by. Long shot. Is this farmer's wife Nancy Cutforth's illegitimate son?' amused Jake.

'Seems far fetched, but as some of you will know, we've been there before.' Inga put her hand up as she stood up. 'We're each taking one aspect of concern regarding this Ronan Colbert. Nicky has already got onto Garda over there and they're coming back to us.'

'The name Ronan Colbert is listed three times on PNC, once with DVLA about driving with no insurance in Worcester and there's one DNA sample on file.'

Inga smiled a contrived sympathetic look. 'Jake. Wonder if you'd go back to Higgins Farm and talk to them about Ronan Colbert. Yes I know,' she said when she saw the look on his face. 'This is a long shot I know, but as I've already said, who else have we got? Remember Rachel for the most part makes up names so as not to cause offence or be sued. Have a feeling this Colbert is different. Appears to be genuine, she was trying to expose. Bit of a pain I know, but think it's best if you do it, than start afresh.' He just grimaced slightly and nodded. 'Does it ring any bells up there?' She then looked past him to Michelle.

'Just a sec,' said Jake. 'Just come to mind. Think it was the farmer's wife Nancy Cutforth said kids used to mess about with the trough in the summer back when it had water in it.'

'Good place to start.'

'Will do.'

'Job for you Michelle on a different tack,' Inga was back to. 'The father Derek Barnard is a bit of a funny devil, but the rest appear to be fine. There's a suggestion boyfriend Sean Joseph is being controlled by his mother.' she pulled a face. 'Is Sean Joseph the issue here we've somehow by passed? Did he and Rachel have a major falling our over it? Is the truth he's a mummy's boy? Can't yet imagine how or why he's protecting his mother but, was…' Inga paused to create emphasis. 'Rachel planning or even already working on an article about mummy's boys?' made one or two suck in a breath.

'Guv,' was Sandy quick as a flash. 'Had she written it and did he think or realize it was aboot him and he thought people would work it oot, knowing full well he still lives at home. What's the chances he handed over all those USB sticks freely, after deleting the mummy's boy one.'

'This is just the thinking we've been missing from this whole case. Well done Sandy, good one. Job for you then,' made him sigh and smile. 'Nip up and ask the Tech Crime Team all about removing stuff from a USB stick.' The DI's phone rumbled. They all watched as she looked at her phone, closed her eyes, sighed and then returned to normal but slightly dejected. 'Toxicology stuff just come though I'll need to look at in detail,'

DS Jake Goodwin had called Higgins Farm and talked to Nancy Cutforth and explained what it was he wished to discuss with them and said he'd be with them later that morning.

As he was heading up the A15 his phone rang and using the hands free took a call from Mrs Cutforth.

'Hope you don't mind,' she said, as Jake pulled over to annoy traffic behind. 'Just had a thought, about that trough business. Nipped round to see Martha Drewry. She'd know if anyone does, certainly more than me as she's lived in village all her life. If anybody knows she does. Said I'll pick her up after lunch, around half two.'

Jake didn't have the heart to say he was already on his way, agreed to call on them later, turned round and headed back to Central.

Back to a discussion concerning the possibility of Sean Joseph being a 'mummy's boy'. Sandy MacLachlan had been to ask advice from the Tech Crime Team and up there Dexter had explained to him. Because the USB drive is an external device, files detected on the drive are deleted permanently rather than going to Recycle. But, he added, if he was given the laptop she used he could retrieve it from there.

'Could be on hers at home they've returned already which means we'd need to get it back.'

'One step forward and two back,' said Jake as he pulled off his jacket and sat down.

'Did,' Inga Larsson said with a look of surprise to see him back so quickly, but went on. 'She use one at work and then the question is, which one. What about she used an internet cafe somewhere if they still have such things or borrowed a mate's laptop? Brilliant!'

'Could be any of those rather than hers at home, particularly if she was hiding it from Sean.'

'You're back,' Inga said to Jake.

'Called me,' he said and pushed out a breath of annoyance. 'Mrs Cutforth's spoken with some woman who might have a better idea. Off back up there later for my sins.'

'Here we go, here we go!' was Jamie Hedley. 'Just thought I'd check about being a mummy's boy. A mummy's boy it says here,' he read from his monitor. 'Will always struggle with the women in his life. Defer to their needs all the time and find it increasingly difficult to say no.'

'Just had a thought Jamie,' said Inga. 'Carry on.'

'A man,' he continued his precis of what was on screen. 'Who regularly gives into a woman's needs, will end up very lost and…' he peered up with a small smirk. 'Angry.'

'Just going to say. Sean Joseph told me or one of us at least, how everything had to be done Rachel's way. Claimed that was what living separate from him was all about. Some notion she had to do with saving money to buy her dream home.'

'Reckon that hits the Ronan Colbert theory on the head,' Jake offered but waited for the rebuke which was immediate.

'You know better than that,' Inga chided. 'You carry on.'

'Boss,' was Jamie back. 'According to this. If they don't get what they want when they want it, mummy's boys are not too proud to pout and throw a temper tantrum'

'Wi' a brick?' Sandy offered.

20

It was mid-afternoon before Jake Goodwin pulled up outside the Higgins farmhouse. There to greet him as soon as she heard his car was Nancy. She ushered him in the backdoor he'd entered before and into the big tidy kitchen. This would be the third time he'd called and so far he'd seen nothing more of the house.

No smell of freshly baked cakes or goodies this time to set his mouth watering.

'This is Martha Drewry,' she said and gestured to an old woman sat on a chair at the big wooden table. This time covered with a red and white chequered tablecloth.

'How do you do,' said Jake down to her and shook her cold small hand.

'Tea alright?' Nancy asked.

'Fine,' he responded to show willing, pulled out a chunky wooden chair and sat down. Jake could feel the old woman looking at him and for a moment or two wondered if there was something amiss.

'Martha's lived in the village all her life,' Nancy explained as she had done basically over the phone earlier. 'Get this tea made and we'll have a chat.'

'You'd have known the farm before Hubert and Nancy moved here,' he suggested to the old woman to create a conversation..

'Yes,' was softly spoken and Jake knew it would be rude to ask her age.

'I expect you've seen a lot of changes.'

'Yes.'

'Martha's late husband worked on the railways,' was Nancy coming to his rescue. 'Not driving or owt like that you understand, worked at Doncaster station mostly tinkering with

160

the trains. Be only steam when he first started I guess.' Nancy brought a mug to the table she placed in front of Martha. 'Arnold worked on steam trains,' Nancy suggested.

'Yes.'

Mugs of hot milky tea for Jake and Nancy herself appeared and sat down opposite him in the same place as she had done previously.

'This is Detective Sergeant Goodwin I was telling you about Martha. He's investigating that poor woman's death on the edge of the woods.'

'This about that Ronan Colbert?' the old woman mumbled back.

'Yes it is,' Goodwin responded. 'Did you know him at all?'

She cleared her throat, blew out a breath and frowned as Jake waited. 'Got to be...thinking 'bout it. Good thirty year or more has to be at least.'

'You're pretty sure about that are you?' Goodwin asked gently.

'Our Billy had to be about ten or twelve,' she said nodding. Jake was about to ask more when she went on. 'See, he's forty three next birthday.'

'Billy is?' Goodwin checked. 'And Billy is what relation to you?'

'Grandson,' said Nancy as Martha had returned to her mug. 'Billy or William if you like, along with Andrew and Stephanie I think it is. Her daughter Amy's kids.' Goodwin scribbled down the names in his notebook as she went on. 'None of them live in the village now, but they all visit fairly regular.'

'Are you saying your Billy used to play with that water trough?' Goodwin was back to.

'All the kids did.'

'How many are we talking?'

This Martha forced a half-hearted smile in his direction. 'Six or seven there'd be, eh?' she then asked Nancy who shrugged.

'No idea love, long before our time remember.'

'But this Ronan Colbert was one of them?' Goodwin suggested, and took his first taste of the tea.

'Group o'lads and lasses.'

'Sort of gang you mean? All went about together.'

161

'Not a lot to do in the village,' said Nancy. 'Bit more of course when we first came here. Not a great deal now youth club got closed down by the do-gooders. Back then they'd not have the internet and all those machine things they mess about with.'

'And in the summer your Billy and this Colbert messed about in the water in that trough with these others?'

'Amy'd get fed up with him getting his clothes in a right mess.' Goodwin took the opportunity as Martha sipped tea to do the same. 'If it'd rained,' was said as she licked her lips and looked at Nancy with one hand holding the mug on the table. 'When was that hot year?' she grimaced. 'One year any road it was all hot and remember hearing kids moaning there was no water.'

'Be seventy six, I think,' was pushed across at Goodwin who nodded.

'Have you always lived in the village?'

'Down Osbournby us came from in me early days,' the old woman pronounced Ozzenby Jake recognized like a local.

'Can we get back to this Ronan Colbert?' Goodwin asked. 'What happened to him at all do you know?'

There was a short pause before Martha replied. 'Can't remember where to. Somewhere down south think it was. Yeh,' she nodded. 'Pretty sure it was.'

'What was down south?' Jake asked as his brain did a bit of mental arithmetic. The old dear had got in a muddle. If her grandson was now 43 he'd not be alive in seventy six let along out with a gang in the summer playing in the trough..

'His work.'

'Who we talking about?' Jake queried.

'Ronan's dad,' she said and looked at him as if it was obvious. 'Lorry driver,' she moved her head about as if struggling. 'Those big ones,' was all she managed. 'Alex he were.'

Didn't sound it, but the question had to be asked. 'Were they Irish?'

Martha pouted. 'No,' she blew out a breath. 'Yorkshire through and through as they say,' Martha looked anxiously about for no reason. 'Alus bragging 'bout how it was God's country.'

'And he moved south with his family?' Goodwin checked with no desire to get involved in a county war.

'Never heard of him again. Working for one of them bigger firms with lots more lorries think it was. Well, somebody said any rate.'

'Just…'

'Long time ago, son,' stopped him. 'Not easy all this.'

'Appreciate that, you're doing well,' he told her.' Just out of interest,' Goodwin continued his thread. 'Were you ever aware of an Irish family in the village or living nearby?' appeared to confuse Martha and she was back to drinking her tea almost as if it was her comfort blanket. Be her age he guessed. Got a problem put the kettle on.

By then Jake Goodwin knew it was a long shot but from his small briefcase he was about to produce a screenshot of a Ronan Colbert the Tech Crime Team clever dicks had produced, when Hubert Cutforth pushed the door open.

'Morning,' he said. 'Hello Martha,' and Goodwin was on his feet to shake hands. 'Want a word with you,' sounded ominous.

'Later Hube, later, ' said Nancy as she got to her feet to boil the kettle again as the farmer disappeared through the door opposite. 'Sorry about that,' Nancy offered.

Back to it, Goodwin slid the picture across the table. 'Do you recognize this man?' he asked the old lady. Martha just looked at the sheet before passing it swiftly to Nancy stood waiting for the kettle. 'Ring any bells, eyes maybe are sometimes a give away.'

'No.'

'How about Ronan Colbert?'

'With no hair,' Martha thought amusing. 'Had big frizzy mop of it back then. No,' she shook her head. Goodwin then placed his hand over the forehead of the man pictured.

There was little point in going into details from his Facebook page as it was very likely the whole concept would take some explaining.

They knew there was a good chance the real Ronan Colbert looked nothing like the person pictured. Not something scammers do, put their latest up-to-date selfie on the internet for all to see.

Fresh mug of tea poured for Hubert Cutforth's return.

'We don't know any Colberts do we?' Nancy asked him.

'Nah.'

'Think that's me about done,' said Goodwin who downed the last of the tea, picked up his notebook, put the picture back in his case and was on his feet.

'Hold up there,' was Cutforth. 'Want a word.'

'Outside!' was sharp from his wife.

'Thank you Martha,' said Goodwin and shook her timid hand again. 'Thank you Nancy, useful,' he fibbed and walked out the backdoor Hubert had opened for him.

'First things first,' Jake insisted to stimy Hubert Cutforth. 'We've got an expert in pollen coming down.,' and saw the look on Cutforth's face. 'Yes I know, sounds all a bit odd. To do with forensics at the area where the body was discovered. Please don't disturb the area around there...'

'Yeh right,' he scoffed. 'What abaht bloody trespassers?'

'How d'you mean?' Goodwin asked as they walked towards his car.

'Sightseers, coming for a bloody gander, Been in me field, one bastard family even knocked on t'door wanting to know if we do cream bloody teas. Cheeky bastards.'

Jake so wanted to suggest it might be a profitable sideline but thought better of it. 'You talking about people poking their noses into where the trough was?'

'Doubt it. Nobody knows 'cept Vonne and Susan Not seen sight of 'em since.'

'This all still going on?'

'One yesterday afternoon. Bastard ga'me a bloody mouthful when I told him to bugger off.'

'I'll have a word. Get patrols stepped up. Carries on, you give me a call. That do?'

'Any closer to solving it?'

'Trouble always is, a murderer looks like anybody. So far Rachel's killer has not been apprehended. Our tape still there?' suddenly came to mind to change subjects..

'Yeh bits and pieces.'

'I'll get rid of it on my way out. Less people know the better.'

'So, whas happening?'

'Several lines of enquiry like the one I was talking to your Nancy about, and this pollen expert, I'll give you a call about.'

'Any good?'

'Got another officer looking into it, I popped up as I know you both. Easier than a stranger knocking on your door. I'll pass on what Martha was saying. All before your time you'll be pleased to know.'

'Good job.'

'Thank Nancy for the tea.'

'Fore you go,' stopped Jake moving away. 'Dave Gibson at Wheatsheaf reckons some copper's been having a look at their CCTV gubbins. That you?'

'Not me,' he could say honestly, at least not at the pub. 'Could be another case, probably traffic related should imagine. Be down from Brigg I guess,' he fibbed. 'See you,' he said and turned.'

Travelling back down to Lincoln Jake couldn't help but allow his mind to return to reminisce the circumstances surrounding one or two other cases where it had been a case of an infuriating one step forward and two back.

21

On his return to Lincoln Central, DS Jacques Goodwin was needing to report no news was bad news about Ronan Colbert, only to discover the case against him had moved on.

Nicky Scoley had received word over from Garda in Ireland, about this Colbert. According to them he didn't have a passport, Irish or British to enable him to visit Lincolnshire to get his own back on Rachel Barnard. They had also concluded the service Madeline Buchanan paid for was to all intents and purposes legitimate and not a scam at all.

What about the illness that sick bastard was talking about? What had Garda done about that? If he was sick, what with, or was he just swinging the lead? Had they done any checks or was this just a case of them fobbing off a yellowbelly rural eejit? If it was Nicky wanted to scream across the Irish Sea at them.

Their investigations had concluded that he was doing the same to other people in a similar fashion on family history websites, but their overarching consideration was that he supplied legitimate information just in the same way other researchers do.

'But he doesn't state he is a researcher and has a list of services with prices as others do,' was an angry Scoley spouting to anyone who'd listen. 'The phone number according to Rachel is false, the address is false and even his country is false. The church he claimed to have visited she paid petrol and overnight stays for never existed. Nigeria it may not be, but it might as well be,' she said and sank her head down onto her folded arms.'

'Very hot dishing out Covid fines.'

'What?' she reacted and sat back up.

'The Irish I remember reading about.'

'Might not be like a romance scam where desperate lonely women hand over their life savings. Can't they see this is not just some researcher, otherwise the lies would not be there, even Garda must be able to see. She in effect gave him her holiday.'

Jake calmly waited for her outburst to end. 'Think I probably did worse than that,' he admitted to his angry and frustrated colleagues. 'Long way for nothing. That's never the same Ronan Colbert, just an amazing coincidence somebody with that unusual name played in that water trough thirty odd years ago. That is of course if this Martha Drewry I spoke to, remembered the name correctly after all this time. Probably find out it's her milkman's name.' He sighed his frustration and went on hastily to explain the circumstances. 'Or an old lady got to be in her eighties at least remembers a name from some place way back when.' Jake turned to Scoley. 'How old is your Colbert just out of interest?'

'Claims thirty, thirty one I seem to remember,' and she went to check on her laptop.

'Don't bother for now. Mine has to be early forties. Woman I've just seen claimed he played there with a gang of kids thirty year ago when this Ronan was ten or twelve same as her grandson who's now in his early forties.'

'The age I quoted is only what he quoted remember. Another thing idiots at Garda have ignored.'

'Don't worry yourself. Mine wasn't Irish he was a Yorkie and they moved down south somewhere with the father being an HGV driver.' Jake paused before he went on. 'Probably not Ronan at all and Colbert could easy be Coleman over time. Anything else happening?'

'Jamie's back on ANPR duties and think the boss is going back through Sean Joseph's interview.'

'We still on this mummy's boy business?'

'Yeh,' was released with her shaking her butterscotch blonde haired head. 'I know some go way over the top about sexism but every now and again I kinda feel it going on.'

'What?' Jake asked quietly. 'Here? How d'you mean?'

'Jamie's been onto ANPR since before you left and all he's doing is checking Sean Joseph's car movements on the Monday and Tuesday evenings.' she pulled as face. 'This is no slight on Jamie, he's good at his job, but chances are I'd have it all done and dusted ages ago.'

Not the first time Jake knew of others reacting far better with the females on the force. Lack of diversity nobody mentions.

'Boss just checking her interview with Joseph you say?'

'And phone tracking she's asked for from upstairs.'

'Looking for him heading for Brigg on Monday or Tuesday.'

'Exactly.'

'Because he's a mummy's boy? Perhaps it's me but I don't see it to be honest. What's he like?'

'Seems pretty decent to me. Talked quite openly to me about how the *Leader* is organized, where they get all the stories from. Like you, I don't really see it.'

'But we've been amazed before. We had any other phone data back?' Jake queried.

'Gosney's. But the odd thing is he never made or received any calls on Monday at all. Tracking says he went to Melton Mowbray on Monday evening as you know.'

'Without making calls,' Jake shook his head. 'Turning up for an appointment on time, getting back around the time his missus expected him. Why phone?' he shrugged and so wanted to comment on the perpetual use of mobiles by far too many. 'We keep crossing names off. Colbert and now Gosney.'

'As I say, news is Joseph's back in the running' Nicky reminded.

'But would you tell the police about her USB flash drives if you were him, with a great deal to hide? Would you choke her to death because you can't stand the way she does the minimum amount of ironing which is not the same as his mum who even irons his shreddies and socks?'

'Even if she is an over the top pedantic, that's no proper reason. Might cause a row or two maybe.'

'What about the others working for the *Leader,* they all knew how she worked surely? Rather than try to keep them hidden or act all innocent, he's dumped the bad USB all about him or he assumes it is and is playing little goody two shoes with the rest.'

'Too much supposition to my mind. But having said that, just might have a look at how many mummy's boys are on the homicide list.' Nicky stretched her arms above her head. 'Better get on and check out more of Rachel's writings, see if another Colbert turns up.'

'Still find that a bit strange,' Jake said. 'Colbert's not a common name, but we have one Rachel mentions in her family history article and it just so happens thirty odd years ago someone with the same name was possibly paddling in the old trough she was dumped in.'

'The Darke boss would call that a coincidence one of his pet hates.'

Jake turned slightly to face Nicky now working her keys. 'Mummy boy murders here we come!'

It didn't take Jake Goodwin long before he was onto websites about killers who were referred by the press as being 'Mummy's Boys.' First up after he'd dismissed the Oedipus complex denoting a child's desire to have sex with a parent and a case recent enough for him to recall parts of it. Elliot Turner who chocked his girlfriend to death in his parents' home was in itself shocking enough. But then he was reminded as he read on, how his parents helped him cover it up. Next up was Jeremy Bamber still inside who some also described as a mummy's boy.

'Listen to this,' he told Nicky when they both took a break from their screens. He with a bottle of water and Nicky with a coffee. 'One I find interesting not just because he was a so-called mummy's boy, but because this Elliot Turner killed his girlfriend and then had his parents cover up for him or at least tried to.' He looked at his colleague.

'We thinking Sean Joseph's mother?' was gasped hand to mouth. 'Be serious!'

'Plus,' he smiled. 'After this Turner's parents came out of prison for perverting the course of justice, the pair of them actually moved back into the very house where their son had committed murder. Just read reports saying his parents who are

169

now out, showed absolutely no remorse during or after the trial.'

'Who on earth would do that?'

'If you doted on your son to that extent it'd probably not bother you, I guess.'

'What do we know about Joseph's mother? How old is she? Can she drive?'

'This Turner's mother is only in her fifties now.'

'Oh my word.' Nicky bit her bottom lip. 'Without checking Joseph has to be in his early thirties if that. Means she could be anything between say forty eight and fifty five.' The look she gave Jake said it all.

'In all seriousness, d'we go to the boss with this idea or is this Joseph woman just another name we'll cross out in a few days because it's too bizarre? Draw a line through Colbert, Gosney and Joseph?'

'If she drives. What was she doing on Monday and Tuesday?'

'Hang on, hang on,' said Jake to stop her thoughts. 'Hang on a tick,' and he was knocking on the boss's small office door and walked in. Within a minute he was back out and sat at his work station next to Nicky Scoley again. 'He claimed he was working from home on the Monday evening, working on a website for a builder.' Jake glanced at his partner. 'He never actually named. Means he was at home with his mother.' He whistled.'Infatuated mother has to be the best alibi any man can get. Working on a local builder's website he could have done at any time we'll have a heck of a job on to prove otherwise, but,' he hesitated. 'According to the boss she reckons there was no mention of Tuesday at all.'

Nicky Scoley fleshed her teeth and sucked in hard. 'What about Joseph's father?' she asked.

'Oh. He died of Covid.'

'We know that for absolute certain do we?'

'Now you're asking,' he had to chuckle with.

Rather than disturb the boss again they agreed to get their heads down. Nicky Scoley back to romance scams just in case and Jake would surreptitiously check up what he could on Sean Joseph's mother. Driving licence first up with DVLA.

With her christian name unknown and with Joseph being a popular Lincolnshire name, after checking what they knew about her son, Jake was onto Lincoln City Council for Council Rent and Tax information with only an address on the Ermine and her surname. He also had the father listed for a Covid death he needed to investigate.

'We ever had a mother and son?' Jake asked nobody in particular.

'Sorry,' said Nicky engrossed as she was in finding the next Rachel Barnard feature on the stick.

Jake Goodwin too was concentrating on his monitor chucking *Mother and son murderers* into Google. 'I'm just saying. Have we ever had a mother and son as killers.'

'Not us,' she replied.

'Got one,' said a pleased with himself Jake Goodwin to disturb Nicky reading. 'Mother and son killed her husband and his father to get their hands on the cash from the sale of his house. Problem was unknown to them he'd changed his will. They got done for murder and in the end got sod all.'

'Nice one,' Nicky just managed before she was back with her evening's reading all planned out..

It was back to sitting back on the sofa, glass of wine on the table beside her for Nicky Scoley, still convinced thr answers were hidden amongst the written word.

22

News about Covid deaths that Saturday morning being higher then a year previous along with reports of more atrocities in Ukraine was never a good start to any day.

After an evening of reading Barnard's columns Nicky would admit she had always admired people who write anything requiring an element of discipline. Writing her popular column which some would say was more in vogue than the paper itself, was something Nicky knew she dealt with week in, week out.

Successful opinion columnists are motivated often incrementally to do their best to stir up debate and appeal to our basest instincts.

First thing, the hard-working Detective Sergeants approached the boss's door first thing the following morning armed with more information. So early in fact apart from Jamie Hadley who seemed not to have moved overnight they were the only two.

'Can you spare two minutes?' Nicky asked when she opened the door. Inga sat up and sat back in her black chair hands behind her head.

'Yeh, why not.' Inga checked her watch. 'Off to link up with Professsor Hewitt so she can take a look at pollen for us, though we've got nothing to check it against.'

'Some people do have strange jobs.'

'Meeting her at Brigg Garden Centre. She's across coming from Leeds and bringing a student with her. Then lead her down to the farm.'

'I'll warn Cutforth,' said Jake and was gone.

'First things first,' was Nicola Scoley in her sunshine yellow shirt stood in front of the desk.. 'Last night I just read more of the romance scams and we're now looking at fraudsters living goodness knows where. Guessing Rachel ran out of anybody local or partially so, but the powers that be must have demanded more of the same ilk. One in Keswick, another in Rushmere and one nasty bastard living in West London who used Covid to swindle some silly woman from the Cotswolds.'

'Got a lot of likes or good reader feedback no doubt, and it spurs them on.' Inga gestured for the DS to be seated.

'Any idea what this Professor woman will do?'

'Be a bit like a bee I assume. But don't ask how. Be interesting though I bet. Shona's meeting us on site. Just hope we get the chance to test her theory.'

'And the student?'

'Got to be work experience.'

'Spoke to Nancy Cutforth,' said Jake as he walked back in and sat down. On the second of the only two chairs in the cramped office facing her. 'Sean Joseph.'

'Go on,' lacked enthusiasm.

They talked to Larsson about the business of him being a mummy's boy and Jake mentioned the Elliott Turner murder where his parents were even involved and the mother and son pairing. He even sneaked in the Oedipus complex to alarm.

'All we have, unless you know different, is Sean saying he worked at home on the Monday. With mummy in attendance,' he gestured his head with a smirk. 'If we asked her to provide an alibi she'd tell us word for word about him working on some builders website to raise extra cash for this house Rachel was after.'

'Been told to go easy on the way we work at times,' said Inga steadily 'Advice is there's more bad news emerging soon about goings on down at the Met. Told to be more caring, for want of a better word.'

'Crims doing the same are they?' was Nicky's sarcasm using a word the boss detested.

Larsson knew the pair were eager to get on. 'Should really have done DNA checks on people like Joseph but we've not arrested him, have no suspicions apart from random suggestions such as you're making here.' She turned her gaze away to her monitor. 'First tox came through overnight I was planning to bring to the table at morning briefing after I've suffered half an hour with Darke. They found DNA on Rachel's clothing, but there's no match on the database.'

'So we could…' the DI nodding and smiling brought Jake to a halt.

'Reasons to be cheerful and reasons to get swabs done.'

'Joseph and his mother we're talking about?' Jake had a need to check.

'What about Rachel's family?'

'Know they're still grieving but now we have a sample, be negligent if we didn't check them all. Maybe not the young son you think?'

'That's hardly what anybody could describe as being over the top.'

'We do this today you think?' an enthusiastic Nicky asked.

'Make the calls and you can split them between you.'

'Not Cutforth the farmer, please.'

Inga blew out a breath. She was tempted. 'Not at this stage eh? He's got to be a long shot.'

'Not as long as some scammer from Indonesia I was reading about last night.'

'Oh by the way,' Jake said. 'Joseph's father did die of Covid. Death certificate has Heart Failure as the main cause with Covid-19 as a contributing factor.'

'We'll stick with those few for now. We can always spread the net wider if they prove negative. DNA testing the *Leader* staff would stir up just the sort of trouble we're told to avoid. I know Joseph's one of theirs, but with him we have a legitimate reason. Elimination, should they ask. Problem is, we don't have Joseph's personal staff details, not being a journalist.'

'Sorry,' said Nicky. 'Didn't bother with the admin, circulation and advertising people. Didn't imagine we'd need their web designer too.'

'That's okay. Sandy!' she called out, and waited. 'Need Joseph's car details. Reg number and anything else you think'll be useful. Head off out to the *Leader* and with a bit of luck you might spot him using it to go for lunch.'

'Unless mummy has made him a pack up,' Larsson ignored but what Jake had eluded to still made her cringe.

'Do'you know which one he is?'

'Car you mean?'

'No, him as a person.'

'Tall one...with sandy hair,' they were amused by when Sandy shook his similar head of hair.

'Och aye,' was all they got and the big man was gone.

'Testing the mother will add to the validity of what we're doing.'

'You get on with sorting those, I'll tip off the boss and we'll talk again in a bit.'

As was the norm, the team in the main were in the process of being refreshed as they listened to the morning briefing given by Jake Goodwin with the DI off up to Brigg. Even those who had not been at work long had brought to go drinks with them, and Nicky had got a black coffee for Jake.

'Something Nicky and I were discussing earlier. Boss warned me of more impeding doom from the Met on the horizon, so we're to take things easy. Play everything, strictly by the book. Second thing. Forensics have discovered DNA on Barnard's clothing which means we should be able to move the case on. Bearing that in mind, we have the boss's full backing to DNA swab the Barnard family and Sean Joseph and his mother we now know to be Susan Melanie,' she said and nodded to both her Detective Sergeants.

'And you never know what this Professor might come up with.'

'How'd all that come about?' Jamie queried.

'Liam one of Shona's team gets serious hay fever but only in particular areas. Stinging nettles is one thing and they're where the sheep trough was, its said because that particular type like damn places. Boss told us a while back about this woman runs a forensic archeological science course in Leeds she met once. Reckons pollen sticks to your shoes and clothing. All we need is a killer we can match the results to.'

DS Nicky Scoley had made arrangements to swab Susan Joseph through talking to Sean when she called him at work, to arrange for her to call and undertake the same procedure with him.

When she arrived at the *Leader* offices he was totally co-operative waiting for her and took her into a communal toilet area off main reception for her to carry out the Buccal Swab.

He told Scoley he had called his mother at work in a local shop where she worked part-time, and she would be home soon after one thirty.

So it was the DS turned up at the Joseph woman's green front door with her warrant card at the ready. She was invited in by a tidy woman with slightly greying hair, dressed conventionally in a tan brown jumper, dark brown skirt and flat black trainer type shoes.

With the swab being the first thing Sean's mother mentioned once they were indoors seemed ideal timing for Nicky to carry out the procedure

Then the DS was offered the choice of tea or coffee by what was turning out to be a very decent woman. They both went for the latter which as it turned out was Instant. Susan Joseph served coffee in mugs in the slightly dated pale green kitchen, although she did offer for them to move into the lounge.

The conversation was not going anyway towards what she and Jake had surmised, with her talking about Rachel with a good degree of kindness rather than about her son. Scoley enjoyed her decent coffee in comfortable enough surroundings whilst waiting for an opportunity.

Was this woman a seriously a suspect? The mother who assisted her son in the murder of his girlfriend? Sat there Nicky Scoley doubted it very much.

'How would you have felt if Sean had moved out to live with Rachel?' she asked gently.

'He wouldn't,' said this trim Susan, and just as Nicky thought she was onto something unpleasant the woman then hastily went on to explain the circumstances for such a statement tweaking Scoley's curiosity. 'Rachel insisted when they moved to the new home they'd buy one with room for me.' She lifted and lowered one shoulder. 'Think some of all this saving business with her was for me. The bit extra I was going to cost them.'

'Was your Sean happy with that, or was this all Rachel's idea?'

Susan Joseph pulled a face. 'Think sometimes he got a bit uneasy when she insisted things were done a certain way, but they seemed happy enough. Known couples not as close as them get married and stay put.'

'That would have been nice, having a new home,' was all Scoley could manage with this turn of events.

'Be honest,' said Susan. 'To begin with I said they didn't need me there cluttering up the place, especially when they were first living together and,' she grimaced. 'Maybe getting married. But Rachel insisted,' she shrugged. 'So,' she breathed out. 'Not happen now,' and the misery of losing her daughter-in-law to be suddenly became evident on her face.

'How do you keep yourself busy?' Scoley delved.

'Got a good circle of friends, some I've known pretty much all my life. Belong to a book reading group locally and Sean fitted me up with that Zoom business so I can chat to my sister.' She stopped to drink her coffee which Nicky Scoley was already doing. 'Sean put me on that Facebook business. Don't use it much except to keep up to date with what's happening all over the Ermine with a group they've got on there. Interesting stuff sometime, but a lot of folk ask such silly things.' Just as Scoley went to speak she went on. 'Bit strange really. Some folk on there still call it Ermine estate, phrase me old dad used to use.'

'Think that's a bit old fashioned Lincolnsheer still hanging around.'

'Any idea when they'll release the body?' caught Scoley by surprise.

'Be a while yet I'm afraid.'

'Just thinking about Millie having to organize the funeral. Know how hard that can be with my Gareth catching that horrid Covid thing.'

'Do you know the family well?' was more probing and a move away from the subject.

'Well enough. Guess had they got wed it'd be better. That Derek can be a bit odd, but Millie's nice enough and her daughter always remembers me birthday.'

'That's kind.'

'Don't deserve it do they, just normal decent people like that. That pair'd not do anybody any harm. See too much of that on the news.' Scoley had never met them but fully understood what Mrs Joseph was saying.

'I take it you read what Rachel wrote?'

'Of course. I'll miss that,' she said shaking her head. 'First thing I turn to, even did before Sean got to know her. Bit like a village newsletter, but less drippy. Famous women in history never read those cosy books I bet. And she wrote bits for other magazines she or Sean got for me. Friends at the book club love her too.'

'I've been reading about those women who get scammed by fraudulent men.'

'I'm sorry,' Joseph said with mug in hand. 'When he starts asking for money you'd be wary but then a second time, sorry,' she smiled at Nicky. 'He'd be on his bike. Wonder why on earth these women do that?' she sipped. 'Is being naive something they've never grown out of?'

'Lonely they say.'

Susan was drinking and Scoley waited. 'Yeh, that's what Rachel says. Get fooled into thinking this is the real thing, love of their life and all that business.' Susan put down her almost empty mug. '£20,000 from one I read not long ago,' she gasped. 'Why would you send that amount to anybody? One I read one time was a retired policeman,' she grinned. 'I've never had that much,' she chuckled. 'So be no good latching onto me,' amused her.

The pair had a good easy conversation which had as far as Nicky Scoley was concerned, kicked any ideas Jake might have had about a mummy's boy well into touch. Especially that nasty suggestion.

She and Jake had agreed to handle the Barnard family together. But it had to be later when Derek was home and their daughter Kathryn could pop round for the swab procedure.

Back at Lincoln Central Nicky Scoley had missed out on major news. Before she'd had time to brief the boss and Jake about Mrs Joseph, Inga was calling the pair into the office on a separate matter

178

'Fascinating, watching Tessa Hewitt at work on pollen profiles. Miniscule tweezers picking off the pollen she put in a tube. Taking it back to the university to freeze it. Reckons it'll stay good for a year.'

'We'd better get a move on then! We need to remember her,' Nicky suggested. 'Being so rural she'll be useful to know.'

'What she called white nettles are found in Europe and Asia but all I know is they sting. Reminded me as we all know we leave a trace wherever we go, but also from her point of view people also take away a trace. Lovely woman and she paid for the coffees. Good choice that Coffee Haven at the garden centre meant we were able to have a good chat first.' Inga looked down at the papers in front of her. 'By the way, your ANPR friends came up with the goods,' said the DI pushing a copy of an ANPR print out across her desk in Nicky's direction.

'This Jamie?' the DS asked quickly and couldn't take her eyes off what she saw.

'Patience is a virtue.'

'What d'you reckon?' was Jamie at the door behind her.

'The boy done good,' and the pair high fived.

'That's what the delay was,' Jamie explained. 'Searching through countless cameras until they came up with one taking an unmistakable shot like that.'

'How did you get them to check every one in such fine detail?' was a curious Nicky when she had imagined he was being fobbed off.

'Used special words,' she waited grinning with her head cocked to one side. 'Murder. Woman,'

The DI sighed deeply. 'Talking of words,' said a frustrated Inga. 'About to share a few with the Darke boss. Here's hoping he'll not throw the latest Met mess at me.'

Just before she'd gone off to have a word with Craig Darke, Inga Larsson had reminded them all of the eyes of the nation likely to be on the police in the near future, and had suggested the pair don't as she put it: 'Nip in, swab and nip out again.' This she felt was particularly relevant in the case of the Barnards as the mother, would still be grieving. To just fob them off would have reflected badly on the Lincoln County force but a mere nothing compared to what was in store to add to the rape, murder and coppers taking photos of dead bodies the whole nation had been alarmed by.

The late afternoon visit with the Barnard family up in delightful Nettleham, was to some extent verging on the pointless, but still had to be done. Cover all bases was the regular suggestion from the boss before she went home with good news ringing in her ears for once.

The family home when they found it, was a three bedroom house complete with garage. Location was fairly close to the A46 north of the city.

Derek Barnard was home and scoffing down his meal when the two Detective Sergeants knocked on the front door out at the property in a village having slowly built up over the years. Ushered the pair into the lounge and offered a hot drink they both had to turn down due to overload and the fact they both had yet to get home for a meal and a possible hot drink.

Nicky Scoley carried out the easy Buccal Swabs with Millie, her daughter Kathryn and even young Harry to keep him happy, but they then had to wait for Derek to finish his meal.

'Getting anywhere, yet?' Kathryn asked with them all sat around after Harry had gone off up to his room as teenage boys do.

'Early days,' said Jake Goodwin acting as dumb as he could. 'Less than a week since I got the call although for you I'm sure it seems a great deal longer.'

'One problem, always,' Scoley joined is. 'Is the fact that a lot of the forensic analysis does take time.'

'We've only just got some toxicology back from the lab today,' Goodwin admitted. 'Forensic analysis is coming in slowly, but they've got a few bits sorted.'

'That's why these DNA swabs have been necessary in order to eliminate you all. Sorry,' said Scoley. 'Whole procedure could be a while yet,' was to avoid raising their hopes.

'Nah then' was Derek Barnard appearing at the lounge door.

Nicky Scoley bag in hand was on her feet. 'Shall we do it out there?' she gestured for him to return to the kitchen which he did so without any hassle. Quick swab round and it was all done. 'I was talking to Susan Joseph earlier,' she said back in the lounge. 'I swabbed her when she got home from work.'

'Why?' was Derek arms folded leaning against the door post to the kitchen.

'Could easily turn out to be Low Template or Familial DNA,' said Goodwin. He knew it wasn't exactly true, but they were not to know. 'May have been indirect contact of course by Sean's mother as well as direct traces being left by Sean himself.'

'Think that's a bit high falutin fer us matey,' was Derek.

'Low Template DNA,' Jake said and wished he'd never mentioned it. 'Is where a very small trace of DNA from say a few skin cells may have been deposited. Familial is usually DNA from close biological relatives. Parent, child, brothers or sisters.,' he hoped would satisfy.

As it was, there were no further technical questions and shortly after Scoley and Goodwin were back out and heading for Lincoln Central.

23

Over the weekend talk had been about Tyson Fury's fight nobody had watched live. With ticket prices ranging from £55 to over £2,000 the discussion had in the main been about how little you'd be able to see in a huge stadium like Wembley for that sort of money.

Monday morning and muscular DC Jamie Hedley had been teamed with tall PC Jason Yeoman off the Road Crime Unit squad for the drugs swipe suddenly and surprisingly approved by Craig Darke and the plan put into force quickly by the DI.

According to boss Larsson, the Detective Superintendent had taken her aback with his decision, and reckoned he was anxious for the case to be resolved as soon as possible due to the inclusion of a high profile member of the *Lincoln Leader's* staff being the victim.

The powers that be she understood were concerned that every step they took was being scrutinized more than normal by the media as a whole. Let alone by the local rag intent on playing their police brutality and law and order cards whilst desperately trying to boost circulation at the same time.

It was for that reason Inga Larsson had been surprised at the decision to allow the false but seemingly justifiable stop.

Guy French as part of his actions had already added to the vehicle info Nicky Scoley had obtained when she visited the paper. Guy had parked up close to the *Leader* offices early the previous morning to note down the vehicle makes, colours and registration numbers.

Back at Central, he'd then gone through the lot with the DVLA information section to obtain detail of the owners along with a quick check on PNC just in case.

With that data in mind Jason Yeoman and DC Jamie Hedley made a quick drive by of the flat in Newark Road in North

Hykeham south of the city, where Elphick lived and then drove on to park up outside the small Co-op store heading for the southern end of the by-pass.

They waited, were tempted to nip into the store for a Costa take-away but thought better of it. Sat there they heard on the radio of a three car RTC close to Holdingham roundabout near Sleaford, they were too far away to react to.

Eventually the red Focus drove past heading south and Yeoman stealthily pulled out and followed. Jamie Hedley called the boss to confirm they were tracking the subject.

Over the Hykeham Roundabout at Pennells and down the A46 they went, keeping a safe distance with Jamie doing the spotting. Elphick turned left at the next roundabout heading for Witham St Hughs just as they had hoped.

Fortunately the traffic going south had been reasonably light and they were pleased not to be on the jam packed Lincoln by-pass at that hour.

Next he took a right into the St Modwen Park industrial estate and pulled into the *Lincoln Leader* car park in front of newer buildings on the right.

Strict instructions to play the whole swabbing process absolutely by the book was clearly in Jamie's mind as Yeoman's Vauxhall Vectra in full Battenburg decals followed Elphick in and parked up close behind.

'Good morning, sir,' PC Yeoman said as Elphick opened his driver's door. 'How are you this morning? Bit sharp there sir, coming off the A46 back at the roundabout don't you think?'

'What?'

'Got a licence have we, sir?' the big copper asked as he removed the car keys.

'Yeh,' was meek from a grimacing and confused individual.

'Please join me in our car if you would,' PC Yeoman gestured and Jamie still sat in the front passenger seat waited for him to get out and trudge the few yards.

'Good morning, sir,' said Jamie Hedley once Elphick was seated behind him.

'Licence, sir if you would?' was Yeoman as he sat back down behind the wheel.

'Not on me, no.'

'You have got a full licence I take it?'

'Of course.'

'You'd be amazed, sir. How many people are driving on our roads without one,' he suggested as Jamie having checked the licence plate with base and receiving feed back in his ear gave his driver a look. 'Insurance,' said Yeoman unaware of what Hedley was being advised.. 'Who would that be with, sir?'

'Hastings,' made Hedley surreptitiously wink to his partner. 'The licence then, sir?' was aimed at Elphick in the back but also in order for Hedley to respond.

'Three points I see sir,' was the answer Yeoman waited for from his temporary colleague. 'All seems in order, thank you. Just a case now of that turn you took off the A46 back there. I'd like you to assist us by allowing us to take a drugs swab.'

'Why? I've not done anything,' for somebody as experienced as Jason Yeomans his words were a clue to being on the right lines.

'Just part of the procedure, that's all sir,' he said as he unwrapped the Drug Wipe. 'No smell of alcohol so we'll not bother with a breath test this time in the morning. That is unless you had a few vodkas with your Corn Flakes. Right sir, just this final check, and we'll be done.'

'And if I refuse?' The look on the young man's face said everything.

'We'll still take you in, sir. You'll be charged with failure to provide if you still maintain that stance when we get to the station. Therefore, I have to tell you in all sincerity it is in your best interests to allow me to carry out the test. Remember,' he hesitated. 'It could as in some cases, be negative.'

Elphick hesitated for a moment sat in the back behind Hedley as if he was considering refusing. 'Alright then,' he sighed with some degree of reluctance.

'Just run your tongue around inside your mouth and then stick your tongue out.' Yeoman went through the procedure. 'Thank you sir.'

'You're not from around these parts,' DC Jamie Hedley suggested as they waited for the Wipe to do its work and come up with an indication. 'By your accent.'

'West Midlands.'

'Big place,' but there was no reaction.

'You work here do you?' Hedley asked.

'Yeh,' he reacted mildly with the sudden change of subject.

'And what do you do then, if you don't mind me asking?'

'Journalist. Well, sub-editor actually.'

'I won't ask,' was cheery and aimed to relax Elphick. 'For the paper I take it?'

'Mostly.'

'Think we all read it, but these days its more of a quick check with your website during the day in case something's been cracking off we don't know about.' Jamie then turned his attention to sport and to Gainsborough Trinity in particular as he was from the town. Even if he knew, this Elphick was chatty enough but not willing to admit if he knew if the new player rumoured to be joining his beloved Blues had actually signed.

'Sorry sir,' said Jason Yeoman eventually, offering Elphick sight of the line on the Drug Wipe. 'Think you'd better explain that line there,' he pointed at. 'Indicates you may be positive.'

'Shit! Fucking shit!' He exploded banging his hands down on his knees.

'You will now be taken to a police station,' said Jason Yeoman casually. 'In this case Lincoln Central for a blood test which will check as many as seventeen substances so I understand. Be such as Ecstasy, Ketamine and Heroin. This one,' he said wiggling the Swab. 'A roadside test will check for Cannabis or Cocaine or both in some cases,' he knew from experience had triggered the Cocaine link.

Yeoman arrested him there and then, whilst Jamie Hedley did the decent thing by talking to the receptionist in the *Lincoln Leader* building without going into details, other than the standard helping with our inquiries business.

Back at Central the pair were told one of the drivers involved in the three car crash near Sleaford earlier had been arrested on suspicion of TWOC (Taking Without Owners Consent).

'Good morning Kevin,' said DI Inga Larsson across a grey table in an interview room with Alisha O'Neill sat beside her. 'I'm Detective Inspector Inga Larsson head of the Major

185

Incident Team, here at Lincoln Central. This,' she gestured with her hand. 'Is my colleague Detective Constable Alisha O'Neill. We're here this morning Mr Elphick to ask a few questions and seek answers to a number of matters.. Do you understand?'

'Sorry,' he pulled a face of confusion. 'It's not like I've seen on the telly,' he said and looked all around the bare pale blue walls.

'Way we do things over this way,' was a get out. 'Let's make a start shall we and you can get back to work. Detective?' she asked Alisha who opened a brown folder and produced two photographs.

'Exhibit 1A,' Alisha tapped. 'And 1B,' she did the same to a second. 'Photographs as you can see are of a motor vehicle and the detail at the top printed automatically has the date and time this was taken by an ANPR camera at the Waltham Roundabout in Leicestershire.'

'Sorry,' Elphick said grimacing and scratching his head. 'Don't understand,' he said and released a pent up breath. 'Thought this was about drugs or something, those er...went on about.'

'We've moved on Kevin, sorry but...'

This was a well tried interview tactic to leave an uncomfortable silence in the middle of a verbal exchange. Someone will feel the need to break it.

'That copper in the car said something about a blood test.'

'Don't worry,' Larsson assured him. 'We'll come back to the drugs you've taken later. You happy with what has been photographed?' she asked and tapped the second photograph.

'Where's this, um Waltham and that other thing?'

'Near Melton Mowbray and what other thing, as you put it?'

'ANP something, was it?'

'Automatic Number Plate Recognition camera.'

'Happy now,' Larsson asked but it only resulted in the slightest of nods as he continued to peer down at the two prints on the table right in front of him. 'Next please, Alisha.' O'Neill opened the folder again and this time produced an A4 photograph of the driver of the same vehicle who was unmistakably sat at the table. 'Talk to me.'

There was no talk, not a single word, just a shrug with his eyes focused on looking at himself sat there driving.

'You?' O'Neill posed. 'Last Monday heading south' She leaned in slightly. 'Something wrong with your little Fiat?'

'What a bastard,' was whispered softly by Elphick to himself.

'Pardon,' Inga asked just as quietly.

'Done it again aint I?' and when he felt a need to look at her Larsson was looking at him unflinching.

Larsson always keen to provide her team with experience just touched Alisha with her elbow. 'Done what Kevin?'

'Cocked me bloody life up.'

'In what way?' O'Neill asked with a continuation of the gentle tone.

'Drugs again.'

'Problem?'

'Not that you'd notice,' he sniggered and looked up at Larsson once more to find her eyes trained on his. 'Got blown outta uni cause of 'em.' He glanced and there she was still looking. 'Bit o'luck when I was in the gutter...now all this crap. Second bloody chance gone for a ball of chalk. Shit!' he said and sat back arms folded head down but something made him peer at Larsson still looking directly at him..

Inga's phone told her she had a message and time to end the strategy which so often made people more than a little nervous. To such an extent in some cases their mind became to embroiled in what she was looking at, other thoughts went by the wayside. 'Excuse me,' she said and was on her feet and out of the room. When she returned she winked at Alisha something Kevin Elphick couldn't see.

'Ready?' said O'Neill once Larsson was back settled down. 'What was the reason for the journey we know you made,' and she tapped the photos. 'What did you do there?'

There was a hint of a smile for the first time. 'Maccy D's and a coffee.'

'Bit of a hike for a Cheeseburger.'

'Bacon Clubhouse double actually,' he said almost arrogantly as if a subject he was au fait with had woken him. One thing in his favour Elphick didn't sport one of those seriously bad Meet Me At McDonalds's haircuts, some low IQs go in for.

'All the way from Lincoln?'

'Yeh.'

'Why?'

'Coz I did. There a law agin it now?' was more spirited.

'No Mr Elphick there is not so far, but you have to admit driving somebody else's car for miles and miles for a bacon double or whatever it may have been, is a somewhat rather implausible story.'

'No comment.'

Her irritation being with the man had partially evaporated until that point. 'Please be sensible,' and Larsson was back to focusing on his eyes. 'Truth is Kevin. You were asked to drive somewhere that evening were you not? You were asked to be away from here for the whole evening. Am I correct?' Inga asked without actual evidence as she racked up the tone. 'Before you answer here's your situation right here and now in a nutshell,' she said tapping the desk with her forefinger.'

'Need a wee,' he said to break away from her look.

His past life, the high he'd felt on getting his A levels with his school mates all around him. The the sight of his proud parents bragging to their neighbours flashed through Kevin Elphick's mind once more sat on the toilet.. Then the downs. The "go on give it a try scaredy custard," suggestion he didn't ignore for once at that lousy bloody party in that cretin's dank flat. The spiral of despair, the dishonour and the cold streets he had stark memories of suffering for months on end. The utter humiliation of begging for crumbs among the constant kicking he got from drunks.

Crumbs indeed from the poor man's table; always the working man who tossed him a bit of change, and then that overcast day it all changed in that one moment.

"Now, just get on and do something bloody useful, son," his father had told him sternly when he'd dared knock on the door to what he had known as home for so many years, and beg for forgiveness, mercy almost.

All part of the Katushabe system he'd had to endure. Repair any damage, make peace with the most important people in his life. Family.

Larsson had taken the opportunity to have Alisha organize hot drinks all round and to check with Craig Darke about his message while Elphick was away.

'This is how it is,' Larsson said now clearer in her mind about what had been going on. 'You could very well be going back to the West Midlands. Your parents will if you have any sense be expecting you,' made his eyes widen and mouth open slightly, pointing a finger at him. 'Now, as if that wasn't bad enough, now you've let them down again, not to mention these good Katushabe people who saved you from a life of goodness knows what, and even gave you a decent job. You'll be back in their fold. Return I dare say to the disciplines they taught you, and your return so I understand could well see you working with two magazines closer to your home…'

'My…place. What about my place?' interrupted her speech.

Inga Larsson held out her hand. 'Keys please.'

'What!' he gasped and just for a moment both detectives thought he was going to refuse.

'As I understand it, people are already on their way here. The Katushabe family will move all your belongings back home for you, and hand the flat keys over to the landlord,' Larsson clicked her fingers as he dragged keys from his trouser pocket and handed them over by chucking them on the table indicating his mood.

'Need my car keys,' he remembered.

'This is what is going to happen. No matter what, you will go home tonight to your parents who are I understand expecting you. As we speak a car is being organised to collect you.'

'Don't understand,' and he was clearly confused.

'It's not what you don't understand it's what we need to understand which will make all these changes possible. You refuse to co-operate and you'll go back with no job. Your days at the *Lincoln Leader* are over. I think you need to be thankful for the extraordinary support you are receiving. Without a car, bearing in mind we of course cannot allow you to drive due to your drug taking and with nowhere to live except at home with

189

your parents means one thing. Almost certainly back to square one. Back to being homeless and destitute more than likely, and if you continue with the cocaine, my reading of the situation is you'll be back on the streets.' Larsson felt like a school teacher dressing down some kid for not doing his homework. 'You comply and you will still have a job, still retain the full backing of your employer, have your old bedroom back rather than back begging on the streets.'

Larsson sat back waiting, arms folded as the young man sat in front of her considered his options. She realized this would not be an instant decision as she assumed he was doing his level best to understand everything he'd been told and then come to grips with the sudden changes to his life.

She fixed him with a stern look. This was all for his sake, yet for a moment or two he attempted to stare the DI down.

She sat there waiting, hoping her words had got through the drug haze. Inga of course had absolutely no comprehension of what the effect of taking drugs felt like. She'd done innumerable courses of course, but for the young man sat there it was real. Not pictures on a screen, or a so-called expert waffling on and on. Was he at that moment in time, seeing life through a haze? Was his sight fine but his brain clogged up?

24

'Hi,' was just about managed before a breath was rushed out. 'Had a bloody 'nough o' this,' said a panting James Gosney stepping over the threshold at the back door of his friend's home.

'What now?' was a deeply frustrated sigh. 'What on earth are you up to now for crissakes?' as he was looked up and down.

'Know that Elphick kid,' said Gosney stood there in jogging bottoms, sweat shirt and trainers out of breath with one hand still on the white handle. 'Kevin, the one the Katushabe shower dragged off the streets, remember all that bollocks?' He had to catch his breath. 'Now they're up to some other bloody stupid Ugandan nonsense'

'Come in,' was gestured. 'Don't stand out there.' Gosney still trying to get his breath stepped into the big white kitchen. 'So Jimmy, what brings you here?'

'Joe public must think we're a bunch of tossers not knowing what's going on with one of our bloody own.'

'Sorry?'

'Always going to happen with that Swedish bitch running things.'

'Attractive woman, I've bumped into a time or two, but not literally unfortunately,' was chortled.

'Swedes always are,' was suggested. 'Look at Abba,' James chuckled. 'Just gets my goat all this.'

'Prop yourself up on there,' he was told as a kitchen high chair close to the breakfast bar was pulled out. 'Now tell me what this is all about?'

'I blame bloody Brexit,' he insisted as he was stepping up and slipping onto the white seat high on chrome legs. 'Thought we were keeping our borders shut to all the rif-raf. What happens? We've been out no time at all and our stupid police take on a Swedish tart.'

'Hardly Brexit my dear man. Leave was and always will be the right choice. Seem to think she's been here a while longer.'

'Whatever,' James sighed and rested his arms onto the breakfast bar surface. 'Trouble is readers don't have to deal with all this, like I'm running a paper clueless.'

'Drink?'

'Sorry. Can't stay long.'

'Coffee?'

'Thanks but no thanks. Just had it all up to here,' he tapped his sweaty forehead. 'In desperate need of a bit of fresh air, blow all this fog away. Been cooped up indoors all day just trying to grapple with all this fuckin' Elphick business.'

'You run round?'

'Yeh why?'

'Just wondered.'

'Needed it, blow the wind out me sails. Got soddin' father-in-law coming round,' he blew out a breath. 'God that'll be bloody boring.'

'So tell me. What happened with this...Elphick?'

'Turned up for work this morning so I'm told. Police car follows him into our car park and apparently there's this copper talking to him. Then after a while puts him in the police car, like you see, you know with all that mind your head crap. Then this other one not in uniform which seems a bit odd, came to reception to say he was helping them with their inquiries bullshit they come out with and were seizing the car. Sarah called me down urgently, by the time I got down there the cop car'd pissed off.'

'Why? What was wrong with it?'

'God knows.'

'How d'you mean, they took it?'

'This second one we're guessing was a copper, got in and drove his car away following the cop car, with Kev in it.'

'Not pissed was he?'

'At half eight?'

'Happens.'

'Next thing I'm getting no sense out the cop shop. Must be three hours later, bloody CX phones me, says Kevin Elphick's not coming back.'

'What?' was grimaced with a breath.

'Gave me some garbage about having a special project for him. What, heading for fuckin' Birmingham in a cop car?' was almost shouted. 'Be in Walsall with that new thing they're working on, but how'd the coppers get involved that's what I'd like to know. Like madness. Why not just say we're moving him?'

'Hang on, hang on. Are you seriously saying the police were acting like a taxi service for the Katushabes?'

'What it bloody looks like.'

'And Elphick himself?'

'Not seen him.'

'You called him, sent somebody round maybe?' he shrugged the questions

'Hey Charlie don't you think we've got enough on? Course I phoned, just went to "Hi this is me. Please Leave A Message After The Tone" bollocks. Five times.'

'And you left a message?'

'Of course. Look, we're too damn busy cobbling together a story. Trying to make sense of what's cracking off. Anyway you know what tossers they are. We do nothing and first light they'll be on to me wanting me to punt over what we've written about it all.'

'But if the Katoshabes are involved surely they'll not let you publish if your headline asks why the police are acting as their chauffeurs? You know better than that Jimmy. You'll have half your front page redacted. Anyway what have the police got to say?'

'Bugger all,' James blew out a breath. 'D'you know what,' was calmer. 'Been five-year-old little blue eyed girl and they'dve solved it all long before now.'

'How d'you mean?' he was asked.

'Way it works Charlie. All PR matey. All about good PR. They create so much bad news, especially down in the Met with all their in-built racism and sexism, stop and search they've got themselves caught doing, they're bloody desperate for one youngster getting herself kidnapped so they can bring out the big guns. Rachel was going on thirty. Bit like poor sods living on sink estates, they get third pickings at best. Dead woman on one o'them they could wait a good day before they get sight of a damn copper.'

'You serious?'

'There's been just one short sharp press conference and they put that foreign bitch in charge. Thought Brexit'd sort all that immigrant stuff out.'

'Yes Jimmy, you said. What's the news about Rachel?'

'Done their damn best to make it all as low profile as possible. I've got a hold the press story I'd normally give my hind teeth for, but it's going precisely nowhere.'

'Why would that be, do you think? Surely this is not just because she's not a little blonde kiddie?'

'So they can get back to what they enjoy most. Stopping some poor sods doing thirty two in a thirty and then blowing thirty six into their tube.'

'Sounds like you're having a series of bad days.'

'You can say that again!'

'Sounds…' made them both chuckle.

'Sure about that drink?' James was asked.

'Better not. Got dozy Eric round tonight; be after something you can bet your life. All I need after the day I've had.'

'Week you've had.'

'Seems an age ago.'

'What now?'

'It's like we're no further forward than we were when we got the first call. No names, no suspects. Almost as if its a deliberate act of obfuscation. All we've actually got are the two women, Basil and the farmer.'

'Basil?'

'The dog.'

'Of course'

'Them two and Cutforth the farmer and his missus we've interviewed, who tell us they've had just a couple of short sharp visits from some copper even though she was found on their land. Good walk away from the farmhouse to be honest Tony reckons, and she was found in a sheep trough. Or rather it was at one time apparently according to Cutforth. Could have done with a shot of that, but those CSI forensic bastards removed it.'

'If she was actually found in it, be where they'll find all the DNA and stuff.'

'All rusty and manky they told Tony and it'd not hold water any more.'

'Where do you as journalists go from here?'

'Just wait for developments, press statements and another press conference wouldn't go amiss. Tony went to the one they did have. Didn't even get offered a cup of tea. One thought though. Not nice for her parents but if this remains an unsolved like that Suzie Lamplugh business and Claudia Lawrence, means we have a story with legs we can keep going back to.'

'Yeh, but they went missing and have never been seen since and no body discovered. Rachel's in the morgue. Does at least mean they can bury her in time.'

'Got a paper to get out next week but right now where the Rachel Barnard latest revelation should be, we have a blank page.'

'Except for Elphick.'

'How d'you mean?'

'Got to be a story link there somewhere surely.'

'What d'you mean?'

'I don't know,' was shrugged. 'Could it have been him who topped her?'

'You're fuckin' joking!'

'Where was he, how did they get on? You could well have a scoop! Be teacher's pet in no time.'

'Fat chance.' James pulled in a breath as he sat thinking. 'Not a bad idea actually, thanks.'

'You upset somebody in the police by any chance? That why they're uncooperative maybe?'

'Just had all the diversity crap with a couple o'dames doing the routine checks, why?'

'They've gone silent with you about Rachel, and now they've grabbed Elphick from under your nose.' He saw the look on Gosney's face. 'What's your thinking?'

'Think you're right. Somewhere there's a story, all we have to do is fathom it.' Gosney sighed and his body slumped 'Know who would be good with this?' wasn't answered as he shook his head 'Rachel.'

'Hmm. Difficult.'

'Better get back,' Jimmy said sliding off his perch. 'That's cleared my head a bit, just talking always does me good, with nobody at home giving a toss of course, as per normal.'

'There's a sure fire way to stay safe James. Take it from me. Stay ahead of the game, jump before you're pushed, take care of problems before they happen...'

'But...'

'Time you made a decision and you know exactly what I'm, talking about, or do I need to spell it out for you?'

'Not easy.'

'I realize that, but your problem now is, if the brothers are involved with whatever Elphick was up to, will they allow you to publish?'

'Thanks,' said James Gosney at the door.

'Now you have an evening with Eric to look forward to.' Gosney pulled the door open. 'Happy days.'

25

Sean Joseph had called Larsson and asked to see her. She in turn had agreed, but with a busy Tuesday morning ahead had nominated Nicky Scoley to deal with him, unbenown to Joseph.

As ever, first thing every morning out in the Incident Room the industrious team were individually opening up their systems as they arrived, checking the overnights in readiness to follow up ineffectual leads and checking a whole galaxy of data each contact crucially provided.

Then as was often the case everything changed.

'Code Red,' said Inga at her door. 'PCSO from Louth called it in. Sandy,' there was really no need to mention him as he was already grabbing his coat and heading out. 'Co-ordinating please as usual. Jake, Nicky if you will.' she said and gestured for the pair to join her. Almost nobody else lifted their head as they were quickly scanning monitors for what Inga was telling them. 'Jamie,' brought his head up. 'If this is good to go, I'd like you to join Nicky on this one,' made him beam.

'Out in the town by the look of it,' said Jake. 'Make a change not being in a field.'

'With a dog!' and Sandy was gone.

'Ah but we don't know that yet.'

'First things first,' was Inga stood behind her desk. 'Got that Joseph heading our way Nicky was seeing, and unless we hear different we'll make a start getting organized for another homicide,' she smiled with. 'Jake, will you speak to Joseph and Nicky I'd like you off to Louth, check what we have and call it in. Sandy's heading out and CSI are on their way any time apparently. According to Kelly Goodyear this PCSO spotted a woman asleep in a shop doorway. Tried to wake her to get her to move on, no pulse thought it was natural causes and that's when she spotted marks on her neck,' she said looking down at her screen for updates. 'Not a rough sleeper vagrant. Casually dressed but without shoes, getting on for middle aged. We'll deal with morning briefing by which time we'll have got a better idea,' she told Jake. 'You've had one after another recently,' she said to Jake in case he was peeved about being left behind.

In truth he was pleased with a break from the tread-mill. Cases for MIT action had appeared so thick and fast of late. So fast in fact the computer was still punting out names of rivers for Ops names. This one was Operation Findhorn, he'd never heard of.

Nicky Scoley knew her Connor would already be on his way complete with cameras and video along with the rest of the Forensics bunch.

Blue sky and sunshine were in evidence when DS Nicky Scoley walked round into Vickers Lane in Louth as it was not a vehicle thoroughfare. Local officers had helped her find a place to park round the corner in a Pay and Display. Location of the incident was no longer a question as it hadn't been as she drove along Eastgate past a crowd of onlookers at railing barriers being held back by two local coppers. Police car and the CSI van with a tent in the doorway of Froggy's Comic Books shop in this Vickers Lane and local police back up the street keeping the voyeuristic nosey parker locals and yokels in Eastgate well away.

'Found it then,' said DC Sandy Maclachlan when he spotted her. 'Get parked okay?'

'Pay and Display round the corner.'

'You didn't pay.'

'Why not?'

'No charge for us with all this cracking off.'

'Thanks for that!' she sighed. 'What we got?'

'Apart from people wittering on aboot access,' he said pointing back up the street.

'Pedestrians only,' she said. 'So why's there a problem?''

'Still got moaning Minnies even oot here, and too far away for selfies.'

In the relative peace and quiet outside the shop, a quick briefing from her big Crime Scene Co-ordinator told Nicky how the local PCSO when reporting her find, immediately requested back-up and initially the response car had been parked across the shop doorway to prevent access to the crime scene. CSI had now erected one of their incitents. Kelly Goodyear the PCSO he advised Nicky, at first glance she had considered the slumped body to be just another dead drug user, but then noticed bruises on her neck.

Having her partner as the CSI chief photographer was always useful. Connor showing her the scene shots on his cameras meant she really had no need to push her way into the small incitent and disturb everyone just for a bird's eye view of the cadaver.

The still unknown victim was as had been reported fair haired and getting on for middle age. What the reports had not specified but obvious by her stature she would shop in the petite section. A cream blouse with a broderie anglaise effect to the collar along with navy blue slacks, none of which had been disturbed, except she had no shoes.

When she mentioned the lack of, Connor flicked through to show Nicky pictures of the soles of her feet which suggested she'd been carried there, with no sign of dirt or damage to her small feet in light fawn socks.

Nicky knew she could leave Sandy MacLachlan to the crime scene role he had been undertaking for some time, in the safe knowledge he'd keep all parties working towards the same ends.

What she needed to deal with was a bloke full of gob, the local police had with them, who she'd been told had arrived just before her.

'Detective Sergeant Nicola Scoley,' she said to him two shops further up the road waving her warrant in his face. 'I'm the Senior Investigating Officer at this time. You are sir?'

'Sam.'

'Sam?' a question he ignored.

'Look missus me shop opens at ten and need to get in there, so some bugger needs to get all this gubbins shifted, like early doors.'

Sometimes Nicky found life easier if she remained silent. Half listening to this guy in his twenties she guessed, jabbering on about his rights was such an occasion. How he paid his taxes and gets bugger all for it. Time you coppers sorted out the winos, tramps and dossers rather than stopping folk earning an honest day's crust and all the nonsense she'd heard dozens of times before.

Allowing people like him to just blabber on, good or bad, was frequently a useful source when investigating a new case. He took a breath.

'Sorry, sir. I'm afraid this is a crime scene, and I should imagine the CSI team are likely to be here most of the day.'

'You fuckin' what?'

'Enough of that,' she insisted pointing a finger right at him. 'You have two choices, you either co-operate or you spend the day at the local Police Station. No. I'll tell you what. If you swear again we'll make it Lincoln Central. Do I make myself clear?'

His cocky demeanour shifted slightly. 'Look, hey, need to get in, that's all like.'

Did she really have to explain to this character how CSI were maintaining the integrity of the crime scene until the pathologist came up with the whys and wherefores they could pursue?

'Name?'

'Sam.'

'Sam what?' she tried again.

'Sam Froggatt everybody calls me Froggy.'

He was slightly shorter than her with a bit of a lager paunch despite his age. A day or two's worth of stubble and his hair was unkempt in a way which suggested he made it look like that deliberately. Probably some comic book character's look.

'Address,' he gave. 'Keys?'

'What?'

'Your keys please sir. Our CSI team need access to your shop.'

'You're bloody joking.'

'No sir,' she said still with her hand out.

'What'm I gonna do about customers?' he said as he scrambled about in his jeans pocket for a bunch of keys he handed over.

'Which is the front door?' she asked and Nicky released it from the bunch. 'You wait there. Don't move. Won't be a sec.' Nicky Scoley walked away to the incitent and poking her nose in handed over the key to Shona Tate the Crime Scene Manager and they had a quick chat about the shop owner. Back to this Froggy she had a suggestion to make. 'Am I right in thinking there's a back way in?' she knew as Sandy'd told her uniforms were already there.

'Yeh.'

'What's at the rear behind the actual shop?'

'Kitchen,' he grimaced as if it was a difficult question. 'Store room, bit of an office and the bog.'

At this very early stage and with no prognosis from the pathologist as yet she didn't see this creature as a killer. Somebody no doubt had heard what was cracking off and given him a call. Anyway, she knew of no other occasion when the killer had dumped his victim outside his own shop. Heard about a good few arsonists returning to see their handiwork though.

'Right. Here's the deal Froggy,' she used his nickname in an attempt to build some sort of rapport. 'Once the body has been removed, the CSI team will gain access to the shop.'

'Wow! Hang on. What....body?' and looked almost excited.

'A person has been found dead in your doorway.'

He flicked his eyebrows at that as if it was part of a knowledge digestive system. 'Really?' he gasped. 'Increds!'

'Yes really.'

'Bugger me.'

'I'll allow you to gain access from the rear, but,' her finger was there again. 'You make absolutely no attempt to gain entry to the front of the shop. Understand?' He nodded.

'Customers come in the back.'

'No. Just you, and I'll put somebody on the door if I have to.'

'You're serious.' Had that only just dawned on him?

'If I were you I'd make the most of this opportunity presented to you. Call the local press, offer to give them an on the spot report, tell them who you are. Go on WhatsApp, Twitter, Facebook anything you like and tell the world you'll be opening, what shall we say?' Nicky looked all around. 'Tomorrow to be on the safe side. Dish out your email and phone number and if this goes viral it could be your lucky day.'

'Who's dead then?'

'Sorry. Too early to release the name as the family need to be informed first; wouldn't be fair. You up for this?' It wasn't exactly enthusiastic but he gestured acceptance.

Nicky was working on the possibility people would react to the publicity he created. Be good if witnesses came forward for their few moments of fame, not just to what had cracked off but anything different, out of place happenings or sight of vehicles involved. It was now gone ten and according to the pathologist the woman had been dead for at least eight hours probably more.

The nerd gathering interest from the Comic Book crowd could provide her with useful information or if not it'd just be the tourism pound and Froggy to benefit, provided he was switched on enough.

Nicky knew she was a long way from having the decisive knowledge from the pathologist who'd trundled up from Boston, into whose care this woman was about to be placed, as he used his skills to determined the cause of her death. Nicky knew she was left with the not so easy bit. Reason.

When Jamie Hedley appeared from Lincoln with Sandy MacLachlan still liaising with the CSI and local police, she had instructed him to check locally for private CCTV. A call back to Lincoln Central had them checking any authority based cameras they could advise about.

Time to check out this Froggy character as he wandered off to gain access to the rear of his scruffy shop. Dressed in denim shorts, red trainers with no socks and a bizarre but poignant black Comic Book t-shirt with full colour "What?" "When?" and "Who?" slogans. Nicky knew he was just the type to wear a baseball cap back to front and come out with that increds nonsense.

Exactly Nicky's own thoughts as the wagon turned up in readiness to transport the victim off to Boston. She was asking the same questions of herself with the addition of 'Why?'

She called Alisha back at base. 'Tell me everything I need to know about a Sam Froggatt, assume Samuel known as Froggy, who runs Froggy's Comic Books shop in Vickers Lane in Louth. PNC and social media, everything and anything we've got you can find.' and gave her this Froggy's home address, or at least the one he'd given. Also told her to keep an eye on social media to see what sort of reaction he managed to generate.

Then Nicky wondered if she could be cheeky enough to pop round and ask this Froggy if he could make her a coffee. Making a brew for everybody was asking as bit much unless he had a shop full of cups and mugs.

When her app told her there's a Cafe Nero in Mercer Row past Market Place she'd driven down, she felt much better. State of the mugs in the shop may well be an issue. Time to open up the street and just cone off Foggy's shop before she thought about that.

'Sergeant Nicky,' she heard accented Scot Sandy call and walked to the tent. 'Doc wants a wee word,' dressed from head to foot in white and pretty blue overshoes, he said gesturing for her to enter.

Sat on the pavement alongside the dead woman the new to her Home Office Pathologist, held up an evidence bag between two fingers for her to peer at but not hold.

'What do you see Sergeant?'

'Nicky, please.' she struggled to see in the poor light. 'Looks like a screwed up piece of paper.'

'This,' he said over top of his horn rimmed glasses, 'was in our victim's mouth.'

'What d'we know about it?' she asked trying hard to get a closer look.

'Not unravelled as yet. Need to check saliva for DNA, fingerprints when it's all disentangled by these guys. What I can tell you is, there's typing on it. As if a type written sheet has been screwed up and pushed into her mouth. Goodness knows why? Post Mortem or forensics we have to hope will solve the conundrum. Love a bit of a puzzle,' seemed an odd remark and Nicky guessed it was more likely in this day and age to be off a printer. He pointed at one of the CSI team. 'And these,' he said for three cards to be handed over in a small purse like pouch. 'Were in her pocket. Judy Marsh, looks local.'

'Thank you, sir,' she said taking hold.

'One last thing,' he said pointing to the bruises on her neck. 'Strangling someone with your bare hands takes time. Likely scenario, but don't take this as gospel, damage to her neck made her unconscious then she was killed in some other way. Likely within the past eight hours but could be ten. PM'll tell me more. All yours Detective Sergeant,' annoyed her but not as much as his gesture to wave her away, as if it was none of her business.

Outside Nicky was checking the three cards when Jamie Hedley re-appeared.

'Made a note. Four places with CCTV close by, but not at all sure they'll show much more than immediately outside the premises..'

'Worth trying. Still waiting for news on East Lindsey's cameras from Central.' She held up the three cards. 'Found on the body, plus a sheet of screwed up paper stuffed in her mouth.'

'You're joking.'

'Why does nothing surprise me these days?'

'What's that all about? Too much telly that's my guess. Our perp got that off one of those noir Swedish things with fifty episodes.'

'Don't let the boss hear you say that,' they both chuckled about. 'Look at this,' she said handing one of the cards to him.

'Meridian Book Club,' he read. 'Judy Marsh.'

'Be one of those groups where women get together to all read the same book.'

'Then pontificate.'

'It's a start,' and Nicky was back on her phone.

'So's paper stuffed in her mouth.'

'Boss,' she said on her phone and began to explain about the paper in the mouth.

'Sandy's been on. We're chasing CCTV but doesn't look hopeful. Sounds very peculiar to me with that paper business.'

'Know who she is now. Got a Nat West Visa Debit card,' she read the number slowly. 'In the name of Mrs J. Marsh. A Shell card and a membership card for the Meridian Book Club.'

'That all?'

'So far.'

'She could get cash, buy petrol and read a book, but nothing else?'

'Not so far.'

'Tell you what,' Inga suggested. 'We'll do the bank and when we have an address get local Family Liaison over to the home as they more than likely know them, so we can all get on. Michelle will check on this book club for you as its local, but hold fire on any of this stuff until the family have been informed.'

'Jamie's got local shop CCTV he's off to check for us, after we've had coffee. CSI have got their brew going, so we're taking a break and when we're done it'll be Sandy's turn.'

'Keep in touch,' and as Nicky was expecting the call to end: 'Paper in the mouth eh? Interesting one.'

Sat in Cafe Nero with Jamie the news came through from Michelle about the victim, and her address.

Before she could think about that her phone pinged again. Message from Alisha back at Central. Any thoughts she may have had about this Froggy being an enterprising young man running his own business were damaged when Alisha told her about his family.

'Guess what?' Alisha posed.

'The dead woman's his mother,' Nicky joked and held her breath for a split second then realized he was Froggatt and the victim Marsh. 'Sorry, sorry, carry on,' she said grinning at Jamie.

'Our Froggy,' she told Jamie once the call was over and read from her jottings. 'Lives at home with his parents Wayne and Shelly Froggatt on Herefrith Farm.' This Herefrith, according to Alisha was a centuries old Bishop of Lindsey, and he was also the Bishop of Winchester.

'Can't be both. No Google back there then of course so I'll let 'em off.'

'This is more interesting. His father Wayne owns many properties in and around Louth.'

'Another poor farmer you'll not see on a bike.'

'Including,' Nicky went on. 'The shop in Vickers Lane, but also,' she slipped in to stop Jamie. 'Cannabis possession and sharing got him a warning, second time somebody was lenient and only told his parents.'

'Not *what* you know, but *who*.'

'Be punishment enough. I can just imagine what my dad would say.'

'So he's not that enterprising, probably runs the place rent free and daddy picks up the bills. Means he's playing at it.'

'Spends all day reading comics,' was possibly not that far short of the mark.

26

Certain situations were always difficult Nicky frequently discovered. Bad enough delivering bad news to family but somehow doing the same to a friend or a neighbour seemed more fraught with danger. Telling a loved one allowed greater elements of sympathy, but taking the same caring approach to a stranger who may not even like the victim was so full of caution.

'You know this for certain?' this Olivia Ranby queried with the pair sat at her dining table in a detached house on the outskirts of Louth along Legbourne Road.

Outside the early morning sunshine had been replaced by a dull cloudy sky.

'Yes we do, and her husband admits she's been missing.'

'How long?'

'Said since yesterday evening. Admitted to our Family Liaison team, but hadn't phoned it in because he knew we'd only take any action after 24 hours.'

'But I saw her yesterday morning,' said Ranby as if that made the whole thing impossible. 'We had coffee.'

'What can you tell me about Judy?'

'Small in stature but not in attitude,' said Olivia Ranby the Meridian Book Club organizer after a few moments consideration. 'Above all else Judy was totally honest and trustworthy. In any organization, and the book club is no different, some members can be quite a challenge. Have to admit in the club Judy was pretty much my go to ally. Somebody I could trust implicitly. Discuss anybody and anything and I know none of what we had conferred about would ever come rolling back to hurt or embarrass me.'

'Did you meet up away from the club?'

'I'm afraid not. Bump into Judy in town we'd maybe go for a coffee. As I said we did just that yesterday as it happens. I was in town and we came across each other and rather than sit alone she joined me. Be some months ago since we last did that.' She sighed and shook her head again. 'This is not real, its...'

'How did she seem?'

'Pretty much like the Judy I've always known.'

'When you met up for coffee would the conversations always be book club orientated?'

'Oh, certainly not. We have too much gibberish about the latest offering from Patricia Cornwell or Peter James at our monthly meetings. Not to mention two who are only interested in fiction claimed to have been written bv celebrities nobody's ever heard of.'

'How long had you known her?'

'Look,' she said as she slapped her hands down onto her thighs. 'I could do with a coffee right now after that news, how about you?' It was not long since she'd had coffee with Jamie, but it might help oil the wheels.

'Yes, fine.'

'Latte, cappuccino?'

'Latte, please.'

Nicky Scoley was left alone to look all around the tidy home and out onto a well kept quite large mature garden. Too many pointless ornaments to her mind and a shelf full of hardback books, some of which she recognized.

There were two free-standing glass-fronted display cabinets given over to a large display of china Otters. Apart from that there was little on display apart from a fancy doily on a round wooden table in the bay window with an empty flower pot sat on it.

Three pictures. One on each wall depicting paintings of old tenement buildings early in the last century. Copies of a much larger originals she surmised. Multi-coloured wall to wall carpet and small rugs each one set against the armchair and small sofa. No wallpaper, no wall lights but heavy navy blue drape curtains tied back.

She took that opportunity sat there waiting to check her phone for messages. Coffees delivered to the table and they were back to chatting.

'You were asking how long I've known Judy. Got to be two years maybe a bit more. Came back from Australia with her husband. Her mother's not at all well...oh my God!' Olivia gasped hand to mouth. 'What about her poor mother has anybody spoken to her?'

'Our Family Liaison will handle all that through her husband.'

'Well I hope you do. Be awful if she got to hear from somebody else. Not in good health, not good at all Judy was saying.'

'I expect her husband will be dealing with all that.'

'If he does.'

'What d'you mean by that?'

'He's a sheep shearer you know. Travis.'

'Is that a problem?'

'No not at all. Just gets so busy at times as you can imagine, could easily slip his mind. Judy was saying he'll be off again any time soon.'

'Excuse me,' said Scoley and got up from the table, phone to ear. 'Boss. I'm with one of Judy Marsh's best friends from the book club. She's just mentioned Marsh's mother is not in good health. Can we just check Family Liaison are up to speed with that, rather than the poor dear hear it from a stranger or on the news. Thanks.' She sat back down. 'My boss is sorting it.' she sat back down and took her first sip of Latte. 'You were saying about...her husband.'

'Travis,' was a reminder. 'Australian you know.'

'Is Judy?'

'No,' she scoffed. 'Went to Australia as a child with her parents. Her father was some sort of engineer they were crying out for at one time. Judy married, had a son and then her parents decided to return back home. D'you know I think I'm right in saying her grandparents became ill back here. Like history repeating itself. But,' she shrugged I might have got that wrong. 'Anyway Judy stayed on rather than disturb her son's education. Then got divorced and think it would be three or four years ago she met this sheep shearer.' Olivia stopped to sip and ponder. 'Look I'll be honest, I'm struggling to piece this all together because their lives were never that straight forward with all this coming and going. Alan and I often wonder if we're really boring living the lives we do, with none of the turmoil others seem to suffer.'

'Or thrive under. But I know what you mean.'

'Anyway,' said Olivia. 'Think I'm right in saying somehow he and Judy got together and my feeling is...oh,' she sagged. 'Forgot. Travis was married with two sons I think it is and divorced. Could be girls, sorry. Or at least she says he was. Anyway, she and Travis got together but as I say always had this feeling from things she's said she was not happy being left on her own for long periods while he was away shearing all those sheep. Excellent money she was saying, and guess that was the incentive for his job. Then Judy's father died, and she flew home for the funeral and soon realized her mother's health was suddenly deteriorating probably as a result, and they both came over here to live.'

'Him as a sheep shearer?'

'It's a year round thing you knows so far as I understand. Travels abroad and all sorts when its out of season here.' Olivia was back to her cappuccino.

'Do I gain the impression you're not that enamoured by him?' Scoley queried.

Olivia pulled a face. 'To be honest we don't know him that well really. Only know from things Judy said, but with Alan it's this sort of Australian in your face macho attitude he can't abide. Good at his job they say.'

'What does Alan do, just out of interest?'

'Landscape gardener,' made sense having been looking out at the lovely garden.

'Any others you meet up with from your book club?'

'Not really, no. We meet once a month, discuss the book we've just read and decide on the next one.'

'These all hardbacks?'

'No, no. Most buy paperbacks and an increasing number of us download these days.'

'Nobody else you can point me in the direction of?'

'Another member you may wish to talk to is Natasha. Now she is different. Reads paperback and hardbacks during the day but at night in bed reads another book on her Kindle.'

'I'd get confused.'

'Natasha Hutton,' Olivia returned to. 'She and Judy were close friends. Met up for coffee that sort of thing on a pretty regular basis. Snack lunch too sometimes. Some members I've never met up with in a social setting apart from our annual Christmas get-together.' She opened her phone. 'I can give you Natasha's number. Judy told me on the quiet Natasha's in the process of writing a book.'

'Do you all do that?' the DS asked.

'Many try, but find it's much harder than you imagine. They do say everybody has a book inside them. It's getting it down on paper's the problem. I wrote short stories and articles at one time, but I think the months of serious hard slog needed is not for me. Here you are,' she said passing her phone to Nicky.

'What else can you tell me about the book club?' the DS asked after jotting down the number.

'Been going close on ten years now. We've got 26 members I think it is.'

'And they all attend your meetings?'

'No, not at all. Probably fifteen or twenty usually. Think some drop out when they don't fancy the book of choice, which is what I meant about the different types I have to deal with. Got a few who are only interested in specific genres, some are into what one or two of us call the cosies. Some of them make a real fuss about coming up against bad language and that sort of snowflake nonsense. Getting a couple of dozen women to agree on one book is not at all easy, let me tell you. Some want love with happy endings, there's the cosy few and others are after mysteries packed with twist, turns and a good deal more like real life.'

'All women?'

'Yes. Had odd men from time to time but think it being almost all females puts them off. As I say, some members can prove awkward at times, often I think for the sake of it. But to be honest we have none of the pretentious twaddle and nasty point scoring I've found in the two previous clubs I belonged to.'

'Anything else you think we need to know about Judy?'

'She had fervent likes and dislikes, and to be honest I don't see her and Travis as a pair. You know how it is sometimes you wonder how on earth people got together, what do they have in common.'

'Opposites attract.'

'Appreciate that. But a lovely caring gentle soul with the big muscular full of himself Australian, I'm not so sure.' Nicky Scoley could sense the traditional gender stereotyping revealing its ugly head and the masculine expectations she imagined were still prevalent down under. 'He's one of those got to be doing stuff. Out helping with football, got a pal she talks about him visiting on a regular basis. Think at times Judy was quite lonely.'

Nicky had early on spotted a habit she had of rolling her tongue around inside her cheek, and had just done it again.

'You mentioned likes and dislikes.'

'Fervent Tory despite that Boris. Absolutely had no time whatsover for the LGBTQ element of society, but then on the other hand was an ardent supporter of BAME and had black and Asian friends.'

If she knew Judy was quite lonely, why hadn't Olivia spent more time with her if only for a regular coffee meet up in town? Nicky's phone rang and she excused herself and went back the way she'd come out through the front door.

'Yes guv,' she said as she stood out on the path.

'Nicky. The husband kicked Family Liaison out, would you believe? Told them in no uncertain terms to get on their bikes and accused them of being nosy parkers.'

'Good job Deanna and Julia are not called Sheila,' Larsson ignored.

'Hardly been there any time at all. Been very obstinate and un-cooperative. Told them and I quote, to rack off, you can look up for yourself if you can't guess. What d'you know about him?'

'Australian, sheep shearer.'

Nicky continued walking to her car all the time explaining what she'd been told by Olivia Ranby. Said all about Judy Marsh going to Australia with her parents, married and divorced then married again and when her mother became ill returned back to England to be with her.

'Been given the name of another member of the book club who was Judy Marsh's best pal apparently.'

'Best if I go off and see this Marsh I think. What d'you say his name is?'

'Travis.'

'Interesting. Where are you now?'

'Still in Louth talking to Mrs Ranby about this book club and Judy Marsh.'

'I'll head out your way and have a word with this...Travis. Might take Jake with me. You finish up there and see the other woman if you would. Bell you later. Just had Jamie on. He's already got one CCTV disk.'

'See you later maybe.' She'd spotted a message on her phone from him.

Nicky wondered how much of this Judy's outdated attitudes were constructed by her upbringing. An educated woman was quite possibly following a preordained way of thinking. Her past gathered at her mother's knee would not allow entry for modern day thinking from a different viewpoint.

Back in the house Nicky Scoley apologized to Olivia, explaining it was her boss on the phone and they chatted until Nicky had finished her drink. Handed her a card and bade the woman farewell with the proviso she may need to talk to her again.

With scribbled instructions she headed off to find this Natasha Hutton who Olivia had kindly checked to see if she would be at home.

27

After the MIT briefing Jake Goodwin had disappeared to find somewhere quiet for this chinwag with Sean Joseph who'd invited himself in. Somewhere down the line he'd been told how most of the material published by the *Leader* was in fact created elsewhere centrally or bought in from freelance writers.

Although not having read so much of Rachel's work as Nicky or the boss had done, he knew she was keen to gain an insight to the workings of the publishers. Settled with an in-house coffee each in a small windowless room used for that type of cosy chat or a place out of harms way to sympathize with relatives and friends of victims. Having explained without going into detail the reason for both the Detective Inspector and Nicky Scoley not being available, Jake Goodwin turned their chat from the weather and troubles in Ukraine to the *Leader* itself.

'When my colleagues went to the *Leader* they were both surprised how few journalists there were. I've got it in my mind that may well be the situation with most papers in this day and age what with technology and dwindling sales in paper form. Having said that, I have to ask why are universities churning out people with degrees in journalism, if there's little or no work?' He grimaced. 'Guess that's the case with everything and why most graduates work in bars.'

'How many banks have closed?' was not the response Goodwin was expecting. 'Universities still run banking courses.' He stopped to ponder. 'Think more and more that's based around financial technology and like us we no longer need shorthand and typing. Well not on a typewriter, and these days of course everybody can,' he seemed to find slightly amusing. 'What you need to understand is,' said Sean. 'As with virtually all the newspapers in the group the *Leader* is in effect a satellite station.

Handling in the main very local news and to a certain extent last minute news appertaining to the county.'

'But in that case where did Rachel fit in?'

'She was just like them initially, but as a sideline before we got together actually, she wrote a couple of really good articles she submitted to the powers that be...'

'The brothers.'

'Pretty much. Not to them directly, but obviously they got wind of them through the Features fella in Birmingham. They liked what she'd written, asked for more and in the end offered her a six week run in the *Leader* as long as they were Lincolnshire specific.' He stopped to sip his coffee. 'Bit ridiculous when you think about it. They buy in stuff and just change it to suit each paper, yet they asked for Rachel to be county distinct. Anyway,' he pressed on. 'Over time as well as becoming a permanent weekly fixture they took her work which was not necessarily local and published them across the group. In much the same way they do with items from contributing editors.'

'Do any of the others out at Witham St Hughs do that?'

'Not that I know of,' brought jealousy to Goodwin's spiky mind as a serious motive. 'In the main the major articles come from freelance contributors. Book reviews tend in the main to be books written by reality TV nobodies, but the word celebrity sells for a reason I've never been able to fathom,' he grinned with. 'Local authors don't get a look in alas, even though they suggest they are a county paper. Gardening articles are bought in. Cooking by a Bake Off heat runner-up whose face doesn't fit gets farmed out to all the locals. Health and Beauty and the rest are all centrally produced and in the main come from elsewhere. Some even from beauty products PR people.' He stopped to drink more coffee. 'These freelancers are in effect the same as Rachel but the difference with her was, she was actually employed.'

Sandy haired, slim and decently dressed, he lacked any of the bizarre attachments many artistic types get drawn to for some reason. With a pale complexion he was certainly not one for sitting out in the sun. His shirt of plain blue had a very thin white stripe which at times was almost imperceptible. Black what looked very much like chinos and matching Chelsea boots. The attraction from Rachel's standpoint was obvious.

'How much of the paper is created out at their place then?'
Tilting his head to one side the DS gave Sean a small smile.

'About twenty five percent at a guess.'

'And as a web and graphic designer but how do you fit into all this?'

'I turn the local news Gosney and his team come up with, combine it with the regular features and anything else Birmingham fob off on them, and turn it into something you can read easily.' He hesitated. 'That's the theory. Tend to work across the whole area's papers mostly, but also some aspects of one or two of their magazines.'

'The web?'

'These days of course the paper version is seen by less and less. Just the old folk in the main. I keep the website up to date as the news has to be more attractive, shorter and punchier than it does paperwise.'

'Advertising I take it is done centrally then?'

'Yes and no,' he responded. 'Birmingham or the Brummies as we call them, deal with the major advertising agents, but we do have a couple here who handle local stuff. The local garage, shops and the like.' He stopped and then said. 'Even the intimations are dealt with elsewhere. Not that many people do these days. Chuck it on Twitter or Facebook and the world knows within minutes. You want to put your grandad's death in, the number you phone is not here at the *Leader*.'

'And Rachel, she went to the office every day like you and wrote her column?'

'Did a lot more. Know this sounds a bit odd but I'm sure Gosney often used her to give dull stories a bit of life. Yes of course she wrote her column but obviously writing that and doing research didn't fill a whole week. As well as doing bits and pieces of re-writing for the *Leader* she did work for other papers and magazines in the group by writing articles.' He pulled in a breath. 'Think you need to see this,' he said. 'Reason I came,' he told Goodwin and from his casual grey jacket he produced a USB stick from the top pocket. 'Found the red one.'

'The missing one?'

Sean explained how and where he had discovered it and after finishing their coffees Jake Goodwin then took him along to the busy Incident Room with people setting the systems up in readiness for the Louth unexplained. There he pulled two chairs close together opened his laptop and plugged in the stick.

'Times I've done this,' said Sean. 'Sat with Rachel reading her work,' sounded so forlorn and Goodwin felt for him having to deal with memories constantly. Sean Joseph guided him through some interesting and intriguing stuff coming up on the screen the DS read pieces of. 'Here we go,' he said as he ushered Goodwin to move down to the next article.

Jake Goodwin sat there reading and in doing so was as mesmerized as he had ever been with the outcome of any case he'd ever been involved in. Sat there open mouthed he had to keep remembering to close, and the words he uttered slowly but surely caught the attention of the whole room.

'My god! That's an absolute shocker,' Goodwin gasped when he finally reached the end. 'On so many levels,' he said sat back staring at the screen hands on the top of his head, mouth partially open.

DI Inga Larsson tablet in hand returning from updating the Darke boss along the corridor, sarcastically knocked on her own office door.

'Come in,' Jake called out grinning when he looked up to see who it was. She took a seat waiting for him to finish a phone call and set his phone down among all the paperwork.

'We need to get off to Louth, talk to this Travis Marsh he's the husband of the our Judy Marsh cadaver.' She told Jake all about how the Family Liaison women had been kicked out by this Australian. 'What about Sean?'

'Gone with Alisha to get another coffee each.'

'He's still here, good.' she said as Jake got to his feet to vacate her big black chair, as Inga waved her tablet at him. 'Got a DNA match hot off the press.'

'I know,' Jake smiled at her as she took his place.

'What?' was gasped with a grimaced look.

'James Gosney or David Petrie.'

'How the f....?'

Jake held up the missing red memory stick. 'All on here. Missing part of the jigsaw.'

'Where's that appeared from?' the DI gasped loudly. 'We were told it was missing.'

'Sean brought it in. It's what he called in about. Rachel's mother was all for offering all her clothes and goodness knows what to a charity shop for any didicoy to just walk in and poke their noses into her business. Sean offered to do it for her. At least deal with her clothes, sort through them. Throw out those on their last legs. Even planned to give some bits a good wash, rather than have people talking on line about her smelly socks.'

'And?' frustrated Inga asked up as she sat down. Jake had just blown her theory right out of the water.

'Little pocket in jeans,' and he slid the memory stick down towards his trouser pocket. 'In there, hidden from view and could easy have gone in the wash or to some rag bag place.'

'That was in her pocket all the time?'

'Nobody knew it was.' Jake waved the stick. 'Like the crown jewels, this is where the money was. These are the big stories, the hard hitting one's she earnt serious money from.' He grinned to annoy the boss slightly. 'Under false names.' Jake bit his bottom lip. 'Her false names and the big one it appears is by somebody she called Burton Dunne.'

'A bloke?' she almost shouted. 'Somebody thought he was getting rid of this…'

'Burton Dunne,' a nodding, grinning Jake responded.

'Oh my word. What d'you reckon, in the dark she gets smacked over the head and suddenly lying there at his feet is Rachel Barnard and not this Dunne.' She looked at Jake. 'That what you're saying?'

'Chances are, ' he shrugged. 'Pretty much sums it up I reckon. Our man discovers who this Dunne really is and hey presto. Plus she also used the name Amelia Odling, very Lincolnsheer,' he emphasised.

'Unbelievable!' His Swedish boss sat there dumbfounded. 'Careful as we go,' she managed. 'This will create more than a bit of a storm, remember.'

'Crossing Ts time,' he guessed she'd not fully comprehend. 'Attention to detail,' was another English lesson.

'Time for Louth and our digeridoo man.'

'Wonder if he's got a decent barbie?'

28

By the time Nicky Scoley reached the home of Natasha Hutton it was obvious she had been called by Mrs Ranby to tell her of the demise of their friend. Judy Marsh.

Invited in Nicky had allowed the woman to sit down first and as she did so she glanced up at the Detective Sergeant with an anxious expression she made no attempt to hide.

Nicky had seen the body of Marsh in the shop doorway and to some extent this Hutton woman physically came as no surprise. It was something Nicky had never understood about pairs of women. The fat with the thin, the quiet as a mouse with the loud mouth, the tall with the short. Somebody had once suggested it was all to do with competition or lack of.

This Natasha Hutton was robust and taller than Nicky, but even so she had perched herself on the edge of her brown leather armchair. Nicky guessed the reason being her need to plant both her slippered feet together flat on the floor with knees pressed together. A convenient place for her forearms to rest with fists clasped.

'Must thank you for seeing me at such short notice,' Scoley started with after talk about her finding the house, the weather and obvious reasons for her needing to visit. 'Olivia said you'd likely be at home.'

'Yes, she called.'

'Appreciate it,' deep breath. 'Are you happy for me to call you Natasha?

'Tasha, please. Yes. Olivia explained,' Scoley had realized already.

'Before Olivia phoned, had you heard anything?'

'No. Nothing.'

'And are you au fait with the circumstances surrounding what happened to your friend?'

'Still trying to get my head round it. Like its somebody on the news but this is real, this is Judy you're talking about. Why?'

'Exactly what we're trying to find out.' Nicky paused. 'Had you heard anything earlier?'

'Used to listen to Radio 2 but the music is just...getting too old that's my problem. Why don't they have good tunes and words you can listen to any more and sing along with?'

Scoley had exactly the same question but no answer save for the dark boss going on endlessly about the day the music died. 'Do you work?'

'Three or four times a week most weeks, at the charity shop. Where I was this morning. People coming in said a woman'd been found dead.'

'That as a permanent job or volunteer?'

'Volunteer.

'Enjoy it?'

'Doing some good and better than sitting round here all day.' This Natasha's fair hair was very fine and looked as though because it was freshly washed she could do nothing with it

'Mind if we talk about your relationship with Judy?' was answered with a gentle shake of her head. 'How long have you known her?'

'Since she came back.'

'From Australia?'

'Well yes, when she joined the club.'

The distinct lack of lucid conversation meant this woman more than likely wouldn't respond well to pressure. Retreating back into her shell was a real danger.

'Did you see much of each other away from the meetings?'

'Quite a bit,' was at least the confirmation Scoley was looking for from what Olivia Ranby had said.

'Would you please explain what you mean by quite a bit?'

'One day a week,' she said and stopped while Scoley was in receipt of another anxious look. 'I work mornings or afternoons whenever they need somebody. Not always same ones as I'm flexible, having no children, no real commitments. One week it'll be coffee on a Tuesday morning, next it could be Thursday afternoon if I've been working in the morning. Sometimes we did lunch.' She looked out of the window as if reminiscing about meeting up with Judy. 'Her not driving meant we didn't meet up as often as we could what with a serious lack of buses.'

'What about at the book club?'

'Don't know why,' said Tasha as she finally sat back, crossed her legs in brown jeans below a loose cream nylon jumper. 'We just sort of hit it off. One daft woman's got this ridiculous idea new members should be allocated a mentor,' she grinned. 'On how to read a book? I ask you.'

'A bit odd.'

'She's odd alright. We like the same books, page turning intrigue, twists and turns and a good dollop of honesty. Not too much grime, though to my mind policemen with a drink or women problems traipsing down dark alleys after a serial killer, appear too often.'

'Are you married? Partner?'

'No thank you,' Scoley waited. 'Did away with all that husband business a good time ago and I'm not into this partner nonsense except I do have to use it in my writing these days of course, or readers'll think all my characters are old fashioned.' she hesitated. 'Like me, I suppose.'

'Have you written much?'

'Three so far.'

'Published?'

'No,' she said sadly. 'First two I realize now are not good enough, but then thirty rejection letters should have told me that. Third one I've got high hopes for.'

'What's it about?'

'About a woman discovering her husband is nothing like the man she thinks he is.' She bit her teeth together and pulled a face. 'Bit autobiographical. First two were subjects I really knew nothing about and told myself I could fudge it.' She shook her head. 'Why I think this one is better. Based on my own experiences to a degree but extended a great deal into a murkier world. Turned a matter of trust into something much much worse.'

'What's it called?'

'Truth Will Out.'

'Do any of the others write?'

'Not that I know of, but then they don't know I've had a try. Except Judy that is.'

'You told her?'

'Sent her a copy of the latest one. By email.'

'Had she read it?'

'Loved it, and with Judy you know she's being honest not just saying that to please a friend.' She smiled broadly. 'She's not seen the other two though,' she chuckled. 'Need a bit of tinkering in places from things she said, but yes I'm pleased with it. Think I might dedicate it to her now.'

'Our crime scene people will be delving into what's on her...laptop is it?'

'Yes. Nice one too. Fairly new I think.'

'Our keyboard clever dicks will probably come across it.'

'Why d'they need to do that?'

'In case Judy received threats on the internet or social media or straight forward emails. You've no ideas what nasty stuff there is about. Got to ask this. What about her enemies? That is apart from anything they find on her laptop or phone, people she'd fallen out with? Any ideas, anything you know about to cause concern?'

'Lot of her life I know nothing about of course. Met her husband once I think it was and she spent a good amount of her time caring for her sick mother.' Tasha shook her head. 'Nobody you would describe as an enemy. Got on with everybody at the club with varying degrees, as we all do.'

Time to move on. Time to head back into town and catch up with Jamie Hedley and his search for CCTV.

29

There was a weariness and a forlorn look to his facial expression the moment Travis Marsh tugged opened his white PVC front door and spotted two warrant cards.

'G'day. Coppers eh?' he then glanced out to the road. 'No divvie van then,' was quite unnecessary.

Inga Larsson had a good idea of what to expect from what the Family Liaison girls had related and from using Google about sheep shearing. Divvie van was a new one.

'Whatever it is yous looking for at a time like this, it's not here,' he said as he gestured for them to enter, then rudely pushing past led them to the kitchen. 'Hey, you guys got no thought for my feelings? Told those other two to...'

'This sir,' said a strident Inga Larsson. 'In case you hadn't noticed is a murder investigation.'

Although the kitchen he'd led them to was a generous size it was to some extent in Inga's eyes too cluttered. Used mugs, empty saucepan, two or three dirty plates, crumbs, knives and forks told Inga a story.

'Right, what's this all about mate?' he asked Goodwin as he stood there. 'What yous after eh?'

'Did we say we were looking for anything?' made him spin his head to look at the woman in the room he'd ignored originally.

Sheep Shearing is a very active, hard, tiring but rewarding occupation Larsson had discovered. A good shearer can earn £2 for each sheep and release the fleece off a good 200 in a day.

She got her first hint of attitude almost immediately. They'd introduced themselves at the door, but once inside he asked again. Larsson saw his eyes give him away. His eyeball shot from Jake to her as he took on board the 'Sheila' stood in his kitchen was the senior officer.

Interviews at this stage of a murder inquiry were for the most part a tree-shaking exercise, just to see what bad fruit dropped.

'We have a duty of care, Mr Marsh. Our remit in the UK is to protect the public and your dismissal of our Family Liaison team has caused some concern.'

'Can't be doin' with mealy mouthed chicks they sent round.' He was either living in the wrong time slot or he was Australian or as she knew both. His look, gestures and arrogance told Inga this chunk of a man's man did not want to be interviewed by a mere woman. 'Anyway why you here and not out grafting lookin' for the bastard what done this?'

'Didn't call for anything in particular,' said Jake Goodwin. 'But as you've drawn our attention to such matters, perhaps in your best interests it would save us time and need for a warrant. Phones, laptops, PCs and any other devices if you would,' and he held out his hand.

'Get away,' he laughed.

Streaked blonde hair, dressed in a black vest with a great tan, baggy camouflage cargo pants and big tan boots indoors. He was so stereotypical to almost be amusing.

'You sir, are the one who needs to get away,' said Larsson. 'Get away and find what we've asked for. Day or two that's all we'll need them for, and we'll bring them right back.'

'And what do I do in the meantime?'

'Many people live their whole lives without.'

Marsh's eyes constantly flicked back and forth between the pair as if he was making his mind up which one it would be best to verbally attack. Larsson however was in interview mode. Every time his eyes flicked in her direction she was looking directly at him.

Larsson had known she could put on her sympathy approach but in this case being wary had proved to be right. Julia and Deanna from Family Liaison would have by essence gone down that route and been shown the door.

'You're bloody serious,' he said to Jake.

Larsson was reminded by the look of him how more than once Nicky Scoley had made reference to the Marsh's being an odd couple as she put it. Or, the long and short, the petite and beefy. She knew personal opinions had a way of clouding her judgement in such an investigation, when a clear mind was essential.

Photographs taken by Connor told her how small Judy Marsh had been, and here in front of her leaning against the smart taupe units, arms folded, legs crossed stood a man well over six feet and chunky with it.

He skuttled off with a sigh and a grunt and the pair stood there looking all around and he came back with one item at a time. First up was a Lenovo laptop, then Inga felt sarcastically he produced what he confirmed was Judy Marsh's Kindle. Then another laptop, an Apple MacBook he claimed was his.

Having fallen foul early in her career, Larsson was switched on enough now to immediately ask for passwords. She knew the Tech Crime Team would still inveigle their way in but it would take time.

He gave the same password for phone and for his laptop, but suggested his wife kept her password secret.

Two things immediately sprung to mind. Number one was Inga's thought of her Adam having a laptop at home she could not gain access to, and secondly Marsh had not mentioned her phone which had not been with the body. Clues were falling into place conveniently, but for a cautious Swede maybe just too conveniently.

'Question we have to ask,' said Larsson. 'Is about enemies, or more than likely people your wife had upset, sent bad tweets to that sort of thing.'

'You didn't know Jude then.'

'No sir, never had the pleasure I'm sorry to say.'

'If you did you'd know my missus didn't do enemies. Anyway she'd been well trained. Her son back down in Aussie land works with technology and warned her against letting her true feelings run riot on those web thingys.'

'On the subject of family. Is there anybody you'd like our people to contact on your behalf? While we're at it we'd like details of her next of kin.'

'Mother's on her last legs. Not done it yet, but I'm off there later.' he stopped and looked at Larsson. 'When I pluck up the courage to tell her. Poor old dear.'

225

'Anybody else?'

'Son knows,' was sharp from Marsh. 'Phoned him.'

'Do you have his details?'

'Yeh, no worries.'

'Could we have it please?'

'What for?'

'Next of kin, being her son. Part of the process, sir,' was always a good excuse.'Always possible you and him don't get on and you keep him out of the loop.'

'Fair enough,' he sighed and wandered off. On his return he had the details written down.

'Australia,' said Larsson when she read the scribble.

'When we came back here or should I say when Jude came back here he decided to stay put. Got a woman, got the surf got the decent weather. What's not to like?'

'Where were you sir,' said Jake in a complete switch. 'When your wife was killed?'

'Man time. Spent an evening at a mate's house.'

'Doing what, sir?'

'Just jawing. This and that. Couple of tinny's like you do.'

'This local, sir?'

'Back in Louth,' he said. Both Inga and Jake knew it had been a good three miles from town out to Elkington village where they were. Drink driving came to Jake's mind immediately with mention of the tinnies.

'And your wife, sir?' Larsson slipped in, but he just looked at her rather than respond. 'What was your wife planning to do with her evening?'

'Be messing about with all that book business, guess.'

'You mean the book club?'

'And writing stuff.' Marsh still had not managed to keep the annoyance from his tone.

'Did your wife write?' she asked aware what that Natasha had told Nicky.

'If you can call it that.'

'You don't approve?'

'Reading's one thing but unless you're a so-called two-bit damn celebrity these days who can put their name to a book some pucker writer's churned out, you can forget it.' He sighed and shook his head as he released his arms and plopped his hands on the work surface either side. 'Told her that, but did she listen?' he just looked at the floor shaking his head.

'Do you read, sir?'

'Bit of facey. Read factual books now and again none'o that fiction business.'

'Do you visit your friend very often?' Jake changed to as part of their technique.

'What?' Marsh's brow furrowed as Jake continued and Larsson was waiting for his reaction.

'Is that something you do frequently or was this just a one off nip into Louth to see your friend?' A case of right place, right time.

'Bit regular,' told Larsson in letters a foot high he'd not read Jake right.

'And he is?' Larsson asked.

'Oh no. No, no not having that. No bloody way. Yous not starting on me best cobber. He's with me I'm telling you,' his hand appeared to point at Larsson. 'Not out bumping off me missus some place.'

'Name if you will,' was Larsson sharp and louder. 'Plus address and phone number while you're at it.'

'Nah bloody way.'

'Take longer but we'll track him through your phone,' said Jake Goodwin pointing at his mobile on the table. 'And read all your emails while we're at it. Or rather, while our keyboard techy wizards are going through it all.'

'Chrissakes!' he gasped. 'I'm no' a drongo matey.'

'Name, and I'm not your mate.'

'Mitch Taylor-Lawson.'

'And?' Marsh sighed again as he tended towards and gave them his address, then checked his phone for the number, Goodwin made a note of.

'What about hobbies?' Larsson moved to.

'What?' she knew was a deliberate ploy to give himself a few extra moments thinking time.

'Do you have any hobbies, like your wife enjoys her book club?'

'Footie. Your soccer not Aussie Rules.'

227

'And what do you do, sir?'

'Local kids team of course, help with training doing bits and pieces when I'm around.'

'What do you mean by that?'

'Job takes me away for long stretches sometimes. Not so much in the winter months these days now I'm over here. Heaps when the season over here starts. Be soon so'll not be helping out with the kids much.'

'You always done this sheep business?'

'Pretty much.'

'What's the system sir?' Jake asked out of sheer curiosity. 'Some farmer phones to say his sheep need a haircut?'

'On the circuit, place to place, going where the work is at different times o'year. Here of course can be hard yakka with your small farms. Back home we're talking thousands of head. This place fills the early months then if you're on the big circuit its a case of your team cross-crossing the nations. USA, New Zealand and back to home in Oz. Even Norway and the Falklands spent time in year or two back.'

Inga Larsson was less interested than Goodwin, but continued to listen politely as what was not said was frequently as important or sometimes more. She had to ensure her look messaged her interest, although he being the sort he was, talked straight to Jake when possible.

'How does your year pan out then?' Goodwin asked to annoy Larsson in need of a break from all this sheep business.

'Back in the day, Straya September through to the end of October and the same with Zealand where I could easy add on a week or two. When we first moved here it meant back to the UK for a bit of a break by February I was ready to start back in the USA for a month before returning for the UK season.'

'Did you used to do it in the winter?'

'Not here. Your winter here but good shearing time down under. Choc a bloc busy.'

'What about as a couple? What sort of things did you do together?' Larsson tried in an attempt to move away from all the wool.

'Not a lot really, neither of us had any notion of being in each other's pockets some go in for. Anyway with me away a lot working, bringing home the bacon, Jude had a life of her own otherwise loneliness is a bit of a bugger what can fester.'

Time to put the brakes on, Larsson decided. 'May we offer our condolences,' made his head pull back. 'Sorry for your loss Mr Marsh,' she said as Goodwin collected the equipment together. 'We'll have them back as soon as we can. I'll get them to check your mobile first, so its not too inconvenient.'

A set of grey hexagonal cork boards had been fitted together on one wall to form a notice board. Looked to Goodwin like any board anywhere at first, but as Marsh was gabbing on about sheep he'd spotted a business card with Travis Marsh printed on it. As he collected up the laptops, Kindle and phone he was closer and spotted it was Marsh offering his services as an odd job man with the strap line *No Job is too odd for Travis.*

'The football club you mentioned?' Goodwin slipped in. 'Just out of interest which one are we talking about?'

'Wolds Colts. Junior team.'

'Thank you sir,' said Goodwin arms too full even to touch elbows as some tend towards.

'One last thing Mr Marsh,' was blonde Larsson who would look great on a sunny beach in Sydney, 'We need you to identify the body for us please. One of the things our Family Relations team would have dealt with for you had you allowed. Would ask her son but guess that's a bit of a trek.'

'Yeh. More misery.'

Inga Larsson had read earlier in the year how in Australia young women face nasty sexism on a daily basis. Some women down there still cow-tow to the myth that some jobs are better suited to men. Jobs over here men take as the norm for their women.

As a nation their gender equality rating puts them down amongst the non-equality bunch of nations, so March's attitude was no real surprise.

'How would you describe the Marsh's as a pair, a couple?' Inga asked Jake as she pulled away heading back to Lincoln.

'It's a relationship of sorts if you know what I mean. But not much more. His absences I suppose has to be like people in the forces. Guess with them the wives have to create their own cluster of friends and activities. Wonder why he came over here? Apart that is from her needing to be with her mother.'

'With all the snakes, venomous spiders, bush fires and sharks its nothing like its cracked up to be. Prawns and sausages on the barbie'd not make up for all that.

'You up to speed with the lingo?' she sniggered at. 'All put on I reckon just for our benefit,' was Jake's opinion. 'Like I was tuned into Neighbours. Heard they sometimes call sausages snag,' made Inga shake her head.

D'you think he could have killed her?' she posed with her eyes on the road and made it sound so casual.

'Capable certainly, but if he's that fed up why not just get on the phone to Quantas and get the hell out of it, sharks or no sharks it's gotta be heaps better than a cell up Greetwell Road.'

30

'Here we are,' said Inga Larsson back just with her basic team minus one, all still bristling with the news and eager for more. 'To some extent as we know this is where the work starts. He's not actually given us a confession, but we're lining things up against him and our efforts now are sure to settle it.'

'Can I just say,' said Jake Goodwin. 'Before we get down to the nitty gritty, just want to mention Alisha,' he just glanced round to smile at her. 'When we walked into Gosney's office, you should have seen the look on his face, when Alisha here of all people read him his rights. Pictures they say paint a thousand words and that was a classic they could use in the *Leader*. Well done you.'

'Thank you Jake. Talking of Alisha,' the DI said looking over towards her. 'Job for you. We have to assume the *Leader* will do its very best to keep a lid on this with their editor incarcerated. What I need you to do is keep a constant eye open for social media and we just might get an internal whistle blower hunting down fifteen minutes of fame through Twitter. Easy be someone down at their Witham St Hughs base Gosney has upset. Getting your own back time is a distinct possibility.'

She'd been taking a break. Sat at her station to rest her eyes as suggested Alisha had been considering something quite silly she'd just read on social media. Some woman had asked why when the bits and pieces of batter you get with a portion of fish and chips are called scrumps, why there was no word for the scratty bits at the bottom of a crisp packet? The dregs most people pour down their throat.

Time for her to return to the here and now and have a look for the boss.

'Can imagine these... Katushabe brothers,' Jake said as he sat there with a degree of intensity. 'Right now are desperately trying to put a lid on it and work out what the best policy will be. Seems to me almost anything they do could quite easily hand too much of an advantage to their competitors.'

'Gosney as you know is in custody downstairs,' said Inga. 'And it won't surprise you to know we are awaiting an express delivery of his DNA results.' The blonde DI then moved a few paces to stand by the murder boards pointing at and tapping her forefinger on the print out of Kevin Elphick at the wheel of James Gosney's Volvo on a roundabout close to Melton Mowbray. 'Zapped by the camera because fortunately for us he was speeding. Which no doubt had we pinned this on somebody else, Gosney would have covered up for Elphick and his boyfriend would no doubt have represented him in court.'

'One thing we could check ma'am,' said Sandy. 'Did Gosney get insurance for Elphick? Had one of the cars picked him up, it wasnae his car. No insurance and he could be in a right muckle o'mess.'

'Nicky if she were here will you tell us what we think happened using what we know for definite from Kevin Elphick here,' she tapped again. 'And her conversation with Raymond Earle the Labour Mayorial candidate.' The blonde Swede walked the three steps to her chair she'd wheeled out from her office, sat down and started on the fresh coffee organized for all who wanted one.

'According to Nicky's report this Raymond Earle,' said a seated Larsson with tablet in hand. 'We will by the way be visiting in the next couple of days once the election is over, to get a signed statement. Was visited by James Gosney on the Monday just as he claimed. What he failed to mention and Mr Earle confirmed to Nicky was, he arrived at around 10.30am and was gone again somewhere after 11.40. He was there as he quite rightly told her personally in his office, to interview Earle for a special issue of the *Leader* they planned to bring out on Friday morning rather than next Thursday, election day.' She hesitated. 'In the morning.'

Once arrested they had access to Gosney's phone and surprise surprise Abby Warriner upstairs had no trouble tracing his GPS down to Melton Mowbray in the morning. Leaving him free all evening and night, when she also discovered he made no phone calls at all and his phone never moved. Put in his home postcode and up the red marker pinged.

Inga Larsson nodded at Jake. 'From what we understand from Kevin Elphick,' he said. 'This nasty piece of work Gosney had somehow sussed the lad was back on the naughty stuff and used that as leverage, forcing the young man to drive his car. We could if required add blackmail to the murder. Quite simple blackmail when you think of it. One word in the ear of the Katushabe brothers and young Elphick would have been in all sorts of trouble. Gosney must have hired or borrowed a similar or identical Volvo to make the journey which is something Jamie has on his list to delve into, had he not moved onto Louth's late night traffic,' she smiled at across the room.' What we already know is, Gosney's Volvo did not pass any ANPR cameras of any kind until just before six that evening.' Inga was back on her feet, tapping Elphick's photo. 'This is young Elphick driving Gosney's car close to Melton Mowbray. Jake,' she said and sat again, but Jamie Hedley beat his DS to it.

'Just a small point. When the boss and I interviewed him after I did the drug swipe with Jason remember, all he could tell us initially was he'd been to Melton Mowbray for a McDonalds.'

'As if.'

'There is still a degree of supposition remember,' said Jake. 'It would appear, on the Tuesday Gosney drove to somewhere close to David Petrie's home and parked it up for over an hour and we suspect he left his phone in the car.' He stopped to shake his head. 'That will give us the GPS Abby is working on when she gets five minutes.'

'Sarge,' said Guy French. 'His excuse for not answering it would be he was busy interviewing that Petrie I guess.'

'Exactly. 'Jake Goodwin scanned the room. 'He did well to be honest. Going to and from Petrie's house from his office he went through it seems to me as many stationery ANPR cameras as he could, to make his whereabouts known. Abby's working with ANPR to link the two together and give us a map.'

'Was this Petrie at home?' Michelle popped in.

'Had breakfast meetings as these sort do,' Jake sniggered with. 'Then spent the day out and about on his campaign trail, covering as many places as he could looking for votes.'

'Remember,' said Inga. 'He told Nicky to her face he'd interviewed this Earle on Monday and Petrie on Tuesday.' She went on. 'But what he failed to say was, and we didn't check,' she slapped her own wrist. 'Was what time.' she glanced towards Alisha, who shrugged and grimaced. 'In truth we now know he interviewed him in the morning and didn't interview Petrie at all,' she grinned. 'He'd have no need to interview his boyfriend had he.'

'Just one thing,' Jake slipped in. 'Reading Rachel Barnard's amazing article about the pair and what they had planned. She was in fact proposing to reveal to the world. Probably to the tabloids under the false name.'

'As an aside,' said Inga. 'Gosney's pet name for Petrie was Charlie, apparently. Darke boss who knows Petrie of course, confirmed it.'

'All stems,' was Jake taking it up. 'From somebody mishearing his name being mentioned, thought they'd said Petrie,' he French accented well, being half French. 'That is French for clown, and a clown was Charlie Cairoli, in a sort of cockney rhyming slang sort of way.'

'David Petrie confirmed to the Darke boss, he had not been interviewed by Gosney at all on that Tuesday. In fact he had not undertaken any formal interview process for the special issue of the *Leader* Gosney had planned. The Tech Crime Team have discovered Gosney's editorial for the post election issue is as if he had actually interviewed both candidates,' Inga grinned.

'What they call pillow talk I guess,' lightened the mood slightly.

'By the way,' said Jake. 'With the election imminent we've agreed not to take Petrie's mobile off him yet for the team upstairs to do their explorations.'

'It's ridiculous really when you think about what had been going on behind the scenes. All the press releases, all the leaflets and what not from Petrie had all been written by Gosney anyway. Which was what he planned to do as his communications bod.'

Larsson checked her watch. 'Time you were off Jamie and Sandy,' she reminded them then saw the look on Jamie's face. 'I know you're waiting on ANPR to get back, but we need this.' Back to the assembled crew. 'We're leading a team made up with a bunch of Stevens crew he's brought together to check for this Volvo,' she said as the big pair sleeved their jackets and scouped up bits and pieces to pocket.. 'Good luck,' she said, as they walked off down the corridor. 'Think that's vital,' she told the remainder of her team as Jake too readied himself for his journey. 'If Gosney killed Rachel, we have to assume he used another car. That's where we'll find DNA to match Rachel's if CSI don't find any at his house. We've swabbed him of course and wait that result. Good barrister will leap on the fact he never went anywhere near Hibaldstow, and tell us to prove it.'

'Brick boss,' was said as a reminder.

'Yes, the brick dust on Rachel's scalp has been cleverly identified by CSI Leicester. This will likely take a day or two but Shona's CSI team going over Gosney's home with a fine tooth comb noticed he'd had a garden room, is it they call them?' Michelle nodded. 'Garden room recently tacked onto the end of the house. They're pretty sure the distinctive bricks used are likely to match the brick dust.'

'Means she was most likely killed there, maybe in his back garden when his wife and kids were away.'

'When she confronted him about his adultery with Petrie.'

'That brings us round to actions to start,' said Inga on her feet. 'Michelle and Alisha will you take Mrs Gosney.'

'Emily Gosney. Will do.'

'Thanks. We need to know if she was at home all that week, if not when was she and when was she not there?' Inga looked across at Jake. 'You're next and guess what?' she sniggered.

'Another cup of tea up at the farm.,' he said and sighed.

'She might give you a slice of the cake you went on about. All we need is a nosy neighbour up there to have spotted a black car, Volvo be our best bet.'

'And if he drove a pale blue Nissan?' he joked as he got to his feet.

'Just something worth mentioning,' said the boss. 'Big question in the back of my mind Nicky mentioned, is why a nice villages like Redbourne and Hibaldstow? I know he's not talking but I can't fathom a reason. This query stemming from her visiting him down at the *Leader* had reminded Nicky of a bike ride she and Connor took down that way. No distance from his office apparently is this weir a couple of miles away between Haddington and Aubourn. He could easily have dumped her there and if not there's the air raid shelters so I understand at what was RAF Swinderby the old training place could also have been ideal.'

'Thinking. Too close for comfort,' Jake offered.

'Off the main roads. Bit of a farmers track apparently Nicky was saying. But it's a public footpath, you have to walk or in their case she admitted they'd biked along. Dump her in the undergrowth she'd not be found if ever, or chuck her into the weir. In fact with a body on board he could have driven down there, you can turn at the end apparently.'

'How d'you know all this ma'am?'

'Nicky showed me photos Connor took when she briefed me. Somebody like him doesn't go anywhere without a camera or two.'

'Still say it's too close to home, or office I should say.'

'But surely transporting a body in your car all the way up the A15 would be more than risky. Choose the right time, be quiet as a mouse down at that weir. Just need to make sure fishermen are not about.'

'Back roads up to Hibaldstow maybe,' Jake responded. 'As I know it's possible to get from the *Leader* offices to Higgins Farm without passing anything of any real consequence.'

'Plus,' Inga added. 'We don't know he used his own car. The car issue is one still to be resolved and it could be he used the other Volvo for it. Time will tell.'

Left on her own with a cold coffee DI Inga Larsson was back to thinking about Emily Gosney again. How her life was suddenly without warning all turned completely upside down. The ignominy of the humiliation she faced. How had she explained that to the school? She'd have given them some sickie story to last the first few days, and was lucky the news had yet to reach the media to show her as a liar.

Shona and her team poking their noses into every corner of her home and garden was Inga knew, a necessary intrusion into people's lives. How would she cope, she asked herself sat in her big black chair when male team members were hunting through her knicker drawer? Then thoughts of her two DCs calling to check where she was. Should she have held them back for a day or so?

The two children were a constant thought which brought her inevitably round to her own family. To her Terése and how something that catastrophic happening because Adam had been a liar and philanderer, would affect what Sandy always affectionately termed the wee one.

31

The wind of change had come over the Tech Crime Team. ASBO as Orford was affectionately known had a Starbucks to go black coffee sat beside him. Pulled faces when Nicky spotted it and a grimace or two from his team told her she was not seeing things.

Her technology mentor for years now had always drunk just plain hot water, and it seemed at times the hotter the better. What was even more of a concern was Adrian drinking the coffee of choice of serial killers. Black.

When Abby Warriner said she was watching a handset IMEI number she knew this was all a completely different ball game, she'd have to get used to. She said there was a strong possibility the Australian could well be using an encrypted app.

Dexter, one of the Computer Analysis guys who was delving into Travis Marsh's phone had surprised Nicky Scoley by finding precious little of interest save for one oddity repeated time and again.

One number he sent text messages to as infrequent as once in three weeks or on other occasions once or twice a week was simply a couple of numbers: 13 18 one day. Then Nicky noted down the week before was 21 and 2 and next up on the day of Judy Marsh's death according to the pathologist's guess at the time were 19 and 3. All such messages to another mobile they discovered belonged to somebody called Taylor-Lawson. Quick nip downstairs to the MIT Incident Room and Nicky had checked he was Marsh's pal, or as Jake jokingly insisted: 'His cobber.'

Word among the geeky set upstairs was this Travis Marsh must have a burner phone, especially when Larsson had said he'd not made a really big fuss about losing his phone for a day. Comprehensive data ordered from the phone provider and they were able to get one of the cars to drop off Marsh's phone to him at home.

Next up for Nicky Scoley was Judy Marsh's laptop she had been looking forward to viewing, and getting a sneaky look at Natasha Hutton's book she'd been sent.

Clever clogs ASBO earwigging her conversation with Dexter set their young Digital Forensic code breaker Hari Mistry to work. While Dexter and Nicky moved onto Travis Marsh's Apple laptop.

Something somewhere at the back of her mind had told Nicky about Judy Marsh's son Richard still living in Australia being somehow connect to computers, technology or something similar. Had he given her a difficult password and explained how to hide it or to make access next to impossible for trolls and conmen?

Fortunately Dexter was able to explain in layman's terms how her laptop could have been configured incorrectly on purpose. That would require repair to the registry via specialized software she didn't fully understand as was increasingly the case upstairs as technology bounded on relentlessly.

Hari Mistry got there in the end and Nicky could forget the possibility of having to call the son in Australia for any info he could provide.

Zyxwvutsrqponmarsh was what they were looking for and once the password had provided access Nicky had enough know how picked up from this bunch of geeks over months and years to sit there and see how much of Judy Marsh's private world she could access.

Carefully she went through the files. Everything from a Christmas Card List detailing who had sent her cards going back two years. What were obviously letters of complaint to a few people and a couple of companies with her address all set up smartly at the top in the same format she could use.

A list of garden plants but with no indication whether they were what she had bought and planted or was in need of. Then she came across one simply titled Roman Way. When she opened it was a book in draft form. No cover, no bumph you usually get, but straight into Chapter 1.

Halfway through the evening disappointment was a real understatement. Nicky Scoley had sat at the dining table reading the draft of the book she'd downloaded onto a Memory Stick, but unless there was a startling transformation this was never the book Natasha said she's emailed to Judy.

This was all about a killer, the police had decided was male through DNA which did not match anybody on the database who was killing people in Roman cities. Not just using places such as Colchester, Bath and Lincoln but leaving reproduction Roman artefacts at the scene and all killings were done by weapons of the time. Pugia and the Gladius short sword. Nothing modern like a cocaine overdose or gun.

This happened to be an interesting read but unless she was completely mistaken it was never the book Natasha had described.

Next morning the only thing for it was to have a word with Natasha Hutton over in Louth, but before that it was morning briefing time.

'We start this morning with the preliminary finding from the Judy Marsh autopsy,' was Inga Larsson sat out with her team, red mug of milky coffee on a desk beside her. 'The unexpurgated version will follow later, but in the meantime these are his basic thoughts on the matter. Dr Latimer says we are supposed to think she was strangled. Bruises around her neck were simply superficial according to him. Says all that will be confirmed when he gets the tox back he has asked to be fast tracked.'

'Boss,' said Jamie. 'What does he mean, think she was strangled?'

'Nowhere near enough pressure apparently,' Inga responded, then stopped to take a drink of her weak coffee. 'According to Latimer,' she read from her tablet. 'Eleven pounds of pressure to the carotid arteries can cause loss of consciousness, which he believes is what happened to provide an opportunity to kill by other means. All he did in effect was to leave marks.' She was back reading. 'Compression of the trachea requires significantly more force to fracture tracheal cartilage apparently.'

'What other means?' Jake perked up with.

'Poison.'

'Poison?' he gasped. 'Now that is unusual, Very small percentage of murders are done by poisoning. We're looking for somebody who knows their way around that sort of stuff then.'

'Big sheep shearer could easy make the marks on her neck,' Inga suggested. 'But unless its something like a sheep tranquilizer think we're looking elsewhere.'

Once the short briefing was over and actions had been set, Nicky Scoley knocked on Larsson's poky office door and walked in.

'Strange request boss, but please here me out,' she said as the Detective Inspector gestured for her to to sit down. 'Will it be alright if I read a book?' Her boss pulled a face. 'Downloaded the book from Judy Marsh's laptop when I was upstairs yesterday and took it home last night on a Memory Stick,' she smiled. 'Wrong book.'

'How d'you mean wrong book?'

'I've just asked ASBO if he can get somebody else to go through all her documents again to see if they can find another book manuscript I missed. If you remember that Natasha Hutton told me she had emailed a copy of her novel to Marsh all about personal relationships. One I read a good lot of last night is about murders happening in Roman cities such as Lincoln of course along with places such as Colchester and Bath. But the killings were as they would have been back in Roman times. No guns or anything like that all knives and spears, and stolen artefacts are left with the body each time. Almost as if its one of those re-enactments some are into. Got to say its a good idea especially as the murders are so far apart it involves forces nationwide.' she stopped to smile. 'Got a lot of our procedures wrong but generally its not bad at all.'

'But the one she says she sent to Marsh was not like that, you're saying?'

'Called something about the truth in a relationship I seem to remember. She told me it was about a woman discovering her husband is not at all the person she believed him to be. Nothing to do with Romans, then or now.'

'But you can see why she chose Romans coming from round here. Any idea where that one came from?'

'No idea, it's just sitting there. Before you suggest she read it and just deleted, Natasha Hutton said Judy Marsh had said she'd spotted a few errors and was going to highlight them and send it back.'

'But she hasn't?'

'Going to call Hutton if its alright with you, and double check she's not had it back, and ask if I can have it sent to me,' she shrugged. 'Just in case.'

'Just in case what?' was a frowned query.

'Dunno, just…' she shrugged.

'At home?'

'Of course. Get her to send it to my private email rather than give my work one out.'

Larsson had yet to fathom the reasoning but as it would be in her own time there was little point in suggesting otherwise. 'I'm after a favour in return. We only know what we know about Marsh from what he's told us and bits and pieces you've picked up talking to the book club women. Not on PNC of course, how many would Alisha need to trawl through social media to get the right one? Anyway she's got plenty on with Operation Greeba. I've put in a request for data from the Australian Federal Police, but just been thinking. Who would know him better?' she queried, then answered her own question. 'Judy Marsh's son Richard.'

'You want…?'

'If you would, but you'll need to check what the time is down there remember, and as you know his address and number are on Judy Marsh's laptop upstairs.'

'Will do,' said Nicky getting to her feet.

'And while you're at it. Things are a bit fraught out there,' she motioned to the main office before she slid a piece of pink paper across her desk. 'This is that Taylor-Lawson's details Marsh gave us as his alibi. Give him a call please.' Inga grinned. 'Enjoy.'

32

First up for Nicky was to make that call to Natasha Hutton in which she explained her predicament.

'Don't understand,' said Tasha. 'Be, well, only last week at the most, Judy said she'd go through it and highlight any errors she had noticed in red and send it back to me. Not received it this end.'

'Can I be cheeky and ask you to email me a copy, please?'

'Certainly,' she responded. 'But on the strict understanding this is for your eyes only. What I mean is police, of course.'

'Of course. The manuscript I've read about Roman murders all over the place what do you know about it?'

'Nothing,' she shook her head. 'First I've heard of it.'

'It's not bad, few mistakes about police procedures but that's quite normal.'

'Oh dear,' Nicky heard. 'Look...if you have time would you tell me anything stupid I've included in mine?'

'Of course. Be my pleasure. We are talking about the one where a woman discovers her husband is not quite the person she thought he was, are we?'

'Truth Will Out. Yes that's basically it, but thinking maybe to be more up to date I'd perhaps make him her partner.'

'Depends if you want her to have more of a hold over him. Partners from my experience in this job tend to be more flighty, less committed. Easy to just get up and go on a whim.'

'Thanks for that.'

'I'll let you know when it arrives and I'll call you about police bits you might want to take a look at, but might be a week or so with all the work we've got on.'

'Send it as soon as we finish. Good to hear from you,' Nicky thought that was it. 'Can I just say many of us have to thank you for the work you're doing on Judy's behalf. We do appreciate it.'

'Thanks. Doing our best. If you hear about a Roman book let me know.'

'I'll call Yvonne and Adele see what they know.'

'Bye.'

Next job on the To Do list for Nicky Scoley was to give this Mitch Taylor-Lawson, Marsh's alibi the boss had lumbered her with, a call. She knew the paperwork at the end of a murder investigation is always more prolific after the arrest than before. Even so. Jake was there at the time, surely he could spare a few minutes to give this one a bell.

Still on her mind was a Facebook message Alisha had pointed out to her soon as she arrived for work. About a woman in Spalding who had received an email saying they had a parcel to deliver. To release it the courier said all she need do was to click a red 'Deliver' square on her laptop as a small token towards the delivery cost.

Blindly she followed the instructions but nothing happened, no parcel was delivered and no further messages were received..

Next event was her Debit Card becoming embarrassingly refused at the till at her local supermarket. Investigation through her bank revealed every penny in her current account had disappeared save for just £15.

For Nicky this was another warning to be ever vigilant, and this was another scam she knew Rachel Barnard would have most certainly highlighted. Being told previously by a friend how a retired policeman had been a victim of the same scam made Nicky and Connor more aware than ever that nobody is safe.

As it turned out calling this Taylor-Lawson was more hassle than a simple quick call and that was the last thing she needed in the mood she was in. Jamie was supposed to be helping her and she thought he was dealing with the CCTV in Louth, only to realize he was back totally wrapped up in the same thing but for Operation Grubber and the journalist woman.

Had to be PR she decided. Murdered young woman from the local paper would give the force more brownie points and help with the Chief Con's promotion prospects, than some anonymous heading for middle-aged woman out in a Wolds market town. The *Leader* would never relegate their Barnard down the pecking order.

This Taylor-Lawson's wife or partner answered the phone. Nicky Scoley explained why she needed to speak to him and was told he was at work, given his mobile number and told to call when it was break time.

According to the woman she spoke to he was a car mechanic or what she referred to him as a Motor Technician, at a local main dealer.

First call he said he was too busy and to ring back in ten minutes which she did.

From the outset he confirmed what Travis Marsh had said, but then the attitude changed.

'If me mate Travis says he was with me he was with me. That a crime now eh?'

'Reason for you being together, sir?'

'D'we need a reason now for a chinwag?'

'Were there other people with you or just you and Mr Marsh. What about your partner?'

'No chance.'

'No chance there were others with you, or no chance as you put it, your partner was there?'

'We was out in me man cave and me missus knows better an' disturb us fellas.'

'And this was where?'

'Me man cave.'

'Yes but where? At home?'

'Where else eh? Down far end o'Crowtree Lane. Remember you can always ask the score but never who's playing. Not get that from some woman. Different world lady, ' was confusing to say the least.'Why d'you wan' him anyway?'

'Nothing in particular, just part of our laid down procedures.'

'For what?'

'Double checking facts. He's given your name as I said as his alibi. Be amiss of us not to check what he said is correct.'

'Said he was here and now I'm telling you too. That not enough eh?'

'What were you doing apart from as you say, having a chinwag?'

'D'you really think you should be hassling a bloke what's just lost his woman? Think about folks' mental health they keep ramming down our throats. That not apply to the likes of you then eh? If that's all, missing me break.'

Her evening call to Australia Nicky knew would be nowhere near as easy. That car mechanic had attitude, but talking across the oceans to a man whose mother had been murdered she knew would not be an easy task.

When it got round to eleven she'd already received the Truth Will Out book from Natasha and called her to thank her. The difference between the two books was like chalk and cheese. Natasha's effort was far more polished and professional and became more enjoyable than just another job for work. The subject matter however was a real surprise.

It was exactly as Natasha had said. This was about a married woman discovering her husband was in effect living two lives. The scene had been set down in Peterborough. The wife held a senior position in education with the local authority and her husband Patrick McCrory worked in London amazingly as the Senior Project Officer civil servant responsible for covert human intelligence sources advising a Detective Chief Inspector running a dozen Child Protection Teams for the National Crime Agency.

Why Nicky had asked herself more than once as she read, would a nice woman living on her own in rural Lincolnshire choose such a subject for a novel?

Travelling down early on a Monday morning and returning home usually on Friday just after lunch, this McCrory character had absolutely nothing whatsoever to do with Romans and a great deal to do with what he was doing on the dark web at night in his Stratford apartment on his own.

246

'Richard Garland?' she said too loudly down the phone, then realized she was shouting for no good reason. Even at her best he'd not hear her that far away.

'Yes,' was very tentative.

'Nothing to worry about but I'm detective Sergeant Nicola Scoley from the Lincoln County Police in England. First up, please accept our sincere condolences for your sad loss and I can assure you we are doing all we can to bring whoever was responsible to justice. It is in that vein I'd like, if I'm not disturbing you, to have a chat.'

'Be honest, look I know its a long way, but if you could call back in say fifteen minutes I'd be pleased to help.'

'Thank you Richard. I'll call back.'

When she did call Australia again Richard Garland explained how his wife was out and he was in the process of putting their young child to bed. Now he could give her his full attention.

'Gday,' had amused her when Richard answered the phone.

'Thank you, appreciate it.' Nicky breathed in and hoped she was approaching this delicate matter correctly. 'Our problem with this murder investigation is how it is exacerbated by the fact one of the people we are obviously talking to is Australian. Don't mean that in any derogatory way of course, but if he was British we have access to a whole number of platforms to provide us with information. Such as the Police National Computer and our National DNA Database to name but two.' This was it. 'With Travis Marsh we have nothing. We can only take what he says as gospel.'

'What has he said?' was difficult.

'Claims he has an alibi we have checked. Didn't report your mother missing in the knowledge we'd not treat it as a missing person for twenty four hours. He's co-operated fully with us, we had his phone checked and our digital forensic people are going through your mother's laptop and his.'

'Where was she found and under what circumstances?'

'By one of our policewomen in a shop doorway in the town. In Louth, don't know if you know it.'

'No not really, only photos. How did she die?'

'The pathologist is still waiting for the toxicology results to come back I'm afraid.'

'So they don't know.'

'Not as yet, sorry', was the best way out of that. 'How well do you know Travis?'

There was this ominous silence for a moment or two, or might simply have been distance delay.

'Easy way to put this. He was mum's choice and there's no way I would expect her to only get involved with somebody I approve of. Couldn't expect the mother child relationship approval in reverse, shall we say.'

'Reason why you're obviously not that enamoured by him?'

'Mother is...was happy, that's all that mattered, but I've always had this idea in the back of my mind he was too controlling and married her for some other reason.'

'Such as?'

'Not sure. Way to move to England maybe.'

'What about his sheep shearing?' she heard him chuckle slightly.

'Do you know that just about sums him up. If I'm perfectly honest he's is a typical old school blonde Aussie. Full of all this tinnie business, passionate about sports but in truth only the two or three they're any good at, especially swimming and cricket. Got to use their own language too often as if they need to constantly prove where they're from. Quite sure he took up sheep shearing to fit his image.'

'Not always been shearing sheep then?'

'No, no. Same as me. Paramedic,' he hesitated. 'My fault really. how mum first met him. One of the lads organized a barbie, and my wife and I took mum along and he was there. He'd left to go shearing by then but one of the lads invited him. Unfortunately. Guess putting a plaster on old ladies knees doesn't have the same image as shearing a hundred sheep a day.'

'There's nothing specific you think we should concentrate on. Does he have a criminal record at all over there do you know?'

'Not that I know of. My dad was unfaithful which is why mum got a divorce. In a way I was on the lookout for what

248

Travis was up to. Since she moved back to look after gran I've had no chance.'

'Thank you Richard, been useful. If you think of anything we might find interesting, please let me know.' she gave him her number.

'What about her funeral?'

'Think that may be a while yet, but I'll make sure whatever happens you get to know about it as soon as her body is released.'

'Pleased to hear it,' he said. 'Look. Him galavanting all over the place with his damn sheep's always been a worry. What else is he up to? What does he do with his spare time? Who is he seeing, more to the point.'

'Might be an aspect we can delve into. We'll do our very best for you. Promise.'

'Thanks.'

33

Sat at her station considering everything Richard Garland had brought to the table, made Nicky conclude there was something about Travis Marsh they'd not come across. Not having met him didn't help.

The DI was in yet another meeting with the Darke boss and DCI Stevens, discussing aspects of the Operation Grubber case. She had wrongly assumed Jamie Hedley was still involved in vehicle tracing for the media woman's murder, until he held his hand up with a yellow Post-it note in his hand.

'Got to be it!' he said and was on his feet and taking the few steps over to her. 'One thirty eight this blue minibus is cleared by ANPR on Eastgate Louth. Just eleven minutes later the same one goes past the other way. Pictures on their way,' he enthused. 'Guess what?' he said down to Nicky. 'It's the Wold Colts minibus,' he then sighed deeply in frustration. 'Driver's wearing a big hat though which is a bit of a bugger.'

'How d'you know?'

'Vehicle's registered to the club secretary.'

'How stupid is that?' Nicky gasped.

'She can't have fallen out with a football club,' Jake turning round offered. 'Somebody missing a penalty'll not put them in good books, but her surely...?'

'Travis Marsh,' said Nicky carefully. 'Coaches the kids sometimes when he's back from shearing. Does he drive the minibus though?'

'Need to check the timing,' Jamie said to Jake. 'Drive from the ANPR camera to the Comic shop and back again, see how long?'

'You're sounding just like a detective,' Sandy joked.

'Off you go,' was Jake approving his suggestion.

'Except,' said Nicky as Jamie slipped his jacket on. 'Marsh's phone says he was at home all evening according to this morning's bad news from upstairs.'

'Carry on,' said Jake to Jamie. 'Need to get that data double checked,' he told Nicky. 'But we also have to consider who else from the football would need to be out and about at that time in the morning.'

'Easy be one of the coaches got his car in for service out visiting a lady friend and used the minibus.'

'Will you do an insurance check on it,' Jake told the Scot. 'Jamie. Leave the minibus details for Sandy.'

'Or Judy Marsh fell out seriously with someone at the club over something. Most likely trivial.'

'Thanks for that.'

'This something to do with a super talented kid's parents expecting him to sign for Man City and play for England? Somebody put a spoke in that wheel his old man'd be bloody angry with all the money sploshing about.'

She'd had a lunch of Corned Beef and Onion filling on her sandwich with an apple and apricot before the boss showed her face again. Previous experience told Nicky to give Inga a chance to settle before having a word about that Richard Garland and what Jamie had discovered.

'Here we go!' said Inga Larsson before she'd left her little office. Tablet in hand she walked the few paces and stood in front of five of her team.

'Dr Latimer was right first time. Tox results are back and he now reveals two things. He noticed an injection mark in her armpit and the results show she died from an overdose of Pentobarbital,' Inga noticed Nicky raise her hand and give a sort of wave. 'Animal euthanasia drug known more commonly as Fatal-Plus,' she went on. 'His conclusion is yes, she was strangled enough to make her unconscious and then with her out cold it was easy to inject.'

'Especially for a paramedic,' Nicky chuckled with.

'You what?' Inga exclaimed.

'Travis Marsh was a paramedic before the started shearing sheep and how he met Judy.'

'How d'you know?'

'Richard Garland told me when I phoned him. That's what he does. He's a paramedic and one of the people he worked with organised a barbecue one time. Garland went along with his wife and his mother, and Travis Marsh even though he'd moved onto sheep by then, was invited.. Got to say since he got together with his mother Garland is not that enchanted by him by a long chalk. Says Marsh is a stereotypical old fashioned Aussie with all his surfing, cricket boasting and drinking Fosters.'

'Proving this'll not be easy.' Inga mused.

'Jamie's gone out to Louth,' Jake informed. 'Found a minibus in the area late that night gone to check the drive time from what's on CCTV the ANPR chaps sent through.'

'Good work one and all,' said the DI. 'Got that Mitch Taylor-Lawson wanting to see me which is a bit surprising to say the least,. She looked across at Nicky. 'Alibi one you spoke to yesterday.' she flicked her look to Jake. 'Was going to suggest you join me Jake, but with what's happened and Nicky talking to the son, think it best if she continues with the same op.' she turned back to Nicky. 'Half an hour he's due.'

Mitch Taylor-Lawson who confirmed from the outset his full name was Mitchell had this just finished work scruffiness about him. Larsson had decided against one of the stark windowless interview rooms and instead showed him to one they used for interviewing people with no connection to a particular crime.

'Look lady, I'm here for a whole host of reasons, not least is me missus who says this gotta be the right thing to do.' He was wearing a pair of scruffy jeans in need of a good wash, a grey and white checked shirt and black body warmer. Larsson went to interrupt. 'Wait a mo,' he said leaning forward with elbows on the wooden table. 'I'm doing this because apart from getting her off me back I knows its the right thing to do, like me ma taught me or drilled into me before I got in any bother. She was right o'course.'

'Is there a but on its way?' appeared to confuse him slightly.

'Know if I go the whole hog and come clean I'm dropping mesen in the clag, but,' he shrugged and pushed out a breath.

'You've got me number, but hell no don't want to be on any list of yorn. Innocent muggins me despite all this, but the rest as they say I'll have to take like a man. Not come here, then I gotta live with mesen and a missus who'll remind me for ever. Truth is I'm best burnt than scolded.'

'What is it you need to tell us, or rather what is it your wife says you need to admit to?'

'Your wife's name,' said Scoley. 'Just out of interest.'

'No bloody way, not fair that...'

'Stop it!' was a loud Larsson. 'If we're to discuss this properly and in an adult manner we need her name Mitch, not *the wife* nonsense or missus.

'Abigail. Abi.'

'Thank you.' Larsson folded her arms and sat back. 'The floor's yours, as they say.'

'Look. My Abi's into gardening and gotta new better shed year or two back for all that potting up business. Kept the old un, gave it a lick o'paint and turned it into me man cave.' No matter what either detective had expected this was most certainly not it. 'Into sport and that, and keeps me out o'her way, get a bottle or two and settle down nicely. Mates pop round from time to time and Travis's been popping in now and again for...well soon after he got here. Met him a few years back when he was over here shearing and knew one o'me mates.' The pair watched as he dragged in his next breath. 'Know this is telling on a mate but gotta be done,' was slower as if he was building up to something. 'Travis weren't with me that night,' he just lifted both shoulders and let them drop, popping out as breath as he did so.

'What night was that Mitch?'

'The night his woman got done.'

'Why did you tell us he was?' Scoley posed across the table.

'Look,' he shook his head. 'Like its a bit of a man thing and that. Travis says he's with me and I say yes. Alibi stops his...stops Judy moaning on he reckons.'

'So no matter the consequences, you confirm his alibi even if its only his wife checking up on him?'

'Yeh.'

'How may I ask,' and Larsson was doing just that. 'Does it work? If we'd come to you and asked when Travis Marsh was with you, how would you know what day and time you're supposed to confirm?'

'Easy,' he said and they waited and the silence egged him on. 'Phones me.'

'Travis Marsh phones you and says will you alibi me next Tuesday evening from eight to eleven. That what you're saying?'

'No, no, no. Text.' They went through the stop phase again and then Taylor-Lawson just dragged his phone from his jeans pocket and flipped it. 'See,' he said and held the phone across for both women to read.

Nicky Scoley realized where she'd seen that before, but couldn't remember whether she'd told the boss about these short sharp messages from Marsh the Tech Crime Team had found on his phone.

'Explain.' Larsson's curt request contained a half-hearted smile.

'See,' said Taylor-Lawson taking back his phone. '8 and 11 would be what you said. That'd be today. If it were to be Friday say I'd get F 9 2 message. Friday 9pm to 2am.'

'Why?'

'Says he did it back in Oz,' he pulled a face. 'Think he musta cheated on his old missus back then. Sort of code she'd not fathom if she poked her nose in his phone like they do. To be fair I'm sure he was up to it again here.'

'Will you give us a written statement to the effect he was not with you at all when Judy Marsh was murdered?'

His 'Yeh' with a shrug was quite solemn as if he was letting down a friend big time.

'Anything else? This what Abi said you need to admit to?'

'Yeh. See, it were her parents wedding anniversary that night. Went out for a meal with them and a few friends, back to their place for a noggin or two. Taxi home got in around oneish s'pose.'

'So you couldn't have been with Marsh and your wife knew that for certain?'

'Yeh.'

'Anything to add, before we look at taking down your statement?'

Time for a big suck of breath. 'This is where I feel a complete prat. Look. Me old man was a big burly brickie, smoked heavy, drank worse, what he called a pucker real man. Know this is wrong but he'd got a real down on gays, gave one or two a right bashing for being pooftahs. That was until he died of a whole heap of stuff.' Both detectives were waiting patiently for something, anything other than that. 'Big guy like Travis reminds me of me ol'dad. No way would I ever dare say no to another pint with him about. No chance I could watch Gardeners' World or EastEnders he reckoned were for sissies, but he was into wrestling which we all know is completely false but he insisted it was real. And stuff like Top Gear. Same with Travis,' he stopped sighed and shook his head as he looked at the table. 'Too weak see, couldn't say no. Like with me old man I'd spent too much time being called a nancy boy, being belittled at every turn.'

'Appreciate all that...' said a frustrated Larsson.

'Listen. Here goes. Used to watch porn in me man cave with Travis an' that.'

'What sort of porn?' Larsson shot at him and he looked at her without lifting his head.

'Yeh, sorry.'

'What exactly do you mean?'

'Shoulda said no, realize now what a complete pillock I was, should've said no way and easy lose Abi now.' His head came up. 'What'll I get?'

It was not uncommon for a person like Taylor-Lawson to admit responsibility for gaining access to indecent images of children.

In formal taped interview after all three had coffee he admitted he was now more scared of what his wife would say and do when he got home.

He was probably right, Larsson said to herself sat there looking at him. His biggest punishment could well be when he gets home and if and when his employer finds out. That was of course assuming she knew nothing about what he had been searching for on the dark net while she got on with the ironing.

DI Larsson from her time as a Sexual Offence Officer in (PPU) Public Protection Unit, had a degree of experience of the issue. If what he said was correct he had probably only been viewing Category C indecent images if that. For that he was more than likely to get a high level community order, but possibly not that when his brief tells the court he had come clean in the end about Marsh's alibi for the night his wife was murdered.

She knew the National Crime Agency would track back the request to the computer it had come from. They would seriously investigate the possibility he may well have interfered with real children not just sat watching videos on the dark net in his old shed supping a pint or two of Doom Bar. To her mind had he been that depraved he'd never have freely walked in the door, overbearing wife or no wife.

Larsson knew just how rife child sexual exploitation is nowadays, with those dedicated to catching the offenders arresting a suspect every two or three days. With thousands of paedophiles on line and in particular on the dark web, but with so few officer handling that major issue they were not likely to be caught.

34

Once Mitchell Taylor-Lawson had been passed onto Inga's colleagues in the Public Protection Unit, both detectives knew they still had a great deal of work to get through.

Jamie was back with the good news having driven both ways along the route he assumed the football club minibus had taken to and from the Cartoon shop. He was now planning to talk to the Secretary of the youngsters' club about use of their minibus.

Nicky had been tasked by Larsson with making contact with Richard Garland again in Australia, now they knew Travis Marsh had a penchant for videos.

On a personal issue but strangely now loosely connected to the case, Nicky was determined to finish Natasha Hutton's draft Truth Will Out book especially after Taylor-Lawson's confession.

There were of course a galaxy of theories going round the team as to why Judy Marsh had been murdered.

'Had she found out what Travis and Mitch were up to?'

'Did Abi Taylor-Lawson realize or perhaps walked in unannounced to that man cave and spotted what was going on and warned Judy.'

'As well as giving her old man a gobfull.'

'It makes sense if Judy found out and was threatening to expose him, tell us or at least tell the sheep shearing fraternity. That'd see him dumped by the gang. Or at least one can hope.'

'Did Travis realize coming up here was one big mistake and she was blackmailing him about the child porn basically to stop him going back down under?'

'One thing being here for a few months shearing sheep in with a gang, was a world he was into. Actually living here thousands of miles from what he was used to is totally different.

Bit like old folk who move to live by the sea where they went on holiday. Never works.'

'And he lost it?'

'Could be.'

'And that gives us a motive.'

'Is the killer maybe pointing us in his direction? Is this racist? Somebody hates Aussies as much as we do apart from when we win the Ashes.'

'Enough now!'

'Hello,' was Richard Garland's partner with a strong Australian twang when DS Nicky Scoley phoned Melbourne again. She passed her over to Richard.

'Sorry to disturb you again Richard but something has come to our attention. This may or may not be relevant to the case so please at this stage don't take this as gospel about Travis Marsh. There is an outside possibility he was into pornography and indeed child pornography to some extent.'

'Bloody hell!'

'Can I just say at this juncture, we're talking viewing videos not actually abusing children as far as we know. Wondered if you knew anything one way or the other?'

'Bit of a shocker that,' he said and she waited. 'Look, I'm in touch with Marsh's first wife Chloe, not much more than an email or two now and again, birthday cards for their kids and that. What I can tell you has nothing to do with pornography. Since he moved up to England he's not paid her any Spousal Maintenance, or at least the last time she was in touch he hadn't. Not for her or the girls. Came into operation of course when their divorce became final.'

'Interesting,' said Scoley as she made a quick note of the term.

'Be in the divorce documents I guess but according to Chloe he was controlling and she suffered domestic abuse to some extent mainly mental.'

'And your mum still married him.'

'Ah but. None of us knew any of this at the time as back then they lived in Adelaide and Chloe still does. It was after divorce was final and they moved up your way Chloe got in touch, and if I'm perfectly honest I think it's her way of keeping tabs on him. Think she's really fearful he might decide to come back.'

'Not if he's not paying maintenance I shouldn't think.'

'He has been back though,' Richard told her. 'He was down here shearing up in Queensland a couple of times two years ago, according to mum.'

'No mention of pornography then?'

'No, thank goodness. Want me to email Chloe, and ask her?'

'Not now, please. Let's just keep all this to ourselves for now and we'll see what happens. Last thing we need is for an unfounded rumour to start. Thanks for all that. How you keeping?'

'We're fine thank you.'

'I'll be in touch about the funeral. Promise.'

'Thanks.'

Jamie had been talking to the football club officials about their minibus. They were adamant it had not been anywhere and the Treasurer had a record of the mileage for all journeys undertaken. No unaccounted for trips out. He was then taken to see it garaged by one of the parents who housed it safely in his builders yard. Jamie immediately realized the one in the CCTV images had no signwriting as the club's vehicle had.

He reported the bad news to Jake on his return. Disappointed at that outcome back in the office pondering his next move and just scanning the murder board for the umpteenth time, and he was back to the boss's office.

'That Taylor-Lawson is a mechanic,' he said. 'The club's minibus has signwriting on it, but when it was clocked by those two cameras it was clean. What if it was not their vehicle at all,' he put up a hand when Inga went to speak. 'Been cloned with false plates,' stopped her. 'And who do we know could easy get false number plates without leaving a trail on the internet?'

'His best friend. His mucker,' even the boss had to smile with.

'Can I phone him?'

'Leave it with me,' she said. 'I'll offer a bit of bait, suggest it will all go in his favour just when he's desperate for one or two. Leave it with me.'

At home with Connor, Nicky checked the Radio Times and was not surprised to find the evening's programmes were just the sort of reality drivel she could not abide, one after another.

So called celebrities taking on sub-zero tasks including facing a blizzard in swimwear was one she'd avoided earlier in the week. *Meet The Khans* whoever they were, was another must to avoid along with something called *Beauty and the Geeks* she could have spent £3.99 a month on.

With her mind still full to overflowing about the Judy Marsh case which they were no closer to solving in a manner to satisfy the CPS, there was nothing for it but to pour a glass of red, open her laptop and have another good read of the draft of Natasha's book. Maybe make a few notes for her along the way.

She'd already read how down in Peterborough this Patrick McCrory character was a well respected member of local society. His friends and family were obviously aware of him being a commuter and working with the police but he had never for obvious reasons explained his specific role,

This McCrory was to his victims on the net a 15 year old girl, across a complex and interwoven web of various well know sites popular with the young. This was a 43 year old civil servant using stolen images of blonde girls spending weekday evenings alone befriending children and becoming a trusted close pal.

All the times he was using techniques he would know well from his day job, none of which would ever trigger his own teams. Keeping McCrory below the radar.

Suddenly Nicky was brought up short and went back to read a page for a second time on her laptop. Realizing what she had read the blonde DS noted where in the book it was, and was back reading with increased enthusiasm

Nicky wondered where on earth Natasha Hutton had got the idea and her draft was so full of detailed information. The blackmailing of children by getting them to perform sex acts with their siblings was something she'd made her main character particularly enjoy.

He was doing precisely what his tight team of undercover detectives were searching the web for every day. The main character the Hutton woman had created in her draft novel was a prolific child abuser, but with insider knowledge.

Then McCrory's deposition was finally planned and executed with a sting operation orchestrated by his own wife. Using a key she had discovered hidden in his brief case by sheer chance, she'd had a copy made and one Tuesday evening crept quietly into his Stratford apartment unannounced.

The address he had given her for his commuter weekday home had been a lie all along. A private detective had followed him from work, out on the tube to Stratford and his secret was no more.

Elegant, charming and to some extent glamorous, wife Alice McCrory had fully expected to find him with another female, but the video he was watching as she walked in was an absolute shock to her system.

A shock to Nicky as well and it was break time at the end of that chapter in Truth Will Out.

Hutton had created a strong story. A husband watching abused children all week at work then calmly nipping across to Kings Cross and train back home to Peterborough of a Friday afternoon for a meal with friends, had all come to a shuddering halt.

Nicky was still engrossed in reading the last chapter when Connor made them both a cup of strong tea. Short break over and soon enough she'd finished.

Yes, some of the police methodology and timings were not quite right but as far as Nicky was concerned it was an excellent book. Certainly worthy of her expertise to tidy up bits and pieces of procedures. As she was reading she'd already decided to seek the assistance of DCI Luke Stevens who had worked for the Met and held a senior child abuse investigation role successfully at one time.

35

Every morning in the Incident Room there was a main topic of conversation. Sometimes weather good or bad, stories from the overnights, events in the news or sports results.

That Thursday as Jake said 'Doing this job I thought I'd heard it all,' when the conversation was all about a Tory MP watching porn on his phone in the House of Commons.

Hearing about a woman in Edinburgh being charged for driving whilst six times over the legal limit was also a point of interest that morning.

Back to the here and now. There had been a request from the Katushabe Group's Features Leader based in Birmingham to visit Inga Larsson and her team to discuss all the issues with regard to Kevin Elphick.

Detective Superintendent Craig Darke was there along with his DI Inga Larsson and DS Scoley sat around a table in the small conference room when this tall dark angular man was ushered in.

First impression for Inga was, he could so easily be a West Indian fast bowler. Although cricket was not a major sport she knew the finer points of, she knew enough simply due to being married to Adam. An avid enthusiast.

Rudolf Toussaint introduced himself to each person in turn by taking the trouble to walk around the table to shake hands as Alisha poured him a black coffee with two sugars. Immaculate in a well fitted navy blue suit, white pristine shirt, matching slightly lighter blue tie and black shoes well polished

'I have been asked by Ginika, Musika and Kaikara Katushabe to visit personally in order to thank you for the work you have dealt with so effectively and efficiently since the loss of Rachel Barnard.' He sipped his hot coffee. 'I have to be in the area for a few days at the *Leader* out at what used to be, so

262

they tell me, an RAF station. Such a timely visit appeared to me to provide an ideal opportunity to visit and make your acquaintance.' He turned to look at Craig Darke. 'I understand it is you I have to thank in particular for the manner in which this whole process has been handled.'

'Might I ask,' was Larsson. 'What will happen to Kevin Elphick, because as we explained, in the end he came good.'

Craig Darke spoke up before Toussaint had an opportunity to respond. 'Can you please assure the brothers how we now have a complete understanding of their culture and methods.'

'We appreciate that.'

'Thank you.' Darke was satisfied enough to turn his attention to his major weakness. Coffee.

'All about concept,' was all Toussaint said, then was back to his coffee as Michelle pushed the plate of biscuits in his direction. After a bite or two he then went on. 'When the family first arrived here they had nothing. They had lost their import business, their home as well as a relative or two.' He took his time, drank a little coffee and the team waited. 'In this day and age there are people who no matter how well they behave still come in for some indescribable rot on social media and the Katushabe family is one such case.' He drank more and licked his lips. 'Yes they are criticized for what some consider to be their strange outmoded ways. I'm sure I can say to you in such cloistered surroundings they are seen in some quarters by many people as weird and freakish almost, and more than once have been likened to some very strange religious sects. Usually by former disgruntled employees,' he offered a cynical look with.

'Amish was mentioned,' Inga offered.

'How some people talk about the family is somewhat akin to the utter nonsense we had to suffer from some quarters about the Covid vaccinations if you remember. People giving completely uninformed reason for not wanting the jab, tittle-tattle of microbes being put into people's bodies in order to control them is along the same fictitious lines as the anti-Katushabe garbage almost permanently on social media.'

'Why is that do you think?'

'Jealousy in some respects. Racism is one aspect of course. Former disgruntled employees started it all apparently before I joined. The internet is damn good in so many ways, yet as with anything there is this downside.'

'Does this hearsay harm the business do you think?'

'In a difficult market we are doing well compared with others, but it's always there in the background.' he responded. 'If I am perfectly honest and I'm just an employee remember, they do have a moralistic background which comes from the Matriarch for want of a better phrase. Mrs Ginika Katushabe sets the standard. Yes back in Uganda around the time of her grandfather what they believed in was not far short of a sect as we know it today. Over time here as in most countries religion has been drawn back from the mainstream of society, but she still retains an overarching theme to her standards of behaviour. No need to swear, no bullying, no need for sexist, homophobic and racist remarks in any form anywhere. Or misogyny come to that. They don't personally drink alcohol but at the same time they put on excellent summer barbecues for staff and one at Christmas where in both cases wine and beer are served freely and put on coaches after.'

Inga Larsson produced a Police regulation USB Stick she held between her fingers. 'This is for you Rudolf,' she said handing it him across in front of Craig Darke. 'Our digital forensics guys have copied this off the secret Memory Stick Rachel used to hide her discoveries which brought us all to where we are today. I'm giving you this because it contains a second article she was working on. About a well-know television news reporter losing close to £130,000 on a scam.'

'Copying this for you,' said Darke. 'Because it has no relevance to the case and anyway to some extent because it was written by Rachel Barnard it is in effect your property.'

'A well know reporter?' Toussaint queried with an intake of breath.

'Hugo Tharpe, more than likely on the Ten O'clock News tonight,' Nicky slipped in.

'The basis of the scam in this,' said Inga. 'Or at least a precis is this. This Hugo Tharpe, celebrity reporter accepts that too many long assignments to notorious trouble spots ended his marriage. Lonely, depressed and to some extent desolate in desperation he decided to try a dating app. To cut a long story short, he finished up talking to, phoning and messaging a beautiful young woman living in a small village just outside Tibilisi in Georgia.' Inga looked down at notes she had made in readiness. 'Natia Saakashvilli,' she struggled to pronounce. 'Convenient, as much of his work took him to Turkey and Russia close by of course. In time they agreed to marry and set up home. Two things happened next. He was told only Georgian nationals are permitted to buy property and when all the wedding arrangements were being made he was brought back to London.' Inga stopped, nudged Nicky and went on to drink her coffee.

'Getting called back to London was just plain unlucky for Hugo,' the DS went on. 'Not checking facts about buying property was his biggest and costliest mistake. Undeterred our man did two things. Arranged to transfer money into Natia's account to buy the flat they'd seen, and gave her money to make and pay for all the wedding arrangements.'

'A week before the great day and our man accepted readily when told it was a tradition for both the bride and groom to go through quite separate wedding rehearsals, particularly with him being from Britain he'd not understand the complex procedure there. That he did, and went through with it.'

'Natia's grandmother acted as bride for his rehearsal and afterwards they and people acting as witnesses went to a local tavern as they waited for Natia to turn up. Which of course she didn't. He next woke up in a hotel room,' said a grinning Nicky Scoley.

'Hugo quickly discovered he was in fact married to the grandmother. He never saw Natia again and has lost all his savings. In round figures, £ 115,000 for the flat which was not even for sale and £12,000 for a wedding that never happened...'

'According to Rachel's notes it was a sophisticated scam from day one. Rachel has not discovered the bank account except one opened and closed in the name of N.Saakashvilli just long enough to receive his money.'

'Rachel was working on the suggestion that Hugo Tharpe had actually paid for Natia Saakashvilli's wedding to her boyfriend. Rather than continue to look for her, she was searching for all the women named Saakashvilli who married around the same time.'

'I do have to say, said Inga. 'The article as you will discover is far from finished. We've gleaned all this from her comprehensive notes. Would suggest more work needs to be done and it all needs more research probably and knocking into shape,' she looked at Rudolf. 'Over to you.'

'That is amazing. Thank you for this,' he said picking up the stick.

'We've only told you the basics, there is a great deal more along with all the contacts she made.'

'No use to us, we could pass it onto Action Fraud and the like,' Inga said. 'But I'm sure you can do that and use what will be a best selling article as a memory to Rachel.'

'Maybe you could calculate what the story is worth,' Darke suggested. 'And the brothers could make a donation to the family to help with funeral costs when the time comes.'

'Absolutely. I'm sure that would have happened anyway.' He held up the USB stick. 'Thank you for this. Thank you,' he looked around the table nodding to each.

'Would you mind me asking, but is Kevin Elphick's story true?' Nicky asked as their visitor tucked into his coffee.

'Absolutely,' Rudolf Toussaint replied, replacing his cup. 'Plus, their attitude is, therefore he will be given a second chance. What you have to remember about the theft of her bag was not the value she may have lost. It is all concerned with the act of stealing and the act of someone being prepared to do good to possibly put themselves in danger for the sake of others. If I'm perfectly honest and I've discussed this with the brothers. They may well have farmed him out over here too soon because of his earlier issues. He is already back in the West Midlands, as you know.' He turned to Darke. 'Thank you in particular for all your efforts, which I have to say is exactly the standards we as part of the Katushabe clan appreciate. Forgiveness and kindness. Back with us we can keep a close eye on him.' He smiled. 'And so can his family of course.'

'Do they do this all the time?' Inga Larsson wanted to know.

'Not all the time, not a case of constantly picking up waifs and strays from every street corner,' he grinned at his own remark. 'I have one who is my personal secretary actually. Let me tell you about her.' It was time to drink more coffee, he finished off and when Alisha offered more he accepted and tucked into a biscuit. 'Lydia,' he said when he was ready. 'Was subjected to the phrase you have over here. She was not to darken her family's door again when she became pregnant. Sad thing is, she was raped by an uncle in inverted commas, for want of a better term. The whole episode was hushed up from the authorities and blamed entirely on her. Somebody somewhere got wind of what had gone on and told Ginika Katushabe about the young woman who by then had given birth living in a one room hovel of a place and she took her under her wing. Lydia is now my right hand man so to speak.'

He talked about racism he had suffered to a degree personally and about being Haitian American originally, but moved to the UK when he was five months old, so Britain is the only home he has ever know.

Rudolf talked about his family saying the UK is a much calmer place than America with all the constant troubles between the races and then surprised everybody by having a knock at Black Lives Matter being too political and losing the message.

A sharp knock on the door and there was Jake Goodwin. 'Apologies one and all. Something's cropped up I think you'll all want to know about.' Inga introduced him to Rudolf Toussaint who then offered to wait outside.

'Right Jake,' said a disgruntled Darke. 'What's so important it can't wait?' Jake took as an unnecessary jibe.

'To be perfectly honest I'm more than a bit embarrassed,' he admitted and took a breath. 'But there you go,' he shrugged. 'Had a phone call just now from an old friend to ask if I'd seen the glamping pods,' he annoyingly hesitated and looked around the table. 'Up on Higgins Farm,' Darke went to speak. 'Please hear me out, sir. Friend of mine's been searching sites for places where relatives could stay over for a couple of nights to attend his wedding anniversary. One of the places he'd come across was Higgins Farm who do what trendy folk call farmcations. Simon'd read about where Barnard'd been discovered, and just wondered on the off chance if I'd seen the place,' he admitted with a wry smile. 'They've got three pods on the farm apparently. Just looked them up.' He put a hand up. 'I know, I know, went there two or three times, spoke to Cutforth and his wife. Absolutely no idea, sorry.'

'Somebody she upset was staying there, you think?'

'No idea,' Jake said. 'Just spoken to Nancy Cutforth and she confirms they are there, but in my defence,' he smiled. 'They are way over behind the farmhouse well out of sight in a small copse and they are only rented out from May to the end of September. Off up the A15 now and I'm taking our suspects photo with me. See if she recognizes him as a customer.' He looked across to Larsson. 'Happy with that boss? Guy's holding the fort.'

'Carry on. Good work and you never know you might get another slice of cake!'

'Thank you,' was a grateful Toussaint who Jake had ushered back into the room as he left. 'Tell me about the situation with the car if you will,' he said as he finished his at best warm coffee.

36

In her comfortable clean Louth home sat at her oak dining table Natasha Hutton had made a cappuccino each for herself and Nicky Scoley using her red Tassimo coffee machine, and had put dark chocolate digestive biscuits on a plate.

Since the Detective Sergeant's arrival they'd been through all the usual chat about the weather and news. Now for Nicky Scoley it was time to get down to her real reason for being there.

'You're good at coming up with a well executed ending as I've recently discovered from your book, and although I can't reveal what it is we know to help you, I've been wondering from what you do know if it was your book, How would you plot the ending? Why do you think Travis killed Judy?'

'I know how I'd have resolved it from your standpoint, bearing in mind I am a bit biased. My book is an important element, because as you say it was deleted from her laptop. Curiosity as they say killed the cat, but I wondered why my book in particular of all things was missing.'

'Equally, to be honest the only thing I expected to find of any real interest maybe apart from the possibility of threatening emails was the one item not there.'

Nicky knew she had to be careful. She was not going to reveal what the Tech Crime Team had since discovered. Such as them using small text files to trace the movement between files they'd followed the route for the book onto the dark web using cryptographic algorithms to then discover it had then been deleted at the final stage.

Nor was she willing to reveal how whilst reading had realized the sheet of A4 screwed into a ball and shoved in Judy Marsh's mouth, had in fact been a printed page from the book.

A book Marsh must have had deleted in an attempt to hide the evidence.

'That's what got me thinking when you told me. Decided he was quite possibly controlling, sadly. Something I'd always suspected from what she's said from time to time combined with my own experiences. Deciding he was indeed from that mindset he'd be snooping at what was on her laptop, who she was texting and all the rest of it.' Natasha hesitated as if something had come to mind. 'Couldn't see he was stalking as it turned out mine was. Anyway, Travis must have known she was writing a book and when by chance I sent her a copy of mine, my guess is during one of his snooping sessions he came across Truth Will Out and decided Judy had written it,' Natasha looked at Nicky. 'Not only had his wife written it, but he assumed she'd also worked out what he was up to and like my Patrick McCrory was somehow planning to expose him and send him to jail. Am I right?'

'Sorry, police business,' Nicky smiled. 'That'd be telling,' she chuckled. 'But how on earth did you come up with all that stuff in your book?'

'There were a couple of programmes on the telly about how your people trap paedophiles. In one they concentrated on the internet and in another one or two they actually physically arrested them at home. I find programmes like that fascinating, not necessarily the subject matter but how you go about it. Forensics is my favourite. One thing struck me was the police doing all the searching on line had to take regular breaks and time away because of how such dreadful scenes affected them. That got me thinking. What if one of them was a paedophile? Changed it slightly of course to make McCrory a civil servant, but still the same thing to some extent.' She pulled a face. 'Didn't want to find out later there's a policeman involved in all that business called McCrory.'

Time for a drink of coffee for both women after that.

'And we've still got no idea where that Roman book came from, unless as you say Judy did write it which got him checking up on her.' Scoley chuckled. 'And got the wrong one.'

'Been wondering about that for a while,' Natasha said as she put her mug down.'

'This job can be tough enough at times without trying to work out who killed Octavius and Augustus up Steep Hill on their way to the castle one cold November night, and why.'

'Research was a bit more than the usual thought provoking. For my wronged wife in the book I hope I've accomplished the way somebody like an innocent wife really would have felt when there was one of those life shattering knocks on the door. From that moment on knew her life would never be the same again. From what I'd read I made it as distressing as I could when they searched her home from top to bottom. Read also how she would have been instructed not to talk to anybody about it.'

Nicky could understand from what the boss had told her about work she had been involved with in the past how your world would come crashing down.

It had almost happened to Judy for real. Had she still been alive. Nicky felt her murder had saved her from the possibility utter humiliation and shame such events can produce. Not a choice any of us would wish to make.

The boss had told her recently how at least ten people a day get 'the knock'.

DS Jake Goodwin was back knocking on a familiar door in a altogether different Lincolnshire district. The Higgins farmhouse between Redbourne and Hibaldstow north of the city

'Sit down son, sit yoursen down,' and under that instruction from Nancy Cutforth the DS did as he was told.

Hubert Cutforth was according to his wife away at the market whatever that meant. Jake was to a degree pleased about his absence in that there was less chance of Nancy moaning about tourists and local nosey-parkers.

Sat at the big old wooden table on the red flagstone floor just as he had done before, they exchanged conversation about the weather and general news as she made them a cup of tea each. Everything clean, controlled and in its place reminded Jake Goodwin how somebody was a good cook. Alas when the tea arrived it was not accompanied by cake.

Time to introduce the subject. Goodwin produced from a cardboard folder a colour photograph.

271

'Do you recognize this man?' he asked as he slid the photo across the table to her.

Nancy looked at the photo of a man's head and shoulders, peered up at Goodwin momentarily and then back to the photo.

'Yes,' she said slowly. 'Well I'm pretty sure I do.'

'In what context?' He queried gently..

'Rented one of our glamping pods,' she said and looked up. 'Really upset me all that.'

'All what?'

Goodwin watched Nancy Cutforth in a pale blue jumper deciding what to say. 'Yeh, sure it was him.'

'And the reason you got upset?' made her suck in a breath noisily as she was lifting her cup up in both hands and again let out a breath obviously.

'Look,' she said and put down her cup. 'Call me old fashioned if you like, but I'm sorry not having that soft of dirty behaviour in my home, thank you very much. Know there's some folk who think all that business is fine these days, but they're not the ones having to clean the place after they've...done their business.'

'Homosexuals?' said Goodwin gently keeping his smirk to himself.

Nancy nodded then sipped her tea which turned into a good drink.

'Be..er.' She pulled a face. 'Pretty sure it were.'

'Thank you for that.'

'Bet you see some sights and have to deal; with the likes of them.'

'One thing I've never had to do is investigate an MP watching porn on his phone in the House of Commons,' he smirked with.

'Heard about that on the radio.' Nancy shook her head. 'You really do have to wonder what is going on at times.'

37

Inga Larsson had called her Detective Sergeants in early to her office and provided coffees. After the usual early chit chat about the news and overnights she became serious after a sip or two.

'Either of you know anything about a DI Oliver Bristow from Grantham?' Both her colleagues grimaced as they shook their heads.

'Heard of him, but that's about all,' Nicky admitted.

'No easy way of saying this, but I'm off to pastures new, and he's my replacement.'

'What?' both Goodwin and Scoley gasped almost in unison.

'Been chosen to be the force lead on rape and serious sexual offence investigations. Working with a fresh SOLO officers team fit for purpose I hope in today's more selfish society. My strap line to be on trend is Taking Women Seriously. Be a good month maybe. Means I'm not off to Newcastle or Gwent so we don't have to move, no change for Terése and Adam's business can stay the same. Just be one floor up. Bit of a win, win.'

'Well done,' Jake enthused.

'Congratulations,' from Nicky was from the heart but not full of enthusiasm if that Bristow turned out to be a berk. At the same time she felt for Jake being overlooked again but guessed they were after a new broom.

'Up to DCI too,' Inga admitted to bring smiles to all three. 'But you'll not see the back of me. Rape serious sexual assault leading to death I'll be back knocking on your door you can guarantee that. Wanted to tell you first, think boss'll tell the team later today or tomorrow.

Time for the big guns. At morning briefing held slightly later than normal, in addition to Inga Larsson was her line manager

Detective Superintendent Craig Darke and sat alongside him unusually, the dapper DCI Luke Stevens.

In addition to the Major Incident Team members working on the Rachel Barnard murder, a few were there who had been brought in to help. There was Guy French and people such as Adrian Orford from the Tech Crime Team which Stevens was head of, along with two or three from the Prisoner Handling Unit normally dealing with the drugged up, shoplifting, drunken waifs and strays of this world.

DS Nicky Scoley not being any longer involved in Operation Greeba was sat there with an air of increasing disinterest. She had a great deal to be getting on with and in particular her need to get upstairs to check what the lads in the Tech Crime Team re-named at the turn of the year, had discovered on Travis Marsh's phone. Jamie Hedley was of like mind with his need to get on with checking out the vehicles the CCTV had pictured in Louth.

Darke was on his feet first.

'What we are about to release to you all, is as yet not public knowledge. Overnight the Editor of the *Lincoln Leader*, James Richard Gosney,' a few sucked in a breath at the confirmation they'd been hoping for. 'Has been charged with the murder of 29 year old Rachel Jane Barnard.' Darke waited for the inevitable reaction to subside. 'Putting it simply, Rachel was about to destroy him, ironically from the inside. The destruction of the major life and career plans he'd lined up for the future, he could not accept without retribution.' Darke hesitated to clear his throat. 'The reason for calling you all together is that as a result of your investigations leading to the arrest and charging of Gosney, it has been brought to our attention that this could very well also have major political implications.'

Inga Larsson replaced him. 'This is the situation as we understand it at this point in time.' she took an obvious breath and wished she'd ordered in coffees. 'DCI Stevens,' she introduced.

'The repercussions from this could be enormous,' he started. 'Since the arrest last evening, some here have worked all night on this case due to the severe implications. Elections next Thursday remember, and as well as the normal Council people standing for the city and the various districts, for the first time you will all be voting for East Midlands Mayor. One of the candidates just happens to be David Petrie, a former County and City Councillor.'

'Just a word,' said Darke interrupting, which from his expression did not go down well with Stevens. 'Can I just say. I know David Petrie personally and he has co-operated fully with our inquiries overnight. Luke,' and he gestured for Stevens to continue.

'Thank you, sir,' had a hint of sarcasm. 'Petrie is also as most of you will be aware a local solicitor, we've all come across at some time in the course of our duties I should imagine.' He looked around the packed room. 'Rachel Barnard had been working on a major scoop for months, and as we understand it she was using a false name to do so. That of a man, which no doubt is some form of diversity these days. This she did we imagine, to protect herself as well as people who might well be implicated. She had made a major discovery the detail of which you will all be able to read about in her draft article after this briefing. James Gosney we charged overnight and the aforementioned East Midlands Mayor candidate Petrie, were in fact lovers. Indeed clandestine homosexuals.'

'Furthermore,' said Darke to give Stevens a break, but the reaction from the room was such he had to wait. 'Furthermore, the new Mayor will need a Communications Director and a Mr Fixit who according to what Rachel Barnard wrote on this,' he waved a USB stick in the air. 'His lover Gosney would fit the bill very nicely indeed. Jobs for the boys, and damn close to nepotism.'

'Good god!' somebody gasped almost under their breath.

'Naughty naughty,' said Jake Goodwin.' The Katushabe brothers'll toss you out for less! Allegedly.'

'Might I just say that being a homosexual in this day and age is not a crime obviously,' Stevens went on. 'Plus I would imagine the majority of us have never seen it us such. That is not what he has been charged with, but Rachel Barnard's tone is that the man cheated on his wife and young family not with some glamorous young thing, but with a man. Then once you begin to dissect his paper's contribution to the local political debate it is obvious on which side his butter was, when his role was to be as impartial as possible. One major talking point over recent weeks I'm sure you're all aware of,' he hesitated deliberately. 'Is the population of the East Midlands ready for a Mayor?' Stevens in his superbly tailored deep brown suit just paused again. 'Now bearing that in mind the question has to be, are they ready and willing to have a gay Mayor?'

'Maybe in the cities,' Jake Goodwin offered. 'But I'm not at all sure I see it in some county villages. Except he's a Tory which local voters still tend to go for when they doff their cap. But having a lover who treated his wife and kids abominably is not quite what folk around here would vote for if they were aware. Reason why all this has to remain in house for the time being.'

'Yes Jake, you're absolutely right,' said Stevens. 'We have been trying to fathom why that old water trough on a farm was chosen when he appeared to have absolutely no connection. Gosney and his lover Petrie spent August Bank Holiday in a glamping pod there. Wandering about he must have spotted the trough and when they asked Cutforth where they could get a more than decent meal, our farmer friend told him he went to the Wheatsheaf in Hibaldstow once a week on a regular basis. Gosney remembered it all when needs must.'

'David Petrie knows which side his bread is buttered and admitted to me how Gosney pretended to his wife he had been chosen by the Katushabe brothers to undertake undercover work for the papers. This meant he had to be away for weekends fairly frequently. Except he was doing nothing of the sort. He was holed up with Petrie frequently at his place up in Bailgate.

'We seem to think Gosney knew if his relationship ever became public knowledge his days were numbered. Chances are Gosney got fed up with the way the brothers ran their publishing business and local newspapers in particular and as a result decided or was persuaded, to change tack and work with and for his boyfriend.' He sucked in a breath. 'Together close to three years, so we understand.'

'The publishers Musika and Kaikara Katushabe,' said Darke once more. 'As far as we are aware are not homophobic. Yes they have strict moralistic views on a good many matters, but so far no such reference has been discovered. Could be Gosney knew different somehow or guessed it all completely wrong. Rachel Barnard's position within the group tends to provide evidence of the stand they took with regard to sexism.'

'Now do you appreciate why?' Stevens asked. 'For the time being we have been asked to keep a lid on this whole matter. Gosney with good advice from his lawyer is co-operating, probably in an attempt to stop this whole business destroying Petrie's campaign, in order somehow retain some form of relationship.'

'Did Petrie know his manfriend killed her?' Guy French stood at the back asked

'We understand not,' said Darke. 'And from talking to him I believe what he says. He had absolutely no idea. Said he'd seen Gosney since Rachel's death on the quiet due to the impending election, but never sensed there was anything underhand going on. Just that Gosney was annoyed by what he saw as police intrusion and,' he stopped to smile at Larsson.

'Interesting sub-text to all this,' said Jake. 'Is Petrie claiming in his election bumph his intention to eliminate cancel culture. Not a good idea now when his boyfriend Gosney will no doubt be demonized. What's the betting that policy will never see the light of day.'

'Be his first policy can kicked down the road. That'll be a good start.'

'The big concern is,' was Stevens back again. 'By releasing this information at the wrong time in the wrong form it very well could have a devastating effect on the democratic process and which other candidates will make the most of from their point of view, a wonderful opportunity being handed to them.'

'When Petrie in effect has done nothing wrong.'

Left alone with her thoughts once that was all over, Inga Larsson gave an involuntary shudder, thinking how she might react were she to discover after what she thought to be a good marriage had in effect been just a lie. Adam having been unfaithful would be bad enough to deal with, but with a man! How would she explain that away?

Had Gosney lied to his wife all along? Lived a permanent lie of utter pretence and total disrespect? Would this revelation leave an indelible stain on their own relationship knowing such a thing is entirely possible.

Such thoughts didn't really bear thinking about and some she ditched almost immediately. Aware how she knew through her close proximity to the tragic slaughter of husbands and wives had no bearing on them as a couple, she was able to turn her thoughts to other matters.

Whatever way she chose, Inga was well aware some lives were being connected to this very case.

Enthusiasm for her work which had always stood her in good stead over the years was how she felt about her man equally.

They'd laugh and joke about it that night when she related the story and sat there alone in her small office Inga told herself it would be one of those crazy "Do you remember when…" moments they could share in the future.

One thing of which she was absolutely convinced was, Adam Kingsley was never a murderer and a homosexual, that she'd bet her career on.

Yes killers were quite often the last person you would suspect, which was confirmed in this case. Gosney had a good job but then so had others before him. Police officers had been convicted one with both rape and murder, as had GP Harold Shipman. She'd been involved in or had heard of murders being committed by military personnel, lawyers, surgeons even, more than one or two nurses, along with chefs and civil servants. Being the Editor of a local newspapers was no big surprise, but as yet she'd not checked the HOLMES computer system to hunt down others.

This whole business had been tragic for Rachel Barnard and her dear family and now it would attack Mrs Gosney, perhaps not with the sudden finality but hit her very hard it indeed would.

That to Inga's mind was quite possibly the true horror of such cases, the distraught felt by the minding their own business totally innocent. The effect would stretch further afield than just Emily Gosney and her two children Rowan and April who would have to live with it for ever, but others too. How would the trauma play out in their mental health decades on when they plan to marry and have to chose a partner bearing in mind the mistake their mother made.

That was for the future. How would these youngsters cope with the relentless horror of being reminded day and night at school by bullies about their daddy being the murderer of a woman, a closet gay and a first rate liar?

One aspect both she and Nicky were determined to resolve was how on earth Rachel knew what was going on. Nicky's theory was that Rachel could well have popped round to see her boss with a genuine query when he didn't answer his phone. To be told by his wife he was away on one of his special assignments for the brothers she'd heard nothing about.

That would have intrigued somebody like Rachel with an an inquisitive mind like hers. Once she knew something was going on there was no need to track him to a weekend away in Cornwall or the Lake District. Bailgate was easy enough.

38

With James Gosney already languishing in jail, it was research and hard work after his arrest which would send him and Travis Marsh to a place with no Fosters on tap.

The Darke boss had risked arresting the Aussie and charging him with child abuse well before all the forensics work on the murder of Judy Marsh was completed. The fear of a well-travelled man absconding to goodness knows where on some sheep shearing expedition, never to return was one aspect of the case CPS also agreed was too much of a risk even had they taken possession of his passport.

In the end they had calmly added murder to his charge when the Major Investigation Team finally came up with what was required to gain a conviction

Sex abuse offences provided the perfect opportunity for the CSI team under the guidance of Shona Tate to dig much deeper into the Marsh's affairs. What was particularly relevant was the discovery of young girls clothing and school uniform in a wardrobe in the spare room, all in sizes big enough to fit Judy.

Jamie Hedley had continued down the minibus route and with the boss coaxing more out of Taylor-Lawson with a feint suggestion it may well help his case.

Travis had switched number plates on his own minibus they found in a compound of garages a few hundred yards from his home. Mitch Taylor-Lawson had arranged to have the number plates made up for him at work. According to Travis's tale some kids had damaged the front one and he wanted new. Put the football minibus plates on his own vehicle and took them off again after the deed. He'd not used the club's minibus he had no access to, but simply used their number to confuse both ANPR and Jamie.

Having been told about his minibus by Taylor-Lawson, it was another job for CSI. At the back of the vehicle behind the rear seats was a metal box stretching the whole width in which Travis stored and transported his sheep shearing equipment and probably similar items for other members of his gang.

As well as an array of Sheep Shearing electric clippers, multiple blades and cutters and what turned out to be foot rot trimming shears for goats, their close forensic examination produced evidence of minute skin tissue providing a DNA match, along with tiny specs of rust on her clothing to indicate how Judy had been transported to the Comic Book shop.

Back to the Cafe Nero in Mercer Row for DS Nicky Scoley to discuss not only the news of Marsh being charged with murder but also to provide her with specific information given to her by DCI Luke Stevens.

To be fair to the man with his highly polished brogues, expensive shirts and brightly coloured socks, he'd taken the trouble to read Natasha's book once she had told him of the subject matter. He had provided a good insight into the processes she had written about.

'What happens now?' Nicky asked, then sipped her Latte.

'Do another final edit with all that, thank you,' said Natasha.

'You are going to get it published surely.'

'If you really think…'

'Please Tash. If it was no good I'd do my best to put you off.' she tapped the notes Stevens had typed out for her. 'This is a top cop let me tell you,. One with real experience of the subject.' She went on tell her how he had once worked undercover on a major crime where gangs were snatching British children off beaches across Europe, bringing them to the UK to be sold to childless couples. 'Go for it and I'll tell you what, I know a good few coppers who'll buy it.'

What was not revealed was how Stevens had used his contacts in the National Crime Agency to assist his Lincoln County child sexual exploitation team with delving deep into the dark web in search of the worst of Marsh's nasty activities.

Almost every one in the room were sniggering or at least smiling with what they knew was to come

'Got to say, he did a really good job,' Craig Darke spoke up. 'In fact two of our team are not here today, not because tracing cars was that exhausting, but. They were both due a spot of leave and during this interim period it seems an ideal opportunity.' He paused. 'Got Kevin Elphick to drive Gosney's car we imagine using drugs as blackmail as his weapon of choice. He then got a friend to buy a similar worse for wear old black Volvo.'

'Can I just say,' was Scoley. 'We as yet have not been able to verify why his friend would do such a thing. We are guessing when we say some form of blackmail was involved, but his friend so far has gone no comment. Sir.'

'Yes. There are a number of theories being banded about, one being that he persuaded this friend of his by saying perhaps he needed to be incognito for an undercover story.'

'We're still investigating all that business,' said Inga.

'That seems unlikely I have to say but it could be the trigger for Rachel. Surely then he would have driven something different. Anything pretty much. Choice of car and colour was part of the plan.'

'Discovering the car boss,' Michelle reminded Darke.

'Oh yes. I contacted the brothers to enquire whether or not there were any other black Volvos in the group he could have borrowed on some pretext. Staff cars and suchlike. During the conversation one of them said they'd check and asked if we could do them a favour. They had just moved Kevin back over there but he had now realized he had left a few of his belongings in a lock up garage a street away he never used, but had lost the key,' he said as Larsson returned to the room and her seat. 'To cut a long story short, when they got a locksmith to get in, there at the back was Kevin's bits and pieces along with... a black Volvo.'

'A crappy black Volvo with DNA from both was easy meat for our CSI team. Registration number made checking it on ANPR very easy, and it had been close enough to the farm.' Inga Larsson stopped to chuckle under her breath. 'Checking CCTV and well as hunting high and low in the next village to where Rachel's body had been dumped. Nosy neighbours were not nosy enough for once, but to be kind it was a Tuesday night, nobody out and about, Cutforth off out drinking with his friends and it was dark.'

'On the other hand our Marsh read a book on the sly he assumed his wife had written about him and took action. Wrong and wrong again.'

ACKNOWLEDGEMENTS

Time to thank my wife and all my friends who are always on hand to assist in many different ways as they encourage and support me. In addition to coffee and sympathy they so often offer up ideas and a great deal of information from their lives and work I am able to use.

My thanks goes out to David Tannock for his original Witham St Hughs location suggestions and to Brŏnte McLachlan for her guidance, information and instructions on the Weir and Air Raid shelters to encourage me to visit Aubourn Weir as part of my research.

In each book a great many people are spoken to. In this case I spent time visiting places and meeting lovely people such as in Lincoln Bailgate, Witham St Hughs, Redbourne village, Hibaldstow of course and Louth getting a feel for the locations and talking to residents many of whom have now become avid readers of the series.

Thank you to Dave Gibson at the Wheatsheaf Hotel in Hibaldstow who was very accommodating with my requests for permission and information.

My research has increasingly over the years become more hands-on. When my characters stop off for a coffee or meet someone in an interesting place, I have for the most part been there and experienced what they do. Some lovely places I've hunted down specifically to fit snugly within the pages, and people are always making suggestions.

I tend to have some very interesting conversations when having completed a complex scenario and take a break to visit a coffee shop.

Where more than once I've been asked what I've been doing all morning. Fact checking the signs for rigor mortis, the timing of body decomposition and checking the correct wording for the Miranda Rights, tend not to be what friends are expecting.

A special thank you to them all, along with my amazing and increasing army of readers and followers. Thank you for your messages, your calls and emails. I read every one.

To discover exactly what it is Lincoln County Police become involved in next, read on...

PREVIEW

Coming your way in 2023

Jake Goodwin knew from bitter experience to follow his dad's instructions explicitly, but even so was not at all sure he'd found the right place. So far there'd been no sign of a farm, even the tarmac had ended and he was now on gravel.

Why does Sod's Law always do its best to choose the most inopportune moment to strike? Like all cops the Detective Sergeant didn't enjoy coincidences, so what this was leading to had to be something else.

A weekend away at his parents with Sally and son Tyler helping them celebrate another wedding anniversary at their place in the village. No more than a good stone's throw from the farm he'd been told to head for.

Suspicious death and likely Code Red phoned alert. Acute instructions from his dad and here he was spotting at last the battenburg decals on the Roads Policing Unit's Skoda, with one of the cops gesturing for him to halt.

Window down, Warrant Card. 'Jacques Goodwin, Detective Sergeant. We have a body or so I'm told.'

'Yes guv. Easy best you park behind us for now and walk.' Jake peered at the gravel road ahead. 'Long way round by road Sarge. Think here'd be best and head that way,' he said as he gestured in between bushes. 'Where Shaun is and the farmer.'

'Thanks.'

'And his dog.'

Momentarily Jake's body sank down as he sighed to himself. How many times had he been called out in similar rural situations to be greeted by some dear soul out for a walk with a dog who'd just happened to come upon an abused body. Jake parked up close behind the police car.

'Body's in the middle of a field and it's all a bit odd, but you'll see when you get there.'

'All I need on a Sunday morning, thanks.'

'Right funny business up there. Just follow your way and you'll see Shaun.''

The route the traffic cop pointed out as a path of sorts, was little more than just downtrodden grass and nettles. Each side of him as he trudged were wildly overgrown shrubs and weeds. He was pleased after a while to see the pathway turn sharp left when he thought he was about to be heading through thorny bushes and gorse spikes. Then within fifty metres there was light ahead through a break in the trees and an opening between two and a rusty iron fence some kind soul had knocked down flat. Stepping over steadily in his best jeans and trainers there before him was this Shaun.

'Hello gaffer. Bit of a trek eh?' he was greeted with as he showed his card again. 'That's him,' dark haired, tall fully kitted up this Shaun said pointing to a figure in shadow set against the skyline a good seventy or more yards away.

'This seriously the best way in?'

'Road for what it's worth goes right through the farm, out the other side to the far end of two fields away. Need an ambo that'll be the way I guess.'

'Thanks fella. D'you know any more?'

'Dog found him and that's Herring the farmer waiting. Not in a very good mood to say the least.'

'Nor am I. Headed here before breakfast.'

'From Lincoln?'

'No. Stayed hereabouts for the weekend now that's that buggered.' Jake blew out a breath. 'What else is new in this game eh? Thanks,' said the DS and set off across an open expanse of field with green crops growing in perfectly straight rows ahead of him.

He walked carefully head down to avoid stepping on whatever the plants were to avoid increased aggravation. As he approached, the man stood legs astride hands on hips, and there beside him was a Collie, tongue hanging out panting.

'Right sir,' Jake said as he looked at the body of a man and at one peculiar aspect in particular. 'Detective Sergeant Jake Goodwin. Major Incident Team from Lincoln.'

'Nah then. Least yer got a shift on, pleased some bugger has.'

There was no point in explaining why he was there so quickly. Next thing he'd ask about his dad, talk about them seeing each other in the pub and they'd lose focus on the priorities. He made do with. 'Mr…?'

'Herring. David Herring.' He waved a hand about and Jake could only think of fish out of water. 'This here's me bread an' butter, son,' was unmistakably glottal Lincolnshire, which could easily have provoked sarcasm from Jake about green bread being mouldy, but this was not the time. 'Need this old bugger shifting a bit sharpish, son.'

'And these are what exactly?' the DS asked pointing to a row of plants.

'Cabbage. Spring Cabbage,' he said as if it was obvious. He was a tubby man Jake guessed to be in his fifties with an equine face, a disheveled mop of thinning brown hair at the front of his head with little beyond.

'How did you come across him?' Jake Goodwin asked as he realized the cadaver's face was known to him. What some these days call an environmental influencer. Widely recognized not only to him but the whole damn nation. Despite years of experience in dealing with some very strange and nasty rural situations, he'd never come across anything like it before in his life. Eyes closed but eyelids are where rigor mortis starts its work.

'All downta Jess,' he was told but Jake was too preoccupied with what he was looking at. 'Got no sheep these days but allus had a dog. So, Jess's bit long in tooth now but she's more a pet. Out for me morning look round and silly bugger scampers off top side o' bottom meadow. Chasing rabbits an' all sorts usually her game. Heard her barking like, but she'd not react to me whistles. Came all the way up here and its a fair walk an' that's what she'd got. Old Alerick, poor bugger.'

From experience Jake was fully aware he was alone with a possible suspect, even though what Herring claimed was entirely possible.

'What're they bringing? Paddy wagon, to cart 'im off in?

'I've no idea,' Jake admitted. Looking all around he knew it would be a good trudge with a stretcher whichever way they came.

'Not want it up here. Needs to come from o'er that way,' he gestured with big chunky fingers. 'Gate at far end there,' Jake couldn't even see. 'They can park it up an' walk. Not ruining this bloody lot that's for damn sure lad.'

'How big is this field?'

'Good seven acres and a touch more.'

'Has Jess touched the body?'

'Just barked for ages. Fair good walk to get here to check wha' all the fuss were about.'

'And you. Have you touched him?'

'What wi' that on there?'

'You know him then?' said Jake gesturing to the man on the ground in what looked like the sort of trousers old Colonels still wear and expensive but battered brown imitation brogues.

'Lives a mile or two off up his big manor place.' A fact Jake already knew as the victim was somebody his father regarded as a neighbour with some pride. 'You seen his missus?' Jake shook his head. 'Tidy piece that and no mistake', and he whistled which was hardly a polite reaction with her husband lying there dead. 'Me lad'll be here soon, wan' me to get him to give us a hand shifting him?'

'Don't you dare!'

'Hang on,' was said back crossly. 'In case yer not noticed this be a working farm mayat and...' his voice to degree was full of sarcasm turning into desperation.

'Excuse me,' was forthright Goodwin. 'This, in case you haven't noticed,' was Jake's own derision. 'Is a crime scene. We'll have a pathologist on his or her way. Nothing happens without their say so. Understand?'

'What'll I do then?'

'What exactly had you in mind for this field today?'

'Well,' he blew out a breath. 'Nowt actually, jus bogglin' about...'

'Thank you. This field stays exactly as it is. Do I make myself clear?'

Herring was contemptuous, turning his back on Goodwin and his next remark was to his dog. 'C'mon Jess. That's all the thanks we'll get. 'Ave a word with Eddie, he'll sort the bugger out and ge' you breakfast.'

The brown shirt Keating–Price was wearing had been cut off at the right shoulder and that bare arm was carefully laid out between the plants.

Jake looked up to watch David Herring and his Jess in the distance walking off the way he'd indicated the farmhouse was situated.

The popular environmentalist's hair was thin and turning grey in places, far too long at the back but although it was hidden from view there would be Jake knew, a ridiculous ponytail. Unless somebody'd chopped it off.

Too conventional even for his age with seriously dated clothing you'd struggle to find at the majority of retailers in town or on line.

With his arm bandaged from wrist to shoulder and sealed with gaffa tape top and bottom, there was a bulge in the crook of his arm. As if that wasn't enough, stuck to the arm in a clear plastic bag with a yellow and black well known skull and crossbones image were the printed words....

Another LINCOLNSHIRE MURDER MYSTERY
by the same Author

BITTER
END

Detective Inspector Inga Larsson is one of the first on the scene of the death of a local woman discovered at home in Lincoln by her young ten-year-old daughter.

The victim, Alyson Allsop, had taken out a series of injunctions in spiteful attempts to stop her ex-husband from having any contact with their daughter.

Is murder by the husband too obvious, too simplistic?

As if all that is not enough to contend with, it is pointed out to Bristow how the local media have suddenly highlighted the anniversary of an unsolved murder of disabled student Donna Steyning, strangled back in 2010.

No one is safe from their past.

Printed in Great Britain
by Amazon

13928037R00169